FINDING
GIDEON

ERIC JEROME DICKEY

FINDING GIDEON

DUTTON

DUTTON

An imprint of Penguin Random House LLC
375 Hudson Street
New York, New York 10014

Copyright © 2017 by Eric Jerome Dickey

LIBRARY OF CONGRESS CATALOGING-IN-PUBLICATION DATA

Names: Dickey, Eric Jerome, author.
Title: Finding Gideon / Eric Jerome Dickey.
Description: First edition. | New York, New York : Dutton, [2017] |
Description based on print version record and CIP data provided by
publisher; resource not viewed.
Identifiers: LCCN 2017002037 (print) | LCCN 2016055134 (ebook) | ISBN
9781101985502 (ebook) | ISBN 9781101985496 (hardcover)
Subjects: LCSH: African American men—Fiction. | Assassins—Fiction. | BISAC:
FICTION / African American / Erotica. | GSAFD: Suspense fiction.
Classification: LCC PS3554.I319 (print) | LCC PS3554.I319 F56 2017 (ebook) |
DDC 813/.54—dc23
LC record available at https://lccn.loc.gov/2017002037

Printed in the United States of America
1 3 5 7 9 10 8 6 4 2

For Carolyn. For Virginia. For Lila. For Vardaman.

Whoever fights monsters should see to it that in the process he does not become a monster. And if you gaze long enough into an abyss, the abyss will gaze back into you.

—Friedrich Nietzsche

FINDING
GIDEON

Prologue

Argentina, Yesterday

Winter. Early morning. Crowded train leaving the Retiro terminal in Buenos Aires.

The assassin Medianoche had been cornered, his team the Four Horsemen temporarily outwitted.

Gideon said, "The gun. Use two fingers. Grip it by the barrel. No fast movements."

Medianoche tightened his jaw, defiant toward the younger assassin, no man's prisoner.

The seasoned warrior wasn't accustomed to being at a disadvantage.

Gideon repeated himself, his voice hard, eyes focused: his last warning.

Medianoche eased his gun out of his coat, business end first. Gideon took the weapon. Tossed it out of the window of the thirty-year-old train as it rambled through the rail yard. Medianoche stared at the rugged young man as the rugged young man stared at him.

Gideon said, "You're older . . . gray hair . . . scarred up . . . but it's you."

Medianoche ignored the rambling description, kept his attention on Gideon's eyes.

Gideon growled. "You were shot in North Carolina."

Medianoche barked out his anger: "Who are you?"

"I'm asking myself *what* the fuck you are."

Gideon struck Medianoche in the face, on the chin, a strong blow that staggered him, moved him back almost two steps. Medianoche adjusted his eye patch and growled.

Gideon stood in front of him, both hands on a gun aimed at the center of his forehead.

Medianoche scanned the crowd, looked to see who was with Gideon. All he saw were people who didn't speak English, but their wide eyes said they understood body language.

Mouth bloodied, Medianoche repeated his question, "Who the fuck are you?"

Gideon said, "I'm the kid who shot you in North Carolina. I'm the kid who killed you. I'm your goddamn son."

Chapter 1

On the Night of the Fire

And their war would continue.

Buenos Aires had been destroyed, from the ramshackle *villas* to the prestigious avenues and high-status boulevards beyond well-known Recoleta, where the streets were paved in gold.

Discomfort increased. Medianoche jerked awake on disheveled sheets, his mind still in battle. He was disoriented, trapped between reality and a restless sleep. Pillows softer than clouds. Sheets white like heaven. Vision focused. He was not in his bed. Not in his quarters on the seventeenth floor of the building that housed the Horsemen. Remembered where he was. He was not far from Avenida 9 de Julio, in a suite of the Four Seasons Hotel in Buenos Aires. While he was in battle, the wretched shit smell of the *villas* had covered his clothing and saturated his flesh. Now the flowery perfume of a mature, intelligent Porteña was on his scarred and wounded skin. He was still in bed with a married Porteña named Caprica Ortiz, a woman as stunning as Sophia Loren when she was the most beautiful woman in the world.

Medianoche felt a sharp sting, touched the cuts and swellings in his face. Lip had been split. Face red, bruised. And his chest. It hurt like hell. Gideon had shot him twice, popped him good, close-range shots, kill shots, but nothing penetrated his Colombian-made clothing, gear that was bulletproof. But still, where the slugs had hit, soreness and pain had been left behind.

Caprica Ortiz stirred, opened her eyes, then sat up. "*Dios mío.* I fell asleep."

She was born in Argentina, but had been educated at Florida A&M University, garnered her degree, then done her Ph.D. in England. She spoke English with hardly an accent. Her English was better than his.

He said gruffly, "I did too. Don't worry. You only slept about ten minutes."

"I was afraid it was close to morning."

"Stay a few more minutes."

"My husband."

"An hour. I want you again."

She hesitated. "I will see if that is possible."

She moved from the bed, took her phone, and went to the bathroom.

Medianoche looked at his damaged hands, opened and closed his fingers. Felt the ache in his knees, the pain in his lower back.

The Four Horsemen had lost a battle on the soil of their adopted country.

The images of Gideon and the other mutts on that team were branded into his brain, still sizzled from the heat. There had been an older Russian. There was a big black guy, the nationality of that tall, muscular bastard unknown. He had moved fast, like a marine, maybe a SEAL.

A Latin Brit called Scamz had been their general, their organizer.

The Scamz Organization. That was the way the Four Horsemen saw them. At least half of the Scamz Organization was morgue-ready on the heels of this fiasco, and the Four Horsemen had lost an ancillary member, Draco, the Beast's loyal servant. The Horsemen themselves were down to two out of four members. Señor Rodriguez had been killed in action. And the Beast, the man many called La Bestia de Guerra, the Beast of War, the powerful, calculating man who had been the leader since the group's inception, was dead.

If Medianoche killed a million of the enemy, but lost one of his own in a firefight, that loss cut down to his bone marrow. There was no reason they should not have slaughtered the Scamz Organization.

And Gideon should be as dead as the Beast. That gaucho and the man who had betrayed Medianoche should be meeting in the halls of hell.

Medianoche turned when the bathroom door opened.

When Caprica Ortiz came back, she checked her watch, put her phone on the nightstand, then slipped back under the covers.

She said, "I called my contact. I told him to get me intel on an assassin named Gideon."

"What's the turnaround time?"

"He will call me back in a few hours. No guarantees."

"Have your contact also look up a man named Scamz. Latin with a British accent. He was their leader. Gideon was his hired gun. And a woman they called Arizona was with them."

She sat up, took her phone again, went to the bathroom, then came back in five minutes.

He asked, "You add those names to the list?"

She nodded, eased back into the bed.

Caprica Ortiz said, "Tell me something, if it is not too much to ask."

"Yes?"

"What nationality are you? What is your true bloodline?"

"My mother was Romanian." He remembered her dying, drowning in the Baldwin Hills Dam disaster and flood back in 1963.

"What nationality was your father?"

"He was mixed. Jack and Coke, easy on the Coke."

"Not a kind man."

"Not at all. Stern and short-tempered, quick to strike. His immigrant father was a rumrunner, moonshiner, and bootlegger. I came from a family of criminals and heroes."

"You were born in the United States, or immigrated?"

"Was born in Los Angeles. Back before they changed laws and fucked it up. Before the liberals took over, it used to be a beautiful place. But now it's ugly and out of control. It's like the *villas* here in some parts. I look at Los Angeles on the Internet. Don't like what I see. Just saw they had gunfire at a house party not far from where I grew up. Three people dead and twelve wounded. Wasn't like that in my day."

She paused. "Where have you worked? No details, but where does a skilled man like you, where does an organization like the one you are a part of, do what you do?"

"In North Korea in Pyongyang, in Thailand in Bangkok and Nakhon Ratchasima, in Venezuela in Bolivia and Caracas, in Honduras in Tegucigalpa and Juticalpa, in Brazil, in Somalia, in Guyana, in Bangladesh, in Afghanistan, on Tuvalu, in Russia, in Jamaica, in Syria."

"'The ever-more-sophisticated weapons piling up in the arsenals of the wealthiest and the mightiest can kill the illiterate, the ill, the poor, and the hungry, but they cannot kill ignorance, illness, poverty, or hunger.'"

"You're naked, smell like sex, and quoting Fidel Castro."

"You have taken your weapons around the world."

"I went where I was sent and did my job as required."

"Your job. The things you have done, it's only a job?"

"Yes."

Caprica Ortiz was a new customer for the Four Horsemen. She lived in an unending war as well. Hers started with Argentina's Dirty War, when the military juntas had kidnapped and killed thirty thousand of Argentina's citizens. Middle-class university students, unionists, journalists, and intellectuals were *disappeared*. Caprica's father was one of the intellectuals abducted and assassinated by the military leaders of her own country. One hundred of those evil men were still alive, protected by amnesty laws until 2003, the mothers and children of the disappeared suffering for more than three decades. Caprica had vowed to be financier, judge, and jury and had hired the Four Horsemen to meet with the men in charge of the Dirty War executions. No man was too old to be put down. They had destroyed families, then gone on to have their own, and that was a slap in the face. Caprica had vowed to see as many as she could find sent to the grave, and hoped their families would finally feel the pain others had endured for decades.

She said, "It was your destructive government and your greedy presidents, until wretched Ronald Reagan, who helped finance the horrors that happened across South America. They were part of the political repression and state terror."

"It was called Operation Condor."

"Your arrogant country was complicit in the deaths of many."

"Don't blame my country for the evil your country practices. People still get disappeared down here. Executions by police still happen every couple of days. People are getting disappeared down here by the police the same way blacks are being gunned down in the States."

"I am surprised that I just slept with you. Our politics are dissimilar."

"A soldier is not a politician. Let me assure you that I am not your enemy. Politicians caused the last meltdown in '02. They are the reason television and computers cost four times here in Argentina what they cost in the UK. Politicians limit the amount of foreign currency Argentineans can buy."

"If a soldier is not a politician, then what is he?"

"Soldiers just enforce the bullshit politicians create."

"Even if that means making people disappear?"

"A soldier follows orders. A soldier doesn't set policy."

"I don't like your answers. They are the same answers Nazis gave on trial."

"I can wipe my dick off and we can return to this being straight business if you want."

She paused, hummed, then whispered, "You kiss me softly like you are using your tongue to write poetry on top of my soul. Then you become feral, so passionate. I like the way you lose control, pull my hair, and fuck me. It makes me feel desirable, beautiful. It makes me feel like I am a very young woman again."

Medianoche ran his fingers through Caprica's hair. "When you get home, act normal."

"I have never betrayed my husband."

"Lots of wives break the Seventh Commandment. And many are military wives. As soon as their husbands are deployed, they group up and have a banana-eating contest."

"I have no idea what that means, but the image in my mind is horrible."

"The navy boys call it that. Banana-eating contest. It's the way it is."

Caprica Ortiz shuddered like she felt a chill, then eased her soft, warm body away from his muscular frame, made his moment of summer become the coldest winter once again.

He asked, "You're leaving?"

"*Vuelvo en un rato.*" She chuckled. "*Tengo muchas ganas de hacer pis.*"

She sashayed toward the bathroom, that curvaceous body breath-taking, amazing.

She said, "You are truly well-endowed."

"Did I hurt you?"

"Did I mention that I will be puffy and sore?"

Medianoche held his cunt stretcher, stared at the wedded woman's ass. She was a polyglot. She was a fucking unicorn.

But he had bedded many unicorns.

When she came back, she cuddled up next to him. "This was supposed to be an hour."

"Too bad you're married."

"Stop saying that."

"Why?"

"Because you might make me regret being married for foolish reasons."

"You said you haven't had sex in a long time."

"Not in five years."

"Can I ask why?"

"That is between my husband and I."

"Understood."

"Now I have done the unexpected, had an affair. With a man I met two days ago."

She touched Medianoche's puffed-up face.

She said, "Were you part of what happened here in Buenos Aires?"

"Why do you ask?"

"I have not mentioned your injuries, but that does not mean I do not see them."

"Had a rough night. Let's just leave it at that."

"The news blames it on Colombian drug lords."

"Colombia is the Mexico of South America. And the news, as usual, is wrong."

"I am glad that you are okay."

She put soft kisses on his sensitive lips.

She whispered, "Like Evita and other great women, I have betrayed my husband."

He pulled the married woman to him, went inside her again as if she were his wife.

She moaned. "North American man, you have a big dick."

"South American woman, stop saying that."

"It's long like Chile and wide like Brazil."

They laughed together.

He stared at her face, her gray hair down, framing perfection. She wasn't ashamed of her gray hair. Usually in Argentina, once a single gray hair reared its head, most women kept a date with Miss Clairol. But Caprica Ortiz was a confident woman. He sucked her nipples, fingered her, then eased inside again. Within three minutes he made her surrender, call out to her god, moan in twenty octaves, and grab the sheets. Another orgasm made her back arch as her legs shook uncontrollably. The way she moved thrilled him to no end. He'd been surprised. She hadn't had sex in half a decade, so he thought she would be a dead fuck. And pretty women were rarely this good between the sheets, on the floor, in the shower, and up against a wall. She showed her yoga moves and pulled both ankles behind her head, let him have her that way. Caprica Ortiz was as pleasing as being with three women at once. She took his mind away from the battle, from the loss, as much as a distraction like this could. He needed to unload his rage and disappointment. Caprica Ortiz announced that she felt so damn good, once again she was near orgasm. Medianoche stroked her into a beautiful frenzy. Tears in her eyes, Caprica Ortiz trembled. Medianoche stroked, never missed a beat, but his mind wasn't in the room. His mind was back in the *villas*, on the avenues, still at war with the Scamz Organization.

He was still at war with the arrogant gaucho who called himself Gideon.

Medianoche laid out yesterday's sequence of unfortunate events in his unsettled mind.

First came a contract from a rich North American fuck named Hopkins, a financier/con man who hired the Horsemen to steal a briefcase from the Uruguayans by any means necessary.

Then.

That mission was accomplished. Many Uruguayan bodies, much blood left behind.

Then.

The briefcase was part of a set of briefcases, was supposed to be one half of a puzzle, and once it was reunited with that second identical briefcase, those devices would be the key to accessing untold fortunes.

The married woman begged Medianoche to slow, to be more gentle. He didn't slow. He was not here to be gentle. She put her forearm in her mouth, bit herself to muffle her cries. Soon Caprica Ortiz trembled again, begged him to not slow down, to not stop making love like that.

Again she sang in *castellano*, toes curling, back arching, hands pulling sheets.

But as he enjoyed her, as he maintained his rhythm, his mind wandered.

After they had taken the briefcase that the Uruguayans had stolen, it all went fast.

Soon came a British Latino named Scamz, another who was in search of the second prized briefcase. He and his team needed the one that was in the possession of the Four Horsemen. And the Four Horsemen needed theirs. The con man and financier Hopkins was dead, so the Four Horsemen could claim the entire prize. That pulled them into the war as if it had been oil in the Middle East. One briefcase was no good without the other.

And time was of the essence.

The Scamz Organization had slid into Buenos Aires and set up base in La Boca. Scamz had several workers on his team, including a knife-throwing pregnant woman named Arizona.

And Gideon. The gaucho who claimed to be the boy who had shot him in the head more than two decades ago.

A group of misfits now known as the Scamz Organization had stolen their briefcase.

The Scamz Organization had won the battle.

And two members of the Four Horsemen were dead.

Medianoche growled, grunted, set free his rage.

Caprica Ortiz begged him not to stop.

Medianoche finished strong, shook the bed good, his final thrusts intense, rapid, making sure he had emptied his voluminous rage. Panting, he fell away from Caprica Ortiz. Glowing, skin flushed, hair disheveled, sweating, eyes closed, she could barely breathe.

He sat up, wiped his sweat on a corner of the sheets, then looked at her.

For a second, the married woman resembled the enemy.

She resembled the French prostitute Thelma. She looked like that gaucho Gideon's whore-mother, the prostitute he and the Beast had had a meretricious relationship with.

Medianoche reached for Caprica Ortiz, put his large, wounded hand around her small, fragile neck, was prepared to squeeze, was inspired to break it ten times. Then the likeness vanished, and he let her go. Eyes closed, still writhing, she put a hand over her heart.

In that moment, he imagined she had enjoyed being strangled.

Caprica Ortiz opened her eyes and without blinking whispered, "That was amazing."

Medianoche opened and closed his swollen hands, the stinging no longer masked.

She took his cock in her hand, held it as if it now belonged to her.

She said, "I wish I could take you with me next week."

"Where are you going?"

"To Las Leñas."

"Skiing?"

"Yes. With my family. It's ski season. The rain here means the snow is good there."

"I've been there. Used to ski the black diamond chutes."

"You took a pretty young woman?"

"No. Last August I went with the man who took your contract for the Four Horsemen."

"The Beast."

"How well did you know the Beast?"

"Not as well as I now know you."

"Maybe you'll bring me back a souvenir."

"Maybe I will."

Medianoche rested next to Caprica Ortiz.

She said, "My therapist said skiing would be a good bonding trip for my family. We have issues, as most families do. But we have a good therapist. I can give you his name, if you want."

"I know. Therapy here is the norm. I prefer to talk my problems over with Jack Daniel's. Everyone in Argentina goes to see a therapist."

"It is no big deal. It is a part of life."

"Argentina is a haven for psychoanalysis. Never understood that."

"We loved Sigmund Freud."

"You get off chatting to strangers about your damn problems."

"Therapy is good for the mind and soul. If you change your mind."

"I won't."

"You and Jack."

"Me and Jack. We've been working out our problems for decades."

"Do you ever go to church, to see a priest, to the confessional?"

"I only confess to Jack."

"I will pray for you. A man who carries his problems needs prayer."

"Then pray for Jack too. He carries the problems of many men."

As soon as Medianoche closed his eyes, the cavern where his left eye used to be ached. It was more intense than it had been before. The sharp pain moved inward, sharpened more, and his brain caught fire.

His brain clicked.

It clicked, made sounds like rusted gears moving, and it was deafening. Part of his missing memory rebooted, came home to roost. He saw part of what had been stolen from him when a bastard child named Gideon shot him in the face.

Chapter 2

The Beast of the City

Medianoche saw the Beast.

He was at least two decades younger. Hair in a military cut. No irregular white patch that made his mane look like the hair on Pepé Le Pew in that cartoon. He saw the French girl from Yerres. Thelma. She looked so juvenile, like she was just a teenager. Her skin was well tanned, had been kissed by the Caribbean sun. The first time they had seen her, they were in Montego Bay. Seemed like they were hardly eighteen when they had gone to that brothel recommended by a taxi driver. It was a brothel that had all the models come out one by one to present themselves. Teenagers there could legally have sex at age sixteen, and a couple of the girls looked younger. After their introductions, the talent lined up in the living room, stood side by side, smiling as if they were in a beauty pageant. Each ingénue waited to see who would become sexually obsessed with her and pay for her services before ever touching her.

In the ninety-degree heat of MoBay, with humidity thick enough to stop a bullet, most of the girls were dressed in lingerie. Some were topless. There was a white Jamaican, her hair in colorful braids. There was a Chinese Jamaican, her hair in dark dreadlocks. Haitian girls. Dominicans. Cubans. East Indian girls. Bahamian girls. Laughter and moans came from down the hallway. Other customers were already there. A cruise ship was in, so they were busy with both married men and young boys who wanted to feel like they were men by screwing foreign women.

There was something about the French girl. Innocence meets sensuality. Her lips were full, her hair long. No pubic hair. Made her look younger. Small waist. Sweet breasts. Very nice pear-shaped ass, as nice as the rotund asses on the sensual Jamaicans.

Medianoche told her, "You resemble the actress Emmanuelle Béart."

The Beast disagreed but still was enthralled. "Your skin is flawless."

They both had wanted the French girl.

The French girl said she could take care of both of them at once, but they both would have to pay the full price. The service would run concurrently. She then brought Medianoche and the Beast laminated menus that looked like they had come from a roadside restaurant, only this was a price list for different kinds of sex.

As the French girl led them to their appointed bedroom, one that had fresh sheets, they heard the other working girls beyond the beads that led to the living area complaining about the French girl being so popular in the West Indian brothel. "We have we youth to take care of enuh, and if we nuh do this, weh we a go do? Walk round and rob people, make them shoot we?"

The Beast. The French girl. The brothel on the outskirts of Montego Bay.

The memory came back clear and strong, and Medianoche relived that day again.

Windows were open. Fans were on, humming. No air-conditioning. Middle of the morning. He smelled her perfume. This was the clearest memory to return to date.

Then the memory skipped, like a record that had been scratched.

Medianoche saw them in bed, the Beast and the French girl, already in congress. She led the way. The Beast was violent and unforgiving with men, but still timid, nervous with girls.

Medianoche told the French prostitute, "You move like a Jamaican."

"Thank you."

"Can you dance like one?"

"I am learning. They dance very sexy."

The walls were canary yellow with light blue trim around the windows. Bright island colors. The bed was just a worn mattress dropped on the floor. For a soldier who had slept on the ground many nights, that mattress looked like heaven. They carried war with them; it was in their blood, left them hyperactive, checking for insurgents even when they were places insurgents should never be. Medianoche looked for exits, in case they were needed. It took him a moment to relax. He had changed, was no longer the boy he had been when he lived in Los Angeles. He had acquired the taste for blood. A red ceiling fan spun and wobbled overhead. Medianoche smoked a cigar as he undressed, took off his military uniform, watched the French girl ride the Beast.

Medianoche asked, "What's your name?"

She looked a little scared of him and didn't answer. He didn't care.

"Call me Midnight," he told her.

"Mr. Midnight. Nice to meet you."

"Can I get ganja here?"

"Yes. I can get you some of the best ganja on the island."

"Wine?"

"Yes. I can get you wine as well."

"I love your voice."

"Thank you."

"You sound sophisticated. Like a college girl. Sound real smart."

"Thank you."

"How long have you been working here?"

She moaned a little. "Here in this home? Two months. Almost three."

"You're the prettiest girl I've seen in a long time."

"Thank you, Mr. Midnight."

"The other girls don't like you."

"We are all competing for the same thing."

"We're going to do you at the same time. You good at that?"

"I'm getting better."

He watched her. She was mesmerizing, generous, not timid in bed. Medianoche and the Beast chatted. Soon Medianoche joined the Beast and Thelma.

He showed the Beast the unforgiving way a man was supposed to take a woman.

The memory played in slow motion. The film choppy. Skipping parts.

Still he could feel Jamaica's humidity on his skin, thick like split-pea soup.

Once, when the three were in a session together, as they drank wine and smoked weed, the French girl asked about America. She was curious. She said she had read about a black woman named Thelma Wright, an American woman who had once sold drugs, a woman the French girl saw as a survivor. The desperate understood the desperate. The French girl said she understood all girls and women who did whatever they had to do to endure in a world governed by the rules of men. She watched the women in poverty-ridden MoBay do it every day. She empathized with West Indian, American black, and African women, with darker women, because they had it worse than everyone else in America and the rest of the world. Racism and apartheid hit the black women the hardest, and the darker the berry, the deeper the abuse.

The Beast asked the teenage French girl what kind of music she liked.

The French girl said she was a fan of Nina Simone, loved her music. And as they lay naked, sweating, ceiling fan rotating over their heads, she sang part of "Ne Me Quitte Pas." She told them how she loved Simone's spirit, said the woman had an inner strength. The Beast asked her about the black women in France. She said that most of the Africans in France were treated horribly by both French and African men. Same for Middle Eastern women. She passed no judgment on women who sold their bodies to survive. She didn't care if a woman did it by choice or to escape physical and mental abuse at home. Selling your body wasn't selling your soul. After sex was done, a man left with only the memory. Memories could not be used to pay bills. The woman had the money. No one could survive without capital, not for long, and could not live well.

She laughed, teased. "The prostitute always wins."

The girl seemed mature for her age but still had the logic of a teenager. They were growing accustomed to the logic of war.

Medianoche said, "Not in Jamaica. Not with this currency. You'll stay poor."

The French girl smiled, but Medianoche could tell she didn't like what he'd said.

The Beast played with her nipples. "A beautiful woman like you, you'd make more in the States. Put on a sexy dress and some high heels, men will spend two thousand American dollars to have you spend the night. You're too pretty to be doing this, at least on this level."

"Two thousand dollars in your country, is that a lot?"

"It's a lot. One night like this, and you could live for a month."

"And that is the truth?"

"It is for gorgeous women. And some make a lot more. If you were with one of those high-class escort agencies, like the ones the politicians and movie stars use, I wouldn't be able to afford you in America."

"I've always wanted to go to the United States. Yes, here you work a lot and make very little. This is not the life I want."

"What do you want to do?"

"I want to go to university one day."

"And do what?"

"Maybe become . . . I don't know what I would become."

The Beast said, "You've only been here a couple of months?"

"And I will not do this for very long. Maybe the rest of the year. I'll save money and leave here. Hmm. Maybe I will make it to America. Go to university there. Become a solicitor."

Medianoche laughed. "You don't have to go to university to sell pussy in America."

"No, that is not what I meant. I used the wrong word? *Avocat* . . . a barrister . . . a lawyer."

Medianoche remembered something else. When she was working in Montego Bay, they did not call her Thelma. She had a French name, one that stood out from the names of the island girls.

He asked, "Why come down here and work in the islands? Men don't come to Jamaica looking for French girls. They come to the islands to get what the island has to offer."

The French girl revealed that she had fled Paris six months ago and come to MoBay. She was an illegal immigrant. She'd tried to find a job, couldn't, and soon she was in the West Indies, alone, famished, and penniless. She had met a nice girl named Margaret. Margaret had befriended her, showed her the trade. Soon she was working at the brothel. Soon she was surviving. The brothel was cleaner, safer, than working the streets. And it was more dignified than working in Saint James. There some girls took men inside makeshift tin-and-cardboard huts, sold themselves in the bushes near the concrete girder bridge along Howard Cooke Boulevard.

She said, "This is better than being like the girls who work under the bridge. Many are mothers that sneak out at night to earn money to feed their children."

The Beast asked, "Where are the fathers of these children?"

The French girl shrugged. "I am glad, thankful to God, that I am not one of them. Forty-year-old women work down there with their twenty-year-old daughters at their side."

"Mothers and daughters work side by side?"

"Yes. Sometimes together."

The Beast laughed. "We might have to find that bridge."

The French girl held on to a smile that had no happiness.

There was a tap at the door. The French girl hopped to her feet, hurried to answer that call, naked, holding her breasts. She opened the door quickly. It was a girl they hadn't seen before. The girl was pure chocolate, sultry, and well-endowed. Her dreadlocks hung down her back and touched her waist. Strong, powerful hair. Her teeth were the whitest of whites. She must've been working when they arrived. She was so beautiful, had the face of a naïve teenager, along with the smoothest skin and amazing breasts. Young breasts. Small waist, subtle hips.

Medianoche stared at her like she was Amaterasu, the goddess of the sun and the universe. The girl had been sent to tell them that their time was up. An hour had passed, a quarter of that spent talking. As if it were a Pavlovian response, or she was afraid to break any house rules, the French girl hurried to gather her things, told them thank you, hoped they both were pleased, to ask for her if they came back, and she would leave so they could get dressed.

Medianoche told the French girl to drop her things and to stay where she was.

He walked to his pants, dick swinging, pulled out his wallet.

He said, "Tell the Jamaican woman who runs this whorehouse we want two more hours."

"She is Guyanese. Okay. I will tell her."

"How old are you?"

"Sixteen."

He ordered, "I want you to come join us for those two hours."

"Another man is waiting for me. A Canadian man from the Carnival cruise ship."

"Not anymore. I want you. Tell him to pick another girl, and I'll pay for his hour."

She looked nervous. Again Medianoche ordered that she join them.

He said, "I want you bareback."

"That will cost a lot more. Twice as much."

"Then I will pay a lot more. Twice as much."

"For you and your handsome friend?"

The Beast nodded, grabbed money from his pocket, money from combat pay, and threw it their way like he was Mr. Big Shot. It wasn't a lot to an American. But it was a fortune to the working girls.

He said, "And bring two more bottles of wine. And wineglasses. Not cups."

The dark and lovely girl took all the American money, left in a hurry, and was back within three minutes. She came in with two bottles of wine and four glasses and placed it all on a small table. She poured four glasses, served the men, handed a glass to the French girl, then pulled off her thong and eased into the disheveled bed, glass of wine in her hand, giggling.

Medianoche asked, "What's your name, pretty woman?"

"Margaret Gayle."

He knew that wasn't her real name. He told her, "It should be Delicious Scrumptious."

She laughed the laugh of a girl who was young, yet cunning. She had presented herself at the door for this purpose, to entice the two rich Americans into paying more money. She hadn't had a customer waiting; she had taken the extra money and kept it for herself.

They were cons. All the girls in the building were cons.

The French girl slapped Margaret's ass and laughed. "She is my best friend here."

"Soignée is my best friend in the whole wide world."

Soignée.

At the ranch-style brothel in MoBay the French girl's name had been Soignée.

Medianoche touched Margaret's chin, touched her breasts. He moved her dreadlocks, kissed the nape of her neck, touched her body, and he kissed her. Then he was inside her.

The Beast and the French girl were in congress; this time the Beast was in charge.

Soon they were a four-headed creature, two of the animals howling as two grunted.

His first orgasm with Margaret had been an outburst that rivaled eruptions at Iceland's Great Geyser. His explosion would have gushed ten feet in the air had he not been inside her. Then they had laughed together. Over and over, he told her how beautiful she was.

She smiled, touched his face, told him he was rugged and handsome.

The memory skipped in time, played on a TV that needed the rabbit ears adjusted.

He saw the Beast again. A hint of white hair showed at the top of his head.

That meant a few years had gone by. Still in their twenties, but seasoned warriors.

Medianoche's memory released other recollections that had been dormant.

He and the Beast had just returned to the States from working in the Niger Delta. Medianoche had wanted to visit a different girl, one who was a mix of Moroccan and Cameroonian, but the Beast had insisted they look up an old favorite first, the French girl, the lovely Parisian, the lassie who smelled like cinnamon and tasted like honey straight from the comb. They'd see the African if they had time and the energy, if any money was left in the pot.

The Beast had kept in contact with the French girl.

She was no longer selling her body in MoBay.

The French girl was hiding from her sins, from her Parisian crimes, in the United States of America now. She had arrived, determined to succeed. She had been there long enough to pick up the way the southerners speak, had managed to mimic their speaking pattern and was able to not sound so French. He assumed for her, that too was a survival skill in the Bible-waving part of the hypocritical country.

Then more daguerreotype memories struggled to rise, came and went like scenes on a movie projector from the silent-film era. There were flashes, and he relived bits and pieces.

The sky turned Carolina blue, very few clouds across the seat of heaven.

The remembrance of the French girl continued.

Now her hair was shorter, dyed Hitchcock blond. Smoking a brown More cigarette. Looked like a James Bond sex siren, but still seemed young enough to be illegal to touch in the USA. She would always look younger than her age. She wore a red satin slip and high heels, anxiously waiting for them, then opened the door to an apartment and kissed them both like they were long-lost lovers. She led them down the carpeted hallway. Light brown carpet. It wasn't close to being the Taj Mahal, but it was much better than where she had worked in MoBay. As they passed a small bedroom, Medianoche looked inside. A kid was sleeping in a twin bed. He was just a shadow underneath wrinkled covers, sucking his thumb. Holding the Beast's hand, the French girl led them into the larger bedroom, her special bedroom, one that made Medianoche feel like he was in a bordello that specialized in dominatrix role-play. It had been modeled after one in Paris where priests were drawn to the crucifixion parlor and Satan's hell torture room.

His brain struggled to heal.

It fought to come online.

Medianoche remembered more.

On that day, the French girl's bastard son was asleep in the next room. She had given him NyQuil to make him siesta while she worked. She closed his door, then went to Medianoche and the Beast. Then congress was in session. The headboard banged against the wall and the snotty-nosed bastard never made a sound. The kid slept through their spirited session, never waking when the French girl took two warriors at once, never stirring as she let out deafening cries.

Medianoche said, "The name on the mailbox outside said Thelma Wright."

She smiled a big smile. "I am using that name now."

"Thelma."

"Yes. I took my hero's name and a man we met made me fake identification. I am Thelma. Now my name sounds more American."

The doorbell rang; then there was a rhythmic knock at the front door. Medianoche stood up. So did the Beast. Prostitution wasn't legal in the United States. They could be discharged from the service, lose all benefits, be demoted, incarcerated, many things.

The French girl told them it was okay. "That will be my friend Margaret."

"The same Margaret from Montego Bay?"

"Yes. Tonight we will have a lot of fun, no?"

When he saw Margaret again, she smiled and ran to him, jumped in his arms, kissing him.

She squealed like a lovesick girl. "I have missed your beautiful lips. I loved how they felt on my body, on my shoulders, on my waist. I am wet thinking about feeling you inside me."

"How much will this cost me?"

"More than in Jamaica."

"How much more?"

"We can negotiate."

Soon the four-headed beast was alive and moaning once again.

Medianoche remembered falling asleep in the well-used bed on top of dark sheets, Margaret in his arms, the Beast resting on the other side of Thelma. When Medianoche woke to go take a piss, he was alone. The Beast was with Thelma, both naked, standing in the doorway to the other bedroom, her back to his chest. At first he thought they were in the hallway having sex, but they were looking in the other bedroom at her drugged rug rat.

They stood nude and held hands.

They looked like serious lovers, like boyfriend and girlfriend. They had that energy, more than client and customer in the middle of a business transaction. They whispered, and in the midst of their conspiracy, one that had been hidden in plain view, she stood on tiptoe and kissed the Beast, or the Beast had kissed her. It had meant nothing to Medianoche. Because he had trusted the Beast. And he was glad to see the Beast kissing the French girl so passionately.

Medianoche asked, "Where is Margaret?"

The French girl said, "She's gone. She left about twenty minutes ago."

"Didn't we pay her enough for all night, or did I fuck her too damn hard?"

The Beast said, "She says you always try to screw the Jamaican out of her."

Still men in their twenties, invincible men who would live forever, they cracked up.

Medianoche asked, "That your kid, or Margaret's, or somebody else's?"

"Mine."

As they stood in the shadows, she sounded like a happy mother, asked the Beast if he wanted to meet her son. He shook his head, told her he wasn't interested in meeting that child.

He had said that it was best that her son never meet them. *Them.* He had used the word *them.* It registered that the Beast was disturbed, only Medianoche didn't know why.

Thelma had sashayed to Medianoche, stood on tiptoe, kissed him the same passionate way she had kissed the Beast, intently, fervently, made his nature rise like the morning sun, then nervously asked Medianoche the same, if he wanted to meet her little soldier.

They were interrupted by a small cry, a bastard crumb snatcher complaining.

The big-headed child sat up, groggy, rubbing his eyes, still nothing more than a silhouette. They crept away, dicks swinging. The gorgeous French girl held her breasts, hurried to her intoxicated tyke, then walked him to the bathroom. Medianoche saw only the back of the trick baby's fat head as he staggered down a drab-colored hallway, across dull and worn carpet toward the toilet. His mother made him empty his bladder and bowels, then gave the rug rat a double dose of NyQuil, made sure he stayed intoxicated, if not unconscious. Even then Medianoche wondered if the French girl's child would have developmental issues. Maybe the bastard already did. Ghetto children ate lead paint like it was potato chips, had many mental problems, and were destined to be criminals.

Then they were back in the bed with the girl they had once called Soignée, the French whore who was now Thelma Wright.

The Beast asked Thelma whose cock was the biggest. She laughed, then playfully said they could get a ruler and figure that out on their own. The Beast suggested they use her throat.

She waggled her finger and said, "That will cost extra."

They all laughed. Sipped wine, smoked marijuana, and soon were once again a three-headed beast. In the middle of their ménage à trois, Medianoche heard a noise, jerked, ready to battle, looked that way.

The bedroom door was pushed open. The bastard child was standing there, had been watching them for a while. Had watched them in silence.

The French girl looked up, saw her child's silhouette, saw that shadow lurking in the room, but didn't freak out.

The groggy child calmly said, "I want a bowl of Frosted Flakes."

"Go back to bed for now."

"I'm hungry."

The French girl said, "Mommy will feed you shortly."

Scratching his head, watching his mother being taken doggie by one man as she fellated another, the unkempt rug rat yawned and did what his mother told him to do. The silhouette left the room and closed the door.

The snotty-nosed bastard didn't react like what he had seen or heard was unusual.

Not long after, Medianoche staggered to the bathroom, again to take a piss.

The kid was sitting at the kitchen table, his back to him, eating a big yellow bowl of Frosted Flakes. He held a banana and stared at the worn, flowery wallpaper like he was a fucking moron. He was the child who would shoot him in the head and try to murder him. He was the bastard child who would kill his left eye and destroy part of his memory. That Frosted Flakes–eating bastard was the snotty-nosed brat who would become Gideon.

After the coma Medianoche had fallen into when he was shot in the left eye, he had recovered in South Carolina, been nursed back to health by a girl from Cape Verde, a willing ingénue of Portuguese and creole heritage supplied by the Beast. Months later he went back to North Carolina. By then the French girl had fled, had taken as many of her belongings as she could, left without paying her rent, left without telling anyone good-bye.

Her scent had already gone cold.

He had hunted for Thelma. Had even gone back to Montego Bay and driven from brothel to brothel, had paid the police at the Freeport police station to contact him if she showed up on the island, had offered the other prostitutes working Cooke Boulevard a reward if they found her and turned her in to him. Medianoche wanted to kill a kid, a child who was no more than seven, maybe eight years old. But that child was already hardened and had the heart of a killer. He wanted to skin the snotty-nosed bastard a-fucking-live and destroy both his goddamn eyes.

His brain set fire again.

Clicked a dozen times.

Then another two-decade-old memory became as clear as the sky in the San Pedro de Atacama region of northern Chile, one of the prettiest places on the planet.

It was a warm day. They were on rue des Bourdonnais, less than a half mile from the Eiffel Tower, seated outdoors at an Italian café, Villa Verdi. They were dressed in dark suits, sat with their legs crossed in an area of boutiques, at a spot where a man could sit and drink with a woman undisturbed. An older man and a much younger woman near them were kissing, making out like high school children. He was well dressed and so was she. He wore a wedding ring. She didn't.

Medianoche took his eyes away from their open-air affair, glanced at two East Africans who were seated two tables away from the amorous couple, then shifted and frowned at other Frenchwomen, felt his anger for the French girl and her bastard son clogging his arteries.

The Beast said, "You know I can look at you and tell what you're thinking."

"You should get a second job as a mind reader with Ringling Brothers."

"You keep touching your injury and scowling."

"I let my fucking guard down. A fucking mutt shot me."

"Let it go, my brother. For now, let it go."

"Let it go, says the man who still has two eyes and all of his memory."

"Brother, that fucking ugly little fuck will probably end up being a fucking thief. He'll get his. The punk will probably get killed while incarcerated in a fucking American prison. I'll bet the little bastard becomes an addict and overdoses. I doubt that the bastard will live through his teen years. Mutts like that with a fucking mother like Thelma, the kid will probably be found dead in a fucking alley with a fucking needle in his fucking arm, or a fucking crack pipe at his side."

Medianoche nodded. "But that should be my kill. Not a needle, not a prisoner. *Mine*."

They had been men of war, had killed many hajjis, many sand niggers, and when the sons of the insurgents had picked up their fathers' weapons, it didn't matter if the boy was ten years old; they had killed the son too. And when the wife ran out to her son's body, she caught a bullet as well. Kill the mother, you kill the terrorist reproduction factory and save a soldier's life.

He had killed for country. Killing for revenge—he was owed that much.

Jaw tight, he tapped his fingers on the circular bistro table at a rapid beat.

The Beast motioned at Medianoche's fingers. He stopped tapping.

The Beast said, "After we leave Paris and move from Jerusalem to

Raqqa to Washington, to help you decompress I'll take you to Languedoc-Roussillon for some more R and R."

"You're taking me back to Cap d'Agde."

"Where the hedonists congregate and fornicate on the beach like it was *Caligula*."

Medianoche's voice trembled with frustration as he touched the patch over his destroyed eye. "Will going there and finding the right fuck hole make my left eye grow back? Will it bring back the part of my brain the doctor scraped out? I have to look at this in the mirror the rest of my damn life. I'd slit that kid's throat with a Ka-Bar, then go eat me a damn ice cream cone in celebration."

"Stand down."

"*I've lost memory*. Chunks of my mind have been . . . destroyed. By that snot-nosed bastard."

The Beast said, "I order you to let it go."

"Pulling rank?"

"You're a Horseman. Act like one."

"You're pulling rank."

"I'm pulling rank. I lead you because I don't make emotional de-cisions. Even in times like this, when your emotions are high, you must control them, lest they control you. What happened to you that day was fucked-up. And I want you to have your revenge. But now is not the time."

"Sir, yes, sir."

"It won't benefit the Four Horsemen."

"Sir, no, sir."

"It was traumatic. It added to your shell shock. To your soldier's heart. That's me talking to you like a brother."

"Yeah, it did. The eye socket aches with the change of the weather. That gives me fuckin' melancholia. It reminds me that I let a child shoot me. I look in the mirror and have the same reminder. I have no left periphery. After all the firefights I had. A fucking child shot me. All I dream about is killing that little fuck."

"And Thelma."

"Especially Thelma."

"Why?"

"I . . . I don't know. I just know I need to kill her."

On that spring day in Paris, as they sipped wine and watched women, some smoking and drinking *café*, as people passed by walking their cute little useless dogs, Medianoche accepted the Beast's logic and command. He agreed to let that costly, time-consuming, aggravating search for the French girl and her snot-nosed bastard child end.

Medianoche responded, "Under your orders, as commanded, I'll let the bastard go."

"Thelma too. Thoughts of her have you distracted as you sit here on this lovely day."

"You'll be a hit at Ringling Brothers. Guessing fat women's weight and telling futures."

"You're looking at women and scowling. You're making fists. You've hardly touched your wine. Brother, I need you to focus on the business of the Four Horsemen, not on the past."

Medianoche inhaled deeply, could smell Thelma. In a city where every alleyway and *rue* held the stench of old piss, he could still smell Thelma's perfume, perfume that had an arousing scent, and it was a scent that did not wash out. He could smell her in the Métro station walkway, her aroma overruling the urine stink the French homeless had left behind. It made him feel as if she were always near. Almost every woman who passed reminded Medianoche of Thelma. Even the ones who were being embraced and kissed as if the stench of piss and canine feces didn't bother them. Shit was all over the sidewalks, hopefully not of human origins, but one never knew.

The Beast said, "It's getting late."

Medianoche took a deep, cleansing breath. "Thanks."

"For?"

"For setting me straight, CO. You're right. Your XO makes emotional decisions. Just like my daddy. Just like my goddamn daddy."

The Beast said, "As soon as you were discharged from service, you went back to Los Angeles to kill the men who offended you when you were a child."

"The thieves had stolen my toys."

"They were boys when they robbed you."

"They had it coming."

"You talked about finding and killing them for years. I didn't actually think you would."

"If I had had the time, instead of just shooting them when they opened the door, I would have injected mercury into their brains and watched them suffer as their heads shrank to the size of a pea. I don't like being fucked over. I don't like losing. Never have. Never will."

He began tapping the table again. The Beast motioned. He stopped.

The Beast nodded toward the amorous couple. "Jesus, that old fuck is going to suck the young woman's tongue out of her mouth. If she doesn't suck his out of his mouth first."

Medianoche stood, looked around, magnificent cathedrals and outstanding architecture everywhere, delicious food and historical attractions galore. He checked his Movado watch and casually strolled toward the amorous, kissy-kissy couple. The older, married man was all but screwing the young woman he was with in public. Medianoche made sure he didn't step in a pile of gooey canine excrement. He could step in a pile of dog poop, slide, and throw everything off. He'd seen well-trained men stumble on a rock, then get taken out in combat.

He eased his weapon out from under his suit coat, one with a suppressor.

The unfaithful Walloon saw Death coming and yelled, *"Qu'est-ce qui passe?"*

Medianoche put two in the married man's head. Two, to be sure. He was a politician out of Belgium, more crooked than Lombard Street in San Francisco. The man's two bodyguards, the East Africans, were gunned down by the Beast before they could react. Three bodies dropped, and the woman who was seated at the bistro table with her lover, his Parisian mistress, screamed and fell to the ground. She scuttled away, actually crawled over a steaming pile of dog poo, and ended up with her stained hands covering her head, trying to hide from the two boogeymen.

They'd laugh about that later. And they would laugh long and hard.

Within seconds, Medianoche and the Beast were in a Peugeot, Medianoche behind the wheel, speeding toward Notre-Dame. One more meeting, then the day would be done. That was the same day they met two other men, who'd joined the Horsemen. Their latest recruits. The week before, the previous two had become members who were no longer of any use, so they needed replacements. The Beast had always been the commanding officer, Medianoche the executive officer. Those were the two everyone feared. Medianoche followed command, but only the command of the man he trusted. When a good soldier had a fearless and flawless leader, he followed every command without question.

After picking up the new Horsemen, it was R & R time, time spent hanging out on the Champs-Élysées, taking in shows at the Moulin Rouge, drinking, snorting a few lines, partying with their new recruits. Then to a brothel on rue Saint-Sulpice in the sixth arrondissement. Medianoche had lost his taste for Frenchwomen. He would kill one before he took her to bed. He went to brothels but would pay to be with only the Africans and West Indians.

Even after the jobs from Jerusalem to Washington, a month later when they were finally back at Cap D'Agde, he avoided the Frenchwomen. Paid for or complimentary, he'd never let another French girl touch his loins. He would have killed them all for free.

Because of Thelma.

The things Medianoche and the Beast did together as young men, as warriors who felt like they owned the world and were entitled to every pleasure and glory, things he would never do with any other man, should have served to bond them but had served only to make the betrayal the Beast had brought to the table that much harder to bear.

The Beast had been in contact with Thelma. He had never been out of contact with Thelma. He had had rendezvous with the French slut. He had impregnated her. They had a son.

Gideon's whore of a mother had had a second son courtesy of the Beast.

When the Beast had gone away on solo missions over the years, he had met with her. He had fucked her in Amsterdam. He had been with her in Germany. That much Medianoche knew for sure. Medianoche had uncovered the Beast's lies yesterday. His commander, his CO, had smiled in his face, shared wine, whiskey, and women, and lied to him for two decades.

That was why, after their war with the Scamz Organization, with emotions high and the treachery exposed, Medianoche had snapped, had turned his weapon away from someone who had been chosen to die and aimed his gun in the direction of his best friend, his brother, and, without pause, had blown his fucking brains out. He'd wanted his brother to know what it felt like to be shot in the fucking head.

Medianoche had killed his brother.

Medianoche had killed the Beast.

Chapter 3

All the King's Men

The recall ended abruptly, like a car slamming on the brakes but still hitting a deer the size of a FedEx truck. Medianoche jerked awake, sweating, heart racing like he was in a firefight, not knowing how much time had passed, hours or days. His eyes went to the clock. Only three moments had gone by. Caprica Ortiz was still in his arms, sleeping, oblivious to his journey.

If he had been in battle and suffered a blackout like that, it would have been certain death. His blackouts were why Gideon was not dead. In the *villas*, the devil had been on his side.

Medianoche shook Caprica Ortiz gently, then whispered her name. She woke in a panic, eyes wide, checked the time. "I must leave."

"I know. Don't want you to get in trouble with your husband."

She said, "Three times in two hours."

"Would make it four if I had the time and the juice."

The gun still worked, though it took longer to reload and it didn't fire as often, but when it discharged, it was a cannon. If time and age were on his side, he would've reloaded and had her facedown, ass up, and given back shots until sunrise, until his cock suffered from carpal tunnel.

She yawned. "*Me pica el bagre.*"

"Yeah. I'm hungry too."

A good fuck took away stress, cleaned the pipes, cleared the head, allowed a warrior to calm and think clearly. But Medianoche knew he couldn't fuck enough to remove the stress this time.

She asked, "May I take a quick shower before returning to my family?"

"Go ahead. I need to take care of some business. Take your time."

She could barely stand. And when she did find her footing, her walk was unsteady. He had her walking from side to side. After she had done a sashay-stagger back to the bathroom, he turned the television on. The president of Argentina was on, her beautiful face contorted, outraged, condemning the violence that had traveled across Buenos Aires yesterday. She said cocaine and *paco*—Argentina's equivalent to crack—were destroying her country, corrupting the rich and addicting the poor, and she vowed to end the drug problems. Medianoche cursed her. She mentioned the damage to the rich areas but said nothing about the damage in the *villas* where the poor lived. The *villas* weren't even on the maps. They were the government's shame. They were areas the leaders couldn't control and wished would disappear. In every other sentence she spoke, the Colombians and their drug wars were blamed. All bullshit. The president knew. He turned the television off, glanced toward his suit, his fedora, his guns.

He was still irritated. Heard a noise in the hallway and jumped, went for his guns. This battle had just ended, and he had no idea where the insurgents were, if Gideon was lurking around a corner, if Scamz or that bitch Arizona were in the shadows. He had to stay on guard. Pussy had been good, but pussy hadn't been enough to dull it all. He wanted to drink too much and drive too fast and kill, kill, kill. Had to concentrate. Sleep would do him no good.

Medianoche had depended on the Beast for decades. Now Medianoche was the commanding officer. He no longer had to take orders from the lying Beast, no longer could be called his lapdog. The Beast was gone, but he had to think with the heart of the Beast.

That memory, that vision, that moment of the past, was like a message from the dead.

He had to deliberate, not like a soldier taking orders, but like a king/warrior.

Earlier, he had sent Señorita Raven, the only other remaining Horseman, on a mission that would take her to the West Indies and the island of Montserrat. He knew now that that had been an emotional decision. That mission was useless, wouldn't benefit the Four Horsemen.

He needed to keep boots on the ground, had to protect his base, not send his only remaining soldier away to handle his personal demon. He picked up his cellular, called Señorita Raven. He hoped she wasn't in the air en route to the West Indies, though she should have been.

But the Punjabi from Saint Louis answered right away, sounded anxious, still wired up.

"Sir, yes, sir."

"Change in plans, soldier. Back to base."

"Why are you canceling the order you just gave me a few hours ago?"

Medianoche said, "Soon I will return to Montserrat and take care of that issue myself."

"Sir, I just arrived at Ezeiza International. I have my boarding pass."

"You're just arriving at the airport? Where have you been the past few hours?"

"Señor Rodriguez, sir. That was a priority. I wasn't going to leave his body unclaimed in the morgue. Gideon killed him and he was left on a train. I went to collect his body, as I told you I would do. I told them I was his girlfriend and claimed his body. I owed that to Señor Rodriguez. And, sir, I expect you to hold up to your promise and send his body home to his family."

"Even if you had claimed his remains, you should have been in the air by now."

"Again, the Scamz Organization, sir. Those motherfuckers served us a soup sandwich."

"Chain of command. The Beast is gone. I'm your commanding officer and you don't make decisions that impact the Horsemen on your own. Do you fucking understand the words coming out of my goddamn mouth?"

"Sir, I understand, sir."

"Return. The Beast kept a list of GIs he'd've used to replace any of us, worst-case scenario. You violated protocol and hacked into the system and no doubt saw the files."

"What file should your executive officer one search for when I return?"

Medianoche paused. "The Disposables. It should be labeled 'Los Desechables.'"

"Why are they called the Disposables?"

He ended the call, not in the mood to explain himself to a problematic soldier.

Three times Medianoche had tried to become a family man. Three times he'd failed. The first two marriages, in the end, were inconsequential. The third had taken root and held him by the heart. Gracelyn was his third wife, the one he'd loved the most, the one he could never forget, the only one who had rejected him when he told her who he really was. When he had come clean and explained to her what he did, when he had told her he was a mercenary, a man other men and countries hired to do their dirty work, she wanted nothing to do with the blood on his hands. The god she praised was a merciful god of peace, not a merciless god of war.

Medianoche was not a man who could let things go. He would go to Montserrat and visit his third wife. And when he saw her again, his would be the last face she ever saw.

Yes.

He wouldn't send a Horseman. He would go there and do it himself.

The bathroom door opened. Caprica Ortiz had her phone in her hand, was ending a call.

He stood and asked, "Any word from your contact on the assassin named Gideon?"

"He has heard of him. Many people have heard of him."

"And?"

"They say he is the son of the devil."

Chapter 4

City Across the River

In Buenos Aires, I'd jumped out of moving trains. Shotgun and I had fallen from buildings. All of us had been shot at with bullets and dodged grenades. But more important, accidentally, I had met the man I knew as Midnight. In the slum of Buenos Aires, I had gone hand to hand against that mercenary. We had gone fist to fist, kick for kick, knee for knee, elbow for elbow, and blow for blow. He was older, but he was fast; he was strong; he was wicked; he was deadly. He had pounded me in ways I'd never been struck before. Every ache and pain I felt now was due to that fight, and I had tried to serve him worse, plus a special dessert.

Midnight and I had battled. I'd fought Medianoche. That was his name in Buenos Aires.

Medianoche.

I'd gone into hell and fought a demon brought back from the dead.

We had brawled in the winter rain. That had been the hardest fight I'd ever had.

He was everything my mother had said he was. And more.

For me, this contract had started in Miami, doing a job for the international grifter Arizona. I had taken a contract that had me dispatching one of her rivals, a man by the name of Hopkins. Somehow he had conned her out of fifteen million, but he had a briefcase that, paired with an identical one, would hold the key to extreme wealth. After that job, I went to meet Arizona and was surprised when she wobbled into the Aventura Starbucks pregnant. There she told me my part wasn't done. Arizona reminded me of a debt. A debt I owed her new lover, Scamz, the man who had taken his own father's name. Once upon a time he had saved my life. He wanted reciprocity for that small favor: getting the other briefcase. That debt had taken me to Argentina, and I had faced a group called the Four Horsemen. Argentina had been ten flavors of hell. It had been one long battle with no pause.

As it rained, we were attacked with bullets and sledgehammers, and the leader of those lunatics was the man they called Medianoche. There was no doubt he was the man I had known as Midnight. But I had killed a man named Midnight a long time ago. I'd killed him to stop him from choking my mother to death. In North Carolina, I'd sat next to my mother and watched him die. Somehow he had defeated Death. And Fate had made our paths cross once again.

My face was swollen, same for one eye, I could barely open and close my hands, and my soul, for the first time, was fractured. My heartbeat was erratic. I anticipated the Four Horsemen would magically appear, guns blazing and grenades flying.

Argentina had been more than traumatic.

It was like being thrown into Fallujah.

The faint echoes from the explosions remained in my ears. The stench from Buenos Aires' Villa 31 remained in my nostrils, and the sewage that had inundated my damaged skin would take weeks to wash away. And the pain from my fight with Midnight had saturated my bones. I felt like Robin fighting Batman, the student against the master. No, more like Robin fighting Deathstroke, the mercenary who could defeat Batman because he had no morals, no code, no honor. He was faster and stronger than I had thought he would be. I wasn't as good as I thought I was, not compared to him. I felt something else. I felt doubt. I was younger, but he was so fucking powerful. I'd never felt that way before.

He still wasn't dead, but I told myself that I was safe for now. That all of my friends were safe. Everything was as normal as it could be for people like us.

Sometimes a man had to lie to himself in order to not lose the plot.

We had escaped Buenos Aires, crossed the river on a yacht that the British con man Scamz and his lover, Arizona, had used to transport both their wounded and their dead. Funds had been transferred. Our job was done. Then I collected my crew and we had gone our separate ways.

We were taking the bus from Colonia del Sacramento to Montevideo, where we would plan our escape out of the country.

I was with Shotgun, the heavyweight boxer turned assassin, and Konstantin, the Russian hit man who many said looked like George Clooney or Cary Grant, depending on the angle. He was also known as the Man in the White Shoes. After going up against the Four Horsemen of the Apocalypse, both were wounded, but both were in much better shape than I was in.

War was hell. And this had been whatever existed on the other side of hell.

Colonia to Montevideo wasn't that far, about 177 kilometers, or 110 miles.

We were only across the Río de la Plata. We were still in Horsemen territory.

We were still trying to breathe while living in the heated mouth of danger.

By the time the crowded bus arrived in Montevideo, Shotgun and Konstantin were both awake and talking in English. Hardly an ear on the bus understood English, and if they did, Shotgun's southern accent and southern-fried colloquialisms would have left them baffled. Konstantin's Russian accent remained as well. I had stayed awake, on guard while they slept the last leg of the trip. The bus had hit a bump and rocked, and both had woken suddenly, like they were having flashbacks, had freed themselves from nightmares and were ready to fight. We surveyed the terrain, took note of any car coming up behind us.

The Horsemen had destroyed *villas* to get to us, so I knew they would blow up the bus we were on, kill everyone, just to satiate their appetite. I'd gone up against many people, had fought for my life more times than I could remember, and I had never met anyone so damn evil.

Medianoche. Midnight. He was the man my mother had told me was my father.

He had a good left hook, if nothing else. He had a chin like a brick and could take a blow.

Rain poured as the crowded bus drew closer to the capital of Uruguay.

A twenty-thousand-dollar Rolex I'd bought in Puerto Rico was on my left arm. Not until then did I see it had garnered attention from the passengers, people who didn't make that much in a year. When I had been with Scamz and Arizona, by their taste, the watch was pedestrian.

Over and over someone pointed at me and said, *"Rico. Eres hombre muy rico."*

The Rolex made them think I was a rich man. The watch meant nothing to me.

I told them, *"No soy rico. El reloj no es auténtico. Es una imitación. Soy pobre, como tu."*

The *paísitos* laughed, nodded, believing me when I told them it was a knockoff, lost interest in my Rolex, and went back to their lives.

In English, my mentor, Konstantin, said, "Gideon. Shotgun. Get ready to roll out."

The bus stopped and the crowd started gathering their belongings. Raincoats. Winter coats. Umbrellas. Some wore plastic or garbage bags to stay dry. Some carried their belongings and had no umbrella, moved as if the cold rain was a summer drizzle. I waited a moment, sweating due to discomfort that wouldn't let me be. When I tried to stand up, the throbbing from the beating grew, then doubled up and hit me like Mike Tyson in his fight with Spinks.

I took short breaths to quell the agony, gripped the backs of two seats to stay afloat.

Shotgun heard me grunt, then looked back and asked, "You okay?"

"I'm good. Just had a moment. Been sitting down on my injuries too long."

"Well, you need to walk to get your blood circulating. Don't need no blood clot."

The moment I stepped off the bus in Montevideo, it felt like the world was made of Jell-O. But I was going to fight it. Collapsing would mean that Medianoche had won this battle.

I asked, "Are we going to try and get out of Carrasco International Airport?"

Konstantin shook his head. "No. They would be on alert. We keep the original plan."

I said, "We exit out of Brazil."

Konstantin nodded.

I said, "Brazil stinks."

Shotgun asked, "How come?"

"They have bad sewage systems. In a lot of the bathrooms they put their toilet paper in a trash can. And when the trash is full they keep throwing more toilet paper on top."

Shotgun said, "Doo-doo paper, like Charmin?"

"Yeah. Doo-doo paper like Charmin."

"That's nasty. Like down-in-the-country-with-outhouses nasty. My granddaddy and them lived down in Grenada, Mississippi, behind a lumberyard, and those outhouses was nasty."

"And to make it worse, they have padded toilet seats that stick to your butt, too."

"Well, I hope the streets there are cleaner than the ones in Buenos Aires. Never seen so much dog doo-doo on the streets in my life. They act like they don't even see it."

"Streets in Buenos Aires are as dirty as its money. They'll fight for the Falklands, but not to make people clean up after their dogs."

I was talking, rambling, to keep alert. The conversation meant nothing.

As we followed the crowd, the ice-cold rain felt good on my heated skin, but pain threw me on a flaming merry-go-round spinning at one hundred miles an hour. I misstepped. Shotgun grabbed my shoulder, kept me from going down to the ground. I got my balance, limped along with Konstantin and Shotgun, moved to the side of the crowd, got closer to the businesses, hardly able to stand, limped to the wall of a nearby building, doubled over, and began regurgitating. It went on for ten minutes. I was sweating like it was the Fourth of July in Atlanta.

The world was a blur. I had too far to go.

I put my hand against the nearest wall, grunted, straightened up.

Shotgun said, "You in bad shape, Gideon. Real bad shape. I can see that now."

Able to see out of only one eye, I said, "Just point me in the direction we're going."

Arm wounded and in a sling, Konstantin was bruised too. They had been in the shootout of all shootouts in the middle of the streets. The Russian had been a true warrior. If not for him, Scamzito and Arizona, his queen Scamz, as well as her younger sister, Sierra, would all be dead.

Arizona's brother hadn't been so lucky.

He had taken a bullet, was killed in the streets.

His corpse was on the yacht with them, a floating mortuary.

Konstantin said, "We need to get Gideon to another doctor."

I said, "I'm good."

"You probably have a fever. You're infected. That's why you're puking."

Shotgun told Konstantin, "It was real nasty where we was, where he had that fight."

As people who called themselves *paísitos*, people from the little country of Uruguay, passed by, I had to lean against another wall. Medianoche had gotten the best of me. I had wanted to leave that motherfucker Midnight gurgling in the mud. If I had had it my way, he would have died of a broken neck, after his spine had been shattered into a million pieces.

Konstantin said, "Big city, places to hide, but we can't stay here too long."

Shotgun nodded. "Buncha people looking at us and talking real fast in Spanish."

I sucked it up and we sped up, hobbled along at the pace of the walking wounded. Konstantin and Shotgun led the way as we traversed through Spanish Colonial and Art Deco structures. It felt like I had hiked a marathon by the time we made it to the open shopping area, the flea market at Plaza Constitución. The side of Konstantin's face was still bloodied. Shotgun was probably in the best shape of the three of us, but he wasn't near one hundred percent.

We were battle worn, but we were also hungry. We grabbed some of the local delicacies, *chivito* and *asado. Puchero* and *pascualina.* Shotgun didn't ask what was in it. He ate like he was starved. We needed the energy. We ate fast, then had to hustle by museums, churches, and government buildings, then rush through the Gateway of Ciudadela and get to Ciudad Vieja.

Konstantin said, "Gideon, son, you're not in any condition to go to Brazil, not today."

"I'm fine. I'll slow it down when we get across the border."

"No, in your shape, you won't make it three more hours. You're fucked-up. We need to make a new plan. I see where you're hurt on the outside, but you might be busted up inside too."

Shotgun said, "He's right, Gideon. Listen to the man. You went twelve rounds over there."

Trying to not sound paranoid, I said, "We're not far from the Four Horsemen."

Shotgun nodded. "They're across that river that looks like the Mississippi on steroids."

Konstantin said, "I'll get us some better hardware. Then I'll get us a place to regroup."

Konstantin had a contact in the area, a man who had ties to an arms dealer on the run. Konstantin ordered us some equipment. Said we could get armed with Steyr AUGs and FAMAS assault rifles, weapons many used, including the New Zealand forces.

When we were back near the artsy shops and galleries, we sat down in a café.

They sat down to force me to rest a moment.

Shotgun was a big man in a land of Lilliputians, so it was hard finding anything in his size. He stood out in this part of the world. Uruguayan kids ran over and tried to sneak pictures with him when he wasn't looking. It scared Shotgun. After what we had been through, anyone who came too close could be the enemy, children included. Children had shot at us on the other side of the river. Children working for the Horsemen had tried to put us to sleep.

Shotgun said, "I definitely ain't in Atlanta no more. Nothing down here to remind me of Malcolm X or Martin Luther King. It's like we landed in a different universe, with all the signs in Spanish."

"It's its own world here."

"Sounded like the Korean folks we passed by were speaking Spanish. Ain't never seen that before. Korean folks in South America speaking Spanish better than Mexicans."

We found some new clothes for all of us. Konstantin even found himself another suit and a new pair of white shoes. I went into a bathroom, redressed my wounds. Two stitches had popped. Those small wounds were too open. Konstantin tried to find a doctor; one could be there in an hour, but we decided we were getting too much attention and moved on.

Konstantin arranged a ride to a place we could lie low for a while. A Brazilian man came to us and loaded us in his small car. It was a tight fit, but we were moving in the right direction.

I sat in the backseat with Shotgun. As soon as we started to roll, I was in and out of consciousness again. I tried to stay awake, especially since I had taken blows to the head, but my body kept shutting down. When I came to, still groggy, Shotgun and Konstantin were talking.

Shotgun said, "We need to get him to an emergency room. Or another doctor."

"We'll get him to a bed and I'll make a few calls. If we're not going to be able to exit as planned, if we're going to be trapped here with the condition we're in, I'll call Hawks and the—"

Then I was gone again. Not all the way. But the world was a blur, their words garbled.

The weather worsened, as did my injuries, and both slowed us down.

I shivered, and the shivers went on for twenty minutes, if not longer.

Konstantin was right. My external wounds were obvious.

If I was busted up on the inside, I had no idea how bad.

I had taken too many hard blows, not just against Medianoche.

I couldn't remember half the men I'd fought, beaten, and killed. I couldn't remember the number of men who had fought, beaten, and almost killed me. Once upon a time, I had died.

Today might be the day I made that journey again.

My vision remained blurry. The trip was like being driven through clouds.

It hurt to inhale. I couldn't breathe. Had to find a better position so I didn't suffocate. When I shifted and moved my body, pain marched in circles, stabbed me with fiery bayonets.

It took a lifetime to make it 185 miles to Punta del Diablo, a sleepy sea town with a population of no more than four hundred. It was good that that was as far as we were going, because the aching became too much to bear. I threw up again, did that until there was nothing in my stomach, and after that it was ten minutes of dry heaving. Where we stopped was like being in the country, more blue-collar, only by the raging sea. The land of the poor, where each home housed at least three generations. Colorful fishing boats were in the sand. Each inhale was the scent of the river.

Konstantin asked, "Can you handle getting him out of the vehicle?"

"I got him. He's a heavy so-'n'-so."

The next thing I knew, I was falling. I dreamed I was being thrown into an open grave, but jerked awake and landed on a bed. Konstantin was on the phone. Sounded like he was talking to the assassin Hawks again. Heard him say *Memphis*. That's where she was. He made another call, and I heard him say something about trying to contact another assassin, the Bajan. The safe house was in an area of fishermen and artisans, was a small hotel, and it helped that this wasn't tourist season.

Konstantin said, "Our new toys will be here within the hour."

Shotgun asked, "Hope we gonna get some bombs and rocket launchers like they had."

"We're not going to be armed like the Four Horsemen, but we won't stay naked."

I had lacerations. And the open wounds had been exposed to the raw sewage and mud in the *villas* of Buenos Aires. I knew I needed antibiotics and more Band-Aids.

We had left all the medicine on the yacht with Scamzito and his half-dead crew.

I stood up long enough to look out the window at the rain.

Again a wave of pain came, took me to my knees, then to the tiled floor.

The room did that merry-go-round number again.

I fell into a warm pool of darkness.

A voice called out, "*Gideon. Gideon. Gideon.* Fuck, did you pass out again?"

When I looked up, Konstantin was there, arm in a sling, trying to pull me up.

I sat on the bed. He made me get horizontal, then played doctor the best he could.

He said, "Somehow Midnight is alive."

"Yeah."

"When you were a boy, you saw him die, right? With your own eyes."

"Yes." I thought back to when I was seven. "I shot him in the head."

"Then what?"

"My mother held me. I held her. He had beat her bad. I remember that. The noise woke me up. He was choking her, had her up in the air, had almost broken her neck."

"Did you check his body? Think back to then. Did you take a pulse?"

"We covered it with a sheet, got away from him. It was a dead body. I was seven. My mother was scared. She didn't want to touch him. We ran away on a Greyhound, had no money. Old folks gave us chicken. Never will forget that. Ended up in Montreal. We were penniless."

I remembered us being penniless, but happier. I remembered my mother buying me a comic book; then I sat on a stoop and read it while she smoked and taught me to speak French. She was calm, relaxed, when she thought Midnight was dead. One of our best days. Quebec was good for us for a while.

Konstantin looked at my swollen eye. "Jesus fucking Christ, son. When did you fight him?"

"After we had the second briefcase, I went back after him. I fucked up."

"Gideon. Fuck. You should have focused on the job. You put us all at risk."

"I know. I fucked up. Yeah. I had to face him. I know he's alive. I know he's real."

"Son, he's a fuckin' merc. We're hired guns. We don't operate on their level. We use a .22 or a plastic bag, or drown them in a bathtub. They think they're fighting a war in Vietnam."

"Yeah, I know. But we managed to beat them. I killed one of them."

"He knows you're alive. He knows you're the one who left him for dead. Your mother—"

"I told him Thelma was . . . told him she was . . . deceased. I told him that my mother . . . my mother . . ."

My voice faded.

That warm black pool came back for me.

This time I didn't fight it.

Chapter 5

Dangerous Profession

Medianoche dressed, put on his dark suit, dark shirt, dark tie, and dark trench coat. He was armed with three guns. Two in holsters, another in an ankle strap. Two blades were in his gear as well. Once he was outfitted in his tailored clothing, all lined in Kevlar, he adjusted what was most important. The black tie stated who he was in the Horsemen. Revelations, chapter six. Loosely interpreted, black was the color of the horse ridden by the lawgiver, the one carrying the scales of justice. He helped Caprica with her dress, then eased on her gray wool coat.

Caprica Ortiz said, "My contact will call me back as soon as possible."

"I know that people down here don't rush, but I need it on North American time."

"Understood. But I am not in control. Only the person in the middle."

"I need more than name recognition and praise for a two-bit hired gun."

"There are rumors that he killed at least fifteen people on the island of Antigua."

"*Rumor* is just a fancy word for *gossip*. I deal in facts. Hard facts. I need my war to go in the right direction. Tell your contact I said that."

"I will get facts. What do you need to know regarding Gideon?"

"Did he leave Argentina? Or did he and the rest of those mutts lay low?"

"I don't know."

He hadn't been thinking like the Beast. He never should have come to this hotel.

The enemy could still be in the city, could be outside his door waiting.

Medianoche hid a gun under the fedora in his hand. Disheveled sheets behind them, he left the room first, then motioned for Caprica to follow. He put her on his left side. She put her arm in his. Even now he treated her like the lady she was. He was thankful that his abusive father had beaten gentlemanly ways and manners into his bones. That drunk bastard did have manners.

On the elevator, alone with the married woman he'd had six ways to Sunday, Medianoche stared at his own reflection in the metal part of the vertical carriage.

He saw the shopworn face of a mercenary.

Like his left eye, his youth would never return.

The elevator stopped. Medianoche stood with the business end of his gun aimed at the unknown. The door opened. A group of middle-aged men got on. Germans. All wore suits. Medianoche's senses caught fire. Each man was armed. Not wanting to be cornered in a moving coffin, he touched Caprica's arm, held her biceps, led her off the elevator, let the Germans have the lift. Once it was gone, he pushed the button, called for another vertical carriage.

She said, "Those men. They stared at me. One looks familiar."

"Stay at my left side. My weapon is in my right hand."

His nine millimeter remained hidden by his fedora. Caprica Ortiz didn't question him. That told Medianoche she was no stranger to violence. Her world was wicked. The next carriage was empty. He told her to get on, and he would meet her in the lobby. She refused to leave him. He took her hand and led her to the stairs. Even then he smelled the scent of bad men. Men like him.

They exited the stairwell at the ground level. Medianoche searched for the Germans he had seen. None waited for him. There was no ambush. He rounded the corner, entered the section with a bar, lounge, and dining area, and there they were. He saw Russians. Frenchmen. Africans. Jamaicans. Middle Easterners. They were in separate spaces, like each corner was a temporary embassy, drinking like they were in Rick's Café.

He saw men who wore Kevlar-lined clothing and traveled only in cars that were bulletproof and had run-flat tires. Caprica frowned at those men, then stepped forward. She looked for faces she had hunted over the decades, searched for her version of Dr. Gerhard Bohne, Josef Mengele, or Adolf Eichmann. She found no one; Medianoche saw that expression of disappointment, anger, and fear; then the tenseness in her body gradually dissipated.

But Medianoche saw a familiar face, a man who had no business in his country.

Eye contact was made.

Medianoche was tempted to go to that man, gun first, but he moved on, Caprica Ortiz at his side. He wanted to get her out of the building, away from trouble, out of his affairs.

He told her, "Don't forget what I need, who I need you to locate."

"Gideon. I should hear back from my source by morning."

"And don't forget Arizona and Scamz. His name is spelled S–C–A–M–Z. A Latin man with a strong British accent."

"I will be your person in the middle, but to be clear, doing business comes at a cost, and that price will be deducted from your fee from my next contract."

"Who is your contact? Is it someone military or in the Argentine government?"

She moved her gray hair from her face. "I will never say. It would not be wise."

She was lean, like most of the women in Buenos Aires, and definitely of Italian ancestry.

Men and women passed whispering, "*Cambio. Cambio.*"

Hustlers exchanged dollars for pesos at a better rate than hotels and *casas de cambio*, but sometimes tourists ended up trading good money for counterfeit bills.

Medianoche escorted her to a black-and-yellow Radio Taxi. He shook her hand as if it were the end of a grueling business meeting, nothing more. He opened the door. She eased inside. Once inside where she could not be seen, she smiled like she wanted a good-bye kiss.

Medianoche said, "I enjoyed you."

"*Igualmente.*"

"*Chau.*"

"*Chau.*"

Her taxi pulled away, blended with a thousand vehicles, most of them driven by shit drivers. Medianoche watched Caprica Ortiz's taxi until it disappeared in traffic that rivaled the madness at the Arc de Triomphe in Paris. He watched to make sure Caprica Ortiz wasn't being followed. It was after one in the morning and the city was just waking up. Clubs didn't get busy until three A.M. and no one had gone to dinner before ten P.M. He frowned at the amazing nocturnal city. Sirens. Horns. Buenos Aires was the Paris of South America, but like no other place in the world.

His gun was ready. It had been ready. He knew a man was creeping up on him.

Without looking behind him, Medianoche asked, "What are you doing in my country?"

"*¿Qué haces, boludo?* You know I came for the steak, *medialunas*, and tango."

"Tienes mas mentiras que el truco."

"Why would I lie to a man of your stature? That would be bad for my health."

"I'd hoped scum like you had come to clean up the mounds of dog shit all over the city."

Medianoche turned, faced a well-built Israeli, a sixty-year-old man no longer welcomed in his own country of warriors. Assad held a trench coat over his arm, a gun in his hidden hand.

Medianoche said, "With your war crimes, I'm surprised you haven't been beheaded."

"Enemies have been many, but fate has been kind, as my escapes have been swift."

Medianoche stopped pointing his gun at Benjamin Assad's heart.

Assad relaxed his weapon at the same time. "Do you mind if we get out of the weather?"

"I have somewhere to be."

"When has anyone in Buenos Aires ever been on time for anything? You show up two hours late, you are still earlier than everyone else. *La noche está en pañales.* Come inside."

Medianoche followed Assad back inside the hotel, into the lobby, toward the Russians, the Nigerians. Assad stopped a dozen feet away before facing Medianoche.

They were far enough away to not be heard, but they could be seen. Medianoche knew Assad could've jaw jacked outside, but he was a man who liked to impress. He wanted to be seen talking to a Horseman in order to elevate his status, his value among the others.

Again Medianoche asked, "What brings you back here?"

"*Rescatate.* Calm down, my friend. The Beast didn't tell you our arrangement?"

"He tells me what I need to know. The important things. I assume it's another auction."

"Of course."

"Of course. And the fees will be paid to our group when all is done."

Assad nodded, evaluated Medianoche's face. "You did not win the prize."

"What prize are you referring to, Assad?"

"The chatter is the Four Horsemen had an interesting day and frustrating night."

"Care to elaborate?"

"When all was said and done, the Four Horsemen were not victorious."

"We are *always* victorious. What we were hired to do, we accomplished."

"A British man named Scamz is telling everyone he bested the Four Horsemen."

"Never heard of a British man named Scamz."

"*De repente tienes una vena.*"

"*Tírame la goma. Tomátela.* I'm not about to blow a fuse."

Assad offered a smile that reminded Medianoche of Lee Harvey Oswald. "You are almost not recognizable. You have taken a beating as if you have been in the La Boca pits. The word is you had a moment with one of Scamz's men in the *villas*. Heard it was quite the battle."

"Are you or someone in this room working with Scamz's cowardly organization?"

"Ah, you do know him."

"Fucking answer me or end up with one eye *less* than I have."

"Scamz is new in the arena and has quickly built his reputation on your back."

"How many of them are dead? Did the pregnant Asian bitch who calls herself Arizona die at the base of *General Justo José de Urquiza*? Did she bleed out in the streets at the roundabout?"

"I have no idea who died where, when, nor why. Only know Scamz bested you."

"He's a dead man walking. Same goes for anyone who comes my way on his behalf."

"Well, I will say this. And I say this in confidentiality. Beware of the Uruguayans."

"Fuck the Uruguayans. *Me chupa un huevo.*"

"Many of their men died here two days ago. You created widows and orphans."

"Unless they have a deal with a coffin maker, they know to stay across the river."

Assad smiled. "We have a planeload of Russian- and American-made weaponry to sell. We have armament that has been intercepted, equipment meant for their allies. No serial numbers. My inventory is deep but will not be deep for long. Come to the auction. An M4 will go for four grand. My AT4 rocket launchers are on special at two thousand. No one beats my prices. Buy a drone. Every man in your business should have a drone. I am offering a General Atomics MQ-1 Predator for three million, a million cheaper than anyone else. Consider buying the drone."

Medianoche paused, stuck on the fact that Scamz had somehow boasted of his victory, and men were arriving here, on his turf, because now they sensed the Horsemen were weak.

Medianoche spoke casually. "If we become interested, you will deal with me."

Assad smiled, as if that had answered an unspoken question. "Not with the Beast?"

"Be glad we didn't meet you when you arrived, Assad."

Unfazed, Assad said, "Maybe we will talk more when I see you in a couple of hours."

"Why would I see you in a few hours?"

"The Beast didn't tell you about our most recent agreement?"

"You tell me; then I will verify what you say with him."

"Colombia was too violent. We grew weary of dealing with the Colombian government, paramilitary groups, crime syndicates, and left-wing guerrillas, so now warriors will come here twice a year and brawl in the La Boca Pits. They are reopening the pits tonight."

"You can go to El Lugar Repugnante and play your games, let your boys be gladiators, but keep this in mind, Assad. You are on Four Horsemen grounds. After the death matches, once you have concluded your arms sales, rinse down the blood, get rid of the bodies, and leave my country as fast as you can. And we expect our cut from the activity in the Pits as well."

"You're not a Porteña. You're an American, an expatriate, an immigrant on this soil."

"Try me. Wise guy, fucking try me. I own wherever I stand, no matter the country."

"The Beast was notified and he agreed. So if there is a change, I need to hear that from your leader, from the Beast, not from his executive officer, who has been left out of the loop."

"If you have heard it from me, then you have heard it from the Beast. I just told you your new walking orders, so let me know if we have a problem, and I'll fix it right now."

Assad, with his Lee Harvey Oswald smile, said, "Be careful dealing with Caprica Ortiz."

Medianoche paused. "Caprica Ortiz is none of your concern."

"She offends people in high places; some say it goes as far as Casa Rosada."

"Not your fucking business."

"Walk away from her. As they say, don't shit where you eat."

"Have a good night, Assad. You have two days to get the fuck out of Argentina."

"If my business affairs are not concluded by then?"

"Buy yourself and whoever is standing at your side a mausoleum."

Assad went back to his cavalry, gun underneath his trench coat. He said something to his Spartans; then he and his Kevlar-suited warriors raised their glasses to Medianoche. As an insult. Again, Medianoche took in the other men in the lobby. Frenchmen. Africans. Japanese. Men from Brazil. They taunted Medianoche's loss. They disrespected the death of his soldiers.

An army that lost a war in its own country was looked down upon.

He walked to the center of the room, stood in challenge.

"You *pussies* have something to say? *Stand the fuck up.* Assad was outside licking my balls and saying that someone in this fuckin' room wanted to challenge the Four Horsemen."

A hush fell across the room.

Medianoche said, "Who wants to stand up and talk shit to a Horseman? We can make this space our new El Lugar Repugnante."

Men who had dared now became nervous.

Before Medianoche was a Horseman, he was a man called Midnight. Midnight had served many men their final darkness. All in the room knew that. He had been legendary in the pits. They had seen him step in the ring and throw one blow. One blow and the fight was done, and his challenger was on the floor, dead. They had seen him battle adversaries with swords, and the man before them won every time with only his fists.

"Have your drinks, have as many women as you can, and have the auction and the fights. Then get out of *my* country. The Four Horsemen will bury anyone left behind. And you won't be dead when your body is put in the ground, *headfirst*. You won't be close to dead."

No one said a word. No one stood. No one reached for a gun.

That was the echo of fear. That was the reverberation of respect.

"And we will expect fifty percent of the take from the games in the pits."

Men shifted, looked unhappy, the fee double the normal, but no one said a word.

Medianoche turned around and left the hotel, loaded gun still under his fedora, ready to pop off a few. He walked beyond where he had put Caprica Ortiz in a taxi. He walked down the avenue, where every building complemented the next, and every man wore proper shoes, acceptable jeans, had his shirt tucked in, and wore a jacket that fit correctly. Up in the States pathetic men wore clothes made for clowns, had their pants sagging, underwear showing, then called that fashion. His father had beat him if his clothes were out of order. Made him proper. Buenos Aires had class, but at the same time it was a city where no one walked and used an iPhone, unless they wanted to be robbed by a hooligan. The city was also filled with horribly dressed tourists, and they always congregated at Plaza Dorrego, Plaza Francia, or La Boca.

He passed a wall that had been spray-painted LAS MALVINAS SON

ARGENTINAS. That message meant that the Malvinas belonged to Argentina, not to the fucking British. That war was a sore spot and left both anger and embarrassment in the air. It would always be about war. Be it your toys or a country, you had to fight for what was yours. You had to keep others from taking what was yours. Or you would end up shot or thrown out of airplanes over the ocean, after you had been blindfolded, tortured, and raped.

Medianoche paused, checked to see if Assad or some other fool was shadowing him, then turned around, moved on, inhaled the endemic corruption in the air. With inflation running at about thirty percent per year, despite everything in sight being built with opulence in mind, he was surprised anyone survived here. It was the land of the rich and the poor. No such thing as a real middle class. Two dog walkers, *paseaperros*, passed by, each being led by two dozen dogs. Dogs were a status symbol—walking dogs and leaving mountains of canine shit behind, an honorable profession. Tourists were easy to spot. Fat ones, Americans. Ones with bad teeth, British. The pale ones were Canadians. Visitors wore tennis shoes. And did a bad job of avoiding the dog shit. Most stayed in Palermo, where people spoke English and drank at Starbucks. Argentine women wore five-inch heels and walked down cobblestone streets like pros. Same-sex couples passed by. No one cared in Buenos Aires. Droves of poor children were out selling flowers and begging, if not stealing. Some had been trafficked and would work until sunrise. By the age of six, children from the villas were expert pickpockets. And dangerous. He passed a *cartoneo* who was separating trash to find cardboard and other recyclable goods to earn a dime. The man's cart was loaded and cardboard was stacked ten feet high, like he had braved the rain and the cold and covered at least twenty-five blocks. Many men worked all day, then spent the night hustling cardboard and plastic.

Medianoche passed them all. None fucked with him.

Bad people knew a bad man. He was the baddest of them all.

A few blocks later, he put the gun away, slid the fedora onto his head, and, dressed in darkness from head to toe, the hue of midnight, kept his arm low, the proper way to hail a taxi. Hailing high was for a bus. A moment later he eased into the next available cab. Their taxis were black with yellow tops. Looked like four-door bumble-bees. A slight headache came on. He attributed that to the stress.

He told the aged and overweight Peruvian driver his destination.

He looked back, checked again to make sure no fool had tailed him, had waited for him to turn his back so they could come at him, guns blazing. He had left himself too damn vulnerable.

His anger came unbridled, and there was an abrupt flash of brightness. Medianoche cringed, reached to hold his head, tried to stop it from occurring again.

As it had been inside the hotel room, Buenos Aires became white light.

Old images went by, the brain whirring, clicking like an old projector.

A thousand blurred images. Everything went blank; then time had no meaning.

Like he had been on the floor of that brothel in North Carolina, he was dead.

Chapter 6

Between Midnight and Dawn

Medianoche heard the aged Peruvian driver shouting. It sounded like the man was far, far away, but with each shout he came closer. Medianoche finally blinked, his only eye coming into focus. He realized they were miles away from where he had gotten inside the Radio Taxi, were parked in front of the penthouse that housed the Four Horsemen.

In Spanish, in a state of fright, the taxi driver yelled, "Mister, are you okay?"

"How long . . . How long have we been double-parked here blocking traffic?"

"Señor . . . I . . . I . . . I called for your attention many times for more than two minutes. I thought you had died. I was going to drive your body to Hospital Alemán."

He had been lost in purgatory for the duration of the ride, from practically the moment he stepped in the taxi. He had died again, this time for at least fifteen goddamn minutes.

He walked toward the building, then stopped when he spotted something on the ground. At first he thought it was a shattered cell phone. It wasn't. It was a broken sensor.

It had been used to track the briefcases. He stepped on it, crunched it under his shoe.

When Medianoche exited their private elevator at the seventeenth floor, eighteen floors above Buenos Aires' concrete jungle, another mercenary waited. He smelled her belligerence and argumentativeness before he exited the lift. The mercenary's given name was Amaravati Panchali Ganeshes. In South America she was Señorita Raven. The Punjabi was the other remaining member of the Four Horsemen. She had survived the battle against the Scamz Organization.

She was the last member to be recruited, chosen by the Beast. She was a woman born in Mumbai, but who grew up in the ghettos of Saint Louis. Wavy black hair. High cheekbones. Dark lipstick. Red winter coat. White sweater. Black skinny jeans. Red boots. Red purse. Señorita Raven paced the hallway. Medianoche exited the ThyssenKrupp elevator and frowned at the Punjabi. Solid woman. Had outrun him in the battle last night. The skinny jeans showed her frame, broadcasted she had just the right amount of this and that to make an old soldier want to lounge eleven inches deep inside her sweet spot for a while. She had enough arrogance for a man to want to get inside and try to break her in half. A dark history lived between them. A recent dark history. Her eyes were bloodshot. He could tell she was oscillating between anger and grief for their lost comrades, her face etched with guilt and self-blame, still a woman in need of a good fight.

He said, "You smell like you took a swim in a distillery."

"Needed something to take away the pain."

"Pain?"

"From the shotgun blast I took to the chest. Big black gun popped me one good."

"You need a medic?"

"I can handle it. There ain't nothing good old Kentucky bourbon can't fix."

"You were fine when you left here, all things considered."

The small gap between her teeth showed. "The adrenaline tapped out. Adrenaline left and the pain arrived. Became my own medic and made friends with Dr. Bourbon at the airport."

Señorita Raven was filled with as much arrogance as her dermis was peppered with shrapnel. Once she was beautiful enough to be Miss World. When she was in the Middle East, she had been too close to an IED. Her comrades had been blown to smithereens: one second on patrol, the next each a jigsaw puzzle being put in at least a dozen boxes. She had survived, but the near-death experience had left her screaming, with scorching-hot metal sizzling into her flesh. *Into her face*. It looked like acne, until a man was up close. Medianoche stared at the damage.

He said, "XO, let's work. Show me the files."

"The Disposables."

She followed him into the apartment that had served as the Beast's quarters.

She said, "The swelling has taken. Your face looks worse than mine."

"With ice and time, mine will heal."

"Touché."

Medianoche stared her down. "Does the damage to your face bother you?"

"Sir, does missing your left eye bother you?"

He nodded. "Your face is fixable. Fix it. Be beautiful again."

"Allah allowed this to happen, so I figured he wanted me close to being FUBAR."

"It's not that bad, but a woman's face is her vanity, even one carrying an M16."

"It's bad enough. For a woman's face, yeah, it's bad enough. Men wear battle scars better. Men get respected for battle scars. I'm not as gorgeous as I once was, and I was a traffic stopper, but still I've seen uglier bitches and they don't have a scar on their skin. I'll survive."

"You didn't seek more corrective surgery at Walter Reed?"

"Sir, when your friends are blown the fuck up, walking into a hospital where soldiers and marines have lost limbs and complaining about not being cute enough to get a Friday night date when you still have both arms and both legs and can shit three times a day and still wipe your own ass—complaining about catching some shrapnel seems very selfish."

"It's your reminder."

"It's my guilt."

Medianoche took in his former friend's meticulous living accommodations, the countless medals and commendations on the walls, things to do on his calendar, as if he intended to return.

Señorita Raven said, "He thought he had killed Gideon."

"What do you mean?"

"When we had cornered Scamz, Arizona, the Russian, and the other guy. The Beast jumped in the fight and killed the other guy right away. He thought he had killed Gideon. I'm convinced he thought he had killed his secret and could continue with his lies."

"I can't argue. The files you uncovered prove he knew Thelma was alive. They made a baby a few years ago. I'm having a hard time digesting that information, but it's in his own words. The Beast had to have known about Gideon. He was still fucking the gaucho's mother."

She nodded, scowled. "You should have killed Arizona. Queen Scamz."

"Hindsight."

"Remember what they say overseas. In Iraq popping a pregnant woman is a two-for-one. No matter how pretty she is, you pop her. You looked at her pretty face and couldn't pull the trigger. The Beast shot her twice and tried to stomp her face into the asphalt. I popped her sister. You should've killed Arizona. If you had killed the bitch, then everything—"

Medianoche raised his voice. "Stand down, Señorita Raven."

"I tried to blow that beautiful pregnant bitch the fuck up."

"Don't let your alcohol and attitude get you dumped in an unmarked grave."

Using the office of a dead man as their hub, they got down to business.

Señorita Raven hacked into the Beast's computer, fired it up, opened files meant for no one other than the Beast to see, the file LOS DESECHABLES.

Medianoche said, "Show me Los Desechables that might fit the bill."

"These are ones who have no problem taking their military training into the private sector. Some have already done that, but never on the level that we operate. Messages have been sent. Five on the list were with Blackwater and were KIA over the last few months. One was in a car accident and is now a quadriplegic. Three suicides. About ten fell off grid, so that means they're homeless and living on the streets somewhere. Messages went out and three replied favorably within ten minutes. Just need more confirmations."

"He vetted them in advance? This many? Did he see a war coming?"

"Uruguay has been a growing problem."

"That they have. They've become bold and crossed the river."

"The Beast was prepared. White supremacists, neo-Nazis, and skinheads who had joined the military to get the talents to overthrow what they have called the Zionist Occupation Government had been filtered out. People who had enlisted to get trained by Uncle Sam so they could get out and kick up shit and start a race war were filtered out, but there are still more than a few crazy 'whiskey poppers.' But you never know what you're getting until you see what you got."

She went through the list of men and women who had committed various offenses, disrespected their superiors, violated regulations. One had made a sex tape with himself and a female superior. Señorita Raven covered twenty in total, but only eleven had been put in the stack for consideration. All had been well trained, fallen from grace, done time, been reduced in rank, lost pay, been dishonorably discharged with PTSD, and then left in the wind, some collecting bottles to eat.

Señorita Raven asked, "Which ones should we consider?"

Medianoche paused. "Bring them all in."

"I didn't think we'd take more than three, four at the most."

"Get the new bullet catchers here ASAP."

"Can we manage eleven?"

"We will manage them. These plus one more, someone not written on any list."

"Who is the twelfth, the one not included on the Beast's list?"

"The Beast already had presented the twelfth one to me."

"Am I safe now? I chose to stay. Will I be irreplaceable once the soldiers arrive?"

"You're irreplaceable. You proved yourself against the Uruguayans, and against the Scamz Organization. I need you. You are a tsunami in battle. A quick thinker. You are fearless like no one I have ever seen. You are important. I can't manage the Horsemen without you."

He said to her what the Beast had said to him many times. He wormed inside of her mind, read her weaknesses. She needed to belong to something. She needed to be favored. To feel smart. It affected her, took the edge off, was what she needed to hear at that moment.

She said, "Thanks for saving my life. Thank you, sir."

"Not only did you break into the files for the Four Horsemen, but you also compromised the Beast's personal files. You knew his secrets. You knew the truth. That is why the Beast was going to put you down."

"I learned things you never knew."

"Maybe I should be thanking you."

"For what?"

"Freeing me from that lie."

"Was just doing my job, sir. Was just doing my job."

"You opened his files and read his secrets."

"I read yours, too."

"You read about things that I am no longer able to remember."

"Your secrets are safe with me."

Señorita Raven walked to the wall, tipsy hips moving from side to side. Slow, feminine stroll, made her Punjabi ass ticktock. She was no longer in soldier mode. She went to a mirror, caught a glimpse of her reflection, then stopped and gazed at her face, frowned at what war had left behind. She touched where shrapnel had burned her flesh.

"If we had had more members yesterday, we would have obtained both briefcases, would have killed them all in the rain at Retiro, if not sooner; then Señor Rodriguez wouldn't be dead."

"Was Señor Rodriguez your lover?"

"*He was my best friend.* Never judged me. That makes him more important than any man who has shoved his dick in me, with consent, and especially any bastard who put his cock inside of me *without* my being in goddamn agreement. He respected me like no other soldier ever has."

Medianoche watched her, evaluated her. He knew her. Could read her every expression. She loosened her mane, let her long black hair fall down as if trying to see how much of her facial injury could be hidden. His words regarding fixing her appearance had gotten to her. He bet that she had done that countless times. She shook her head, perturbed. She had more alcohol in her body than blood. She was kerosene looking for a match to set her on fire. She looked at photos of the Beast in uniform, deliberated her former CO. Powerful man, hard yet calm, debonair with a swath of gray in his dark hair. She stared at the picture of the man who was going to kill her, hatred rising, and frowned deeply.

Done obsessing, Medianoche asked, "Is there an issue?"

"Does Gideon look more like you, or more like the Beast?"

"Stand down."

"And since the Beast was a closet gunsel—"

"Don't slander him. The man was a cock hound. You know he was."

"The Beast betrayed you. He told you lies. For years. If not for me, *sir*, you'd still be in the dark. He was going to assassinate me to shut me up. He knew I knew what he had done to you, and he knew that one day I'd open my mouth and say the wrong thing. My former CO was going to kill me to protect himself, not because of anything I had done."

"Stand down, soldier."

"He sure protected that bitch Thelma. He sure in the fuck gave her another baby and kept it a secret. I trusted that man. He looked me in my face, told me that there was no problem, then came to pop a cap in my head. He deserves to be slandered. I bet that *pathicus* knew who that motherfucker Gideon was. I *bet* he knew."

Medianoche took a harsh step toward the unarmed Señorita Raven.

She took a step back. "It's the bourbon talking, sir. Hard to keep my thoughts to myself."

"More than bourbon is in your blood. And don't fuckin' lie to me."

"Captagon, sir."

"You're on amphetamines."

"I was yesterday."

"When we were in battle."

"Sir, yes, sir."

"Why?"

"We had been going for days, sir. I needed a little help."

Captagon was the drug of choice in the Middle East. It stimulated the central nervous system, kept a soldier alert in battle, helped with concentration, took away fear, and made warriors feel invincible.

Opening and closing his hands, he asked, "Why are you here?"

"Why am I here? You called and ordered me to return to base."

"No, Señorita Raven, why are you here? Why were you in the goddamn military?"

"You know my family history. My father killed my cheating mother and her boy toy in a fleabag motel. I'm a middle child. Older sister is insane. You know my struggles. You know my shames. You know what I don't want anyone else to know. You know I suffered a breakdown."

"You wanted to kill yourself."

"Something like that. But that's behind me now."

"With your IQ, you could be a doctor, lawyer, business executive, professor, or scientist. You could have been a well-paid bad case of hemorrhoids for any Fortune 500 company."

"Not all people with an IQ on my level are those types of professionals. There are many intellectual slackers in the high-IQ crew. People bore us. Not much excites us intellectually."

"You need the military to survive. You need to be told when to get up, when to take a shit, when to eat. You need someone to come into your fucked-up life and give it order."

"I needed order and structure, but I know when I have to take a dump."

Medianoche looked at the quarters of a traitor, then looked at Señorita Raven. "Do you need something medicinal or prescribed to help you control your mood?"

"Maybe I'll call my Tres Josés. Let them try to fuck me senseless."

"If that's what it takes."

"I had respected you and desired you, had wanted you to be my *amigovio, mi amigo con derecho*. I didn't want to be . . . *noviazgo*. Not that serious. Just for relief. To scratch an itch. I've grown tired of going to the *milongas* alone, waiting to see if a guy will hit on me. Lots of soldiers become friends with benefits while deployed. I'd been one. Every soldier wanted to bang the hot Indian babe. I had to fight off guys who had that rape-ish look in their eyes. Until the IED. I was foolish for wanting you. But that's why a woman has her Tres Josés on speed dial. Less drama. But you know how that goes. You had your Tres Marias."

He nodded. "You're wired and two shots past drunk."

"Yeah, the bourbon has kicked in and the Captagon is fading."

"You're swimming in alcohol, drugs, grief, and anger. Some things I will let pass tonight."

"Of course you will. Your *son* killed my best friend."

"*That gaucho is not my son.* Never let those words leave your mouth again. *Never.*"

"Then explain this to me. This is bugging me. You said you can't have children."

"No, I can't."

"Yesterday, why did you freak out and pull out of me before you came? The time before the misunderstanding."

"Why are you bringing up what we agreed to put behind us?"

"You pulled out. I am bringing that up because that's not what a man who can't have kids would do. It surprised me when you did."

That had been before the skirmish with the Scamz Organization.

He said, "We agreed that whatever happened between us was a mistake. We agreed to let it go and deal with Four Horsemen affairs."

"I'll let it go. I'm done with it. It was a mistake. The second time more than the first."

"If there had not been a first time, then there would not have been a second."

A tense moment passed. Again he channeled the spirit of the Beast.

He said, "Your performance in the field yesterday was exemplary. You handle firefights and never back down. Firefights are sheer terror because you know you could die at any second."

"Thank you, sir."

"Some people shut down. Can't think. Can't see. End up in body bags."

"I'm just doing what I have been trained to do."

"We need to have each other's back. Twelve new members, if that works out, won't be the same as there being four. We will have to manage twelve different personalities."

"I look forward to being in a leadership position and welcome the challenge, sir."

"Not all will make the cut. Is that clear? For some it will be a one-way trip."

"I understand how you and the Beast work, sir. Now better than before."

"I set the rules. You follow command, without question, without hesitation."

"I understand. Rules are not for leaders. Not for kings, only for paupers."

She continued to test him. Medianoche didn't let her pull him into her rolling fury.

He snapped, *"Attention."*

She lost her attitude, stood at attention, quickly, sharply, a Pavlovian response that had her knees together, chin up, chest out, shoulders back, stomach in, eyes front, and no speech.

Medianoche puffed on his Cuban cigar, craved something stronger.

All the things she felt, he felt them on a much higher level.

He watched Señorita Raven, at attention, struggling not to wobble.

Four moments of absolute silence passed before he said, "Dismissed."

She turned on her heels, head high, face moist, cleared her throat, and marched out of the room of a dead man, a man who had been assassinated in front of her eyes for his crimes.

Soon he would have to do the same to her as well. Soon, but not too soon. Not before he had the reorganization under control. She was going to be too much of a problem. He hated problems.

Chapter 7

The Long Wait

Medianoche returned to his quarters.

It looked like a disgrace. A mess. His usually pristine apartment had been tossed. Books and newspapers from the *Buenos Aires Herald* and *La Nación* were scattered. His anger had gotten the best of him a few hours ago, after the loss, after he had downed the Beast. He had had a tantrum, lost it, screamed, gone berserk, and kicked over everything that wasn't nailed down.

After the loss, he had been emotional.

Now exhaustion toyed with him.

Dealing with Señorita Raven had drained him.

He needed more energy.

He did a line of Peruvian marching powder, then went into his kitchen, ate the final piece of leftover steak. He stood out on his balcony, saxophone in his hands. He played a song, a tune sung by Frank Sinatra, then put the sax away. Anger manifested. He opened a Quilmes Cristal, massaged his mostly gray goatee, and stared out at the lights twinkling in Buenos Aires, scowled toward the *villas miserias*, the villages of the miserable, where their final battle had occurred.

His cellular rang. It rang twice more before he answered. It was Caprica Ortiz.

"Scamz was sighted at Puerto Madero Yacht Club. Not long after all the gunfire and damage across Buenos Aires. He boarded a ship that was leased, but it is owned by an African, a petroleum and aviation mogul from Lagos. The same wealthy Nigerian had arranged for a private plane to bring three people here from North America yesterday in the middle of the night."

Medianoche knew those passengers who had been snuck into his country were the Russian, the black, and Gideon. The rest of the Scamz Organization had already been here.

He asked, "Where is the ship now?"

"The yacht is gone. But Gideon, the black man, and the older man in white shoes left the ship at Colonia del Sacramento and boarded a bus to Montevideo. They are wounded."

"Are you sure? Is this intel good?"

"This is very good intel. The yacht left Colonia without Gideon and those two men."

"And you are one hundred percent sure they took a bus to Montevideo?"

"Yes. They remain near there in the area. The bad men are across Río de la Plata."

"Do you have a high-speed boat or helicopter at your disposal?"

"No. No, I do not. It's storming in Uruguay. The river is restless, very angry."

"In the military, this storm would be considered nothing but a breeze. I will take it from here."

Medianoche ended the conversation, then made another urgent call.

"Assad."

"What can I do for you, Medianoche?"

"*Tengo un quilombo de novela*. Where are you?"

"La Boca. You should be here."

"You're in the pits."

"Tonight, the fights are already amazing. Can you hear the men cheering?"

"How many men do you have at your disposal?"

"Medianoche, I am an entrepreneur. I procure whatever men like you need. At a fee."

"Cut the shit. You're an arms broker. You've killed more indirectly than I have directly."

"And at times, a friend like me is the only friend you need."

"I need a dozen armed men. I want the best, men like me, not rookies."

"I can get you whatever you need."

"We also need a high-speed boat or a helicopter, expeditiously."

"How soon?"

"An hour ago. I'm tracking an insurgent."

"Scamz?"

"That's not your concern."

"Where do you need to go so urgently?"

"Uruguay. The other side of the river. Can that be arranged?"

"Answer one question."

"What the fuck do you need to know?"

"Are you the leader of the Four Horsemen now?"

Medianoche paused. "After today, I will wear the red necktie."

"Then the Beast is gone."

"I am the leader. That is all that matters. I run this yard."

"In that case, I am at your disposal. Anything you need can be arranged."

"And I need more weapons. A launcher. And more flash and bang."

"Your standard weaponry. Of course. The people across the river are a little perturbed."

"And if they get in my way, they will be more than a little dead."

"Well, they ordered the same weaponry, but you didn't hear that from me."

Chapter 8

Hangmen Also Die

"*Gideon.*"

I snapped awake, gun aimed, finger tight on the trigger, unable to tell what was real.

"*Gideon*, put the gun down. *Stop acting like a damn fool.*"

A tall woman was near me. Her skin looked Mediterranean and Native American, now with a Puerto Rican poolside tan. Her haunting green eyes came into focus, eyes that always reminded me of Sharbat Gula on the cover of *National Geographic*. I saw her beautiful face. She wore Levi's, not too tight, but she filled them out well. Stonewashed Lucchese cowboy boots.

I lowered the business end of my gun, exhaled hard, and said, "Hawks?"

"Glad you remember my gosh-dern name."

I tried to smile. "Hey, babe."

Hawks was one of the people Konstantin had trained. She was one of the best in the business. Hours ago, when my crew challenged the Four Horsemen, she was working back in the USA, had done a last-minute job for me in Memphis, and was going to take in Beale Street.

Shotgun called out from down the hallway, "Y'all all right in there?"

Hawks called back. "Don't ever wake this fool up suddenly, that's all."

Her highlighted hair was in a tight braid that roped its way down her spine to the curve in her tight little butt. Sitting on her sweet chest was a bedazzled T-shirt with Elvis Presley's image on the front, that dead legend sporting prison gear from the movie *Jailhouse Rock*. Her suntanned Mediterranean and Native American features made her one of a kind.

"Hawks, what are you doing here? You were in Memphis when I talked to you."

"I'd expected a warmer welcome, considering all the hell I went through to get here from Tennessee. After I took care of your little blackmail problem, I followed my gut, got on a plane, and headed this way, because something told me this was not going as good as you claimed."

The rain came down harder on the Switzerland of South America. Frigid winds blew into the darkness. Our safe house was somewhere backpacking college students could crash for a few bucks a day, and made a Motel 6 along Route 66 seem as swank as the Parker Meridien in NYC.

Hawks said, "Almost got yourself beat to death. *Again.* Do you have a death wish?"

"Hawks, don't irritate me. Not right now."

I pulled on a tight-fitting celeste-blue Uruguay national football team hoodie, tugged the sleeves up to my forearms, then hobbled to the window, each step followed by a dull grunt.

Small boats were docked in the sand, vessels used to catch both fish and sharks, and colorful homes of wood or stucco dotted the land. In the distance, a white lighthouse stood tall.

I didn't see any sign of enemies, but enemies never wanted to be seen.

A bowl of fruit, half of a cold empanada, leftover *asado* with *achuras* and sausages, and half a bottled water were on the nightstand next to pills for pain and bandages for wounds.

I sipped water, cleared my throat again, and asked Hawks, "How did you find us?"

"Got to Argentina and contacted Konstantin, and he told me y'all were one country over, so I had to fly into someplace I can't pronounce to save my life, then arrange a ride up here. The *Spanish for Dummies* I studied ain't doing me a bit of good. Not like I know more than ten words."

"We had a rough time down here."

"You and Shotgun fell off a building?"

"Long story, but yeah, we fell off a building. And that was the easiest part of the day."

Hawks said, "Their cute little lady president ain't happy with the way y'all left her country. Y'all messed up some famous landmarks and people were left dead on the side of the road."

"It went sideways fast. We were attacked as soon as we got here."

"Like in Antigua."

I asked Hawks, "How long was I out of it?"

"Shotgun said you were down pretty much all day. Your body shut down."

"I noticed."

"You have another serious infection." She motioned at the dresser. "Bon appétit."

I saw the medicine. Knew it was for me. I picked up the antibiotics, tried to open the childproof bottle, and couldn't. Hands were swollen, and each finger like a balloon about to pop. Hawks took the bottle from my hand, opened it with ease, did that to prove a point. She gave me the pills, dropped them in the palm of my right hand, and I popped two.

I said, "Déjà vu."

"Being your nurse, this is me saving you like that time in Atlanta all over again."

I nodded. "Konstantin and Shotgun, where are they?"

"Our boss is resting. The new guy, Shotgun, is out front. Met him earlier."

"This is his first rodeo. He rose to the occasion. Was worth his weight."

"Seems like a nice guy. The other guy is just as big, but he's a lot darker than Shotgun."

"What other guy?"

"Green eyes. Wavy hair. Pretty skin. Smooth and black, like expensive chocolate."

"The African we met a long time ago, after I worked in North Hollywood?"

"Not him. This guy is West Indian. The one that trains everybody how to fight to kill."

"The Bajan?"

"Yeah, the Bajan." She nodded. "He's been standing guard with me and Shotgun. Konstantin was trying to help, but I made him go get his butt in the bed and rest."

Guilt and embarrassment replaced pain. I asked, "What'd I miss?"

"Been real quiet so far. Police passed by three or four times, but they never stopped or slowed down. We kept it dark in here so we can see what's out there. Hardly a light on."

"Where is Konstantin?"

"Told you, resting."

"He's okay?"

"From what Shotgun told me, all of you had an Italian tune-up, but Konstantin ain't like he used to be. He has *cancer*. He's the closest thing I've had to a daddy in a long time, and I bet that goes for you too. This little field trip was too much for him in his weakened condition. You and I know he ain't the man he was fifteen years ago. You never should've involved him. What were you thinking? I have a lot to say, but I'll hold my tongue. *El jefe* ain't looking good at all, to be honest. But he has risked his life, looked out for you. He made a few calls and new toys showed up."

Hawks stood in the window, a nine millimeter in her hand, another tucked in the small of her back, a blade strapped to the hip of her jeans, and a high-power rifle two feet from where she stood.

She said, "I hate this pneumonia weather. And this safe house stinks like rotten fish."

"Guess you liked our downtime in Puerto Rico better than this smelly shit hole."

Again she paused. "But you know that sort of thing between us will never happen again."

"What do you mean?"

"We'll talk. Once we get back to the America I know like the back of my hand, and everybody is okay and you're safe, we can meet in Nashville, find a spot that plays some country-sangin', banjo-pickin' music, have a few beers while we listen to Chyyanna Lee sing that country song I like, 'Older Men and Whiskey,' and then we can talk."

"I'm not an older man."

"But you're my whiskey."

"You think you're not mine?"

"We'll finish this chat in Nashville. Now ain't the time."

"Don't bring it up and drop it."

"Konstantin needs me. Shotgun does too. See these guns? See the expression on this face? I know I'm wearing sexy underwear, but that's how I roll, and don't be fooled. I'm here to work. I'll be professional."

"Hawks, you've always been real with me. Don't stop now."

She shook her head, took a breath, and said, "We can address Arizona some other time."

"What's the issue?"

"Don't get Konstantin and everybody else wrapped up in your personal shit."

"This job was about settling a debt. This was business."

"I'm calling bullshit on that one, partner. I heard you on the phone with her. I happened to be in your arms, and you happened to be inside of me, balls deep from what I remember, so I felt the difference, felt what you felt for her, heard how your voice changed when you talked to her."

"This was about a debt."

"I am professional, and you know that. The business part of my head understands that it comes with the territory, but the woman part of my brain, the real shrewd part that seems to malfunction when I get around you, it didn't like that too much. Yeah, I guess I felt like a fool when we left from down there. Well, *up there* now, since I'm *down here* and the world is as upside down as you had me while we were naked. I got drunk, let you go three for three. No man has ever gone three for three. That won't happen again. Hate to say it now, but yes. We are so goddamn done. After this, you go left and I go right. It's for the best. We can't be bed buddies no more."

I took a breath. "Hawks, I don't want us like this."

"Ain't no us. Ain't never been an *us*."

"What have we been, then?"

"You serious? We've never been anything like boyfriend and girlfriend. You're just a guy I met, got hot and bothered over, and had a few good nights with, might've even had the wrong kinda fantasies about. But thank God I came to my senses when I realized he was a total jerk."

"So, we're not friends?"

"We're still friends. Just without the benefits. No more *irrumatio*. At least not with you."

She checked her guns once more, pulled her long, butt-length braid to the side, and let it hang down over her breasts. She sniffled, coughed, wiped her eyes, then cleared her throat.

She said, "Now, with that spoken into the universe, anything you need to say to me?"

"I asked you for a favor as well, or should I pass that search on to someone else?"

"Jeremy Bentham from Smyrna. Nathalie Marie Masreliez from Yerres."

"You didn't forget."

"You know my character. I keep my promises."

"I won't hold you to this one. When we get back to America, I won't trouble you."

"I will do like I promised, and those two names you gave me, those two people you want tracked for whatever reason, I'll get what information I can as soon as possible so we can be done. I will keep my word and look for Nathalie Marie Masreliez and Jeremy Bentham."

I hesitated. "Both have to do with Catherine."

"Catherine, who used to be Thelma. The woman who swore to God she wasn't your mother, then you forced her to take a DNA test, and like it was an episode of *Maury*, you just verified she is your mother?"

"Both of those names have nothing to do with this job; both are personal."

She shook her head. "More lies from your momma who wasn't your momma but is now officially your momma whether she wants to be your lying-ass momma or not?"

"They never end. With each untruth uncovered, ten more deceits are born."

"Good Lord. How many falsehoods can one heifer tell in one lifetime?"

"No idea. Just have to check on a few things. I need to know who she was in Paris. In Yerres. I have no idea where I was born. I've had a dozen birthdays. It changes with each passport. And I need to know who this new man is in her life. I need to know who is around the boys, my little brothers. We have too much to lose if whoever she is seeing ain't legit."

"You just confirmed she's your mother a few hours ago. She has lied to you since you were a little boy, told you your real momma was a two-bit whore named Margaret, and said Margaret was killed by a madman and left to rot in a Dumpster somewhere in the Bible Belt. Catherine lied and said she took you in and took care of you out of the goodness in her heart, then dragged you from here to Montreal and back, only to have to confess she is your real momma. I'm confused. What kind of woman would mind fuck you like that for the majority of your life? No wonder you're messed up. I swear, I don't understand some people."

"There is more to her. She's still lying. I just don't know about what."

"She's crazy because she's French. French people ain't normal. They eat snails."

"Well, I'm half-French."

"And you're half-crazy."

Hawks knew I had grown up in brothels. My mother had fled from Paris, reason unknown, and at some point she'd used the name Thelma. In North Carolina, she was the Frenchwoman many men and women went to see. I had seen my mother doing things a son should never see his mother doing, and I had seen it for so long that it had become normal. That life of watching people being pleased for funds became normal. Another friend of hers had almost been beaten to death, and that beating had reminded her of what had happened to Margaret, so she had said, and my mother sent me to kill the man who had assaulted her friend. The friend was a woman for hire who had paid to have that job done. That was the first job I had as an assassin. My mother had lied about how much I was paid and pocketed most of the money. She had used me.

I was a teenager, trapped between nature and nurture.

My mother had opened up a new darkness inside of me.

When she was Thelma, she showed me my own midnight. And one night when she was drunk, while I was sleeping, she had come into my bedroom. She showed me hers.

I will never understand why.

I said, "When we were in Puerto Rico, you seemed okay with the Buenos Aires job."

"Had time to think that over. I was trying to be a big girl about it at the time. But I realized that I was just lying to myself. And when you lie to yourself, you make a fool out of yourself."

"Want to share those thoughts before we leave?"

Hawks said, "For starters, I keep my word and I have never used you."

"I've never said you used me. And I've never used you."

"I've never disrespected you."

"I didn't disrespect you, not intentionally. I had to take that call."

"You talked to her while you were sexing me up, and I was professional. I didn't get girly. I didn't press the issue. But the thing that got to me, and it got to me good, was I have never insulted you and hung up the phone in your face. After all that, after being considerate, and after all I've done for you, you gave me the goddamn *click*. I've always respected you on all levels."

"Is that what this is about?"

"The day after we left Puerto Rico, you hung up in my face like I was nothing to you."

"I was stressed, Hawks. I was being blackmailed. I was dealing with Scamz."

"I'm a hired gun, one of the best liquidators in the world in my opinion, and even if I am a hatchet person, no matter who I've left facedown in a bathtub, I'm a human being too. I got feelings. I might've overlooked all of that. But you treated me like I was shit. You don't have a woman putting her lipstick on your dipstick, then just hang up the phone in her face."

"I was STFO when I hung up on you."

"I've looked out for you time and time again. I rescued you in Huntsville. I had your back in Antigua. I was your nurse in Atlanta. I've dropped everything to help you at every turn. And you hang up in my goddamn face? That was so damn disrespectful, even if you were STFO."

I took a breath. "Come here."

She hardened her tone. "You'd be dead in the ground. If not for me, you'd be in an unmarked grave. I was the one who tried to get you out of danger, not put you in jeopardy."

"Thanks, Hawks. I mean that."

"You are welcome. I mean that too, even though I'm not smiling."

Silence passed between us.

Hawks said, "Nathalie Marie Masreliez and Jeremy Bentham."

"Catherine said Nathalie was her name in Yerres."

"So now Catherine used to be Thelma and Thelma used to be Nathalie Marie Masreliez."

"I have no idea if it's another lie."

"Well, she had a real pretty name when she was in France, if nothing else. Even if she stole it off a grave, it's real pretty. What's that have to do with Jeremy Bentham?"

"Jeremy Bentham is the man she's seeing."

"Has this new Romeo been vetted?"

"I don't know jack about him. Just found out about him when I was on the way here. She said she met him at a bookstore or something."

"Anything else?"

"I guess that's all."

"You sure?"

"I'm sure."

"So we're done."

I looked her in the eyes, knowing what she meant. "This is your decision, not mine."

"It's for the best."

"Okay."

"And to be clear, this is about the lack of respect, not Arizona. She means nothing to me. I know you think I'm one of the boys, but I'm not. You don't put your dick in them and they don't suck you dry. So I expect a little more respect than you're able to give. That's why we're done."

"Okay."

"So we're straight?"

"As a ruler."

"We can move forward."

"Always."

She exited the room.

But she came right back; her eyes avoided me and mine avoided her.

She said, "Forgot. Brought you something. Copped it in Memphis."

Hawks tossed me a small blue-and-white box. BC Powder. Pack of fifty.

She said, "Cost me ten dollars and eleven cents. Want my money back."

Before I could thank her, Hawks's boots were marching down the hallway.

I'd taken her for granted. That date we'd had meant more to her than it had to me because I was preoccupied, and going to Puerto Rico was just one more thing on the list. I had been stressed the fuck out.

And I still was stressed the fuck out.

But right now she had other concerns and my problems were ocean deep.

Hawks started talking to the Bajan, chatting, then laughing. Even in stressful moments, we laughed to keep from going insane. Only a man with no soul never laughed. The Bajan had a reputation. He was a strong man, a well-built gun for hire who knew how to use all weapons, and could turn anything within reach into a deadly object. He could paper-cut a man to death. But the way he fought, his body was a top-shelf weapon as well. He was a killer's killer. People said he would pull out a man's spine while he was alive. I'd done horrible things, but never that.

Shotgun marched the hallway. He remained on the lookout.

Hawks's voice carried when she asked the green-eyed Bajan, "You have any kids?"

"Yeah. What about you?"

"I was married once, but no kids, no family, none worth mentioning twice."

"Your ex-husband, he was one of us?"

"He wasn't in the business. He was a regular guy with a regular job living a regular life with regular people. We went to happy hour or movies most Friday nights, and we had dates every other Saturday. Had a nine-to-five. Family barbecues and church once every other month."

"You only went to church once every other month?"

"Well, I'm the kinda girl who likes to have fun on a Saturday night, so I preferred being in bed butt-naked with my husband. Had my own kinda church service, praise the Lord. If it was football season, we stayed home and watched games all day Sunday like normal people did."

"Sounds better than the services at the Anglican church I grew up in, in Barbados."

"Marriage didn't work for me. Too many lies. I can't stand a man who lies and can't keep his word, and he sure had a problem with that. Don't make me promises and don't keep them. Clean up behind yourself. And if I cook Sunday dinner, be kind enough to wash the dishes."

"I enjoy the conversation, but let me check on our transportation. They're late and I'm getting a little worried."

"Take care of that, and let me know what I can do to help. We'll have plenty of time to chat and get to know each other better."

"We'll be on the road almost twenty-four hours."

"Well, ride with me and I'll talk your ear off to keep you awake."

"And if we're not sleeping, I'll sing a few soca songs."

"You can sing?"

"When I grew up I wanted to be a famous soca singer."

"I know nothing about soca."

"See you in a few minutes. Go check on the others."

Hawks came down the hallway, headed toward the bathrooms. I called her name. She ignored me. I picked up a gun, went to the window. We'd been here too long. Because of me.

When I turned around, I saw I wasn't alone.

A hired gun waited at my door.

Chapter 9

House by the River

Holding a nine millimeter in his hand, Shotgun stood in the doorframe of my small room.

The big man tapped on the doorframe three times to get my attention.

The former pugilist asked, "Got a minute?"

"What's wrong?"

He came a step closer. "You done told Catherine about Midnight and all this trouble?"

"After I make sure you and Konstantin are on a plane, I want to resolve this myself."

"You want to fix this how?"

I opened and closed my hands. No answer came. Only more confusion.

He said, "You need to tell Catherine."

"No."

"Why not?"

"She'd take the boys, run away, and we'd never hear from her again."

"But still, they have a right to know. If they want to run and hide somewhere, help them run and hide. The Four Horsemen—you saw what they can do. They kill anybody in the way."

I paused. Angry because Shotgun was right and I knew that he was right.

He said, "If this was the Mob we were dealing with, like *The Sopranos*, or like them boys in the *Godfather* movie, I know families are off-limits. I know that much. The Mob didn't touch nobody else but other mobsters. And snitches. Was kinda like they had morals. I know that much too. I've just started doing this, and I'm new to this kinda life, and I know that I can't read that good right now, but I didn't make it this far in the world being as dumb as people think that I am."

When he paused, I went to the other side of the room, checked out the window, saw three vans pass by. Hairs on the back of my neck stood up, but the vans didn't slow in front of our safe haven. A bus passed by. It didn't slow. After that no other traffic came down the road.

I nodded. "I'll let Catherine know the boogeyman ain't dead. Maybe you should talk to your family too. Move them to some other place for a while. Until you feel comfortable."

"Already done did that. My wife done loaded up my family and they heading over to Alabama. We got some folks two hours away, not far across the state line."

"I'll call Catherine before we get out of here."

I limped to the bathroom, did that to get away from him the way I wanted to get away from Hawks. I needed some space. I looked at the abrasions, cuts on my face.

Over and over, in frustration I whispered, "Midnight."

When I shuffled out of the bathroom, Konstantin addressed me in Russian. I raised my swollen eyes and faced a man in a dark suit and white shoes, a Moscow-born man resembling George Clooney, at times Cary Grant. He was the closest thing to a father I had ever had. His right hand was still wrapped, and the right side of his face was still red, swollen.

Still talking in Russian, he said, "Thought I had lost you."

In the same language I replied, "I'm fine, and I'm more concerned with you."

"I've never been better. Will be better when I get home to my wife."

"She's worried."

"I am going to be in the doghouse."

"I'm sorry. Had no idea what I was getting all of us into."

Konstantin said, "Everything will be all right. We can fix this problem too."

I nodded. "I need to get all of you out of the danger zone and back home."

"Shotgun talked to you about contacting your mother and your two brothers?"

"Have to figure out how to tell Catherine about this shit we went through."

"I doubt if you'll find the right message on a Hallmark card, so just tell her."

Two battered pickup trucks stopped out front. I reached for the AR-15 that had been allocated to me, and Konstantin grabbed his own. Shotgun had a gun in each hand.

The Bajan called out that it was okay. Our ride had arrived.

We went down the hallway toward the rustic lobby. The Bajan went outside and spoke in Spanish to the Korean man and woman who had come from Busan and were hired to drive us into Brazil. By then Hawks was with Konstantin, coming down the hallway. He was doing the talking and she was listening. She looked surprised, then stared at me with a cast of disbelief.

He had told her about Midnight. I would've told her myself, given the chance.

But telling her would have made it seem like I was asking her to save me again.

She had been right about Arizona. Every accusation had been on point.

Hawks moved away from our boss, cowboy boots hard on the tile floor, and rushed over to me. I was in the front, staring out the window, making sure the Four Horsemen didn't sneak up.

Hawks said, "Your daddy's still alive some kinda way and did this to you?"

"You want to call child services?"

She looked like she wanted to reach and touch my injured face, but I walked away from her. The Bajan came back inside, soaking wet—a man who didn't have any fat on his body. His skin was as dark as the night, glistening with rain. I went over to the Bajan, shook his hand.

In that strong Bajan accent, he said, "You in 'nuff pain? It hurting bad?"

With a passable Ichirouganaim intonation, I responded, "I in 'nuff pain."

Konstantin, Hawks, the Bajan, and Shotgun carried two sidearms and either AR-15s, Steyr AUGs, or FAMAS assault rifles. We followed the willowy Korean woman. She was an Asian Audrey Hepburn. She held an umbrella and wore jeans, construction-worker boots, and a raincoat over a yellow sweater. She led us to a man who was about five foot five. Her husband. Jeans and construction-worker boots, same as the wife. We had seen three or four Korean-run karaoke bars in Montevideo. They had a small presence here.

She led me and Shotgun to an old truck used to transport fish. The Bajan, Konstantin, and Hawks followed the woman's husband to another battered truck used for the same purpose, only it was larger, had front and backseats. Korean writing was on the side of each truck.

I used a throwaway and called Catherine's cellular. Only had two bars on the phone. The storm had killed the Internet connection hours ago. If I'd had Wi-Fi and a smartphone, I could've connected to the hidden cameras I'd installed in the house in Powder Springs and looked in on Catherine and the boys, could have seen if they were up or sleeping before I called, or if Catherine's boyfriend was over and she was entertaining.

She had a boyfriend. She went on dates. She had children she cared for. She went to PTA meetings. She had a regular life. That new life she had, it was the life she'd always wanted. She had become one of the squares. She had left her old ways, her old life behind. I envied her. I had tried to leave this world behind me more than once, had met women and run away from this world and created my own hedonistic paradise, but each time this vocation put its claws in me and pulled me back into the belly of the beast. Catherine had left Thelma behind and become free of her past. I had made it possible for her to get off her knees and live a good life. And now with a phone call, I would take that all away from her.

She answered on the first ring and sounded stressed. "Hello?"

She sounded like she was crying, and she rarely cried. Our last moment before I had left the land of Uncle Sam had been an argument, a huge blowout, but I had to steamroll past that issue for now.

In French I asked, "What happened?"

"A boy at Robert and Sven's school was found dead in the Chattahoochee River."

"What happened?"

"He was murdered. Beaten and then drowned."

I didn't have time for that. "This is urgent. Between us. I need to tell you something."

She paused. "What is going on?"

It took all I had just to say his name. "Midnight is alive."

"Midnight?"

I said, "He's alive. A few hours ago, I saw him in Argentina."

"What are you talking about?"

"The man you told me is my father—he's still alive. I saw him a few hours ago."

She paused for several seconds, her breathing congealing with trepidation.

I said, "You there?"

"Tell me that after the issue you gave me with the DNA, with you and your brother Andrew-Sven, with the little lie I told, tell me you are doing this because you are angry, and you want to get mean with me."

"This has nothing to do with any lie you ever told, or anything you've done to me."

"You saw someone who reminded you of him. That is what happened."

"No. It was him. He's a mercenary. A one-eyed mercenary with a group called the Four Horsemen of the Apocalypse. He's older, has more scars, but it's him. He's alive."

"Tell me again. Tell me where you saw him, and if you are sure it was him."

"It was him."

No matter what I said, Catherine had the same response. "This cannot be true."

Something broke inside of her. Even in the storm, I heard fear crack some part of her wide open. She wasn't Catherine anymore. The light inside her went out; darkness awoke.

She exploded. "What the hell have you done?"

"Did you know he wasn't dead?"

"Why would you find him?"

"Did you fuckin' know he was alive?"

The connection went in and out, the call crackled, splintered.

I yelled, "Catherine, are you still there?"

The old flatbed truck rolled through mud and took to the rugged road, pitching and yawing while the wipers were in their own battle, struggling to slap angry rain away. We had piss-poor visibility, but the drivers knew the road. They knew every pothole, dip, and blind curve.

I called out to Catherine again. And again. And again.

As soon as I lowered the phone, Shotgun asked, "You told her?"

"I told her."

"What's she gonna do?"

Again I remembered being a child in North Carolina, shooting Mr. Midnight in the head, his body falling, the panic that ensued, fleeing and heading north, on the run until we landed in Montreal, my mother at my side, people on Greyhound buses giving us chicken. Then she took on strange men to make money. Soon I had killed a police officer who had beaten her in Montreal. Then we were on the run again. Seven years old, and I shot men like I was born to kill.

I knew what I had become. I was aware of who I was.

I didn't want my brothers to be like me.

I was scared for my brothers, scared of what they would become if Catherine went on the run, ran out of money, struggled to survive, to feed them, and became Thelma again.

I said, "She's resourceful."

As we rode, the heater on low, radio off, our driver glanced at my injured face.

In Spanish I asked my Korean driver, "Everything okay?"

In perfect *castellano*, no Korean accent, she replied, "You are Gideon."

"How do you know?"

"People in Montevideo talk. When you arrived, with your friends, they knew where you had come from. The news spread fast. We know what happened in Buenos Aires. A dozen men from this side of the river died there. The husband of a friend was thrown from a building."

"They went up against the Four Horsemen. We're not part of that group."

Her voice shook. "When this is done, my husband and I will be okay, no? Nothing bad will happen to my husband or me, no? We have a daughter. We have a little girl waiting at home."

"What is your name?"

Almost too nervous to form words, she said, "Soon-Bok Kim."

"Your husband?"

She swallowed. "Chung-Ho Kim."

"You come from a family of Korean fishermen. That's odd in this part of the world."

"My family came here in the seventies."

"Fisherman. Dangerous job. Hard work. Little pay."

"My family knows. We have lost loved ones. Two years ago three of my relatives were killed in an explosion. We were devastated. It was an accident on board a fishing boat."

Then her husband tapped his brake lights, tapped them several times. She did the same and we slowed to a crawl, her husband's truck ten yards in front of us moving at a snail's pace.

I raised my gun, let her see it in my hand. "What's up there in the road?"

"I swear on my grandmother's grave, I do not know."

Shotgun spoke up. "I don't know what y'all saying, but we got some trouble."

Bright lights kicked on in front of us. We were forced to stop. Ambushed. Too far from the Chuy border crossing. Right underneath a road sign—REPÚBLICA ORIENTAL DEL URUGUAY—a four-decade-old, red-and-white, forty-foot-long city bus had been used as a barricade. In front of that bus were four black vans. The four vans faced us, headlights bright. Two armed men exited each of the first two vans. Then four armed men stepped out of each of the last two. A dozen men, a dozen weapons. More could be inside the vans.

Soon-Bok Kim became a statue. Fear widened her eyes.

While they tried to blind us, unseen gunmen sprayed shots into the sky.

That told me that it wasn't La Policía Nacional de Uruguay.

Eyes focused, Shotgun asked, "Four Horsemen?"

"Might be."

"You still ain't in no condition for a fight. You can't even walk ten feet without falling."

"I'm as good as I'm going to get until I get better."

"Me or the Bajan, if it come down to it, we fight Medianoche. Not you. It's decided. We done already had that talk while you were halfway dead and in a coma. Didn't know a showdown would come this quick."

Soon-Bok Kim closed her eyes, said rapid prayers in *castellano*, beat the steering wheel, begged God to save her and her stupid husband, said they would become better Christians.

The truck carrying Hawks, the Bajan, and Konstantin backed up until it was next to us. I pushed my door open so we could roll out. Shotgun didn't hesitate, followed my lead. Hawks, the Bajan, and Konstantin did the same.

The welcoming committee sent shots into the air.

We sent shots into the air, a response to their call.

Only it had sounded like thirty of them, at least. Didn't know if they had a sniper. Or two. I was half-past dead and now we were outnumbered and outgunned. Shotgun and the Bajan aimed their guns behind us, in case we'd been surrounded. We couldn't tell. Didn't know if this was what was left of the Four Horsemen, or bloodthirsty surrogates.

Soon-Bok Kim leapt out of the truck, and she dashed toward the enemy, ran in the storm, the wind pushing against her petite frame, and she screamed one word over and over. The bitch was shrieking out my name like she wanted that team to know they had brought the prize.

Chung-Ho Kim shouted after his wife. He tried to take off running, but the Bajan did a spin kick and dropped him hard to the road. Konstantin snapped and pointed his weapon at Chung-Ho Kim's head. The Russian in Konstantin came to life. He became the Man in the White Shoes, a man who had created business for many gravediggers.

The kindness in the Bajan was gone too.

The Bajan yelled, "We need to flank, move to get a better position."

Konstantin commanded, "We don't have the numbers."

I said, "We don't know if we're already surrounded."

Soaking wet, Konstantin had his weapon aimed at Chung-Ho Kim's head. *"Are we surrounded? How many are there out there? Talk or I'll blow a hole in your head right now."*

Hawks was in sniper mode, had her weapon trained on the running Korean woman as she ran into the storm. Hawks was steady, calculating wind and distance, ready to drop her before she reached whoever was waiting.

The Korean woman and this sniveling man were part of this ambush.

They were decoys, pawns who would be sacrificed to achieve a goal.

The panicked man at our feet knew he was already dead.

The woman who claimed to be his wife would die too.

Then we'd kill as many of them as we could while they tried to kill all of us.

Chapter 10

The Strange Woman

Soon-Bok Kim screamed and ran into their headlights. She was about fifty yards away; then all of the lights turned off at the same moment, and darkness showered us, forced us to let our eyes adjust. The lights came back on, blinded us again. Moments later our driver came back our way, stumbling backward, two men with her. Neither was very tall, but they wore dark uniforms. I'd have bet they were bulletproof. One of the men marched at her side as he held her arm and guided her, had what looked like a Glock pointed at her head, her back into our headlights. The other walked behind her, held what looked like an Uzi, ready to spray and pray.

Hawks had cover behind the truck. Weapon up, she maintained her aim, ready to return fire. She hadn't taken the shot. The wind. She wanted to save the bullet for a sure shot.

Konstantin called out, "What can we do for you on this cold, rainy evening?"

Soon-Bok Kim yelled into the night. "*Gideon. Please. Tell them you are the Gideon.*"

The Bajan and Shotgun, like Hawks, kept their weapons trained.

The Bajan said, "Someone looking for you especially."

I asked Konstantin, "What did the other Horseman who attacked you look like?"

"He was older. About the same age as Medianoche. Had a patch of gray."

"That's not him?"

"No. His accent was American. I'd say West Coast, but military has influenced his speaking pattern. These are not Americans. The other man, Medianoche's leader, we left him with a knife in his back. They called him the Beast. He's too fucked-up to be out here."

I went to Chung-Ho Kim, grabbed him by his neck, and forced him back against the truck, growled when I propelled him hard. I expected him to fight back, and that fight would be a quick fight that wouldn't end in his favor, but he covered his head, terrified, fell to the ground, was praying and shitting his pants. I told him he had one chance to answer, one chance only, to tell me who that woman was who had driven me—the woman who was so inquisitive—and tell me who had paid them to sell us out, and who the men were on the other side of those headlights. They were the barrier between us and our escape to Brazil.

He told us she was his wife. They had a child.

He told me the same things she had told me.

That meant nothing. It could have been rehearsed long before.

I asked, "Then why did she run? She abandoned you and ran."

He said, "My wife is afraid. And she does impulsive things. I love her, but she's stupid."

I left him on the ground, and I stood up, groaned, and felt the weight of the rain.

I walked to my team, told them to cover me.

They looked at me like I'd gone mad.

I said, "They want Gideon. I'm going out there. Unarmed."

Hawks stepped in front of me and barked, "Don't take stupid to a brand-new level."

I moved around her. The Bajan told me to think twice. Konstantin said the same in Russian, but it was too late. Arms stretched out to my sides, fingers spread apart, I went toward them, strode through puddles, took easy steps toward the woman who was in the rain, a gun held to her head, losing her mind and screaming my name like I was their target.

Hawks had been right. I had pulled them all into my personal shit.

I knew they all would die to save me, but I'd rather die to save them.

I marched through puddles, moved at an even, nonhostile pace, arms extended, anticipating being shot by their version of James Earl Ray. Then I was less than five yards shy of the armed men. Both were dressed in all black, the attire of a Spanish militia. Both had lean builds, strong upper bodies like champion brawlers, from what I could tell. My face cringed with pain and I limped the last few steps, rain weighing my hoodie down.

I told them, "*Soy* Gideon. *¿Me buscan, caballeros? No llevo armas.*"

I asked the gentlemen if they were looking for me and said I was unarmed.

Arms still extended, fingers wide apart, I looked at one, then the other, to see who was the leader. No response as they sized me up. Two against one. They had the guns. They knew they had me. Again I told them that I was Gideon, repeated that I did not have a weapon.

I said, "The girl is afraid. Move the gun from her head."

One hard-ass finally found his voice and spoke up, said, "Fuck you, asshole."

"Put the gun on me. This is between us."

The other one found his voice and echoed, "Fuck you, asshole."

She said, "I beg them, tell them you are not the Four Horsemen, that none of you are the ones they want, that you are the one they call Gideon and you are running from the Horsemen."

I took another step and the taller one moved his gun from her head and pointed it at my face. His friend was broader, looked powerful. He did the same, pointed his gun at me.

I told Soon-Bok Kim, "Go back to your husband. Tell my friends to not shoot. But if they do, to try not to shoot me. Especially the girl. She might shoot me to get a laugh."

Eyes wide, body shaking, she looked at the men. She was soaking wet, cold, beyond terrified.

I repeated, "Go back to your husband. *Run*."

She did what I told her. The stocky man redirected his gun at her, ready to pop her as she fled, but I stepped in the path of the shot. That angered him. He came closer. He pointed his gun at my chest, stabbed me with the death end of the weapon, and I kept my hands up, submitting. I closed my eyes and he laughed. He thought I was wounded and afraid. Called me a coward. Then I moved so fast it was a blur, grabbed the barrel of the gun with my left hand, gripped the slider, then hit him twice with my right fist. That hurt my already damaged hands. Two moves later his nose was bloodied, and I had his weapon pointed at his face. He didn't know what had happened. Neither did his coworker. Before he could raise his gun and take aim, I had my newly acquired weapon aimed at the center of his head. He cursed, surrendered his gun without saying a word. I put his gun in my waistband, then clocked him with the butt of the gun I was holding, clocked him hard, and he was on the ground with his homie, his mouth twice as bloodied.

I repeated, "*Soy* Gideon."

They stood up, wiped rain from their faces, looked at each other like they were in trouble.

I asked, "*¿Dónde está tu maldito jefe?*"

They pointed toward their headlights. The big boss was out here in the rain.

I said, "Let's go to Oz and have a talk with the wizard."

The taller one asked, "*Por favor*, first, may I have my gun back?"

"Fuck you, asshole. And if you plan on asking the same question, fuck you too."

We walked about halfway, and I stood behind them, used them as human shields. I had my hostages call out, tell their boss that Señor Gideon was here seeking an audience, and he was pissed. A moment later there was movement on their side. It looked like a huge shadow came my way, but it was a large figure and a smaller figure. The larger figure was almost seven feet tall, very tall for a man in this region, and carried a black umbrella. When they were close I saw the smaller figure had hips and curves. She wore a gray winter coat, one that was impermeable, over a black dress, fancy black tights, and heeled boots, hair pulled into a tight bun. She was very presidential. In heels she was five-six but thought she was six foot five, had about forty years of attitude inside of a body that couldn't have been more than thirty. She was attractive, in a dark way.

The fashionable woman calmly said, *"Buenas noches."*

"Buenas noches."

She stood in the rain, expressionless, a woman of steel.

The short woman wearing diamonds and pearls evaluated my existence in her world.

I asked, "Who are you?"

"I am the one who will decide your fate and the fate of all who wait behind you."

"Since I have the guns, I will be deciding your fate as well."

"May I borrow one of my men's guns?"

"Do I look crazy?"

"Trust me. Not trusting me is a bad way to start a negotiation."

I handed a gun to her but kept the second aimed at her.

Without hesitation she shot both of her men. Cranium shots. With their dead bodies resting at our feet, she shot them again. Shot each two more times, then sighed and handed me back the smoking gun. She did that, then adjusted her coat as if nothing had happened.

She said, "See? Now we have established some level of trust."

The big man next to her, he feared the small woman. It was in his eyes. Weak links dead at her feet, like she was Dame Judi. She saw that the over-the-top display didn't rattle me.

"Señor Gideon. Who do you work for on this lovely evening?"

"Yesterday, when we were in Buenos Aires, I worked for a capo named Scamz."

"And today? Señor Gideon, which capo do you work for today?"

"No one, Señorita. No one. Thinking about filing for unemployment."

"Why are you in my country if not to challenge us on our own land?"

"Just passing through to get to Brazil."

"Why Brazil?"

"I want to meet that girl from Ipanema everyone sings about."

She remained stoic. "Let's talk serious."

"Let's."

"For a man named Scamz, you met the Four Horsemen of the Apocalypse."

"Three Horsemen of the Apocalypse. One of them is dead. I killed him on a train."

"The Beast or Medianoche?"

"A young guy. Well built. Spanish. Frowns when stabbed. Can't take a punch."

"Señor Rodriguez. He was a very handsome man."

"If you say so. That Horseman did his last gallop on the morning train."

"If that is the truth, the Beast and Medianoche won't rest until you are dead."

"Well, they are my adversaries of the week."

"They are our adversaries as well."

"But are we adversaries?"

"At the moment, no."

"You're blocking my way on this *carretera* in a very comprehensive and hostile manner."

"I have allowed you to come this far. I could have destroyed all of you in Montevideo. The long-haired American girl, I could have had her executed the moment she landed in this country. We could have attacked you when you were resting in the hotel. Understand?"

"Look. It's cold. I'm wet. I'm tired. We need to cross the border into Brazil."

"The girl from Ipanema."

"You know it."

She said, "As a courtesy, you may continue."

"But?"

"All of my favors come at a price."

"What's your price?"

"One day I will reach out to you and call in this favor."

"I don't want any bullshit. We could just battle it out right here."

"We could. But it wouldn't serve either of us, other than for ego. The briefcases are no longer in play; therefore, I have nothing to gain by wasting ammunition at this moment."

"You've already lost enough men over in Buenos Aires."

She smiled. "I'm being generous. Don't be ungrateful."

I said, "You'll let my crew pass *sin problema*."

"You are *the* Gideon. Your word is all the currency needed."

"And what do they call you?"

"Abeja Reina. I am the Queen Bee."

"Looks like you have a militia. I'm one man. Nothing I can do for you."

"But some things are out of my jurisdiction."

I told her, "Once. At my discretion. I won't go on a suicide run, not like yesterday."

She shook her head. "Once. You will not get to choose. That is not how this works. You don't come to my country and tell me what you will and will not do like you're my president."

A second passed with us staring at each other. Not friends. Never would be.

With a handful of friends behind me and an untold number of guns in front of us, instead of popping her in the head, then doing the same to her guard, instead of starting a firefight on this road in the freezing rain, I gave a stone face to the expressionless woman and capitulated.

This wicked business was determined to not let me leave, at least not alive.

I told her, "Once. To get my associates out of your country. Once and we're done. My friends are not involved, will not be involved, and will never owe you anything. They don't exist to you. They are invisible. This fucked-up deal will be between me and you, no backlash for them."

"I will decide the manner in which this debt will be paid. I write the *fucked-up* deal."

"Write it, but only put my name on it. No compromise on that. I don't care how many guns you have hiding in the dark. It will be paid by me. *Once.* Then our business will be done."

A moment passed before she said, "This will be between us."

I asked, "How will you find me when you need to call in a favor?"

For the first time, she grinned. "I will contact someone who knows how to find you."

"I doubt if we run in the same circles."

"Queen Scamz. You know her as Arizona. She will contact you on my behalf."

My blood became as icy as my skin.

We looked in each other's eyes, shook cold hands.

She said, "If I were smart, I would require that once to be now."

"A storm is coming."

"I am sure it would love for you to be here when it arrived."

"Sorry. A tall, tanned, young, and lovely girl from Ipanema is waiting."

"I am sure she will be waiting for you in a *terma.*"

"*Estamos hasta las manos.*"

"*Igualmente.*"

She came closer to me, stood inches away, then raised her small hand, gently touched the side of my wounded face. She tightened her jaw, then touched my arms, squeezed my muscles, nodded. She licked her lips, stepped away, looked behind her, signaled that everything was fine.

She turned to me and said, "I believe you have something that belongs to me."

"I don't think so."

"We must maintain the trust we have created."

I handed her the guns. She held one in each hand.

She said, "Same arrogance. Same rhythm. You walk like one of them."

"One of who?"

"One of the Four Horsemen."

"The Three Horsemen, unless they kept a spare in the closet."

"You walk like you have testicles the size of coconuts."

"That explains the chafing."

She tried to see past my injuries, compared me to a Horseman.

Before she could make a connection, I turned around, jogged toward my crew. Every step let me know how bad I had been injured across the river, but I put on a show, pretended pain wasn't attached to me like a tick. The anxious, foolish men on the other side fired rapid shots into the air. Men and women. As I jogged, the bus started up, I heard that engine crank up behind me, and the vans revved their engines in response. All moved and cleared a way so we could pass.

I didn't learn it until later, but thirty minutes after we crossed into Brazil, there was a firefight back at the blockade. The Queen Bee knew they were coming, had been waiting on them, not us. She wanted a fight. She wanted to defend her land like she was part of a street gang in South Central Los Angeles. Medianoche had arrived looking for us, the woman they called Señorita Raven at his side. The Beast wasn't there. My assumption was that he was wounded. Medianoche had different people instead, a crew who didn't dress like Horsemen. The mercenaries had enlisted guns for hire. Half the people we had seen at the blockade were long dead by the time I boarded a plane in Rio. So were most of the men that Medianoche and Señorita Raven had brought along.

The Queen Bee had scarified all, run the Horsemen back across the river. Their fight was personal, not on my behalf. Still, part of me wished I had let my crew go without me and stayed behind. Our victory in Buenos Aires had been Pyrrhic at best, even for Scamz and Arizona. But it was my duty to make sure my team made it to safe ground.

I'd died once. And a man named Midnight had been killed once.

Both of us owed Death. We had cheated Death.

Like father. Like son.

Medianoche would find me and seek revenge for what had been done to Midnight.

Or I'd find him before he found Catherine and the boys.

That was already written in the books of hell.

I don't know why he tried to kill my mother, but even when I was seven years old I knew that Medianoche and I were not meant to walk the same earth. Every ache in my battered body confirmed that. One of us would die again. Mine or his, that second death would be the last.

Chapter 11

Black Angel

Raincoat over his Colombian suit, black umbrella up high, one gun resting in the small of his back, two more inside holsters underneath his coat, and two blades on his person, Medianoche stood under the enormous rubber tree, the famous *gomero* in Plaza Francia.

He was near Café La Biela and where prostitutes worked inside the discos, close to the drove of tourists going into La Recoleta Cemetery to give their respects to Eva Perón, not far from McDonald's and Village Cines.

The rubber tree had been planted in the 1800s by the Recoleta brothers and now was twenty meters wide and fifty meters high, a shade tree, much needed in Argentina's brutal, humid summers, that now served as an umbrella that kept much of the rain from falling. Much. Not all. A young woman with the hue of a Moor stood with Medianoche and looked up at the tree.

Luggage at her side, umbrella in hand, the former soldier was absolutely amazed.

She said, "I've never seen a tree like this, sir. It's ginormous, as wide as a park."

When she spoke, he could see the braces on her teeth. He took his attention from her and watched as city buses, tour buses, trucks, and a million cars raced along Avenida del Libertador. The Four Horsemen had chased the Scamz Organization down that boulevard, guns blazing, what felt like a few hours ago.

He whispered, "Gideon."

They had been so close to catching that gaucho in Uruguay.

The young woman broke his gaze when she said, "Sir?"

He faced the recruit who had just arrived from North America. She shivered in the weather. It was twelve degrees Celsius. That would be about fifty degrees Fahrenheit. He'd grown used to the metric system. The USA had been stubborn and not kept up with the times. Like an aging soldier. The dampness made the air feel colder. He thought about Caprica Ortiz. Las Leñas. Had to be good snow at the resorts.

The recruit said, "It's both an honor and a pleasure to finally meet you, sir."

He let her stand in the rain, in the cold, in uncomfortable silence.

She added, "And I am sad to hear the Beast is no longer with us."

"I am your commanding officer. Will there be an issue?"

"No, sir. The Beast spoke highly of you during our last conversation. He said that you were an outstanding soldier, a warrior, a fearless man who was the best executive officer."

He had come to meet her alone. If it did not go well, if she was not to his liking despite her résumé and having already been vetted by the Beast, he would put her down. She wore a military-style jacket over two wifebeaters, Old Navy gear that stood out as North American apparel. North Americans had become slouchy, had become a nation of bums. Men disgraced suits by wearing tennis shoes and called it fashion. He took in the recruit. The women in Argentina did their eyebrows differently and were all about brunette hair. They did not like their mane short and didn't like it to be seen with gray.

This girl had big hair, a curly, feral Afro, thick like wool, wild like a forest of black kudzu. Toned body, but not masculine.

Medianoche stood before her and asked, "What is your government name, soldier?"

She held her own umbrella, took a breath, and said, "Quiana Sapphire Savage."

He asked, "Where are you from originally?"

She told Medianoche she was from New York but had been born in the West Indies. Dominican. Identified with Carib, Quisqueyano, or Taino Indians, depending on the day of the week.

Medianoche asked, "What issues did Uncle Sam have with you?"

"There was an unauthorized absence when I left post to go hook up with someone."

"Hook up?"

"To have sexual intercourse, sir."

"You left your post to go get laid. You put your men in jeopardy to go cock chasing."

"I also violated a general order and attempted escape from custody when I was arrested."

"Tell me about the fight that happened when you were confronted."

"Took four men to subdue me. Three of those bitches couldn't do the job."

"How did that turn out?"

"Broke a couple collarbones, not mine, broke noses, again not mine, broke an arm, not mine, when they came to drag me to the brig. It took them twenty minutes to take me down."

"You were wrong. You left your comrades at risk. Then fucked up three or four more."

"I am embarrassed for doing so, sir. But what they did was no way to treat a woman."

"Was the fuck worth it?"

"No, sir. Not worth it. Two minutes of pleasure for a life of trouble. Didn't even nut, sir."

"There is a time for everything. Understand?"

"Understood."

"I would have put a bullet in your head for abandoning my team."

"Should I leave? Should I head back to America?"

"You're in America."

"I'm in Argentina, sir."

"You're in America. Argentina is in South America, and South America is just as America as the America from where you arrived. These are the Americas. From the top of Canada to the end of South America is America. The USA isn't the only America. Don't forget that."

"I won't forget that, sir. But can I explain what led to that bad decision?"

"Explain why you were *irresponsible* and put your comrades at risk."

"My older brother had died in Iraq. I had to get away. Having sex was just a way of medicating myself. Had to do something that made me feel alive and connected to the universe. I know that's no excuse. But that's what I did. That's why I was so angry I fought everyone who put their hands on me. I wanted to fight the entire world. It was wrong. Very wrong. But I had lost my only sibling in Iraq. We all grieve differently."

"What was the verdict handed down?"

"Dismissed with a Bad Conduct Discharge. Reduction in rank to pay grade E-1 and was locked up for nine months. Because I had one bad night, made one bad decision."

"How many bad decisions does it take to cost lives?"

"One, sir. One."

"You're a fuckup. Own it."

Medianoche pulled out a gun, silencer attached. She stepped back, afraid. Medianoche motioned toward the entrance of the Cementerio de la Recoleta, toward the city of the dead that was a potpourri of everything from neoclassical, neo-gothic, art nouveau, and art deco.

"There is a man inside. Gray suit, black tie. Was a soldier here in the eighties. The cemetery is a well-planned town for the dead. Neat city blocks with street names at every intersection. Walk past the feral cats. The directions are in red. He will be near the space marked number ninety-five, the grave for Rufina Cambaceres. The target's wife is buried in the adjoining mausoleum."

Without questioning she responded, "Yes, sir."

"Tell him you came to see him on behalf of the missing thirty thousand."

She repeated, "The missing thirty thousand."

"Then blow his fucking brains out. If anyone is with him, send them on the same trip."

He handed her a nine-inch tactical combat bowie knife sleeping in its sheath.

"Bring me his ears. And his tongue. Proof of death."

Without hesitation she took the knife. She put the gun in the small of her back, then put the knife in the pocket of her jacket before she fluffed her wild hair. She picked her umbrella up and took the stone walkway. She passed by a waiter dressed in black, carrying a silver tray, taking fresh coffee to some lazy fuck who wouldn't come out in the rain. Medianoche watched Quiana Savage as she passed by the waiter and others without a second look, watched the way she moved until she disappeared into the city of the dead.

She was focused. She had blocked out everything but that which was important.

Then a teen carrying a baby came to Medianoche, one of the tens of thousands who lived in the Argentine slums. Girls like her sat on every corner, in front of every shopping area, on every street, baby in arms, hand outstretched. He gave her his pocket change.

She thanked him, became teary-eyed, and moved on, hand outstretched to others.

Medianoche took out his phone, called Caprica Ortiz.

He said, "It's being handled as we speak. Another one will be in hell soon."

"Good. I have more intel for you."

"More information for me, or another contract from you?"

"The woman you say is the mother of Gideon. She is living in Atlanta. I have her passport information. I have an address where she lives. She has two sons living in her house."

"Is Gideon one of those sons? Is one of them an adult?"

"Both are boys in primary school. Nothing more on Gideon yet."

"Photos?"

"She is not on social media. But I will ask for photos."

"Keep trying. I need to be one hundred percent sure it's her. Just like you want to be sure that the men you send me to visit are the right men, I want to be sure about the woman who has been to me what evil men have been to you. I need to be sure that the right one is found."

"If that is what she is to you, then you will kill her."

"I will kill her like I have never killed anyone. I lost my eye because of *esa mierda puta*."

"Then I will check again and let you know. I will make sure she is the right one."

Chapter 12

Kiss the Blood off My Hands

Ten minutes later Quiana Savage exited the cemetery. She casually walked by religious Argentine women standing in the rain offering hugs for free, past children selling flowers, by other sidewalk vendors. This area was the tourist epicenter, the part of the city that felt the safest during the day. When Savage stopped and faced Medianoche, she opened a bag she carried. Inside were the ears and tongue. Blood was on her clothing, on the backs of her hands.

He took the bag, dropped it in the trash, then said, "Good job, Savage."

"Thank you, sir. The cemetery is amazing. Breathtaking. This area is off the chains."

She picked up her luggage and followed him with the cadence of an eager soldier.

He asked, "Are you hungry?"

"Famished, sir. I've been on a low-cash diet for the last six months."

"Well, your starving days are about to come to an end."

She exhaled like she wanted to cry. "Thanks for the opportunity, sir. I will prove to you that I am no longer a fuckup. I will earn my keep."

"I'm sorry about your brother."

"Thank you, sir."

"Nothing hurts like losing a brother."

Ten minutes later they were on Posadas, inside of the swank restaurant Fervor. Savage had gone to the bathroom, cleaned herself up, and come back wearing a Lakers hoodie.

He said, "This will be your last day dressing the way you do."

"Sir, yes, sir."

"You won't dress like a hooligan."

They were seated across from each other, underneath chandeliers at a white-tablecloth table. Argentine steaks had been ordered. The new recruit was looking at the people, the city, eyes wide, amazed by everything she saw. Medianoche looked at her. Black and beautiful. He never understood why gorgeous women wanted to be in the military. He never understood why so many blacks lined up to fight for a country that would never fight for them. The USA's military was to maintain dominance of the white man, and no one else. That was what his father had told him many times, usually when he was in a flag-waving, drunken stupor.

The new recruit took to the steak and vegetables like she hadn't had a meal for three days, maybe hadn't had a decent meal in as long as three weeks. It was like watching a poor child in a Dickens novel. It was sad. This was what became of many when war was done.

The door to the restaurant opened. Several suited men entered, marched in from the rain. One flipped the sign on the restaurant door from ABIERTO to CERRADO. From OPEN to CLOSED.

Another moved forward. He was Nigerian.

Medianoche stood, faced them all.

Savage stopped eating and did the same, stood by Medianoche's side, showing her commitment to the Four Horsemen of the Apocalypse.

Medianoche handed her his second gun. "Shoot those bitches in the heart."

She shot five times. Those five rapid shots popped five guerrillas in the chest.

The five guerrillas stumbled backward into the others, then looked down at their clothing, touched where the bullets had hit, pulled their hands back. There was no blood. Then one by one, four of the five laughed. The release of nervous energy. Just as many were behind them. The other men and women laughed too. At that moment, as if on cue, the suited mercenaries moved to the side.

Medianoche adjusted his bloodred tie.

Dressed in her Colombian suit, wearing the black tie of a Horseman, Señorita Raven marched by them all. Her walk had authority. She turned and regarded her squad.

She walked from one to the next, their second-in-command inspecting her team: Six-six, 235 pounds. Albino. Called himself Tiburón. The Shark. Born in the islands. Had six fingers on each hand, six toes on each foot. He was a great fighter, a sniper, could handle most weapons, especially the one at his side. The man next to him stood at five-seven. Dr. Spots weighed 160. He had vitiligo and could be brown-skinned or white, achieved by applying makeup to either the light patches or darker patches of his flesh. He was a good follower. Behind him was a broad-shouldered black man. The Butcher. Next to him was an Afro-Nicaraguan. Black Mamba. They moved to the side and once again Ibo the Nigerian came to the front. He stood at six foot nine, weighed a solid 390. The Cobra appeared next to Ibo. All muscle, had more strength than Lithuanian strongman Žydrūnas Savickas. There was a British soldier, Clutterbuck, six-one, athletic, 180 on the scales. Next to him was a woman from Dearborn, Michigan. She was a Pakistani woman named Javeria. She had joined the military on court order to avoid doing time for an armed robbery when she was a teen. Two tours of duty under her belt. There was an Israeli woman, Rayna. She was out of Newhall, California. She had worked as an assassin since her Dishonorable

Discharge and had a dozen more kills under her belt, outside of the twenty she had earned for Uncle Sam. There was a Mexican who called himself Chico Blanco. A soccer-playing pussy chaser. He had come home from Iraq and Afghanistan with PTSD as a souvenir. He stood next to a woman who wore a gray Colombian suit and white preacher's collar. Curvy and blond, built like South African actress Charlize Theron, only with a Cajun accent. She called herself Preacher. The only thing Preacher loved more than war was God. The Bible told her all she needed to know. It was all she read.

All had left the military on bad terms and had been uncertain about their futures. These were his bullet catchers. His new set of disposables.

Medianoche said, "Horsemen. Be seated."

Señorita Raven nodded. "Let's break bread and tell war tales."

Medianoche listened to the new Horsemen bond, talk about battle experiences, about the Middle East, about atrocities, about the things that soldiers had done to Middle Eastern women and their children, about the walking wounded, about the men and women who wouldn't make it home, about those who had and now were sleeping in storefronts.

His phone rang. It was Caprica Ortiz. He stood to the side and answered. The enemy had been located.

She said, "I know where he is hiding, but he is moving, and he changes his location very often, once a day, so you must be quick."

Medianoche called Preacher to the side.

He said, "I've reviewed your files."

"Sir, yes, sir."

"Three tours of duty."

"Sir, yes, sir."

"I read about the incident."

"The men who were involved, there was no punishment."

"You ended up in California."

"Working as a security guard at a Mexican food chain out in West Covina. But I did wet work as well. Small jobs. I wanted to get on with the LAPD. I wanted to become a Special Weapons Tactics officer. Or become part of the Sheriff's Department. But . . . my military record."

Medianoche nodded, didn't want to get into the details of her past, and moved on. She was sleek, fierce. Healthy. Good skin. He had seen her legs yesterday. She had strong, amazing calves and a tight ass. And she had kept busy doing assassin's work. She was ready.

"Preacher, I have an assignment for you. You will be team leader. You have to go back to the States. I'm not sure where yet."

"No problem, sir. I'll be returning to US soil as a Horseman."

"I will let you pick three Horsemen to complete your squad."

"May I pick Señorita Raven? Her reputation precedes her."

"So does yours, soldier."

"That's not what I was implying, sir."

"My XO stays here. We have to get all of you acclimated to being Horsemen and to South America. Outside of the issue in the States, we have other international work to be coordinated. Important work. But before we move on, we need to take care of some old Horsemen business."

"I won't disappoint you. I've never failed a mission."

"You're confident."

"'Blessed is the one who trusts in the Lord, whose confidence is in him.'"

Medianoche countered the biblical quote with one of his own. "'Pride goes before destruction. And a haughty spirit before stumbling.'"

"You know the word of the Lord."

"My father beat it into me. Church every Sunday from early morning until late afternoon. He was as religious as he was alcoholic."

"Never would have guessed you'd be able to quote anything besides *The Art of War*."

"Believe in God. But watch your six and trust your weapon on the battlefield. Everybody has a god, and a man's god or Allah or whatever he believes has never stopped anyone in any religion from dying in combat. Trust your gun during, then thank your God you survived after."

"Sir, yes, sir."

"I will let you know when the time has come. It may be tomorrow, it might be a week, could be a month. In the meantime, get to know your fellow Horsemen. Be ready to choose and create a secondary team."

"Sir, yes, sir."

"And you are to destroy all. Is that a problem?"

"I will destroy all like they are the Amalekite nation."

"Dismissed."

Two hours later Medianoche exited a Radio Taxi on Avenida Pueyrredón. He walked a block, made sure no one was on his tail, then took a private entrance into Hospital Alemán. When he turned around, Señorita Raven was there, not hiding, but tracking as she had done in the past.

She was in point-blank range before he said, "You're following me?"

"Is there a contract here? Like the one you just had Savage do in the cemetery?"

"Why are you trailing my every move?"

"I'm protecting you. We know the issues you have."

He snapped, *"Vamos a los bifes."*

"You freeze. I'm concerned. I'm doing my fucking job as your XO. I have your back. Do what you have to do, and I will be here, locked and loaded. I will make sure no enemy comes up behind you while you are vulnerable. Just let me do what your XO needs to do, sir."

He conceded. "Wait in the hallway."

"Is this another part of the Caprica Ortiz contract?"

"No. I have an appointment. Nothing major."

"I will, sir. I will stand sentry. You made your decisions, but since we're not with the others, I have to say that I should be your driver as well, just as you were the Beast's driver. From here out, I drive you. That is not negotiable. Walking in the open like this leaves us vulnerable. We're back in the Mercedes, rocking bulletproof windows and run-flat tires. You are our leader and must be protected above everything else."

He nodded. She was right.

Then he moved through the hospital's private section.

Medianoche was there for a fucking brain scan. The pain in his missing eye was without pause. He'd had too many blackouts. Like the best plane, battleship, or tank, the body could last only so many wars. Damage had been done. The older a man, the longer he took to heal.

He felt the injury when he inhaled, felt it when he exhaled.

Each ache took him back to Gideon.

He heard every lie that gaucho had told while they were in battle.

That son of a whore Gideon had claimed that Medianoche was his father.

Either a lie that had been told to him, or Gideon had simply chosen to tell a lie.

The whore's son had looked too much like the Beast to be anyone else's mutt.

Chapter 13

No Questions Asked

Konstantin, Hawks, and Shotgun escaped north to the alpha global city São Paulo.

The Russian was the only one in that bunch who spoke any Portuguese and understood the culture, so they had to depend on him. They kept it moving, no time to take selfies.

A contact there arranged new passports.

And in Rio de Janeiro another contact was doing the same for me.

Shotgun headed to Atlanta. He wanted to drive by Powder Springs, see if he could find out where Catherine and the boys had gone. My only hope was that she wasn't dead and stuffed in a freezer with the boys. I worked in that kind of world. I knew because I had been paid to do worse, more than once. The things I had done for money would not be televised.

I was back to depending on Shotgun.

Once my coworker and friend checked on Catherine and tried to find out where she was with the boys, he was going to stop being

Shotgun, become a hardworking blue-collar man named Alvin White again, then speed two hours east on I-20, get to Alabama, and check on his own family. Hawks stayed with Konstantin, made sure he made it back home. The Russian's wife was impatiently waiting, and so was an appointment to get another round of chemotherapy.

He was still in the ring fighting cancer. Still refusing to lose to man or God.

Before we parted ways, Hawks said, "I haven't forgotten those two names."

"Jeremy Bentham from Smyrna. Nathalie Marie Masreliez from Yerres."

"Either I'll be in touch or I'll pass what I find on to Konstantin."

"I still owe you for the BC Powder."

"Pay Konstantin and he'll get my money to me."

The green-eyed Bajan stayed in Rio at the safe house with me. It was a three-bedroom apartment in Leblon, the most affluent neighborhood in Rio. After the cold and damp safe house in Uruguay, stepping into a spot with white walls and comfortable furniture felt like I had died and gone to a hit man's heaven. The beach was right outside our window, across the street. I could hear the rhythmic roar of the sea. The winter here was about twenty-four degrees Celsius. That made it about seventy-five degrees Fahrenheit during the day, and the temperature dropped at nights to a balmy eighteen degrees Celsius, which was sixty-four degrees on that same Fahrenheit scale. It had weather like Southern California. The humidity was low, very tolerable, not like in the ATL. I saw people jogging all day, especially around noon. I was going to go to Angra dos Reis, but Rio was better. It would be easy for us to vanish into the area with more than twelve million people moving back and forth outside our door. Besides, I was hurting. It felt like I had broken every part of my body in that fight with Medianoche.

I should have killed him again. But I wanted him to admit he was my father first.

I wanted something my mother had told me since I was born to be true.

The Bajan said, "I want to train you when you get better."

"You think I need training? I kicked ass from the moment I arrived until I left."

"You can always be better. We fall into bad habits and don't realize we have done so. You say you kicked ass, but you didn't walk away clean. You almost lost an eye."

"I took a few hits."

"The point is to not get hit at all. Or suffer minimal damage. I teach my daughters how to fight. They are almost untouchable. If you are close enough to hit them, then they are close enough to kill you. I don't teach them to trade blows. I teach them to end the fight. To win."

I understood. They had sent the Bajan with me for a purpose.

I said, "So, I take it you're my bodyguard, more or less. An assassin's assassin."

"No. Not at all. I am here until morning. Have to get back to the Bahamas; then I have to go home to California."

"You have daughters?"

"Two. They haven't met. One is in the Bahamas. One lives in the States."

"You have any more kids?"

"I's a Bajan. We have kids everywhere."

That made me laugh. "It's like that sometimes."

"You?"

"No kids. Never been in one spot long enough to think about that. Well, I thought about that once upon a time with a girl I met at a pool hall near Los Angeles, but that was years ago. I was a different man then."

"I'm training both of my daughters. I've trained them for years."

"Just to fight? Or to do what you do?"

"To be able to survive. To never back down. To always win."

I nodded, then said to the green-eyed man, "Haven't seen you in a few years."

"You didn't have a name when I saw you last."

"I was new at the game. I might have still been a teenager."

"Now you big man in the business."

"Now I'm Gideon."

"I like that name. Wish I had thought of it first."

I said, "I thought you had left this business, one way or the other."

He nodded. "I did collections, some contracts for some powerful people in the US. It is a dark company called RCSI."

"Never heard of them."

"They are known as the Barbarians in our profession."

"Still, never heard of them."

"I am beginning to wish I hadn't. It has turned out to be a problem. They don't like it when an employee wants his freedom once again."

"You're telling me that you're on the run?"

"You could say that. But a man know when he catch me, he catch big trouble."

It sounded like he needed some help with a problem. But I was knee-deep in my own.

I said, "We'll talk. When this settles down, when it cools down, we can sit and chat."

"No need to worry about me. I make a man regret the day he catches me."

"I'm that way with women."

We laughed.

When I woke the next morning, the Bajan was gone. The West Indian man with the green eyes, smile, and Caribbean accent who had made Hawks's panties wet had left the safe house. He left a note. Told me he would be in touch, left a number to reach him.

I wanted to call Hawks, to apologize again. But I didn't. I stayed in Rio de Janeiro, called Catherine over and over. Never got an answer.

Konstantin had set up for me to go to a doctor and get X-rays. I'd taken a lot of blows to the head. Not just in Rio, but since the start of this career in wetworks. I'd fought rappers. Politicians. A man with a broken nose. A red-haired assassin and his wife. I'd fought too many fights. Each fight was a fight to the death. But I felt okay. My vision wasn't blurry. That merry-go-round had stopped going at one hundred miles per hour. So I blew off that appointment.

I wore clothes that were on the level of the people in my surroundings, dressed like the locals, and stuck to the south, the Zona Sul neighborhoods of Copa and Ipanema. My Portuguese made the tourists think I was Brazilian and respectable enough to make Brazilians think I was an expatriate living in their country. An old man asked me what happened and I told him I was attacked by a gang out of the Rochina favela, said I had gotten too close to the biggest slum in the world.

He told me I was lucky to still be alive.

I agreed.

Within two days, with the help of BC Powder, I was moving much better.

Konstantin called. Funds had been transferred.

In Russian he asked, "Are you up to working, or should I pass on the Rio job?"

"Send me the information."

"Do it; then I will send you somewhere else. You've been there too long."

"I don't want to run. People have been chasing me for years. I'm tired of running. The Horsemen are a mission for a thousand, or a mission for one, and I can sneak back and be my own Seal Team Six."

"You're not running. If it was only Medianoche, you could handle that. You're capable. But one man can't defeat an army. You're a man with a gun fighting a battalion of rocket launchers. Let's not be insane. They would have destroyed everyone in Buenos Aires to get to us."

"I need to know where Catherine and the boys are."

"Be patient, my favorite son. Be patient. You are injured."

"Now let's talk about you. How's that cancer?"

"Like we did the Four Horsemen of the Apocalypse, I will kick its ass."

"If you don't kill it all, it comes back, sometimes stronger."

"I may have a little cancer, but cancer does not have me."

Chapter 14

Estafador

Scamz had outsmarted the Four Horsemen. He had spread the word across the lands.

He had not garnered as much as he had hoped, but in Buenos Aires, he had won.

Now he was with his team on a seventy-million-dollar super-yacht, one that had a six-cabin layout. The main deck was the master deck, and the upper deck was VIP.

That was where he sat. Leeward. Sipping champagne, an AR-15 and Glock at his side.

He had sixteen hired men, all in suits, all armed in the same fashion.

They guarded the boat in shifts. Underway, astern, or resting, they moved from stern to starboard to bow to port and back to stern. No man ever sat or stopped moving. Men who moved couldn't fall asleep on the job. If one did, he had to swim home. They covered all three levels of the pleasure boat. Wherever Scamz went, two armed guards stayed near. No one spoke to Scamz. When he slept, they patrolled outside his door.

No one had made him run before.

No one had ever made him live in the middle of an ocean, too nervous to return to land.

It was nighttime. In the distance a cruise ship went by, unaware of his presence. Scamz's vessel was not trackable. The automatic identification system had been disabled. Maritime authorities couldn't track his position, speed, location, or movements without AIS. The primary function of AIS was collision avoidance. But Scamz had his crew track the position of other ships, especially any heading in their direction, and moved accordingly. They also used their eyes. At night they could see the lights on other vessels. But now lightning was in the distance. Beautiful lightning. There was a storm out on the water.

Winds picked up. And on the open seas, there were no buildings to block the brunt of it.

When darkness hit and the rainfall touched his area, Scamz moved inside. Polished wood. Marble. Made the Presidential Suite at the Four Seasons seem like a retreat for paupers.

The yacht was the type of water transportation that would be used by a man who drove a four-hundred-thousand-dollar Bentley Mulsanne Speed that had a champagne chiller with three glasses and iPads built into the backseats. This vessel cost more than most made in their lifetimes.

Life was about comfort, if nothing else.

His six-bedroom home in Pacific Palisades and his Kensington Palace Gardens address were testaments to his taste, to where and how he existed in a world of losers. When he flew, if he wasn't in a private jet, flying instead with commoners in order to facilitate a scam, he traveled first class. Tickets were as much as twenty-one grand, but those were paid for by his lovers, women with addresses in Chelsea, the Boltons, Compton Avenue, Park Place Villas, Courtenay Avenue, Manresa Road, Victoria Road, and Notting Hill. Beverly Hills, Hollywood Hills, Park Avenue, Honolulu, Atherton, and Sagaponack.

He was a good-looking man, tall and Latin, dressed well, and smelled like success. He was *Scamz*. The con man of all con men. He had taken his deceased father's name in the game. He had taken his father's reputation. He was better than his father ever dreamed of being.

His father ran grifts out of pool halls in North Hollywood. Credit card scams. Rent scams.

But Scamz the younger went bigger. His long-deceased Ecuadorian father would be proud of all Scamz had done. Of all of the children his father had created, Scamz had been the one who had garnered the most success.

He had even seduced his father's favorite concubine. He was a child when his father had Arizona in his bed. And now he had had her. And her sister. The same as it had been with his father.

He knew his father was in his grave laughing. His son had conquered Arizona.

His father had summed up life in two words: *pussy* and *money*. Whoever had one had access to the other.

The man who had taken the name Scamz had been at sea since he left Colonia, Uruguay. He had brought the dead body of Arizona's brother on board, had done the same with Arizona's almost-dead sister. Arizona was wounded, her face scarred up and bloodied, in no shape to do anything but lie on a bed and suffer as she cried and mourned. Scamz had left Gideon and his friends in Uruguay. He hoped they had been found and were dead.

Nothing would upset Arizona more. Nothing would please Scamz more.

He had won the battle. He was safe. He was a long way from Buenos Aires.

The point of being at sea was to be able to see danger before it arrived. His men were paid to be on guard. Especially at night. Without city lights, the ocean offered nothing but darkness.

The night also made it even harder to judge speed. On the open sea it felt like the recreational vehicle wasn't moving fast. Not until something fell overboard could you use your eyes to judge the speed of a ship by how quickly something or someone faded into the distance.

But seeing someone fall overboard, and fight to stay alive, was terrifying. It made grown men scream.

And that was what happened when a harpoon appeared in the chest of a guard at the yacht's stern. Only after he fell, the waters swallowed his scream. The splash was hardly noticeable.

Seconds later one of the patrolling bodyguards spotted people boarding. Scamz's guard called out, and they fired at him. The enemy's weapons had suppressors. The guard fired his AR-15 back, and that sounded the alarm. He screamed out to the others. Shots came at them from the darkness that reached out from the bow. Not until then did the protectors of the Scamz Organization see how this had happened. A small ship was in the water, right under their noses. It was dark, reflected no light, and had little water resistance, and its hull was propped up on two narrow struts. The struts made the ship look like it was standing on legs. It resembled a plane and moved like an aircraft on the sea. It was called a Ghost. A fast-attack stealth boat with low radar and heat signature. Jet propulsion. They wouldn't be able to outrun the bitch.

The water vehicle was military, made to get soldiers, marines, SEALs, and pissed-off Horsemen of the Apocalypse to battle. In the darkness, they had appeared out of nowhere.

One of the guards snapped, "They are trying to board aft."

Another fired shots and screamed, "And bow."

"They're all over the bloody ship."

Chapter 15

Apology for Murder

Gunfire lit up the night, the racket and clamor deafening.

Señorita Raven led her team's charge, the albino, Tiburón, and Quiana Savage at her six.

"Fuck! Shoot that bitch!"

"Pop all of them motherfuckers!"

The Horsemen wore helmets that could stop shrapnel and sniper fire. Four-tube night vision goggles. Body-armor plates. Carried M4 rifles. SIG Sauers, Glocks, and .45-caliber handguns. Had M79 grenade launchers and M67 hand grenades. And Daniel Winkler fixed-blade weapons, the Rolls-Royce of blades. Salomon Quest boots. Crye Precision combat uniforms.

There were no tailor-made Kevlar-lined Colombian suits tonight. There was no need to dress in a way that didn't terrify the public.

One of Scamz's guards yelled, "We're being flanked!"

Another howled in pain. "I'm hit! I'm hit! I'm hit!"

"Right *there*. Port side!"

"I saw two more of them starboard!"

"Is anybody else hit?"

Underneath the stars, as the rain fell, the guards retreated. A set of guards fled past the swimming pool, stopped by the sauna and returned fire, tried to keep the Horsemen from controlling the top deck. The ship's engine stopped and all went dark on board. The Horsemen controlled the engine room. The guards needed to rectify that.

Suddenly an explosion rocked the ship. A bomb had been set off in the engine room.

The superyacht was no longer super, just an oversized ship dead in the water.

Señorita Raven yelled, "Reloading."

Tiburón shouted, "Moving."

Quiana Savage responded, "Set!"

There was no room to perform a bold flanking maneuver, so they pressed on. It was a brute-force attack. Close quarters. The stealth part of the operation was over.

"Splash in five seconds."

Five seconds later, there was another explosion.

Scamz's guards were unable to reverse their course, were forced to retreat to the Jacuzzi. Smoke bombs hit the deck and obscured everything the shining stars made visible. They were on the top level, a very open area made for lounging and catching sun, clothes optional. This part of the Scamz Organization was forced from aft to bow on the twenty-meter sundeck. They lost four guards, then fled to the lower decks to regroup. The Horsemen hounded their prey, but two stayed in case someone was forced to retreat back up the stairs. If it was the Horsemen being forced back, they'd have support. If it was the Scamz Organization, they would be cornered.

If a distress call had gone out and a rescue helicopter appeared in the night and tried to make use of the touch-and-go helipad on the foredeck, they were ready for that action too.

Past mistakes had been teaching moments. This had been mapped out.

As the guards fought along port side, they were compromised at starboard by Medianoche. Medianoche led Cobra, Clutterbuck, Javeria, and Rayna, guns blazing.

A wounded guard called out, "We need reinforcements!"

"They're hitting us on two levels at once!"

"We can take these arrogant motherfuckers!"

Flash and bang followed the guards, and gunfire from the Horsemen kept them retreating forward into the main salon. Bullets destroyed rich woods and carpet and damaged expensive marble. The elevator opened and three members of the crew were gunned down.

The superyacht no longer looked like an award-winning house in the Hamptons. The sofas, coffee table, lounge chairs, large television—everything was destroyed. Windows were blown out and the sea breeze came in strong. Scamz's men were forced to hide behind a wall of polished wooden cabinetry that separated the dining area from a section with white leather sofas, reclining chairs, and flat-screen televisions. On the formal table for twelve, Scamz's half-eaten five-course dinner was left behind.

In the main salon, where that part of the battle was enclosed, the cacophony was deafening. The gunfire, the yells from men paid to protect a grifter, the screams, were in an echo chamber.

Medianoche reloaded, heard the enemy yelling, each hired gunman telling his ill-prepared comrade they had to do something or they wouldn't survive the fucking onslaught.

The intense firefight continued.

One of Scamz's men was on the floor, holding his ears. Blood covered his hands and painted his face, both of his eardrums ruptured by the concussive force of a flash grenade. He had become a liability and was left behind. They were in full panic. Every man for himself.

Medianoche double-popped the enemy in the head and moved by him.

They came up on more men, men who had been incapacitated, who clung to their weapons and chose to take shelter from enemy fire. They were bleeding out on the beautiful floor. Horsemen gunned them down.

Medianoche moved on, weapon trained, searching for Scamz.

Behind him the Horsemen double-popped more of the enemy.

The Horsemen had covered two levels of the 157-foot yacht from aft to bow.

Medianoche's team met Señorita Raven's team and they proceeded together.

The Scamz Organization sought protection, scrambled to avoid the hail of bullets. The gunmen from the Scamz Organization took whatever shelter they could find and returned fire.

"Arrrrrrgh!"

"I'm blind; I'm blind!"

"There are more of them behind us!"

"Help me. I'm hit!"

There would be no escape. No rules. No holds barred.

No fucking United Nations setting the limits of war.

Señorita Raven called out, "Surrender and I promise not to kill you."

"Fuck you!"

"I'm hit! Fuck, fuck, fuck. I'm hit!"

Guards fled across wood and marble. Across luxury meant to entertain.

Medianoche said, "Grenade!"

He tossed one ahead of his squad, and more gunfire followed.

Medianoche felt alive. This was where he was the most comfortable. This was where he excelled. He moved better and faster than Horsemen who were almost half his age. In his mind, he was still a young man in war, killing for his country, each kill a celebration. Once a man had been in war, the rest of his life was war. The hired guns on board were good, well armed, as determined as marines who refused to be taken by Taliban fighters. Trapped at sea, on a ship that had become a floating kill zone. It was life or death with no chance to catch your breath. Men breathing heavily were all around him. The enemy wouldn't give anyone a minute to aim. It wasn't a game. No one would magically heal if they sat for five seconds. No one would spawn like they did in the games Señor Rodriguez used to play. This was real life.

Half of the men from the Scamz Organization had caught bullets. There was also a crew of thirteen. Since they were indistinguishable from the enemy, they were shot on sight.

Scamz hadn't been found. Not yet. The yacht was enormous—plenty of space, many rooms, but it had a limited number of places to hide. The con man was still on board.

Scamz had fought well on the streets of Buenos Aires. This was different. There would be no car chase. There was no escape. Most of all, there would be no mercy for a pregnant woman. Medianoche wished he had double-popped Arizona the moment he met her.

Scamz was trapped. Even if he tried to flee the yacht on one of the smaller boats the superyacht carried, it would be futile. If Scamz boarded a speedboat, then tried to flee this battle, the Horsemen left on the Ghost would blow him out of the water. Just as it had detected the superyacht, the radar on their Ghost would detect if a minisub left the yacht.

The tangos were pursued. Soon there were more Horsemen than tangos.

The yacht had been boarded and now was destined to be overrun.

Medianoche was impressed, as impressed as he had been during the skirmish in Buenos Aires. The Scamz Organization's guards fought bravely but were eventually overcome.

The ship had become a mortuary rocking with the waves.

The two twin cabins on the lower deck, the two queen staterooms, and the VIP stateroom were all secured. Flash and bang were thrown in, followed by turning each room into a shooting gallery. Be it hired gun or crew, they were all terminated. They didn't chance a guard pretending to be a crew member. They wanted no witnesses. With the ship under their control, Medianoche told them to watch their six and go to the spot each had been assigned.

He told the other Horsemen, "Do your designated tasks. Set the explosives."

Señorita Raven went with Medianoche, side by side, weapons drawn.

The ship rocked and rolled with the ocean swells.

Medianoche stopped at the door of the master suite.

Señorita Raven said, "Sure you're okay?"

He took a breath, sweat dripping. "I'm good."

"He might be armed."

"I want him alive."

"Is that optional?"

"Not optional."

Medianoche kicked open the door, and they entered guns high.

The superyacht's layout had said the master suite was accessed via the owner's private office. King bed; walk-in wardrobe; entertainment center; Jacuzzi tub and shower.

They found Scamz in the private office. He was dressed in a white suit. While his men battled, he had changed clothing. He smoked a cigarette that smelled like cloves.

He said, "The door was unlocked. There was no need to break it down."

Señorita Raven went to Scamz, patted him down. While Medianoche kept his weapon trained on Scamz, Señorita Raven checked to make sure the elusive con man was alone. Then she checked the cabinets, made sure no weapons were in reach, before she walked back to Scamz, stared him down, anger as high as adrenaline.

He coolly said, "You must be the lovely Señorita Raven."

She treated him to a head-butt. Then she gut-kicked him, tried to break a rib. When he staggered, Medianoche hit him on the chin and Scamz dropped to the floor.

Scamz said, "I take it that you are not here to capitulate. If you are, help me to my feet and I'll make us all a cuppa while we lay out the policies of your unconditional surrender."

Señorita Raven kicked him in the gut once more. "Motherfucker, you think this is a joke?"

Medianoche stopped her from kicking him again. Her rage was strong but controllable.

Eyes on Scamz, as the ship rocked and rolled, Medianoche said, "Watch my six, XO."

Breathing heavily, Señorita Raven moved back to the door, halfway in, halfway out, gun in each hand. Medianoche waited, watched Scamz pull himself to his feet again. Nose bloodied, the con man straightened his white suit, then looked at the blood on his hands.

Medianoche said, "Scamz."

"Medianoche. So our paths have crossed again."

"They never uncrossed."

"Obviously."

"'Attack where your enemies are not prepared; go to where they do not expect.'"

"*Art of War.*"

"Of course."

"'If your enemies have advantage, bait them; if they are numerous, prepare for them; if they are strong, avoid them; if they are angry, disturb them; if they are united, separate them.'"

"What you managed to accomplish in Buenos Aires."

"You outgunned us, but we outsmarted you."

"A fuckin' clerisy will never be smarter than my gun."

"I'm a bit curious, Señor Medianoche. May I ask how you located me so expeditiously?"

"Spectrum data from satellites. They used exactEarth to estimate your position."

"Brilliant."

"Still wasn't easy. Didn't know if you were spoofing and hiding outside the EEZ."

"Any particular reason you're here? Need a ride somewhere? Did you sign up for a three-hour tour? Would you like some caviar, perhaps?"

"We are here to defeat the enemy and avenge the fallen."

"Are you still the Four Horsemen? Or did you become the Three Musketeers?"

"We will always be the Four Horsemen, and this is your apocalypse."

"You arrived in a much larger number than anticipated."

Medianoche nodded. "You had the courage, just needed more firepower."

"Yours was a well-coordinated, concerted sneak attack."

"Did you expect a Hallmark card sent by carrier pigeon or warning shots?"

"Cleverly orchestrated. Tonight your attack was as brutal as it was clever."

Medianoche paused. "Was the assassin called Gideon one of your bodyguards?"

"Unfortunately not."

"You decided to stay at sea."

"Oh, I hate being at sea too long. When I am on a ship for a week, I suffer from *mal de débarquement* tremendously. It's horrible. Disturbs my eyes, ears, and throat, and for days I feel as if I'm still at sea. The persistent rocking, swaying, or bobbing feeling becomes endless."

"You won't have that problem this time."

He smiled. "I suppose not."

Medianoche adjusted his eye patch. "We have business to settle."

Scamz nodded. "The Beast? Where is that convivial fellow?"

"He paid the ultimate price."

"Arizona's knife appears to have done more damage than anticipated."

Medianoche shot Scamz in his left shoulder. The shot made the British-born grifter grunt, then spin as he fell. He fell hard. Didn't see the shot coming. The pain came after.

"Medianoche, my good man. Was that necessary?"

Señorita Raven came back into the room. She pressed her boot against Scamz's face, almost stood on his head, tried to press his face into the floor, same as they had done to Arizona on the streets of Buenos Aires. At the same time, Medianoche used his foot, put his weight on Scamz's wound. He pressed hard, put all his weight on the injury, and when Scamz had screamed enough, Medianoche put his Glock in the center of the con man's head.

Upstairs there was gunfire. Single pops. The sound of Horsemen putting bullets in the skulls of the lifeless to make sure they were really dead. There would be no witnesses.

Soon that would include the con man in the room.

Medianoche said, "Where is Arizona?"

"Could you ask this beautiful woman to get her smelly, bloody foot off my head?"

Medianoche nodded. Señorita Raven went back to the door.

Scamz's pained expression turned hostile. "Now. What about Arizona?"

"She's on board?"

"We parted ways hours after the event was over."

"Pregnant?"

"She gave birth to our precious baby in Buenos Aires."

"Premature and worth a king's fortune."

"You figured it out. Kudos."

"A fake pregnancy."

"Survey says, that's the number one answer."

"She had the device we needed hidden in her belly the whole time."

"Oh, we wish we could have seen the look on your face."

Scamz laughed like he was showing two middle fingers in the face of defeat.

Medianoche raised his foot and stomped down on the bloody wound, then pressed harder than he had before. Scamz gritted his teeth, sweated, wanted to howl.

Medianoche barked, spit flying, "I figured it out. I fucking figured it out."

"Just . . . not . . . in . . . time."

"Oh, it's not too late. If I have you, I have the money. I don't need the con woman. But before you take your last breath on this ship, you will tell me where to find that bitch. By the time the Horsemen are done with you, you will scream what I want to know. And you will give me the big black guy's info, the Russian's info, and you will give me that gaucho Gideon."

Scamz heard someone come down the hallway. A broad-shouldered Horseman entered, a man who, like Scamz, was in his twenties. He had a smile on his face and held surgical blades in his hands.

The Butcher.

Chapter 16

Kiss Tomorrow Good-bye

I wore dull jeans, a worn baseball hat, work boots, a winter coat, and shades. I took to the streets, shadowed a businessman from his job, followed him as he hurried from Senhor dos Passos and Avenida Presidente Vargas down into the Uruguaiana subway station. The stench of sweat, urine, sick, and something that reeked like stale cardboard violated my nostrils.

Disillusioned business partners wanted him out of the picture for good. And as I stood on the crowded platform waiting to shadow him to the killing point, someone crept up behind me, took slow steps.

Someone tapped my back and said, "Jean-Claude?"

When I turned around, I faced another part of the past.

Eyes wide, wearing a blue dress and high heels under her coat, sporting dark lipstick and a darker look of surprise, she repeated, in Spanish, "Jean-Claude? It's you? It's you. It's you. It's you."

"Angelina Maldonado?"

Her surprise changed to dislike. "Jean-Claude. It is you."

Once upon a time I had gone to the End of the World and done a job for a grifter. When that work was done, I had met a beautiful engineering student who was enrolled at the Universidad Nacional de la Patagonia San Juan Bosco. We had become lovers. She stood in front of me now. I had lived with her for two months, had been her lover for almost a season, but it became too heavy and I left one day and never went back.

Tears formed in her eyes. She said, "I thought you had died."

All I could say was, "Angelina. Wow. You look amazing."

"You went for a walk one day and . . . *poof* . . . you disappeared."

Her lips turned down, bitter, disappointed, pissed off. Like a bride who had been stood up at the altar. Surrounded by people, inhaling the staleness of the tunnel, forgetting what I was there to do, I saw the damage that people like me left behind. I had killed her inside.

I couldn't tell her that being with her was a liability in my cluttered world, that I had to be cold and walk away because it could have been too much. I couldn't tell her that I'd been trying to earn a million dollars to be with another woman, a woman who had long since rejected me.

It was pithy, not close to being enough, but all I could say was, "Sorry if I hurt you."

"Why did you leave?"

"I had to."

"Why?"

"I just had to."

"Was it me?"

"No, it was me."

She motioned. "Your face. What happened?"

"Got mugged."

"You have to be careful here. This is nothing like where I grew up."

"I've learned to keep to the main streets and not take any shortcuts at night."

She wiped her eyes, firmed herself. "Where are you going? On the train?"

"No, I'm going back to my hotel room."

"You're not getting on the next train?"

"No. I'm . . . I was . . ." The target was next to us. I turned around, gave him my back so he couldn't see my face; then I asked Angelina, "You want to go to a coffee shop and talk?"

She paused, considered it—I saw memories flash in her eyes— then shook her head and said, "I have to rush home."

The crowd swelled, pushed us closer. I asked, "You live here?"

"Yes. I have lived here since after I graduated from university. You?"

"Visiting. Have to be at the airport at four A.M. I leave on the first flight."

"Then back to Quebec?"

"Will be heading to Dubai. Then home to Quebec."

"I looked for you there. In Quebec. In all of Montreal. Couldn't find you."

"I don't Facebook."

"No, I went to Quebec. About a year later. I looked for your face everywhere. There are many Jean-Claudes in Quebec. I think I met them all. I prayed to God to let me find you and that you were safe. All sorts of crazy things were in my mind. Maybe he was kidnapped? Crazy things."

"I had no idea."

She took a breath, swallowed, too close to me; I was beyond un- easy. "You have a family?"

"No, I'm not married. I have brothers. They are with my mother."

"Didn't you tell me your mother was dead? You said you had no siblings."

"It's a long story."

"Who do you work for?"

"Independent contractor for the Hanso Foundation."

"Never heard of that company. Is it around here?"

"It is, but it's hard to find. Most people get lost."

"Well. I'm glad you are alive. I can let that part of my mind rest."

"The train is coming. Shit. Look. Maybe I can change my flight and stay another day. We can meet later, get drinks, and talk. Let me take you to Rio Scenarium, or we can dance the samba at Carioca da Gema or Clube dos Democráticos. I know you still love to dance. Or if you want to talk, we can do that at Bip Bip. We can drink, talk, listen to music. It's up to you."

"We danced so much when we were together."

"At that Irish bar at the End of the World. The sun was out until after eleven."

"Galway was the Irish bar. El Nautico was the other place we went all the time. The one with the DJ."

"Where we could dance and see the lake."

"We ended up at both of those places every weekend. We did a lot of hiking, trekking, rowing. We snow skied in Ushuaia. Tierra del Fuego. We worked out almost every day. I lost so much weight. After class I looked forward to seeing you. You were the ideal man for me."

"I looked forward to seeing you too. You taught me how to speak Spanish. You got me started."

"We talked about going so many places together. To the United States. To London. To Canada. To Los Penitentes on the highway between Santiago and Mendoza in Chile. I had imagined it all. Then you were gone. People at my church wondered what had happened."

"Iglesia de la Merced. Your Catholic church."

"The things you owned, you left it all behind. When you left, they spread a rumor that you were married and went back home to your wife."

"No, I wasn't married."

"Was there another woman?"

"No. I didn't leave you for another woman."

"Was it me?"

"No, it wasn't you. You did nothing wrong."

"Some said you were a criminal."

"I wasn't on the run from the law."

"That is good to know. Then I will feel like less of a fool."

I asked, "So can we hook up later tonight?"

"Hook up?"

"I don't mean it in that way. Can we meet and chat for a while?"

She blinked, remembering, then raised her left hand. "I'm married."

"Oh."

"Two months ago."

"You're a newlywed. Congratulations."

"Jean-Claude. This . . . My heart is racing right now. This feels like a dream."

"It's real."

"We met in Ushuaia. You left. And now I find you in Brazil. Here in Rio de Janeiro."

The train and the rumble of the people kept me from having to say anything.

She hesitated, looked uneasy, then took out a business card, pushed it into my hand.

Now she was ANGELINA MALDONADO DE LEÃO DE ALBUQUERQUE.

She paused a moment, as if she expected me to reciprocate and give her my card.

She nodded, bit her lip, said, "Don't change your flight."

"It wouldn't be a problem."

"Please don't. I don't need to start to feel . . . angry and confused all over again."

"We could meet for lunch tomorrow. I owe you a better explanation."

She shook her head. "Well, Jean-Claude, just call me when you have a moment."

"I will call you. I'm serious. I should have called a long time ago."

"I wish you had. One call would have meant so much."

"I will call you. I know I keep saying that. I will."

"If you don't call, it was nice to see you one more time. This has been both a surprise and awkward for me."

"For both of us."

"And since you are the one who left me, it has been more awkward for me than it has been for you. I wish you safe travels."

Her voice had cracked at the end. Tears returned to her eyes. She kissed me on both cheeks, still polite.

She said, "*Chau.*"

I said, "*Chau.*"

Then she was rushing, wiping her eyes and moving with the swarm to get on the congested train. I stuffed her card in my coat pocket, then waved good-bye. Out of all the subways in all the towns in all the world, she walked into mine.

My target got on the train, unaware. The doors to the train closed. He didn't notice me. The greatest trick the devil ever pulled was convincing the world he didn't exist. My best trick was being able to stand in a crowd, right next to a target, and never be noticed. But I had been noticed. By an old lover. As it pulled away, Angelina stood on the crowded train, stared at me until she couldn't see me anymore.

I hurried back up to street level. I made my way around the area, watching my back, using the reflections in glass to see who was behind me, memorized the crowd, made turns, made sure no one else had made the same turns, made sure the hunter wasn't being hunted.

I took to Rua Roldolfo Dantas and stopped at Sofá Café. There was a Kraft Café near the safe house, but I didn't want to go back in that area. Sofá was a small, colorful coffee shop, the owner very attractive, with a smile like a morning sunrise.

I sat in a yellow chair at a table for two, had a French press and a sandwich, and looked over what had been sent. The package had included the target's personal information and all of his habits, his routines. He would be on Rua Xavier da Silveira later. He slept at his girlfriend's apartment twice a week. I bet that pissed his wife off. Or maybe she didn't care.

I picked up a newspaper. Flipped the pages as I ate. The news item that made me pause was about a kid. A fourteen-year-old had been captured. News said the kid was a reluctant hit man for the Mexican cartel. Mexican cartels had become the top source for US meth. He said that he had been forced to work as a hit man, kill or be killed.

El Ponchis. The Cloaked One.

The kid claimed that he didn't have any parents. Had been in the killing business since he was twelve. He admitted that he had assassinated at least seven people at three thousand dollars a pop.

Child assassin. It was like reading about myself, part of my biography in black and white. I nodded. Sending a child out to commit murder was a form of child abuse.

The kid was being paraded in front of the news media, his face exposed, his fifteen minutes of abuse now international while everyone who guarded him, with guns, stood around the diminutive killer with their faces hidden behind masks. If that kid was who he claimed to be, his days would be numbered, despite his age. This business didn't care if he were eight or eighty. Once you were a marked man, death followed.

The world would be surprised how many assassins weren't old enough to obtain a driver's license. I had been in the business since I was seven. That had been the first time I picked up a .22 and shot an evil man in the head. When I was a child, I killed a man who was trying to kill my mother. Many days I had wished that I had let my mother die.

But I had done what a child was supposed to do, protect his mother, right or wrong, and I had killed her aggressor. That man was my father.

That was what my mother had told me.

But my mother was a woman of many lies.

If I carried Catherine to the top of Mount Corcovado and placed her before the statue of Christ the Redeemer, Jesus would close his eyes and turn his back on her. If she touched his feet, the six million stone tiles that covered the religious figure would catch fire and fall like a fiery rain.

My mother had fooled many, but she was no saint.

I put the paper down and considered my environs.

The Four Horsemen could be in Brazil by now.

I might walk out into the streets and get triple-popped.

The stress kept my heart rate up. Kept my paranoia strong.

Paranoia kept me alert, and that was what kept me alive.

I left the café, went into the center of Rio's business district, and found my way to a place where businessmen went to hide from the world from two in the afternoon until midnight. I went to Quatro por Quatro. I climbed the narrow stairwell and paid less than ten dollars US entry fee to get in and see the stunners they had to offer. They took my credit card, the one with the North American name, verified it against my bogus passport, kept the card, then gave me the key to a private locker. Anything I paid for would get charged to the card associated with the key. Women who looked like they should be holding briefcases on *Deal or No Deal* walked to and fro, only they were dressed in lingerie.

While Brazilian music mixed with music from the USA and the people jammed hard, I went to the locker room and undressed.

I showered. Stood naked. Looked at my body. I touched places my skin had met a blade. Touched where I had been shot. My body was a road map of trouble.

I eased on a white robe and slippers. I felt naked without a loaded Glock at my side, almost as naked as the women who were walking around the building. But my body was a weapon.

Two men found four women who looked like movie stars, and right away they were heading upstairs to claim one of the fifty beds.

I saw women who reminded me of every woman I'd been with, even as a teen. I saw Arizona. I saw Miki Morioka. I saw Jewell Stewark. I saw Lola Mack. I saw Mrs. Jones. I saw the first women I'd slept with. I saw women my mother used to send to my room to please me. I saw three women who looked like Angelina. And I saw Hawks's doppelganger. I'd known women, but no woman was waiting on me anywhere in the world.

There was an area with a small stage for women to show off their stripper skills. A well-built Brazilian girl held on to a bar built into the ceiling and did an upside-down Chinese split. Deep brown skin, small waist, with an ass that could make Serena and Beyoncé bow down.

Six feet tall and wearing six-inch heels, she was an Amazon come to life. She had a wide smile. That girl stole the attention in this *terma*. She twirled around the silver pole, was in a jovial mood, kept laughing and flirting, and then she slapped her bottom over and over.

With a wide-faced smile, she laughed as she yelled, "I need a man wit a *bik* hard *deck* to *fook* me in my arse."

There were admirers but no takers. She made her offer again, laughed at the cowards. Then she was upside down again, holding on to the bar in the ceiling, doing a Chinese split, spinning in circles. She was solid. Athletic. Blazing like an out-of-control forest fire.

She was too beautiful, too fit, and too much for the average man.

I searched for that girl from Ipanema. Needed to get the last of Arizona out of my heart. I needed to get Hawks out of my head too. And running into Angelina had thrown me off.

For two months I had given Angelina the BFE—boyfriend experience. I had grown up in brothels, had slept with whores before I was a teen, had learned twice as many ways to please a woman as I knew ways to kill. I had shown all of those ways to Angelina.

No. It was deeper than that. Regardless of the name I used, I had been her boyfriend. I had met her friends. I had met her family. She had invited me into her life and home.

Then funds had been transferred. There was another job. That night we had sex. The next morning, I went for a walk, and minutes later I was in the wind. Many days I wished I had stayed, but I knew the end would have been inevitable. I just didn't know when it would end.

That was the problem when people in my corrupt world dealt with squares.

I walked from room to room in Quatro por Quatro, more comfortable in a place like this than I ever would be in a church. The women knew I was different. Not desperate. Not afraid. I looked at them like I saw their humanity behind the makeup and heels. I saw daughters, young mothers, girls trying to survive. Paranoia made me check out the place. I needed to make sure I saw everyone except who was doing the up-and-down in the fifty small bedrooms. Was still tense. Medianoche wasn't in this brothel. The woman called Señorita Raven wouldn't be in this space. To me she had never been more than a blur. Shotgun had faced her. But if that wicked bitch was here, the way Shotgun described her damaged face, she'd stand out.

I opened and closed my hands. They shook, not with fear, but with worry.

I had a mother. I didn't like her because I didn't trust her. But that was irrelevant. Like her or not, trust her or not, she was the mother the universe assigned me. By nature, or nurture, this was where I was. And I had brothers. Robert and I had had different mothers and fathers, but he was just as much my brother as Steven. Steven was the name he used, but the name he'd had in London was Andrew-Sven. Steven and Robert both had lived in London's red-light district. They had lived on Berwick Street in brothels, in rooms barely big enough to turn around in. Steven and I had the same mother. Robert's mother had been killed because of me. That blood was on my hands. I owed that boy everything I could possibly give. We were a bunch of misfits and rascals. Steven had no idea who his father was. I understood how he felt. Robert had no idea who his father was either. He had connected to Shotgun more than he had to me. Shotgun could explain racism to Robert, what to expect, how to handle it, much better than I could. Shotgun had become my best friend. It was my first time having a best friend, and I saw how important it was to have someone to rely on.

That was why Robert and Steven needed each other.

I needed them too. They were all I had.

I'd find Catherine. I'd see my brothers again.

I told myself a bushel of lies, more than I had in a long, long time.

When I felt safe, I went back to the main area, moved to the spot where they had the stripper pole and the bar recessed in the low ceiling. I passed meek men and faced the dark-skinned girl with the body of all bodies and the Julia Roberts smile. I told the solid Amazon to come down from the stage. She wasn't average, and neither was I. I reached for her hand.

I said, "You're beautiful. I would think men would fight to have a second of your time."

"They prefer girls who look European. Or girls who look like they are from Spain."

"They're missing out. What's your name?"

"I'm black, and I like to be called Black. I am proud of my beauty and my color."

The magnificence she had to offer was billed at 150 reals; forty-six US dollars an hour.

She sat with me, chatted while we shared a drink. She smiled a lot, had a nice laugh.

She told me her real name was Rojane Carvalho, but she wanted to be called Black.

She told me that once she came in those doors, Black was her name.

She asked, "Where are you from?"

"The States."

"American?"

"As far as I know."

"You don't sound American."

"I've been around. Travel a lot. For work."

I warmed up to her, the best I could warm up to a woman in her profession. She warmed up to me the best she could with a man she'd never seen before. She touched my chin. Flirted. Made me smile. Put me at ease. I decided to patronize the goddess, take her up on her bodacious offer, and see what kind of fun we could have in a room upstairs. Then I would find a plastic bag to put over a man's head and watch him die.

Chapter 17

Murder by Contract

After Brazil, I was sent to Iceland.

I did what I was paid to do near Hallgrímskirkja Church. Then I geared up, put on warm clothing, rain gear, and hiking boots, and carried my lunch. I found Road 221 and parked my Jeep in the parking lot at Sólheimajökull Café. I was heading for the Sólheimajökull Glacier. I picked up ice gear and safety equipment, got ready to hike for the next four hours. This felt therapeutic. I moved by ice sculptures, water cauldrons, ridges, and deep crevasses. I was doing this to leave the world.

If I had known if Catherine and the boys were safe, I might've stayed on top of that glacial mountain and enjoyed the effects of global warming. Or just gone to Reykjavík, used my new name and bogus cards to rent an apartment. Her voice was inside my head, our last shared words.

She had snapped like she was Thelma once again. "What the hell have you done?"

"Did you know he wasn't dead?"

"Why would you find him?"

"Did you fuckin' know he was alive?"

One hand in a fist, the other with its trigger finger moving over and over, I nodded.

There had been anger. There was surprise, but not the kind that outweighed her rage. That wasn't the way a person would react when someone they loathed had been resurrected.

She knew. She had known all along.

For years I thought she had been running from me because of what she had done, but she had been running, hiding, from Midnight.

Now I had kicked the dirt off his grave and pulled him out of his coffin.

Other hikers were in the area, part of their own four-hour tour, all being led by Icelandic mountain guides. In the group were kids as young as ten. I didn't pull my nine millimeter from my back. I took out a satellite phone and dialed a number that was at least seven thousand miles away from where I stood. Konstantin answered on the first ring, then told me something that made my heart skip a beat.

He told me, "Scamz is dead."

"What happened?"

"The yacht he had, it exploded, went down like the *Titanic*, and it wasn't an accident. The only reason anyone knows is because a cruise ship off in the distance saw fireworks and called it in."

A chill ran through me and I said, "The Four Horsemen tracked him some way."

"After what I saw them do on the streets, that's where I'd put my bet."

"Scamz's body?"

"Fish food, like everyone else who was on board."

My breath fogged from my mouth. "Arizona and her sister, Sierra?"

"We left them with Scamz. Assume the worst."

I took a breath, shrugged off a useless emotion. "What's my next job?"

"You sure you're in shape to move on? I'm talking mind, not body."

"I'm sure. Tell me about the next job. Get me there."

"You need rest."

"Rest is for the dead."

He told me about the next contract. Everything was already in place. The job had been triple verified so I would know I wasn't being set up, being sent to where the Four Horsemen wanted me to facilitate an ambush.

Then I hung up, stood on the glacier, too stunned to see beauty.

This was too much. I needed to be a square, if only for a moment.

I needed to be back in the Cayman Islands with an attorney and an actress.

I needed to not be Gideon. But Jean-Claude had done as much emotional damage.

Guilt rose and I called Angelina, the Porteña I had met at the End of the World. When she answered, I hung up. I'd broken her heart. I'd seen that leftover pain bringing tears to her eyes.

I had nothing to offer a square but another helping of the same.

She'd only been married for two months.

My mind went back to the place I had tried to free it from in vain.

Scamz was dead. At the bottom of the sea.

And Arizona and her sister were probably consigned to the same sepulcher as well. Both were at Davy Jones's locker with the son of the man who had been their lover.

The son was Arizona's lover too, and he was probably her sister's bedroom bully as well.

The hunter was hunting. He was vicious. And he wasn't alone.

I took the nine millimeter from my back as I hiked down, not trusting anyone.

Exhausted, I left the land of the Vikings and disembarked in Athens, Greece. It was around twenty-seven degrees Celsius. That made it just a bit more than eighty-one Fahrenheit. The temperature was going up to thirty-three on the Celsius scale, so that meant it would be at least ninety-two degrees Fahrenheit.

For days I'd dressed in boots and trainers, so I changed it up. I put on a single-button gray suit, brown shoes, gray shirt, pink necktie, and frameless glasses and soon carried a briefcase that had been handed off to me after I cleared customs. I left the international airport looking like a respectable but overworked businessman.

The briefcase had good weight. Now I had weapons: two Glocks, blades, brass knuckles, and poison. After I visited a rapist who had been on the run from his victims in North America, I went to the safe house, a penthouse in Athens in Davaki Square in the Kallithea area. I rested a few hours. Then I went to France, where it was just as hot as it had been in Athens. Was there one hour before I mixed with sweaty and smelly migrants from Calais. I herded with men desperate to get into London, paid the price, and prepared to be smuggled into the Big Smoke, the place economists were now calling Reykjavík-on-Thames, in the back of an overpacked lorry.

While we were waiting for the lorry to show up, I stepped away and called Shotgun.

The man born with the name Alvin White said, "You still alive?"

"I'm aboveground. Still on the move. Not sure how far the bastards are behind me, but I know they're trailing me."

"If you can smell the dog doo-doo on their shoes, keep moving."

"I'd say they are running a day behind me. About to change that."

He said, "Heard about Scamz. Arizona and her sister. Was worried."

"I have to run in a minute or two. Anything urgent?"

"You shouldn't be traveling by yourself."

"I'm bad milk for everybody."

Shotgun paused again. "You talked to Hawks?"

"She can take care of herself. She's smarter than all of us combined."

Then his worry deepened as he asked, "No word from Catherine?"

I paused. "Let's hope for the best."

"I'm going to go by there again."

"That spot could be hot. Don't go by there. Let her make first contact."

"I know all the cars that 'pose to be in her cul-de-sac."

"This ain't like the trouble I had before. So stay out of that area."

"Okay. I understand."

"But everything is good with you?"

"Well, I been back in the gym, been training hard. Mixed martial arts and boxing. I'm working on getting stronger. I go out to Woodstock and shoot a nine millimeter and my shotgun. And I'm still working on my reading. Did the homework Catherine gave me to do. Got me a workbook and a CD at Barnes and Noble by Cumberland Mall. I ain't sleeping much, so I keep my mind busy studying. Doing pretty good. I bought a John Grisham book when I was at the airport."

"You're reading Grisham already?"

"Not yet. I bought *A Time to Kill*. Was going to buy the book *The Reader*, but my man Samuel Jackson was in the Grisham movie. My goal is to be able to read every word in that book in six months."

"You can do it."

"Then I'm going to buy *The Reader* and read that. I'm sticking with it. That movie made my wife cry. I'm going to do like the woman in that film and learn to read. Then my wife won't be the only one reading the bills when they come in the mailbox."

"Catherine will be proud. Whenever she comes out of hiding, she will be proud."

"No idea where she went?"

"By now she could be hiding in Switzerland, or in an igloo at the North Pole."

"When I see her again, I want to surprise her. She's really made a difference in my life. She taking the time and out of the goodness in her heart she was teaching me to read."

"Make sure you tell her that. She needs to know she's done something positive."

"So have you, Gideon."

I had turned a failed heavyweight boxer, an illiterate man who was driving a taxi for a living, into a man who would never see the pearly gates of heaven, but he saw me as a good thing. He had blood on his hands, but he had money in his pockets. He could feed his family.

I could have said a lot, but just replied, "Thanks, Alvin. I appreciate that."

"I ain't never had this much money at one time."

"Spend it bit by bit."

"Oh, I know. I finally got my wife under control. Last time she spent it all up real fast."

We laughed like brothers who didn't have a care in the world.

He said, "Never got to say it because we was kinda busy, but I had thought being down in Buenos Aires would be like being in the islands."

"Not even close."

"I thought black people were all down there."

"Used to be in the 1800s."

"What happened? Where they go?"

I told him that millions of African slaves had been imported to almost all of Latin America. From what I knew the Portuguese settlers intermarried with both the Indians and the African slaves.

He said, "Jungle fever been around a long time."

"I guess so."

We laughed a little.

He said, "That's messing me up. Being somewhere and ain't no black people. I was happy to get off that plane up here in the ATL."

"Used to be more than fifty African nations in that area."

"For real?"

"Augunga, Kisama, Maravi, Monyolo, Mina Nago, Sabalu."

"What happened?"

I told him that Africans had been enslaved and put on the front line, sent to fight somebody else's war. Most of them killed while the people who started the war sat back and waited for the outcome.

He said, "Making slaves fight was genocide for the Africans. I bet they tried to kill off my people to make their money. Had no idea."

"What the war didn't kill, some say yellow fever put in the ground."

"What, nobody was left?"

"They think that the surviving Africans got out of Argentina."

"Did they leave Argentina to go back to Africa?"

"They migrated across the river into Uruguay."

"I would've kept going until I got to Africa."

"They stopped in Brazil. Intermarried. Had babies."

"Well, that explains why Brazilian women are shaped like that."

We laughed.

Talking to a friend about the things he cared about calmed me.

A couple of sentences later I became serious, told him I would be in touch within the next forty-eight to seventy-two hours, but if he hadn't heard from me in ninety-six, to not come looking for me.

Eleven days had passed since escaping Uruguay.

Twelve since the battle that spread across Buenos Aires.

They'd found Scamz's yacht in less than two weeks.

I climbed on the truck and kept my eyes on the desperate strangers. Being still gave the exhaustion in my bones time to settle, and the way the truck rocked didn't help my case. I didn't want to, but thirty minutes into the trip I closed my eyes. Each eyelid weighed a ton. I hadn't planned on sleeping, just needed to stop blinking for a couple of minutes. Sleep captured me, and soon it dragged me into a nightmare. I was back in the *villas*, covered in sewage and mud, and Medianoche was in front of me. It was as it had been. He faced me holding two nine millimeters.

The dead bodies of all my friends surrounded me. Scamz. Arizona and her brother. Konstantin. Shotgun. Hawks. Sierra. The Bajan. I looked at their corpses, and when I raised my eyes to Medianoche, he was no longer alone. The Beast, Señorita Raven, and Rodriguez were at his side. I'd never seen the Beast, so his face wasn't clear, but I knew he looked as powerful as his name. Each Horseman carried two guns. They raised their guns and fired at the same time.

I jerked awake, panting, ready to kill. The immigrants in the truck moved away from me. Some laughed a nervous laugh. Some called me a madman. I downed a BC Powder, ignored them all, and made myself stay awake. I didn't want to see Horsemen, not even in my goddamn dreams.

Chapter 18

The Tattooed Woman

London was hotter than normal. The heat wave in the Great Wen was part of global warming. I was on Queen Street in the area for postal code EC4R, near the site of Saint Thomas the Apostle Church. A placard said the church had been destroyed in the Great Fire of 1666.

The safe house was on the top floor of the Marlin Apartments, over a Domino's Pizza. My window faced Cannon Street. Bicycles were down below. The section of Queen Street that ended at Cannon Street was blocked off to through traffic, only allowed pedestrians. I needed to know all of that in case I had to leave in a hurry, had to chase or was being pursued.

In the land of red phone booths, I stood at the window eating a mayonnaise-thick seafood sandwich from Sainsbury's, binoculars in my right hand, wearing dungarees and a plain white T-shirt. There was an iPad that picked up the feed from the CCTV cameras right outside the building. I used the binoculars to see what the cameras didn't show. CCTV cameras had blind spots. The television was on.

The screen showed me what was in the lobby of the building, let me see who entered, and showed me what was going on in the hallway outside of my door.

I took another bite of my seafood sandwich. Nasty, but not nasty enough to toss.

The Brits put mayo-fuckin'-naise on everything. Might even be in the water.

I watched the massive crowd trudge toward Saint Paul's Cathedral and in the opposite direction toward London Bridge. For the last hour there had been so many professionals walking in the heat I thought a white-collar protest was going on. Double-decker buses were packed to the windows. People looked miserable and murderous. Something bad had happened. But no one was running, no one was panicked, so they weren't reliving the terrorist bombing of 7/7.

At the appointed time, my contact appeared in London's financial center.

She came from the direction of the restaurant Thai Square. She had two backpacks. She carried a black one, but she wore a heavy Arsenal backpack that had a red teddy bear hanging from its strap. She came down one of the mews leading to the Mansion House tube. Konstantin had told me to expect a young Hindu woman sporting an aquamarine Mohawk. As she passed the row of bicycles, someone on the crowded mews bumped into her and she snapped, said something harsh, then brandished two middle fingers. She was in a fucked-up mood.

She took out her phone, punched in a number. I waited for my phone to buzz. Nothing. She was chatting with someone else as she looked around, frustrated. She wiped sweat from her neck with the edge of her T-shirt. A ginger who looked like Nicole Kidman paused next to her, smiled, said a few words; then the ginger walked away, left in a hurry.

The woman I was waiting on punched in another number.

My cellular rang. I answered, "Sam I am. Green eggs and ham."

She replied, "One-eyed, one-horned, flyin' purple people eater."

With the passwords done I said, "I want to do the transaction inside."

"May I ask why the change?"

"CCTVs are all over."

I wanted her inside in case she was followed by cameras. There were almost six million CCTV surveillance cameras in the UK, so the bobbies could sit in a cool room, eat fish and chips while they watched a screen and tracked your every move. As long as those moves were made on the street, they had you. Inside a building, they didn't have access to the cameras.

I said, "Come to the front entrance at 30 Queen Street."

I stared at the screen on the iPad. I spied on my contact. No one came over to her. That meant nothing. I checked the cameras on the television. A woman who could pass for Julia Roberts came into the frame. She wore a dark suit. She paused by my contact long enough to ask the time, then moved on. She moved on in a hurry. Every black suit reminded me of the Four Horsemen. It felt like I was looking out at a thousand Horsemen.

My clothing was plain, subdued. I dropped a Beretta in my brown leather messenger bag and headed downstairs, still watching my contact on the iPad. She was at the door, fanning herself, trying to stay in the shade. She was fit; I could see the definition in her arms, and her legs were toned. I was between the Mansion House and Bank tube stations, an area where many wore dark business attire as if they were headed to a rich man's funeral, and she wore military boots paired with tight jeans, and a cropped shirt with the brand FCUK across the front. She was five feet tall and a cross between the Joker's lover Harley Quinn and Lisbeth Salander, the Girl with the Dragon Tattoo.

I opened the glass door, let her and a blast of hot and humid air that was mixed with carbon monoxide come inside. Now all she carried was the heavy Arsenal backpack.

She said, "Hiya."

"What happened to the other backpack?"

"Handed it off to a customer who was supposed to meet me an hour ago at Embankment."

"The dirty-blonde in the business suit?"

"You saw?"

"Who was she and what was that about?"

"She is Swedish, new to London, and rents a flat down in Brighton. Russian Jewish neighborhood." She mimicked sniffing cocaine. "Sold her something for her and her friends' sinus problems."

Her hands were empty and the backpack was zipped shut. There was a bulge in her pocket. I told her to show me what she had. It was a wad of money and an Oyster card.

She followed me but paused on the second-floor landing when her phone rang. The moment she answered, she had an argument in French. Her French was good, and it was the French of the streets. She told whoever was on the other end she never wanted to see him again, and no matter how well a woman treated a man, she could ride his dick, swallow his come, be monogamous, and he would still fuck some slag from Ukraine.

In English she snapped, "Oh, I'm a cunt? Fucktard. Pube quilt. Go bother your latest atrocious sperm burper, *dickhead*. I bet she's a jizz jar. You're wanking every volde-moron between here and Vladivostok, and I'm the slag? Fuck you, you fecal muncher."

I leaned against the wall, hand in my bag, on my gun, finger on the trigger.

She yelled, "And Kanye West to you too, you clown dick ignoramusgigantotous."

She hung up on him, then readjusted the backpack.

Feeling the heat in the stairway, I asked, "You okay?"

Anger lit her face. "I'm fine. I just lost one hundred and sixty pounds of rubbish."

Her phone rang again and she answered, spoke in Russian, politely told whoever it was she was not available to talk business at the moment, would call soon, then ended the call.

She apologized. "Been pretty busy today. Errands are done. Should slow down now."

"We should be done in twenty minutes."

She turned her phone off and followed me.

Once we entered the flat, she put the heavy backpack on the sofa and, without asking permission, crossed the small white-walled room and took in my view, without looking at me.

She said, "This flat is great. Not a lot of bits 'n' bobs, but you have air-conditioning."

"What's going on out there?"

"Very nice chessboard on the table. That's from the House of Staunton."

"Why are all the businesspeople walking by like it's a parade?"

"Someone committed suicide. Jumped in front of a train, so a tube is closed. Traffic is tailing back no matter which direction you are going. So much for going to Seven Sisters."

"What's at Seven Sisters?"

"I get my hair done down there. The Jamaicans are the best stylists."

I took a breath. "Want a bottle of water? A cuppa? I can put a pot on."

She motioned toward the Arsenal backpack. "Please look over the order."

"You took the tube with this care package?"

"I don't drive into Central London during the day. Congestion charge."

She remained fascinated by the chessboard. Went over. Touched the wooden pawns. She had a kidlike smile as she appreciated the details of the pieces. She wasn't angry anymore.

I asked, "You play?"

"Couple times a week at Waterstones bookshop."

I unzipped the Arsenal bag. I took out an Oyster card and a small box of Saran Cling Plus Plastic Wrap. I dropped the Oyster in my pocket and put the Saran Wrap on the kitchen table.

I took out the hardware, went over the gun and ammo. Looked at the blades.

She started popping her lips over and over as she looked at her phone.

I thought she was about to turn it back on. Could tell she wanted to. She didn't.

I took out the rest of what she had brought, powered up the new MacBook Pro. Did the same for the new sat phone. The most important thing was a pen drive with information, and hard copies of what I needed. I went to the wall in the kitchen, picked up a roll of Scotch tape. Soon that section of the apartment looked like it was a war room. Security cameras in various parts of Buenos Aires had taken all of the shots; most were stills made from video. Images of car chases in the rain, everything too blurry, impossible to make out the details of any one face.

I asked, "This is the building the Horsemen are housed in?"

She stopped popping her lips. "They have the seventeenth floor. Private elevators."

"Images from their floor? What's the layout?"

"No cameras are up there, at least none that are part of the system to the rest of the building. I would assume they have security as good as Parliament up there."

I went back to the images, flipping slowly, studying, heart still beating strong.

"Can you hack into their system?"

"My hacker mate has been beavering away at that for hours. She's a bit of a chancer. More than I am. Makes me nervous doing this for your handler, but I need the money."

"You're being rewarded handsomely for your efforts."

"Hopefully you're happy with this bit. The money won't come unless you approve. But still, I don't want to use the money to buy my own coffin. They don't take too nicely to being hacked."

"What do you have on their leader, the one they called the Beast?"

"Will try and get his military records. My hacker will have to break into the USA's military system, but she'll bounce the signal, make it look like Putin is fucking with them again."

The Four Horsemen's building was near where we had fought. I asked, "Any other properties around the globe? Or are they only set up there, in Buenos Aires? Any bases anywhere else? Like here in London?"

"Wasn't asked to check." She nodded. "Will text my hacker, so give me a day."

"I don't plan on being here more than a few hours, so sooner would be better."

There were images from the aftermath of a battle they had had near EZE International Airport down there. Looked like a war zone. Vans on fire. Dead bodies on the asphalt. A mercenary group called the Seven Jamaicans had challenged the Horsemen, and those skilled Yardies didn't last two minutes. The Horsemen had attacked them hard and fast.

I asked, "You okay?"

"Stressed. A bit off. I just found out the sky's not blue."

"Sure you don't want a drink?"

"I shouldn't. But I think I will. Yeah, I will have something to correct the course of my mood. I don't want to get sloshed, even if I do feel like going all out and getting lashed."

She went to the kitchen, grabbed a lager, opened it, went back to her cool spot.

I paused, thought about the girl I had met at the End of the World. I thought about Angelina. I was sure she had felt the same way when I vanished as I did when I left, that the sky in her world wasn't blue.

I cleared my mind, returned to the task at hand.

The images were taken before we had gone there and battled.

In the photos, the Four Horsemen moved across the cobblestone walkway of tourist-crowded La Boca. It was daytime. Colorful buildings were in the background. Cafés. Restaurants. Looked like a tourist trap. They were in regular clothing. Medianoche walked like he was second-in-command, his position slightly behind the other mercenary. Several feet behind them were two more soldiers, a man in his twenties and a woman of about the same age. Both wore jeans and military-style boots. The lackeys carried backpacks and motorcycle helmets. Both wore riding gear. The dark-haired woman could've been any one of a dozen nationalities, but the muscular man at her side was definitely La-tino. I'd seen him up close right before I put a blade in his chest.

I turned to the next set of photos, which showed Medianoche and Señorita Raven with a group of people I'd never seen before. They had been taken the day after the battle.

I raised a photo and asked, "Who are these people?"

"No idea. They showed up within hours of each other, but not together."

"My handler was sent the same package?"

"The images, yes. About ten minutes before I arrived here. Did it in transit."

There was a shot of all of them leaving together. Suited up. Medianoche was in front. Señorita Raven at his side. The rest followed. I counted at least a dozen people. I didn't see the one they called the Beast. That was two days before Scamz's yacht was attacked at sea.

Maybe Shotgun was right. We should all be in one place.

The local arms dealer stayed in the window. Her back was to me. Modest hips. Toned. I watched her for a moment, my bag at my side, my gun a quick movement away, already loaded, bullet ready to fly. Wondered if she was signaling someone. She didn't have any weapons. No bracelet that could be equipped with piano wire sharp enough to cut a throat. No chopsticks in her hair. Colorful fingernails, each a different hue, but they were short and dull. She put her hands to her mouth a few times, so that told me the tips of her nails weren't poison. Sized her up again. I could hit her once and she would die twice. She rubbed the back of her neck, then smoothed her hands over the curve of her ass.

I asked, "Everything okay?"

She pointed up, indicated she was standing underneath a vent. "Enjoying the breeze. Feels so good it took my mind off wanting to play *Candy Crush* or *Words with Friends*, at least for the moment."

I picked up my phone, sent a message to Konstantin. Told him the package was good. The small-time arms dealer turned her phone back on. A moment later she received a message.

She said, "Funds transferred. About time something good happened today."

I nodded, watched her struggle to squeeze her phone back into her back pocket.

She finished her lager, put the bottle on the counter. "Terrorist by trade?"

In Russian I answered her question regarding my vocation, said, "*Mokroye delo.*"

In Russian she responded, "I've met people in your line of work. Most don't live long."

"I've met a few in yours. And neither do they."

She nodded and returned to speaking in English, lips pursed, her anger not hidden. "So every day, people like us must seize the day because YOLO and it can end abruptly."

She raised her T-shirt to wipe her chin. When she raised her T-shirt, it exposed more of her colorful tattooed skin. She caught me looking at her body when she turned around. I didn't move my eyes from what had unexpectedly fascinated me.

She went back to the window, found her spot under the vent, closed her eyes.

She said, "I don't have air-conditioning in my flat. Tubes are down and I'm stranded."

"Feels like it's at least one hundred degrees."

"Impossible. That would boil water."

"Was talking Fahrenheit."

"No one uses that system but the USA. What they have against metric?"

"No idea. The Bahamas, Belize, the Cayman Islands, Palau, and the United States are behind the curve on that one. But that would be more than thirty-seven degrees Celsius."

"We use the pound for our currency. And across the pond they use *pounds* for weight, not stones. How many pounds equal eight stone?"

"About one hundred twelve."

"I would weigh about one hundred and twelve *pounds* in America."

"More or less."

"Bloody hot out."

"Yeah. Bloody hot."

"Mind if I stay a couple of hours? Until sundown. I promise to not be much of a bother. We can get a pizza from Domino's and kick it like we're old chums, play chess, if you like."

"We can get a pizza. Haven't played chess in a while."

"I can break for my elevenses. Usually I have tea or coffee, but I'm in a rather foul mood and need something stronger. You have alcohol. I'll buy the pizza. How's that sound?"

I nodded, then asked, "Do you know how to remove stitches?"

"You have scissors and tweezers?"

"Yeah. Right over there on the table with a bottle of alcohol. Was going to do it myself in a little bit, but it's always better to have someone else pull them out, especially in the back."

She nodded, then went to the sink and washed her hands. She used the alcohol to sterilize the scissors and tweezers, then washed her hands again, brought everything to me.

I removed my baseball cap and sunglasses, then pulled off my T-shirt.

She said, "Nice arms. Bet you do two hundred push-ups before breakfast."

"Thanks. And I do three hundred."

"How much can you lift?"

"I can bench four hundred. That's about twenty-nine stone."

"MMA fighter?"

"When I need to be."

"Never use a knuckle when a bullet will suffice."

"I'll remember that next time I'm in a fight."

I straddled a chair. I had three sets of stitches on my back and two on my stomach. She used the alcohol to clean the wounds before she started. She had done this many times before.

She said, "I'll pull the thread slowly. If the skin bleeds, I'll stop. And I'll mind the knot."

She pulled her chair up close to me, then ran her hand across my back, did that over and over. She took a deep breath, focused, then snipped and tugged the stiches out one by one.

She said, "Turn around, if you don't mind."

I did, and we faced each other, inches apart. She looked in my eyes for a moment. I returned the favor. She ran her hand over my abs, shivered, licked her lips, then smiled a little.

She got on her knees in front of me, worked on a stitch.

I asked, "How old are you?"

"Older than most of my friends have lived to see, but not close to being a pensioner."

"You're a cheeky one."

"I'm beyond the age of consent for penetrative sex, oral sex, and mutual masturbation."

"How long you been in this business?"

"Since before I had penetrative sex, oral sex, or engaged in mutual masturbation."

Then she was done. We faced each other for a moment. Again, she licked her lips.

She said, "I'll call down and order the pizza. I'll pick it up too."

"Let them deliver. Get it at the door. Pay cash."

"I don't have cash."

"Then I'll pay. You can pay them at the door. Avoid the CCTVs."

She patted me on my legs, looked me in the eyes as she eased away from me. She broke the stare, went back to the sink, washed her hands over and over again.

I went back to the wall, evaluated the Four Horsemen.

An hour later we were eating a medium pizza. We had ordered a large, but they came to the door with a medium. Most of the order was fucked-up, but we ate what they brought. We finished our third game of chess around the same time. She'd won two out of three.

The arms dealer finished her second London Porter, then said, "Love your voice. Such a man's voice. I bet you bleed testosterone. Your accent is very soothing and attractive."

I finished my Sprite. "I thought you were the one with the accent."

She laughed. "Yankee, you're the one with the accent, not me. I sound normal here."

"I stand corrected."

"Like music?"

"Yeah. Of course."

She motioned at her phone. "Mind if I put on some of my jams? I love Fela, Bob Marley, King Sunny Ade, and Ebenezer Obey, but this Nigerian singer named Asa is so amazing. Can't get her lovely songs out of my head. Extremely talented, but I think she is very underrated."

"Never heard of her."

"She's a bit more serious and classy and doesn't perform half-naked."

"That'll do it. Performing fully dressed is so old-school."

"Asa sings the beauty of Africa. Beautiful voice. Reminds me of Adele."

The music started. The arms dealer sang along, a song about a prisoner and the prison guard both being in uniforms, not that different, a powerful song. She fell into the social commentary.

I asked her, "Want another lager?"

"I'll never say no to that, not on a day when I found out the sky's not blue."

I opened another. She drank her brew warm. Asa sang about a fire on a mountain. The arms dealer swayed and rolled her hips. Inside every woman lived a bit of Beyoncé.

She asked, "Expecting company?"

"Why?"

"Really am enjoying your companionship."

She finished her lager, then went to the kitchen and helped herself to another, then went back to her spot, back to dancing slowly. "Might be our only chance to get to know each other."

"No, I'm not expecting company. Anyone who shows up at that door is bad news."

"That sounds scary."

"Will be for me, then scarier for whoever is on the other side of that door."

"Well, I still feel a bit yucky from being on the tube with all the nasty people."

"Go take a cool shower. There is soap and a few towels. Deodorant. Lotion."

"Don't tempt me. With the food and lager, I'll end up clean and might have a kip."

"No one is coming by. Take your time. Shower. Take a nap."

"Shower and a comfy bed? If that's the case, then do me a favor."

"What's that?"

She grinned as she pulled at her hair with both hands. "Having kittens. Can feel my heart hammering in my chest."

"No need to be nervous. Just say what you need."

"And since I am the chess champion, the grandmaster of the flat, you should comply."

"Depends."

She said, "There is a spot on my back I can't quite reach when I bathe alone."

"Where is that spot?"

"It would be up to you to find that spot."

"You've had one lager too many."

She pulled her top off. Took off her boots. Wiggled out of her jeans.

I went to her and put my hand on her stomach. Battle scars and tattoos. Tattoos were being used to cover up a few marks. I traced two six-inch scars where she had been knifed.

"Got into a little row in South London near Elephant and Castle. Dangerous there. Edgy, has a lot of state housing blocks and high crime rate. Horrible mall. Ugly during the day and after nightfall it turns into something out of a Stephen King novel. Not a place for a female to walk round there late at night. But I did. Got attacked. Not long after 7/7 over here. Some crazy man came up to me and started screaming at me about how he hated Allah, and before I could tell him that my family was part of the Catholic Church in India, he knifed me. Left me to die."

"This scar?"

"Ten or fifteen of us got into a street fight at Elephant and Castle."

"You really need to keep away from that area."

"I know. I was almost run down on Elephant Road. One of the guys in the fight got his car and tried to run everyone over."

"Recently?"

"Nah. I was a teen."

Then I traced more of her flesh, down to her thong. Her stomach had a love affair with sit-ups and crunches, while her backside was enamored of doing squats. She was solid.

She closed her eyes. "You have strong hands. I like that."

I touched the edges of her breasts. She shivered.

I pulled her to me and I kissed her scars. Kissed them because I knew what that near-death moment was like. She opened her eyes, her expression much softer than it had been since she arrived, very vulnerable. Women looked vulnerable when aroused. That was why hard women didn't like men to see them that way. She ran her hands over my scars, where bullets had broken my skin, over my chest, then again over my abs. She stayed on my abs the longest.

She stood on tiptoe and we kissed. I picked her up and she put her legs around my waist while we let our tongues get acquainted. It was soft, slow, went on for a moment; then she put her feet on the floor, eased away, took my hand, and I followed her tattooed body toward the bathroom.

She turned the shower on while I undressed. I put the gun and iPad on the counter. On that same iPad, YouTube played, gave us Wilson Pickett's greatest hits on low.

Then I went back to the arms dealer, picked up where we left off.

She kissed me again. "You have a bulletproof vest?"

"As in Kevlar?"

"As in euphemism for condom."

"In the bedroom. They came with the place."

"In that case you can come with me."

Her cellular rang. She answered and talked to another customer.

She said, "Six Glocks. Two days. Can't get ten. Six. Embankment. Car park. Same fee. No, I can't go any lower. See you then."

She put her phone on the back of the toilet, eased into the shower. While we were under the cool water soaping each other's bodies, kissing and touching, the images I had seen stayed in my mind. There were a dozen Horsemen. They could be a dozen places at once. After the arms dealer and I had kissed and showered, we went to the bed, making out. The arms dealer took me in her hand, stroked me while we kissed, but it didn't rise. She went to her knees and took me in her mouth, was as wicked as she was thorough, and it didn't rise.

The arms dealer asked, "It does work, right?"

"Just give me a moment. This doesn't usually happen."

"Is your todger rejecting me?"

"My trouser snake is not rejecting you."

"The stress?"

"Yeah. The stress."

"Want to talk about it?"

"Just kiss me again."

"Up there or down here?"

"You can choose."

"I'm already comfortable where I am."

I focused on her, and in a matter of moments, things were working the way they should. She eased away and I put on a bulletproof vest, then eased between her thighs. She worked to get me inside. She was tipsy and aroused, full of desire for sex, and she wanted that sex to be with me, but I had a hard time getting her to open up. I pushed the tip inside and she cringed. She made sounds like she was in pain.

I said, "I think your vagina is rejecting me."

"Sometimes penetration hurts."

"Want me to stop?"

"Just give me a moment."

"Want to talk about it?"

She laughed, then eased me in bit by bit. Panted, tensed until I was most of the way in. I pushed and she moaned like fire, hooked her feet around my ankles, put her hands on my ass. When I went too deep she jerked, made a sound of pain dancing with pleasure, and pushed me away.

Lots of kissing, our groove slow. She brought her right leg around, turned over, and we did it with her being on her side, my strokes long and intense, like I was swimming inside of her. She turned more and was on her stomach. Soon we transitioned to doggie without disconnecting.

She craned her neck to see me, mouth opened as she panted. I got up on my haunches, held her waist, pulled her into me, and she was astonished. She weighed nothing in my hands. I pushed her forward, made her get off her knees, put her flat on the bed. She was on her belly and I straddled her, pressed down on her waist, rode her strong and hard. She was a loud one, no words, just erotic sounds. It sounded like she was being tortured, like she was dying, and all she could tell me was to give it to her harder. The iPad beeped and I stopped mid-stroke, moved away from her and monitored the screen as I reached for the gun. It was the Ethiopian couple who lived two units down. Happily married. A kid on the way. I knew everyone who should be in the building, especially on this floor. The information was here at the safe house before I arrived.

I put the gun back down, then told the arms dealer, "Sorry about that."

Her eyes were closed, and she took curt breaths, rolled over, rocked from side to side.

"You okay?"

"You going in and out to the bellend is maddening."

Her phone rang. She growled at the ringtone, then grabbed it and answered with a whip.

"What now? Bugger off and stop ringing my bloody phone. What am I doing? You left me gutted and have the nerve to ask me what I'm doing? You know what? I'm going to tell you *exactly* what I am doing. I had some top-notch lager, was getting the last of you out of my system, and now I'm chock-full of penis. I'm not taking a piss. That's right, ya blagger. I'm wanking with an American whose pork sword is larger than yours, you bloody cunt fucker. An American with a stonking wanker. Barely gets in. Put tears in my eyes. Had to be a big girl and take it all at once like medicine. And it's hard, not half-hard like you. No blue pill needed. Oh, I'm not joking. Yeah, American. You expected me to sit around like I was a Billy no-mates crying? I'm no munter, so you think I have a problem meeting handsome men? *Arsehole, this is not cheating.* What a nutter. *We broke up two hours ago.* Wankstain, at least I waited until *after* we were done with that farce of a relationship to wank someone. I met him today. Yes, a stranger. Yes, an American. You think I'm joking? Oh really? You think I'm having a piss?"

I sat on the bed, and she came to me, mounted me, put me inside her, and began getting her freak on. She was smooth, she was ready, and I heard her wetness. Revenge aroused her. She became intense, made erotic sounds, surrendered to what she felt, to what my being inside of her made her feel. Maybe being inside her was more therapeutic than amorous, maybe riding me, maybe this new pain she felt, made her stop feeling something she didn't want to feel right now. She moved up and down like she was long-stroking me, moving up until I was almost out of her, then gliding back down until flesh kissed. My toes wanted to curl. Her butt slapped my skin each time she came down, and each time she surrendered a soft and low moan. The sex wasn't polite. It was rude. Again I was sleeping with a stranger, chancing waking with an enemy, and it felt wonderful.

I moaned with her, moaned away the angst in my troubled soul.

She told him, "Thanks for cheating on me. I mean that. Goodbye . . . and good riddance."

The arms dealer dropped the phone and lost her religion. She bit my lips, sucked my lips. She was a bucker, a kisser, a scratcher, and it felt like she was a woman who could have a powerful orgasm.

I asked, "You like this?"

"Fuck yeah."

She leaned forward and put her hands back on my chest for balance. With my hands on her waist, she continued her rise and fall, and when her leg started to shake, she put her mouth on my neck, bit me to muffle her sounds. Her teeth clung to my skin; then she sucked hard. Her moans were erotic, like a flutist playing jazz, and then the purrs of a randy cat.

She asked, "What's your name? Is it okay to ask that? You don't have to say. Just give me a name to moan. Tell me you're Doctor Who and I'll moan for the Doctor. Tell me you're Freema Agyeman and I'll definitely moan for her. I was coming and didn't have a name to call, and that was odd. Made you feel a bit abstract when what you were giving me was so concrete."

She moved her butt well, had the rhythm of hip-hop and the sensuality of Hindu, went from being passive to aggressive, and made me want to come, but I maintained control.

She grinned. "I can feel your donkey dick all the way up to my bloody rib cage."

Someone barked her name, then cursed her name. I stopped, became alert, ready to rumble. She had jumped alert too. Her ex was still on the phone, shouting like a maniac.

She shouted down toward the phone, "The perv is listening and wanking off."

I picked up her phone and ended the call. Her problems were her problems.

With contempt in her voice she said, "I think the unfaithful bloke is a bit jealous that you're with me getting your end away. And hopefully you'll get your end away a second time."

Her phone rang again. She laughed a tipsy laugh but turned serious when she took the business call. I sat on the bed, kissed the tattoos on her body, went down on her.

"Yes . . . I can get you what you need. Two days. Cheers."

She finished her call, dropped her phone again, held my head, guided my tongue. When I stood up, she pulled me to her and put my cock between her breasts, gave me eye contact, bit the corner of her lip.

I said, "Gideon. My name is Gideon."

She panted, then paused. "Gideon?"

"You okay?"

"My name is Zankhana."

"Nice to meet you, Zankhana."

"Some call me Zed. Few knob heads call me Bolshie."

"If they call you Bolshie, has to be because of your rebellious attitude."

"It is."

"I'll call you Zankhana."

She smiled. "Okay, Gideon."

I took the arms dealer's hand, pulled her to me, felt her skin on my skin as I grabbed her waist, lifted her like she weighed as much as a slip of paper, and gradually turned her body until she was upside down.

I positioned her thighs on either side of my head, and she panicked, squeezed her thighs tight, had no idea what I was doing until I pulled her throbbing sex to my anxious tongue. I held her tight ass and tongue fucked her as blood rushed to her head.

"Bloody hell bloody hell bloody hell *ooooooo* bloody hell."

At first she put her hands on my belly, then held my thighs. She realized I had her, that she wasn't going to fall, and she trusted me, relaxed into what I was doing.

"Bloody hell ooooooo bloody hell ooooooo bloody hell ooooooo."

She was a honey-sweet-sticky-mildly-salty bonbon, better than a nutritious confection. Soon she was comfortable upside down, and she took me in her mouth, sucked me like a sweet lolly. Even upside down her blow job was noisy, wet, sexy, intense, and uninhibited. Soon I took her to the mattress, and we danced all over the bed, in a dozen positions.

I remembered when Arizona had told me that I didn't know how to make love. She said I knew how to fuck, and the better a man fucked a woman, the more she was convinced she was making love. I fucked one woman and thought about another, about how she had made me feel so good that I had been convinced she had fallen in love with me.

I'd loved her the only way I knew how.

She had fucked me in more ways than one.

A half hour later, while the arms dealer slept under cool air, I went back to the war room. Gun at my side, I ate a slice of cold pizza, sipped soda, and reviewed the Horsemen while I kept the iPad on my lap. I left it on the house in Powder Springs. The cameras for this building were back on the flat-screen television in the small living area. The flat was UK-size, small. I could walk from end to end in twenty steps. I monitored the front of the building, the rear, and the hallway. It beeped as people left the floor too. All was quiet. Quiet left me unnerved.

I watched Powder Springs to see if Catherine had left a clue in the home.

The FedEx truck was leaving the neighborhood.

I was going to call Shotgun, but I told myself I was being paranoid. I was distracted when my phone buzzed. FUNDS TRANSFERRED. The London job was a go. I opened a file, went over the details. Saw which entrance and exit had been set up for me to get in and out without a problem. Then I read about the target. A white male, city worker who rose up the ranks. Middle-aged. On his second marriage. Two kids. I read why someone wanted him put six feet under.

She whispered, "Hey."

I looked up. The arms dealer was standing in the doorway.

I closed what I was reading and said, "Hey."

"That was something else. Being eaten out while upside down was quite a dizzying experience. Makes me wonder what other sexual positions you are capable of doing."

"That position was a tamer one of the lot."

"Wish I had walked with my motorcycle helmet and kneepads."

She came over to the sofa and straddled me again. Right away she kissed me, sucked my neck, masturbated me. She took me in her mouth, made my eyes water, and weakened my knees, made me moan the way I had made her moan. She used hands and mouth, kneaded me, set my nerves on fire, and I thought she was going to suck a two-pound orgasm out of my body. I was hard enough to slide inside her. She showed me she had a bulletproof vest. She dressed me, then trembled and moaned while she worked me back inside her body. I put her on her knees, and with one foot on the floor, I took her from behind. I fucked her the way I had fucked Arizona at the Parker Meridien. I fucked her the way I had fucked Hawks in Puerto Rico. I fucked her the way I had fucked Lola Mack and Mrs. Jones at My-Hotel in Bloomsbury. I fucked her the way I had fucked the Jewell of the South. I fucked her the way I had fucked Miki in Miami and fucked Angelina for two months. I fucked as if I might never get a chance to fuck again. When I came, she told me to pull out, and she took the bulletproof vest away, then took me down her throat, made me climb the walls. I howled when I came. My toes curled. Lights flashed behind my eyes. She made me witness something better than the aurora borealis. I had to close my eyes until I was back to normal. She eased up from the sofa, wiped the corners of her lips, and walked away.

She looked back and said, "You make me feel like being disgusting. I've had lager and become aroused by a handsome chap like you, and now you make me want to be disgusting."

"I'm not complaining."

"It's cooler now. I promise I will leave soon. Before the last train."

"No rush."

"I'll kip a bit longer and try not to bother you again. Can't promise I won't."

"No bother if you do."

"The disgusting bit I just did. Wanted to pay you back for the wicked upside-down thing. I'm a bit competitive. Hope that doesn't bother you."

"Touché. And well done."

She went toward the bed.

I headed back to the wall, resumed studying the Horsemen.

Chapter 19

The Woman in the Window

It was ninety-five degrees in the shade, but with the humidity it felt like it was 102.

Shotgun was down in Atlanta's Old Fourth Ward on Decatur Street Southeast, sipping green tea at Marlee's Coffee Tea and Tapas. The café was named after the owner's granddaughter. Shotgun always stopped in and grabbed a cup after he got his hair cut at Master Groom Barber Salon. Every once in a while, if he had the money to spare, he would eat at Bento Hut. That was the first thing he had done after Gideon had paid him for watching over Catherine a while ago, long before Argentina, when some other folks were trying to get to Gideon and put him in the ground. Alvin White had been paid to look out for trouble, had outsmarted that trouble, had made some money, some real money, then brought the wife and children to Bento Hut. Alvin had loved the sushi. His wife and children had looked at the sushi and turned their noses up like he was trying to get them to eat raw monkey brains. His family wanted to go eat at the Chick-fil-A on Cobb Parkway, then catch a movie at the AMC and go bowling. He did what they wanted.

Making money made him feel like a man. A man who had value in the world.

That first job, Gideon had given him sixty thousand dollars. When Alvin had come home with that much money, his wife's eyes got as big as saucers. He told her they couldn't put it in the bank, and if they did they couldn't put in more than nine thousand at a time, because the IRS would ask questions at the ten-thousand-dollar mark. But if a man who hadn't ever made thirty grand a year suddenly had nine thousand in the bank, red flags would fly. So they paid cash for everything. And that much cash had set his wife's pockets on fire. Had heated up his pockets too. Sixty thousand dollars. Bills were paid. He had been driving an old car for the last decade. That car had doubled as his illegal taxi. He could stop being a taxi driver now. He spent three thousand on an old truck he saw on Roswell Road, then bought a better lawnmower and some gardening tools so he could get back into landscaping. He bought his family some health insurance, paid that up for the year. Now they didn't have to go to "Shady" Grady Memorial Hospital and stand in line behind gunshot victims and people who were half-crazy just to get seen when they came down with the flu. Everybody got a trip to the Great Expressions Dental Center on Cascade Road. Before they didn't go to the dentist unless they had to get a tooth pulled. They got their teeth cleaned and cavities filled. He let his wife get her teeth whitened. They came out real pretty. His wife cried. That night was like being on their honeymoon all over again. Actually it had been better. In that new lingerie, that night his wife had put on high heels and done some things he could only see watching porn. He chuckled, smiled thinking about that.

Then the smile went away. Things weren't safe now. He knew that. That was why his family was hiding out in Odenville, Alabama. He should have been over there too. Maybe they should move there. But he needed to make sure Catherine and those boys were safe.

He sipped green tea loaded with honey. A lot of GRITS were out today. Girls raised in the South. He hadn't seen that many GRITS in a long time. Definitely didn't see nothing that looked like GRITS in Buenos Aires or Uruguay. They probably called the girls in South America *empanadas*. They were nice, good-looking, but too skinny, couldn't touch the sisters in ATL. A lot of the girls grinned at him, gave him a little flirt. His body was sculpted, lean, with hard muscles. He'd been working out hard and eating right. Had started training with MMA boys in Buckhead and was studying Krav Maga too. Just in case he had to fight like Gideon and Hawks.

Marlee's was one block from the King Memorial MARTA station, not far from Ebenezer Baptist Church and Auburn Avenue, where Martin Luther King Jr. had lived as a child.

Here he wasn't Shotgun. He was just plain old Alvin White. He wasn't even the former boxer. He was just a blue-collar man who picked up work wherever he could find it.

Alvin White had on Levi's, a worn Atlanta Hawks T-shirt, and work boots that had seen better days. He could sit in the window and watch the GRITS all day. Alvin White liked them thick, heavy on the bottom, with breasts real soft like a pillow. That was what his wife looked like. First time he saw that Coke-bottle-shaped 'Bama girl in the Atlanta Underground, she sashayed by in jeans and a Prince T-shirt. He was with his brothers. They had dared him to holler at that bad mamma jamma. He left them, ran over to her, told her he hoped she wasn't married because he was looking for a wife that looked just like her. That made the 'Bama girl laugh. She had a body like one of those girls who worked at Magic City. He drove over to Odenville and met her crazy family the next weekend. A month later they were shacking up. Six months later that small-town 'Bama girl was his wife. A year after that they had their first child.

He had done good boxing for a while, never was rich, but had enough money for a man to take care of food, clothing, shelter, and have a little fun. Then all the money was gone.

Was harder being broke when a man had a wife. Then had a kid. Then another kid. His wife had worked hard and no matter how hard

Alvin was on himself, no matter how many times he told her she would do better with another man, she told him to hush and she kept the family together. So no matter how much money he brought home, she had the right to spend it all.

He looked at his wedding ring. It was a cheap piece of metal, but it was his; his wife had given it to him, and that ring meant more to him than two diamonds the size of his fist.

A white woman wearing a preacher's collar came in from Decatur Street. The café was crowded. A large group of folks were practicing speaking in Spanish. Some sort of a weekly Meetup group. The room could hold fifty people, and about that many were there.

Lots of rumbles, lots of laughter, as they ate and drank.

All the brothers stopped speaking in Spanish when the white woman came in. She was a curvy blond woman. Had a body like Ice T's wife. Women like that could confuse a lot of black men, make them forget where they came from, make them forget about the struggle.

Alvin White heard her order a cup of tea; then she stood by him, eyes out the window. She was close enough to Alvin White for him to smell her perfume. It smelled expensive.

Alvin smiled at the member of the clergy. "Good afternoon, Reverend."

The woman with pale powder-blue eyes responded, "Good afternoon."

He was going to ask her about the perfume, was going to buy it for his wife. But his wife had a lot of perfume. He turned, went back to the news. A report on the war that never should have been started. People who had supported the war at first were jumping ship left and right.

He pondered, "Wonder how long this here new war gonna go on."

Without looking, the minister said, "War never ends. 'The Lord is a man of war.'"

"America sho' likes tearing up other folks' countries. They was doing that long before 9/11. At least the way I see it. That's why this terrorism thang just gonna get worse. America is over there messing with them folks and them folks are tired of it, so now they are over here."

He had almost told her what they had said at the barbershop, that the terrorists were going after the white folks. Black people had been terrorized since they came to know white people. Black people were enslaved and kidnapped, and no one was ever charged for the crime. And soon the safest place in America was gonna be a black area.

But he kept the barbershop talk to himself, would save it for other black folk.

The minister asked, "You're military?"

"No, ma'am. But I lost two uncles in Vietnam."

"You never served."

"No, ma'am. Never signed up. My daddy had the same philosophy as Muhammad Ali."

"You're Christian?"

"Yes, ma'am. Baptist."

Dark clouds in the distance rolled in their direction, devouring sunlight.

The minister asked, "How long before you think the storm gets here?"

Alvin White turned to the minister. "Well, ma'am, it gonna hit soon. News said this one was gonna be here two hours ago. Gonna be thunder and lightning and might be some flooding."

"What kind of work you do?"

"Landscaping. I drove a taxi for a few years, but now I'm changing over to landscaping. Gonna try that awhile. Was supposed to go to these people's house in the Cascades and work, but the weather looking bad. They want some color added, so I was going to put down some marigold, add some vinca, a little begonia, coleus, zinnia, impatiens, and maybe some pentas."

He had a hard time pronouncing half those flowers, but he knew what they were. When a man couldn't read, he had to memorize everything. He depended on his memory to survive. Even as a taxi driver, he had made it work. He knew almost every street in ATL, all the Peachtrees. There were more than seventy streets in Atlanta that had *Peachtree* in their names. He had made it to every destination by landmark. He'd gotten lost only a few times, but those times he gave the passenger the ride for free. That was how he had met Gideon. He'd needed a taxi.

Behind them chairs screeched against tiled floors when people started to stand. The Spanish Meetup group was done. Members were shaking hands, joking, giving hugs, cleaning their tables, preparing to leave.

The minister stood in silence, the people behind her laughing and talking, now mostly in English. Alvin White felt like the minister was admiring more women than he had. ATL was like that. People had moved out from LA and down from New York and brought their parades.

Alvin White asked the minister, "You from N'awlins, Reverend?"

"What's it to you?"

"You sound creole."

"Bourbon Street and Bourbon are in my blood."

The minister took out a slip of paper and put it in front of Alvin White.

He asked, "What's this, ma'am?"

She said, "Read the note."

That made him nervous. Even when he took his reading and writing lessons from Catherine he was nervous. It was easier for him to get in the ring and fight fifteen rounds than read for fifteen minutes. He looked at the note, pretended to read, tried to see how he was going to get out of this moment without confessing his ignorance, then said, "It's a Bible scripture. I think."

She shook her head. "No, it's not a Bible scripture. You can't understand the message?"

"My eyes are real bad and I don't have my reading glasses."

"Reading glasses?"

"Oh, you're from the church. I don't have any money to buy anything or give a donation, not right now."

"This note is not asking for a donation."

Alvin rubbed his big paws together and whispered, "Read it to me, if you don't mind."

The minister looked perplexed. Didn't get the reaction she had anticipated.

She whispered, "Jesus Christ. I'm not reading the note to you out loud."

Then Alvin White could tell she understood his handicap, his setback in life. And she shook her head, like many had done. No matter how smart he was, too many times he'd been called anything but. He could build a house, fix anything, and for some folks that wasn't enough.

She said, "So you're a landscaper."

"A pretty good one too. At least my customers think so. Started my own business."

"A landscaper who claims to have bad eyes."

"Just read it to me, Reverend. Sorry I forgot my glasses. Sho' am sorry I did."

The minister was called for her order. She took her tea and walked out the front door, went to the left, then disappeared. Alvin White twisted his lips, felt embarrassed.

He missed Catherine. He needed her. She had been teaching him how to read.

She was a real nice woman.

She was the first Frenchwoman he'd ever met. She was real smart. And patient. Kept a clean house, and when those boys were home, made them three meals a day.

Gideon had told him about her when she was a woman named Thelma. Was hard to imagine Catherine any other way than being a mother with two little boys.

He wished he knew where she had gone so he could go protect her.

Maybe he could get them to Odenville. His in-laws had another trailer home. But like Gideon had said, Catherine and her two boys had to be in Sweden, someplace like that, by now.

Then Alvin White turned and looked at the television.

He saw a truck like his in someone's driveway. He went and stood close to the television so he could hear. Something had happened in the city of Marietta last night. Not too far from Dobbins Air Reserve Base, a family had been slaughtered. Someone had broken into their home around two in the morning and killed a family. The family had last been seen eating at Tassa's Roti Shop on Powers Ferry Road. One neighbor across the street said he was up past one and didn't hear anything. The news called it another home invasion.

Alvin White stood and looked at the truck in that family's driveway.

The family's truck was behind the newscaster as she reported.

There was no license plate on the truck. Some people never noticed that.

Alvin White shook his head. "Naw. No way. Don't let me be done did it wrong."

He had gone to Cumberland Mall two days ago and driven around. When he saw a truck like his near Costco, he had taken the plates. He had swapped plates in case he was being followed. He had stolen the plates from some man's truck, a man's truck that was the same make and model as his. And now that man and his family were dead. That wasn't a coincidence.

Alvin White watched behind him, studied the streets for trouble.

What was left of the Four Horsemen could be in the ATL.

Alvin White sat in the window, phone in hand, thinking about calling Konstantin.

If what he thought had happened, then someone had followed him at some point, saw his stolen tags, then got the information and gone to that house and killed everybody and the dog. Alvin White knew that if that was true, that could have been his wife and children heading to meet the undertaker. He called Konstantin and got the answering service. He stammered, then left a simple coded message. It sounded innocuous, but it meant to call him back.

Opening and closing his hands he said, "Jesus, I done messed up some kinda way."

Alvin thought back. After he had switched the tags on his truck, he had put on a Braves baseball cap and gone by Catherine's home in Powder Springs. He had driven to the end of the cul-de-sac and turned around. Thinking back, he remembered a FedEx truck had been parked in the cul-de-sac. He didn't remember seeing any packages on anyone's porch. The FedEx truck was just sitting there. What had struck Alvin White as odd was there were two people in the FedEx truck. Two women. He knew they weren't black and they weren't Mexican. He'd never seen more than one person working a FedEx truck. But he had dismissed it.

Whoever was in that FedEx truck could've gotten the stolen tag number on his truck when he passed by. They might've used a cell phone and taken his photo when he passed by too. Angry at himself, Alvin White rolled his hands into fists, and he lost his congenial smile.

He whispered, "Nah. I'm just jumpy. Making up thangs in my head."

Raindrops appeared on the windows. Cars went up and down Decatur Street, windshield wipers on. The rain was coming a lot sooner than he had hoped.

Within five minutes, the skies darkened.

Alvin White thanked the owner for the good tea and good service, told the owner's pretty wife and beautiful daughter to have a good weekend, then left the back way so he wouldn't have to get wet before he made it to his truck. He took the rear door by the bathroom. That exit led to the stairs for the lofts in the buildings at the Pencil Factory Flats and Shops. He jogged one level up to go to the covered parking garage. It was bare bones, concrete. It smelled like damp cement and humidity mixed with a stale, dusty, nothing scent. The residents parked to the immediate left, and they had a security gate. Everyone else parked straight ahead and down. It wasn't until customers turned left in the structure that they realized it was a great place to get mugged. But a man Alvin White's size didn't worry about that too much.

The winds had picked up already. That meant the roads would be slick.

The former heavyweight boxer slowed down when he saw a group of people standing by his old truck. There were two foreign women. He didn't know that one dressed in jeans and sneakers and holding a big purse was a Pakistani woman named Javeria. The Israeli woman next to her was Rayna. Rayna wore slacks and heels. Her purse was a duplicate of the Pakistani's.

Those were the two women who had been in the FedEx truck he had seen.

There was a young Mexican man with them. He had a goatee and a military haircut. He was overdressed for the heat and humidity. The minister was with them. She had the sheet of paper she had given him in her hand and was waving it at the people she was with. She was pissed off. He heard her use words like *motherfucker*, *bitch*, and *bastard*.

Alvin couldn't read more than a few simple words, but he was sure those words weren't in the Bible.

The minister's coat was open. Alvin saw part of a gun holster.

The Mexican sweated like a pig, but he kept his coat buttoned.

That told Alvin White the man had to be hiding his gun holster.

The other women put their hands in their bags, their intent expressions a tell.

A man didn't have to know the alphabet to be able to read bad news and trouble.

Alvin White stared at them and they glowered at him. Like cowboys right before a showdown at high noon.

Preacher said, "Landscaper, come ride with us. Show us around Atlanta."

"Wish I could, but I have to be somewhere right now."

"Come with us. I insist."

"I need to go buy some flowers."

"When we're done, we will buy you flowers."

Behind him a dozen people came out of Marlee's and were heading for their cars. They were all parked near Alvin White; some were by the minister. At the same moment, an APD vehicle came into the garage from the end closest to the King Memorial MARTA station.

When APD showed up, the minister and her congregation went toward a black SUV.

Alvin White got into his truck and drove away in a hurry.

His gas light was on. He was low on fuel. He had meant to fill up earlier, but he didn't want to be late to get his hair cut. He'd had an appointment. Hated to be late for anything.

He doubted if he had six miles' worth of gas.

Rain came down harder. In the distance thunder crackled.

Alvin White took to Decatur Street, broke the light at Hill, then crossed over I-85. Georgia State University went by in a blur. Alvin White sped through the area with the pedestrians and tourists going to places like the Center for Civil and Human Rights, the aquarium, the World of Coca-Cola. Thousands of tourists were out. And the streets were crowded with hundreds of cars. He got caught by Philips Arena. Drove after drove of pedestrians crossed, coming from Centennial Park and the Ferris wheel, half of them already soaking wet, but not from the rain. They had been in the spouts that shot streams of water up from the ground before the rain had started. Just as many came from the CNN building. The black SUV had caught up with him. It was about six cars back.

When Alvin White saw a break in the crowd, he ran the light, did that in an area that had droves of policemen. The SUV did the same, whipped into the opposing lane, sped around traffic, broke the light, and was almost on top of him when he passed Uptown Comedy Corner.

This was the only day in his life he'd run a light and APD hadn't pulled him over.

He changed to Marietta Boulevard Northwest, but they were there, aggressively following him, chasing him how they had been chased in Buenos Aires. By the time he was at Crest Lawn Memorial Park, he knew he'd be out of gas soon. There was no way to call the Russian.

There was nothing Konstantin could do for him on the phone.

Hawks was in Nashville. Nothing she could do from there.

He didn't know how to get in contact with the Bajan.

He made a hard left and zoomed up Bolton Road, skidded, but corrected before he spun out. Driving the two-lane road was like being out in the country. It had a lot of older homes. Most hadn't been modernized or kept up. That narrow road led toward Mableton and Smyrna.

He had hoped he'd have distance between him and the SUV to bail out in this area, because of the homes and the many trees, but the SUV was trying to tap his bumper and make him lose control. He floored it, put some space between him and the suit-wearing devils.

He reached under his seat and clicked a button, and a hidden rifle rolled out to his heels. Alvin White, former boxer, husband and father, that kind man, was gone, and the hired gun called Shotgun was in his place. He had handled two men before, in both gunfights and fistfights, but had never fought four. When there were four, you needed to outrun them, no matter how good you were. In a fistfight he'd never take on four men by himself.

Same rule went for a shootout.

Three miles later he made another hard right on Cobb Drive. The Waffle House was on the left, and a gas station was right there, taunting him. Riverview Road was a mile away, at the next light. A quarter of a mile down, as he approached the overpass for the Chattahoochee River, his truck stuttered, and the engine died. He tried to start it back up, but it was futile.

The street was six lanes wide on this strip. Little to no traffic. It was probably the only spot in the ATL that was wide open. He looked for trees and kudzu. A small subdivision was to the left. It would be impossible to run there for cover. There was a cemetery on the right, but it was the kind without large tombstones. If it had been like Oakland Cemetery, he could have tried to make a break for it and used the tombstones as cover.

On South Cobb, there was nowhere to run, and no one to cover him if he tried.

Preacher's voice shook with rage as she screamed, "Landscaper."

Shotgun yelled back, "What can I do for you, Reverend?"

"Medianoche would like you to come with us so he can have a word with you."

"Oh, he ain't nobody I'd wanna talk to. I done seen how that crazy man talks to people."

"Talk to me. You seem like a reasonable man, so talk to me, pray with me. The Bible says, 'Put your sword back into its place. For all who take the sword will perish by the sword.'"

"The Bible you got looks too much like a gun, so I don't trust your scripture."

"Give us Thelma, give us Gideon, and I won't make your heat fade out right away."

Thunder. Lightning. The world became a shadow sending down a summer storm.

Alvin White took a deep breath.

He thought about his wife. Her name was Betty White. Like the actress. She always told people her full name, then said she was the *other* Betty White, the sexier one.

He thought about his boys. Since they were born, he'd tried to be a good dad to them, and even though he couldn't read, he didn't let their friends know, never embarrassed them.

He used his cell phone, called his wife, but only got her answering machine.

"Betty White, I love you. Don't ever forget that. Your man loves you. I love them badass chirren we got too. Tell 'em that. Make sure they know that they daddy love 'em more than—"

When the street was clear for a half mile in both directions, the end came.

The Horsemen left their SUV in a hurry, came at Shotgun like an insurgent group. Shotgun dropped his phone without turning it off, the message still recording as he rolled out, stepped into the rain with his shotgun creating its own powerful thunder.

He stepped into the fresh storm. He was fast, like Chuck Connors on *The Rifleman*. He gifted his enemy a 240-grain jacketed hollow-point .44

projectile, fresh from a Winchester lever-action .44 Magnum rifle. Thirty-inch barrel. Fifteen rounds were in the tube. Shotgun popped the Mexican and the Israeli assassins without hesitation. The .44s exploded and detonated inside their skulls. There was a flash, like fireworks starting off; then their heads opened up like watermelons dropped on concrete. The blond minister and the Pakistani killer fired as they flanked, and Shotgun fired twice at the clergy. Today she was the head of the snake. Something about her told Shotgun she had more rattlesnake venom in her body than blood.

The minister yelled, "You're a dead motherfucker now."

He unloaded more shots, didn't get distracted, didn't talk, didn't pause. Konstantin had told Shotgun never to hesitate if he faced a woman with a gun. A woman with a gun was a killer.

Wingtips or high heels, an assassin was an assassin.

If Gideon and Konstantin had been at his side, this would have gone differently. The four people in that SUV would be handled, and Shotgun and his friends would be speeding up the road and getting on 285.

He had flown on a plane for the first time in his life. He had flown on a private jet and had the prettiest flight attendants, who would have done anything to make him happy.

He hoped his wife never found out about that. She'd put him in the doghouse.

He thought about Buenos Aires. About Montevideo and Colonia del Sacramento. He had seen Brazil. He had finally left the country, had seen some beautiful things while they had been on the run.

None of his family had ever been out of the country. He had done that before them all.

He wished his pretty wife and badass kids had been with him. They would have gotten a kick out of feeling South American winter in North American summertime. Though if they had been down in South America a week, they would've missed the good food at Sweet Auburn Curb Market, complained about there not being a Chick-fil-A in sight, and come back home. There weren't enough black people down there for his taste. And down there it seemed like they had never heard of Martin Luther King Jr. or they just didn't care. Hadn't seen one T-shirt with his face on it.

The minister fired. Shotgun returned fire.

Still, Buenos Aires had been an adventure.

They had been like Jack Bauer, James Bond, and Jason Bourne.

Bullets hit his secondhand pickup truck, burst open the back window.

Shotgun got in another shot, made his rifle erupt, saw the Pakistani assassin's face get blown away, saw her lifeless body drop. He had a chance. God had woken and given him a chance. But he saw the minister, that rattlesnake's face in a rage. She was screaming some damn Bible verse about "he who smiteth a man." The minister was yelling, her gun popping. Popping. Popping.

Shotgun tried to fire back. He was out of ammo.

He'd spent his load.

Thunder roared, winds blew, and rain fell.

He'd been hit hundreds of times in the ring, had fought men who went on to become world champion, but had never felt pain so unbearable.

Shotgun was hit by eight rounds: four in his leg, one in the chest, one in his arm, one through his shoulder, and one through his left hand. The big man staggered back and flipped over the concrete railing, fell like rain, dropped thirty feet into the murky Chattahoochee River.

Chapter 20

Chase a Crooked Shadow

In an accent decorated with agony, the bloodied capitalist asked, "Were you abused?"

That paused me. I adjusted the bloodied brass knuckles. "Why would you ask me that?"

"You're acting like a radge."

"I have no idea what that means."

"A *maniac*. This deplorable violence seems . . . personal."

"Maybe it is. But this is what I have been paid to do by someone who didn't have the guts to do it themselves. A rich man pays others to do his dirty work. Same for rich women."

In the thick of the balmy night, as rain fell, I was in the financial district at 30 Saint Mary Axe, on the thirtieth floor of the pickle-shaped edifice people called the Gherkin. The landmark had been built on the site of the historic Baltic Exchange, destroyed by a Provisional IRA bomb back in the nineties. The new phallic-shaped structure resembled a strap-on made of glass and steel.

British people were too kind to call the skyscraper the Dildo. The phallus that cost 600 million British pounds had forty floors. Thirty-three were office floors. Five hundred and ninety feet from top to bottom. There were 1,037 steps in the building. London Zoo was to the north, Tower Bridge to the east, Tate Britain to the south. Fenchurch or Liverpool tubes were the closest, if I needed to exit in a hurry.

The target worked inside a large glass penis. That was as sick as he was.

I eased the bloodied brass knuckles off my hand, dropped them on top of a glass desk next to the box of Saran Wrap and the plastic bag for carrying a luxury suit from Charles Tyrwhitt. My jeans and hoodie had traces of his blood. The middle-aged man crawled across the floor, pulled himself up, struggled to get back in his chair. I guessed that chair was his symbol of power, where he was the king. The British man tugged at his two-button suit coat, tried to make himself proper. He reminded me of Scamz. What he had done took me to a bad place as well.

He repeated his question. "Were you abused?"

I paused long enough to glance out at London, the view as spectacular as his life.

I whispered, "Sure. I'll tell you. It's just us boys. It was my mother. Was my *mum*."

"Ah. The Greek tragedy comes to life."

I said, "Now we're the best of friends."

"That we are."

"You have two nine-year-old kids. Fraternal twins. Boy and girl."

"I've *never* harmed my kids. Wouldn't dare. I am a great father. Great at my job, mediocre at marriage, but great with my children. I would never subject them to such a thing."

"But you would harm the kids of others. Have done so for decades."

He shook his head. "This resentment is because your mother abused you."

I opened and closed my hands.

He laughed. "You put your *todger* in your mum's fanny and wiggled it around?"

Hair stood up on my neck, goose bumps moved across my skin, but I didn't say anything.

He snapped, "If not a shag, then what?"

Still nothing. I thought about *Oedipus the King*. That tale mirrored my life so far.

He chuckled. "*Ohhh.* Your mum slurped you when you were a wee lad."

I shifted and my nostrils flared; my trigger finger became itchy, real itchy.

He sang, "Your mum sucked you off. Sucked off by a woman old enough to be your mother, and it was your mother. Oh, this is *good*. Tell me more about the guilty mother, *Figaro*."

The target taunted me, ridiculed me, laughed like it was the best joke he'd ever heard.

He cackled. "Tell me, how was that? Did you come in mum? Are you a *motherfucker*?"

I put the brass knuckles on again, hit him three times, put him on the floor, and when he tried to get up, as he wobbled, two roundhouse kicks put him on his back. Then I went back to the window. It took him longer to crawl back, was harder for him to pull himself up to his chair.

I eased my gun from under my jacket, screwed on the suppressor.

He waggled his finger. "Many mothers are sick. Women are as sick as men. Especially the schoolteachers. A few are getting knocked up by thirteen-year-old boys. Very attractive teachers too. They groom a young boy, and soon they've turned him into a lover. Imagine that, you have your first orgasm with your teacher. You must think she is God when she makes you come. It takes a sick woman to know that, plan that, and get into a boy's head that way."

"You're one to talk."

"Sod off. Go sex your mum. *Motherfucker.* You know nothing about me."

"I would trade my life to be a square like you. To be able to work in an office like this, to be able to go to lunch with friends, to watch Arsenal play without watching my back. To not jump when I hear a siren, to be able to sleep with both eyes closed and without a gun at my side. To be able to sit and have a cup of tea with a woman I love, and not worry about who's coming in the coffee shop, and not beating a man half to death to protect her from her enemies. You have no idea how lucky you are to have a home, to own things, to have a decent woman in your bed who loves you. Your new wife looks like a young Helen Mirren, a woman many men would kill to have or die to get just one kiss, yet you're a fucking pedophile."

"Yeah, yeah, yeah. Stop waffling about and get to the point."

"How can a man have a woman like your wife and still want to bugger a child?"

"You kill people. I think that qualifies as being a tad bit lower, don't you think?"

"I go visit those who seem to have forgotten right from wrong."

"I know right from wrong," he barked. "I know better than to go online and seek out children who . . . who want adults to . . . to . . . It's wrong . . . *corrupt* to do the things that I do. If only you could see inside my heart and my head. You'd see how this faulty machine I live in, this body, how damaged it is, and this *addiction* is a making that is beyond my control. Don't you think I want to wake up next to my lovely wife and be as normal as she thinks I am? Why would I choose to live this pathetic double life? Only a fool would choose to have these cravings. I go long periods and I am normal. Still, despite what I have done, I am a good father to my mollycoddled children. A decent husband to my wife. They've always been taken care of, at least financially."

His uninterrupted diatribe ended. I didn't respond. He was shaking. So many tears were in his eyes. I handed him a tissue. He waved me away, wanted nothing from me.

He wiped his eyes on his sleeves, sounded like a kid when he asked, "Why me?"

"Some people deserve to die."

"Then you should have killed my father for what he did to me. *My father.* That rugger bugger would play rugby, drink until he was steaming, then come in my room. You should have killed my rat-arsed father for what he did to me. So you want the bloody details? Should I tell you about him putting the dog in the bathtub? My mother knew he put his cock in my mouth and blamed me. She had a perfectly good mouth and he chose to put his cock in mine. She blamed me and I believed it was my fault. You should kill *my* mother for what she allowed. Living like that gets in your head. I was bullied from primary until sixth form college. You should have mercy on me for what I have endured since I came out of my mother's pathetic womb."

"You should have contracted me. Not touched other children. You fucked up."

"In my head I am still that child, acting out what was done to me. I am stuck at that age. I am stuck in that moment. Don't you think I want to be free of those bloody memories?"

I snapped, "Then you should have gone to talk to a shrink."

"Look at my face. Why didn't you beat your mother until she was unrecognizable?"

"This is about you. You are an irredeemable pervert. You're a predator."

"I've never, never, never done anything to you."

"If you had, you wouldn't have lived this long. And your death would be different. It would have dragged on for weeks. By the end, you would have begged for a gun and one bullet."

"In that case, if you have such sound *morals*, why didn't you kill your mother? She sucked your wanker and left you screwed up in the head. Why me and not that skank?"

I went to him and forced a dirty sock in his mouth, shut him up, tried to shove it down his throat. With him gagged, I wrapped his face in Saran Wrap. I wrapped his face so many times he looked like a mummy. He struggled to pull it away. He failed. He urinated himself. His bowels made a stench. When the plastic stopped rising and falling, I kicked him over.

I said, "You don't get to call my mother out of her name. You don't get to call her a skank. You don't get to judge her."

My eyes watered, but I wiped away the angst.

As he transitioned, I wiped down anything I had touched.

I turned on his computer, put in the password, and inserted a memory stick. A video of him abusing children played. I could look at dead bodies and feel nothing, but I couldn't bear to look at the heinous things he'd done. Those were videos he had made and posted on dark sites that attracted mentally ill men like him. It would play on a loop, the software making it impossible to turn the computer off. That filth had been sent to my handler by the target's bitter ex-wife.

I spray-painted the word NONCE across his desk, UK prison slang for sex offender.

I grabbed the dead man by his large feet, dragged him toward a window. Nine aircraft warning lights glowed red, an alert to planes overhead. If anyone was in Searcy's—the club on the top three floors—they wouldn't hear the target as he plummeted. The dead never screamed.

Within a couple of minutes, I made it to the ground level and exited the building. The hoodie and jeans were gone and I had on a gray-check, slim-fit British Panama luxury suit, collar open. Looked like my name was Mr. Bespoke. A car alarm screamed. The target had landed on top of a parked Peugeot. The owner and others ran out of the building. Some became paparazzi and took rapid photos. Without looking back, I kept my head down and took a slow stroll to where a UK-branded Mini Cooper waited. The arms dealer was parked where I had left her.

I eased into her car. She drove away from the scene of the crime at an unhurried pace. She zigged and zagged, eventually went past a few sleeping policemen. Now she wore a dark skirt, hose that had holes in the knees, and a sleeveless blouse. Her face was made up. She looked like a different woman. She was more attractive than I had realized.

I asked, "Did you get the video?"

She stopped eating Walkers crisps. "I watched the idiot fall. Recorded it on your phone."

I took the phone, sent images to the number the ex-wife was using, that too a disposable phone. A one-word reply came. RECEIVED. Then I took the SIM card out of mine, broke it in half, then dropped it and the disposable phone out of the window, let them bounce on the high street.

She said, "I have extra clothes and can stay over at your bolt-hole, if you want company. Might be convenient in case my hacker calls in a few hours with more news on the Horsemen."

"It's a muggy night and you just want to sleep in a flat with air-conditioning."

She laughed. "It would be nice to put my head down for a kip and not wake up swimming in my own sweat because of the bloody weather. I know you have a lot of work to do. Don't want to be a bother."

She handed me her bag of crisps. I ate one.

The city was filled with the fast drivers who only came into Central London at night, after the congestion fees were turned off until morning. Bright lights, big city. We crossed the Thames. Went down, turned around, crossed the Thames again. Made sure no one was following us.

She did that without asking. She was small-time but had never been caught.

We had about twenty minutes of riding with the radio jamming KISS FM. She sang every song. When she finished wukkuping and backing up Rihanna on her latest dance tune, the arms dealer said, "I can get us in this posh club in Mayfair. Their sound system is bumping."

I opened the glove box. Took out another Beretta. "As long as I can take this."

"Then maybe we should just find a pub. There are about seven thousand pubs and I've only been to about five hundred. So tell me what kind of place you like, and I'll know where to go."

"I need to be able to see who's coming and going, and have a secondary exit."

"I'll drive us over to New Cross and we can pop in the Rose Pub and Kitchen. But we could get a glass of Guinness at the Sea Horse. Or drink a few wife beaters. I can afford to double-fist a few Stella Artois now. The pub is by the Millennium Bridge and we could drink and decompress and be back in your flat in five minutes or less. Won't be crowded at the Sea Horse."

Sirens were all over Central London. Gun in my lap, I checked the rearview, then scanned the horizon. Expected a Horseman to leap out of the shadows like they did in Buenos Aires. She touched my hand and I jumped. Jaw tight, I took a few deep breaths.

She asked, "You okay?"

I gazed at my watch, stared at the floating hands on a Rolex bought in Puerto Rico.

It was twelve A.M. Midnight. Our fight in the *villas* flashed before my eyes.

Watching the second hand glide, I replied, "I will be okay in a minute."

When the minute passed, I checked the cameras at the safe house.

Then I checked the cameras at Catherine's home in Powder Springs, Georgia. The treadmill and EFX machines sat untouched. So did the thirty-two-inch flat-screen and the Wii equipment. I looked inside the panic room that had been built by Alvin White. It was big enough for ten people to sit. I made the lights come on inside. I had left four guns in that room. Four nine millimeters. Two were missing. Wherever she went, she didn't go empty-handed.

My driver's phone rang. Her hacker.

She answered, "What's the craic? Brick, you sound pissed and knackered. I appreciate you sorting this out for me while in Belgium. Bollocks. Yes, you can. Because you're the best. Tell me what you found so far. I was driving. Not out on the pull. I'm with the client. Yeah. He's the American. I copped off with him. No, I wasn't plastered. Innit? We broke up. That wazzack. Yeah, today I behaved like a twenty-four-hour trollop. Back to the matter at hand. Buenos Aires. Tell me now and whip around when you get back. I'm good for it. He's good for it. Don't be trampy."

She pulled over near Trafalgar Square, where everyone went to protest everything from climate change to the war. She pulled into a car park on Spring Gardens, not far from Downing Street and Horse Guards. They talked. My trigger finger was itching, moving back and forth.

While they chatted, my satellite phone rang. It was Konstantin.

"Gideon, you okay?"

"What happened?"

He told me about Shotgun.

He told me he had been ambushed in Atlanta.

I wasn't ready for that news. I wasn't fucking ready.

Almost sunrise. I stood to the side of the window over the mews, the one over Domino's facing the high street, weapon in hand. The iPad monitored the hallway. The laptop was connected to the cameras inside Catherine's home. Felt so many emotions I couldn't define. I dialed Shotgun's number hoping for a miracle. Someone answered on the first ring.

In a low snarl I asked, "Who is this?"

They said nothing as gospel music played.

Ten tense seconds passed before I repeated, "Who is this?"

She said, "Gideon, son of Thelma, is this your sweet voice I finally hear?"

She had my attention. "Who is this?"

"Your day will come soon. Like it came for your friends, yours will come."

"Señorita Raven? Bitch, is this you? Answer me. Answer me!"

"No, no, no. I am called Preacher. One by one, all will fall. One by one."

"I have some news for you. You won't be the first preacher I've sent to see Jesus."

"We were right behind you in Brazil. Same for Athens. Next time, you're mine."

"Tell me where you are, and I'll come there. I'll fucking come there now."

She hung up the phone. I went to the wall, to the war room, tried to guess who the bitch was. Had to be the blonde. She was well-endowed and dressed like she was going to do humanitarian work. A woman of European heritage sporting a preacher's collar had the opposite effect of a Muslim woman wearing a hijab. She used her privilege and the favored religion to make herself look like a golden child. I sat on a kitchen chair, head in my hands, bouncing my legs, talking to myself. Then I broke down and dialed Hawks's number.

She said, "I just heard. I have Konstantin on the other line."

"My best friend . . . *fuck*. Worried about his wife. His kids. He watched my back from the day I met him. I fucking failed him. I never should have taken him with me to South America."

"Might be a bad time, but I have other stuff to talk to you about."

"Then it's a good thing I called."

"Jeremy Bentham from Smyrna. I found an address for him, and it's off Campbell Road in a subdivision on a street called Oakwood Trace. He rents a townhome owned by Nia Simone Bijou. She lives in Los Angeles most of the time and it's rented through a property management company. Three bedrooms. Three levels. Condo costs two hundred and forty thou and he pays twenty-three forty-nine a month. But something is not right about this man. One, that's the name of an English philosopher, jurist, and social reformer from the 1800s. And it's also the name of a character on the TV show *Lost*."

"Coincidence? Or somebody fucking with my life again?"

"Unlikely to be a coincidence. This Jeremy Bentham didn't exist five years ago. Nothing on him anywhere, not in any of the fifty states, and his info says he's an American."

"Okay. So that rules out his parents naming him after a philosopher, jurist, whatever."

"And I know for certain he's not the character from the TV show *Lost*."

"Where does he work?"

"That's another thing. I can't find a job under his name."

"Okay. So, it's not adding up. Nothing ever does with Catherine."

"And Catherine's other name. Nathalie Marie Masreliez from Yerres, France. Yerres. That's a community about eleven miles from Paris. Southeastern suburbs of Paris. Sounds like it is to Paris what Franklin, Tennessee, is to Nashville. People from there are called Yerrois."

"I knew that. The last part. I knew she claimed to be a Yerrois."

"Well, it's all new to me, so pardon me for trying be thorough. Place sounds like Dallas, Georgia, with a French accent. You sure you gave me the right name for her?"

"I'm sure. My mother said that was her name when she was in Yerres."

"Well, we know half of what she says ain't true and the other half is a lie."

"What did you find?"

"What I found was that there were two of them. Both had the same address in Yerres."

"Two?"

"Maybe mother and daughter? Women name their daughters after themselves sometimes, but not often. That name thing is about male ego and lineage."

"Mothers naming daughters after themselves is common overseas. The Irish had a set and complicated naming tradition. They knew what every child would be named even before a couple met and had kids. It's not the same as it is in the States all over the world."

"Well, you learn something new every day."

"So there are two Nathalies."

"One of them is dead. And she died twenty years ago. Could be her mother. But I would think your mother would tell you if you had a granny and other folks over there in France."

I rubbed my head. "No, she wouldn't. She ran away from her commune and her name."

"Were you born there?"

"I have no idea where I was born."

"Your birth name?"

"I have no idea what my name is on the birth certificate."

"This is the part where I refrain from saying something bad about your momma."

"Appreciated."

She asked, "Well, you want me to fly across the pond and check it out? I could fly into Paris; something called the RER Line D goes from there into Yerres. Has to be a short trip. And I looked up places to stay. There is a B and B called Crosne Plazza and Spa."

"You don't speak French. And too many French aren't kind to those who don't."

"I can manage. I can make it work. They have to have a city hall over there."

I said, "Hawks, I don't have time for this right now."

"Don't hang up in my face."

"I have no idea where Catherine and the boys are. I just need to know where she is. I need to know she's safe. I need her to be in a refuge with the boys. They weren't with Shotgun. And I have no idea how the Horsemen found Shotgun."

"Do you think she would have gone back over there to hide from what's over here?"

"She told me she ran from over there. She ran, changed her name, the whole nine. The life we led, what she ran from had to be bad. She never mentioned them. No matter how hard times were, she never called or reached out for help. I had never heard the name Nathalie until a few days ago. So far as that goes, she could have made that up too. She lies to cover lies."

"How did you know about her and this Jeremy guy?"

"The cameras in the house. I looked at the film, saw him come over late one night."

"Were they intimate, or was he someone snooping around?"

"Intimate. The boys were asleep. Didn't meet him. She messed around with him in the living room, then took him to her bedroom."

"What was going on?"

"She said it wasn't a cash-transaction thing."

"So he's a boyfriend? A booty call? A one-night stand? I mean, can't fault her for that. A woman gets lonely. She's in the USA and ain't got no friends. She's a mother, but she's still a woman, Gideon."

"You're taking her side now?"

"Just trying to be professional and objective."

"That's what she said. That she's a woman. She has needs. He is the new friend she has to tend to those needs, after hours. But now you say he didn't exist five years ago."

"Other things are more important."

"Much more important. I should have been there."

She paused. "Again, sorry about what happened to Shotgun."

"Thanks for everything. Thanks for getting me out of Uruguay."

"I was there for Konstantin."

"Well, thanks for the BC Powder and the wake-up call."

"You still owe me for the BC Powder."

"I'll pay you as soon as I can get you the eleven hundred pennies."

"I stick to my word. If I can't do something, I won't promise it at all. And if I promise something, I will do it. I have to let you know, even on bad terms, my loyalty doesn't change."

"Thanks, Hawks."

"Let me get back to Konstantin. He's still on hold."

"Is something going on I need to know about?"

A phone rang on her end of the line. Soca music played as a ringtone.

Hawks said, "If I find anything, I'll get in touch. Or Konstantin will."

We hung up.

Wherever Hawks was, she wasn't alone. A phone had rung in the background and I had heard a man answer another call. The soca music was enough, Red Plastic Bag singing "Something Happening," but I also heard his voice. It was the Bajan. His accent was distinct.

He spoke a few languages, one of them being French.

Hawks was with him.

That gutted me.

When I raised my head, the arms dealer was standing in the doorway. She had on my dress shirt, the one I had worn with the gray suit. It was open enough to see she was still nude.

She said, "Sorry about what hap'd to your mate across the pond."

I opened my mouth to say something, but words escaped me.

She yawned, stretched hard enough to pop her back. "Anything I can do to help?"

Again I had no response.

She straddled me, rubbed my head, rubbed noses. Then she kissed me.

The Four Horsemen had managed to find Shotgun. Scamz was dead. And he had taken Arizona with him to Davy Jones's locker. Konstantin said he was safe, but I wanted to fly to him, and I needed to get back to Atlanta, see if there was a hint of where Catherine had gone.

I couldn't be in two places, in two states, at the same time.

I couldn't be in two states of mind at the same time, either.

She whispered, "Revenge lines are in your forehead."

My jaw remained tight and my nostrils flared. "Yeah. I can feel them pulsating."

She said, "You're thinking a thousand thoughts, none pleasant."

She told me to relax on the sofa. She rubbed on me awhile, then went down on me, made me rise. She went to the bedroom, came back with a bulletproof vest made of latex. She rolled it on me, then straddled me again, wiggled me inside of her. She had tightened up and put me in slowly. She sat there, inhaling, exhaling, adjusting to me being inside of her to my balls. Her fingers traced the lines in my face, rubbed like she wanted to erase them. Then she tried to ease my pain.

In a soft, caring tone she said, "I know you're hurting. I don't know what else I can do to help comfort you. Is this appropriate? Should I stop?"

"Don't stop. This is fine. For now, this is fine."

She rose and fell, became passionate, and found her way to heaven. Then she worked hard to get me back to that same place. When I was close, she took the condom away, fellated until the ending was happy.

When that was done, she rested with her head in my lap.

She wiped the corners of her lips, shifted around, then whispered, "You're still thinking a thousand thoughts a minute. I can tell."

My eyes refused to blink. My trigger finger moved without pause.

My mother had told me I was the son of a mercenary, a man who jumped out of airplanes, a man who had killed many people. My mother had told me I was Midnight's son. That was the blood I had running in my veins. The blood of the devil and the blood of a whore.

I said, "I know what you can do to help."

"Tell me."

"Radically Invasive Projectile. Heard of those bullets?"

"The bloody RIP ammo? It's called RIP for a reason. The round splits into nine needles of solid copper on impact, puts holes through skin, muscle, lungs, heart, all vital organs. That bullet was banned by the Hague Convention. They don't let soldiers use those in war."

"Each bullet splits nine times."

"One pop, you drop."

"And when you drop, if you don't die right away, it will be worse than getting shot nine times. One shot, and there is no going back. You'll lose more than an eye."

"That bullet is hatred on steroids."

"That's where I am right now. Hatred on steroids. What's the cost?"

"Almost two pounds for *one* RIP bullet, but you can get one *hundred* nine-millimeter bullets for fifteen pounds. That's why most buy the cheaper nine millimeter. That, and for some reason popping someone with a nine millimeter is seen as being just a tad bit more humane. Even a hollow point is more humane than the RIP bullets. I've seen the video of what the RIP does to a man's insides."

I asked, "How many can you get me? And I could use a VSS Vintorez in a briefcase."

"A VSS is okay. But the M24 claims to be the most powerful sniper rifle in the world."

"The Russian VSS is easy to transport."

She popped her lips, thinking, then said, "Sure. I don't know anyone who is having a jumble sale of that sort. But I can make most of it happen. I have to deal with someone I'm not that fond of. Bloke has an issue with my ethnicity and the religion of my parents. But if the money is right, I can make it happen much faster if I deal with this particular bloke."

I told her my complete order, my wish list. She picked up her phone to make a call.

She said, "My jaw hurts."

"That's called *irrumatio*."

"This has a name?"

"I have BC Powder in the bedroom. Take one."

"Oh, I'm not done yet. More *irrumatio* to come. Once more, with me on the bed on my back, head hanging over the edge, if you please."

Two hours later we left the safe house, her hand in mine. She walked with me down the mews toward Queen Victoria Street and Cannon Street, then down the stairs to the hot, stuffy Mansion House tube station. Tube stations had their own smell. This one was one of the oldest tube stations in London, so it reeked like a combination of hundred-year-old dust and cast iron.

Nibbling on a digestive, she said, "I hope you enjoyed the British fry-up."

"I did. Thanks for cooking breakfast. You're a good cook."

"Since I was a small child. Since I was a sprog, had to take care of myself. And I should thank you for the protein. *Bally*. Sorry. Bad timing on that joke, with what happened to your mate. Didn't mean to joke about having it off with you and jizz when I know you're in a bad mood."

I smiled the best I could. "It's fine. Hope I helped put some blue back in your sky."

"Wish I could do the same for you. You look like your skies are the darkest black."

She handed me the rest of the round British biscuit. I ate it in one bite.

The loaded Arsenal backpack hung from my left shoulder. I was back in jeans and trainers and sported a plain blue T-shirt. At least twenty people were there, waiting on one of the three trains. Once I felt comfortable, and since no hairs stood on my neck like my Spider sense was going off, I hugged and kissed the arms dealer as we stood on one of the three platforms.

I said, "Nothing bothers you, yet you're very sensitive at the same time."

"Nah. I grew up in council housing, lived around the most notorious gangs in the UK. Saw people get beaten and left stabbed in the roads. Before you're a teen, you're already used to violence, murder, drug deals, guns, knives, that sort of thing. The things I've experienced and the things I've done, London will never erect a blue plaque on a wall in my name, that's for sure."

"How you grow up can put calluses on your soul."

"This is who I am, calluses and all. But this isn't who I'm supposed to be, if you know what I mean. DNA predisposes a certain behavior, but if your environment doesn't support it, then that behavior won't manifest. When people don't have opportunity, they have to create their own opportunities. I would've been someone different. Maybe an architect. I think I would've liked it."

"It probably would have been boring, but you would have been safer."

"How did you get into your business?"

Again I thought about Catherine, about the day she came to me and told me a friend in her business needed help, and she put a knife in my hand and sent me to kill a man. That was years after I had shot Medianoche. That was years after I had killed another man for her on the streets of Montreal. Then I was a teenager. I went to public school but kept to myself. When you live in a brothel, you don't want anyone coming to your home. When your mother does what mine did, you don't want her at PTA meetings. I had thought killing was behind me, but my mother told me I was needed again, and we needed the money to survive, so I stopped doing my homework to go see a man my mother said didn't deserve to live to see another day.

That time hadn't been in self-defense, or because a man had beaten her.

She put a weapon in my hand and made me a killer.

I had killed a man, then went back home and finished my homework.

I didn't want to talk about my own faulty programming.

I responded, "Long story. Next time I see you, maybe I'll tell you all about it."

"So you think there's going to be a next time? So I'll be able to show you London, take you to the most beautiful tube stations. Westminster. Southwark. Saint James's Park. Gants Hill. East Finchley. Cockfosters. So, you're telling me this chance meeting wasn't a bloody one-off?"

We yielded tentative expressions, one made heavy by reality.

She pulled her lips in. "I'm never going to see you again. We both know that."

"I won't lie to you. No. You won't."

"And if I did, it would probably be donkey's years. Would be yonks."

I didn't say anything.

I didn't want to tell any more lies, not even to myself. A woman like her was every hit man's dream. Knew how to take the troubles away with her body and knew the right questions to ask and didn't get all emotional when you disagreed. And she liked pizza, chess, and lager.

She sighed, then forced a small smile. "Be careful, Gideon."

I ran my fingers through her aquamarine mane. "You too, Zankhana."

"You're going to visit your guv'nor."

"For the last time."

The sound and gust of wind that came when a train was approaching blew over us. It whooshed warm, turbulent air that smelled of metal, engine oil, warm tarmac, and maybe dirty, wet clothes. We had a final kiss as the train approached, its wheels grinding on the track. The ear-splitting screeching noise didn't make her pull away from me. She held me and gave me her tongue. The way she tasted, even the dust, and the scent of cast iron, would stay in my mind. The din of the crowd and the *clickity-clack* of the train coming through the tunnel were ignored.

The kiss ended and she looked me in my eyes. I thought she was about to ask me to stay, to give up my world, and she'd give up hers, and we'd run away, start all over.

She whispered, "May God, Allah, Yahweh, whoever you believe in, may they be on your side. May they guide your sword and keep you safe. This I pray for you, Gideon."

"Same to you."

"You're wrong. Everything bothers me. And most of the time I am afraid."

"You hide it well."

"I don't have a choice. It's about survival."

I hopped on the Circle Line but kept my eyes on Zankhana, wanted to blow a kiss, wave until she disappeared. But Zankhana headed up the stairs, head down, never looking back.

I thought she knew who I was but didn't say. The moment I had told her my name was Gideon there was a look of recognition in her eyes. We'd never met, but she would've known my name. She had worked for an arms dealer named Sam when she was a teenager. He had been on the opposing team when I was here in London being hounded by a man with a broken nose. The man with the broken nose was a hired gun, and he baited me and killed me here. I had died here. And I had been resurrected. That happened on the floor of a flat near London Bridge. Someone else had taken care of the man with the broken nose. I had gone to visit Sam in Hackney. She knew I'd beaten her old boss half to death to get information. She didn't care. That had been just business.

This was something else. It was something I needed to get away from.

I sat on a train that reeked like someone who hadn't showered, then sprayed on cologne that stank like old fish 'n' chips and soured chicken tikka masala.

I focused, used my phone, and looked over the new information I had on the Horsemen, information that had come an hour before I left. I stayed on the tube for hours. There were eleven train lines that spread out over 250 miles. I could sit where no one was behind my back, move from tube to tube, hide underground, ride the funky trains until the tubes closed for the night.

I called the number I had for the con woman Arizona. Queen Scamz.

On the first ring, as it had been with Shotgun's number, someone answered.

Chapter 21

Behold a Pale Horse

Medianoche barked, "Five. We've lost five soldiers since this bullshit began."

Señorita Raven said, "Since the Beast took that contract from Hopkins."

They were in Medianoche's pristine quarters. Plaques and awards were on his walls.

Medianoche held a wood-veneered *mate* cup. He sipped from a metal straw called a bombilla. The bombilla also served as a filter. This *mate* was of herbs and whiskey. He looked out the window at the traffic eighteen stories below. Ice fell on snow as cars crowded the streets. It was 1.6 degrees Celsius in the city of Buenos Aires. With the wind chill, it was 1.7 degrees below zero.

Dressed in a black suit and black tie, Señorita Raven took the cup from Medianoche, sipped the bitter *mate*, then said, "Señor Rodriguez. Draco. Chico Blanco. Rayna. Javeria."

Medianoche adjusted his bloodred tie and added, "And the Beast."

She nodded, held on to the secret. "And the Beast. The Beast makes six KIA."

Behind them a video played. Gunfire. Screams. The echoes of war.

Medianoche said, "I should've sent you to Atlanta as team leader."

"If I had known the bastard who shot me in my chest was there, I would've been there. I'd pegged him as being British, like Scamz. Maybe from some part of Africa. Not a country boy."

"Preacher called him the Landscaper."

Seated across the room, Ibo the Nigerian said, "Instead of being here and wasting time at Reina Loba and Anchorena, I should've gone along with Chico Blanco. As team leader."

The Butcher nodded. "I should have gone as well. Not three women and Chico Blanco."

Señorita Raven turned to them and asked, "Are you saying women are weak?"

Ibo said, "Does it look like I give a rat's ass they were women?"

"Just because a man can lift more weight does not make him stronger."

"Let's not start with you bringing up your friggin' IQ again."

"Stay off the haterade."

"Since I arrived, have I said I have a problem with women? They were good soldiers; at least I thought they were. This is about competence. Incompetence has no gender. Incompetence is incompetence. Two out of three of those bitches got themselves killed."

Señorita Raven barked, "Stand down, African. Stand the fuck down."

"XO, this *Nigerian* thinks they were careless. The conclusion verifies my assumption."

The Butcher huffed. "The assignment was simple. To find and track a civilian woman."

Ibo said, "It was a no-brainer. And they accidentally found the Landscaper."

Medianoche adjusted his eye patch, touched his goatee, hair that was mostly gray with a few strands of black, and said nothing. He sat back, hands steepled. Listened. Observed.

The Butcher said, "They should have trailed him longer. They spooked him. If they suspected he was the mercenary who was here to battle, they knew he was no Joe average."

Ibo said, "But they went in for the kill. They should have waited until oh dark thirty."

The Butcher nodded. "That decision was unauthorized and made by Preacher."

Ibo said, "If all Horsemen didn't return, they fucking failed."

The Butcher cosigned. "They left the situation totally and royally fucked-up. She left there trying to get away and ran over a pedestrian crossing at the East-West Connector. She had a safe house off Buford Highway near Norcross, but after the accident, she had to dump the vehicle and steal another. She's sloppy. She'll be rotting in jail up in the ATL, if they catch her."

Ibo said, "I heard pretty white women don't go to jail in the South."

"So now you think she's pretty? Going to bring her back to the home team?"

Señorita Raven handed Medianoche the *mate*. "How long will Preacher stay in the US?"

The Butcher said, "I don't think Preacher's effective. This is where the Peter Principle kicks in for her. Her team went down in a matter of seconds. Four against one civilian, and she lost three members. There is no way in hell *one* tango should have taken down *three* Horsemen."

Medianoche paused. "What do you think happened? Talk to me. Make it good."

Ibo said, "The idiot was probably too busy running her cock holster and spitting out Bible verses when she should have had her pussy-eating mouth shut and been spitting out bullets."

Medianoche handed the *mate* to Ibo. Ibo sipped and handed it to the Butcher. He sipped and passed it back to Señorita Raven. She put the cup on the edge of Medianoche's desk.

Ibo said, "Pisses me off that we don't know what happened up there."

Medianoche nodded, agreed with his soldier. "There is no video for us to critique."

The Butcher said, "There was supposed to be a dashboard camera in the SUV."

Señorita Raven said, "She doesn't know what happened to it. Said it vanished."

The Butcher huffed again. "That's pretty convenient, considering the mission was CATFU."

Ibo shook his head. "Preacher is a garratrooper. She's good at practice, but the bitch loses it on the field, where it counts, and it costs lives. She probably saw a big black man with a gun and her dick beaters couldn't pull the trigger on her nine millimeter until it was too late. Bet her dick skinners were shaking. And she needs to lose weight. She can barely run two miles in fifteen."

Señorita Raven said, "Stop with the damn insults. She's your equal, *not a bitch*."

Ibo went on. "Or *my equal* was too busy admiring the butts on the pretty little girls."

"Show respect. Last time, Ibo. You're about to earn a GI party. Piss me off, disobey me, disrespect me, one more time and I'll have you in your quarters doing PTs until the windows cry."

Ibo smiled. "Didn't mean to offend you, XO. Just calling it like I see it."

Medianoche sat back, let the conversation run, did as the Beast used to do. Medianoche took a page from his dead friend's playbook and observed with minimal intervention. Señorita Raven was overaggravated, as Medianoche had been, and Ibo the Nigerian supplied most of that frustration. There was an energy between them that would play itself out. The anger would lead to shouting, drinks, being half-drunk, then naked, trying to fuck each other into submission.

Señorita Raven woke up the resentment in men.

All eyes went to the video playing on the flat-screen. The skirmish on the yacht.

When they were five knots to nowhere, they had eradicated more than a dozen bodyguards on Scamz's yacht. Horsemen had worn mountable GoPro cameras on their helmets. Each had walked the ship after the melee. Each dead insurgent received a close-up.

They had recorded Scamz. Had the man say who he was so the people in their world would know. He sat in a chair, naked, their POW, beaten, bloodied, suffering as the Horsemen laughed, smoked cigars, ate his caviar, and drank his wine. Medianoche pummeled him with punches, then let his men do the same. Looked like he had lost two pints of blood and his dignity.

Medianoche said, "We will send two more Horsemen to Atlanta. One will relieve Preacher of command, and the other will assist. She will follow the new leader's orders to the letter."

Ibo asked, "May I be on the team? I can lead or I can follow. I have no issues."

The Butcher raised his hand like he was in a classroom. "Same for me."

Medianoche offered his men Cuban cigars. The Hoyo de Monterrey Double Corona was a cigar that had an excellent burn, a pleasing aroma, a mix of cocoa and coffee with a subtle spicy aftertaste. The Butcher lit his cigar, puffed, then made a comment about how he was finally living the life a man with his skill set deserved. He pointed at himself in the video, torturing Scamz. He laughed at Scamz's pain, smiled like he was more than happy with himself.

He moved toward Medianoche's balcony. "You have a king's view of the South American dystopia. So this is where the Nazis were welcomed after they tried to liquidate the Jews. I heard they were set up in some part of Argentina like it was their second kingdom of Bavaria. Also heard that when a Nazi died, they gave him the full Nazi send-off, in uniforms and all."

Ibo said, "Nazis were Christians and it's still the religion of white supremacy. They have used Christianity to control the black man by giving him a lie to cling on to as hope."

"Don't start, Ibo. Don't start. You and Savage and your black conversations are trying."

"I like Quiana Savage because she keeps it real. We know the truth. The black man has been manipulated by the offspring of the evil bastards who kidnapped and enslaved his forefathers. A black man using the white man's Bible is the best example of Stockholm syndrome to date. If blacks are in a white man's heaven, they are janitors and maids."

"You're not fun to be around when you're not drunk. When you're sober you're depressing. You're a fun drunk. You dance, you sing, you tell jokes. Sober, you're a bitch."

"I guess no one wants to talk about how Hitler didn't die in Germany, didn't commit suicide, but fled here in a submarine and lived out the rest of his days. The FBI knew he was chilling at the Eden Hotel. Argentina and Nazi Germany were kissing cousins who wanted to finger fuck the rest of the world. Argentina was storing uranium for the Nazis and was trying to help them build a nuclear bomb. Bet you didn't know all of that, did you, Butcher Man?"

"Who gives a fuck? Somebody, get the delusional African drunk. I like him drunk."

Laughter spread around the room.

Ibo stretched, yawned, went to check out the view, see what the Butcher could see.

Medianoche picked up a remote, put the skirmish on mute, then turned on music, let Frank Sinatra sing "The September of My Years," allowed that song to score the battle.

Medianoche's cellular rang. It was Caprica Ortiz. He was to meet the Porteña at their regular hotel for two hours. It was his downtime, personal time to get away and relieve stress.

Señorita Raven adjusted her tie and asked, "Was that Assad with our new shipment?"

"Not Assad. Has to do with the other contracts. The Nunca Más contract."

"Caprica Ortiz."

"Yes, Caprica Ortiz."

"Another meeting?"

"Yes, another meeting."

There was a tap at the door. Quiana Savage entered, hurried, greeted her superiors.

She said, "Some fucktard is trying to hack into our systems again. Looks like it's out of Russia. But I think the signal is being bounced around the globe. The system is secure now."

Señorita Raven cursed. "Did they get anything? What's the damage?"

"Dr. Spots shut it down immediately, but he wants your eyes on the issue."

Medianoche looked to Señorita Raven. She said, "I'm on it. Give me two minutes."

His cellular rang again. It was Preacher.

Medianoche took a beat before he said, "We thought you had gone Elvis."

"I've found her, sir. I've found Thelma. She uses the name Catherine Rousseau Gautier."

He stood up. "It's confirmed that it is her? I don't want it to be anyone else but her."

"It's confirmed. I used her home address to find her cellular provider, and then I accessed her cellular records. She only called a few people, and one was in the area. Recently she called the number several times a day. I reverse engineered the number and retrieved the home address, then came to the area and parked. The garage door went up and one of the cars inside is registered in her name. Sir, there is no doubt in my mind."

"Where is Thelma hiding?"

"In Smyrna. Hiding in a townhome rented by Jeremy Bentham. She's outside Atlanta in the burbs. Pardon the noise. A train is going by. Railroad runs through this area."

"Gideon is there?"

"He could be hiding inside."

"You're on surveillance?"

"I've been sitting here."

"We already lost three down there. I want to send someone up to take charge, but that could cost precious time. Can you handle this assignment? Don't bullshit me, soldier."

"I have the layout of the townhome. Pulled it up online from when it was listed as a rental. The management company never took the ad down. I have all the info I need."

"Good. Drive on. Do nothing before oh dark stupid. Don't make a move in daylight and fuck it up like you did with the Landscaper. *Do you understand?* Can you handle this by—"

At that moment, the Butcher reached to open the patio door so he could step outside into the cold, maybe to check out the view toward Río de la Plata. The glass door shattered. Something whizzed by Señorita Raven and destroyed the lower part of the wall.

Ibo and the Butcher were one behind the other, almost in Ranger file.

That was how they fell.

A hole was in the Butcher's neck, had destroyed most of his neck, and that same bullet had continued, destroyed the Nigerian's heart.

It had barely missed Quiana Savage's left knee. She felt its energy. She screamed, then realized they were under attack.

Medianoche hit the floor as he pulled out his sidearm. *"Get down."*

Another projectile destroyed the patio door. A round blew a hole in the wall. Two more rounds destroyed furniture. Quiana Savage tried to pull the fallen Horsemen out of the line of fire.

Señorita Raven shouted, "We're getting hit with fifty-caliber rounds."

They were attacked like they were Black Panthers being raided by Hoover's FBI.

The gunfire paused.

Medianoche commanded, "Savage, get a fix from another room, and be fucking careful."

Quiana Savage had frozen, had lost her training, was in a knot.

Many well-trained soldiers did that in combat, when death was so close.

Medianoche barked, "Savage, get off your black ass and get a fix on the enemy."

Quiana Savage took three deep breaths, and she complied. Weapon in hand, she stayed low, scurried, backed out of the apartment. Medianoche and Señorita Raven moved to opposite sides, came together at the shattered window, weapons in hand, searching for a target, and tried to get a fix on the sniper. They didn't know if it was the Russians, the French, or the Men from Uruguay. They saw their enemy. Their antagonist was in the building across the street.

The renegade with the death wish stood next to a sniper's rifle.

He wasn't hiding. He wore all black. He pulled the black hoodie back from his head. It was a side zip-up, long sleeve. He wore a mask. Then he pulled away his balaclava.

It was Thelma's bastard son.

Gideon had returned.

The fucking gaucho was back. And he had become a beast.

The gaucho began shooting again.

Chapter 22

Some Deserve to Die

Twenty floors above the ground, charges blew the hinges off the door.

Horsemen threw flash and bang into the apartment where the gaucho Gideon had been holed up. Horsemen entered, locked and loaded, weapons high, mentally back in the Middle East, in Iraq, in Fallujah.

Carrying a ballistic shield, Medianoche moved in first. He wanted this kill to belong to him. Señorita Raven was right on his heels. Medianoche could tell his XO was anxious to empty her clip in the bastard she was convinced was his son. Tiburón, Dr. Spots, and Black Mamba came in behind their XO. They were geared up, nervous, angry, hyped, and dying for revenge.

The windows had been left open. Boot prints were on the floor where he had moved around. The room was freezing. Nothing was in the small apartment except scattered shells below the window. A prepaid cell phone was on the counter in the kitchen. Next to the prepaid phone was a package of BC Powder. Both sat on top of an unsigned Father's Day card.

A worn paperback was on the floor by the window. *Ten Little Indians* by Agatha Christie.

Señorita Raven said, "He's on the run."

The bastard who had left Medianoche dead on the floor of a whorehouse in Mecklenburg County, North Carolina, had snuck back into Buenos Aires and was hunting the hunters.

Señorita Raven picked up the cellular their prey had left behind.

She said, "It hasn't been used. There is one number programmed in memory."

Medianoche took the phone from her. He shoved it in his pocket.

Black Mamba asked, "What does the book mean?"

Dr. Spots said, "*Ten Little Indians?*"

Black Mamba said, "So he set up shop here and was reading a mystery novel, waiting for the right moment."

Medianoche told his men, "Sweep the floor. Someone go downstairs, be with Cobra, Clutterbuck, and Savage. And be careful. Keep away from windows. He has a fifty-cal."

Señorita Raven pointed at two Horsemen. "Black Mamba. Dr. Spots. Go downstairs and work your way up floor by floor. We will work our way down and meet in the middle."

Black Mamba and Dr. Spots hurried out and boarded the elevator. The elevator had opened as soon as they pushed the button. It didn't have to come up from *piso cero*. Medianoche paused when he saw that. The elevator had been here, waiting for them. As soon as the elevator door opened, his men rushed on. Medianoche remembered something.

The novel. His mother had read that novel when it was called *Ten Little Niggers*. The title of the Agatha Christie novel had changed over the years. *Ten Little Niggers* became *Ten Little Indians*. Years later, when political correctness had taken root, it was called *And Then There Were None*. But it had also been called *Ten Little Soldiers*.

No matter the name, it was the same story.

Someone had been offended, and one by one everyone in the tale died.

He had remembered all of that in the blink of an eye, and his panic set in.

Medianoche screamed and ran toward the lift. "Get off the lift. Don't take the fuckin' elevator."

The elevator door closed hard and fast. Unusually hard, unusually fast.

There was an explosion. All the Horsemen fell into defensive positions.

Dr. Spots screamed loud enough to be heard through the doors, "Fuck was that?"

Then a second explosion came from above them in the shaft.

Medianoche heard his men in the elevator. They were alive. They were shook up but uninjured.

Medianoche and his team struggled to pull the elevator doors open, tugged until he could see a sliver of the inside. He saw his men inside doing the same, fighting to open the doors.

But it was like a steel trap. They would need the Jaws of Life to open it fully.

Black Mamba was sweating, shaken, but composed under fire. He assessed the situation. His temperament remained stolid, phlegmatic, as he fought with Dr. Spots to open the jammed doors.

Black Mamba said, "We're okay. We just got rocked a bit. The explosion was above us."

Teeth gritted, still tugging, Medianoche said, "These doors have been tampered with."

Señorita Raven yelled, "We'll get you out. We got your six. Trust me, we got you."

They heard something break in the chute above them. Some debris fell on the roof.

Dr. Spots panicked. "The wiring snapped. I heard the fuckin' wiring—"

The elevator slipped two feet. They fought to open the door. It skated downward again. They dropped weapons and used all of their muscle. As a group, they had it opened only eight inches. Black Mamba tried to force open the car-top escape hatch, but it wasn't like in the movies. It had to be opened with a fireman's key, or from the other side.

Black Mamba trained his gun on the hatch and fired off a few rounds.

That solved the problem. When he opened the hatch, gunfire erupted from above. Six fast shots. He had been hit in the clavicle. He dropped and screamed like they had never heard a man scream before. He screamed like he had been shot nine times.

Dr. Spots returned fire, sent bullets up into the darkness, heard his shots ping, ricochet. *"Get me the fuck out of this elevator. Get me out. Get me the fuck—"*

The lift slipped again.

Dr. Spots looked at Medianoche, pleading to be rescued.

The lift slipped another nine inches. Then fell another foot.

Dr. Spots looked at the other Horsemen, his plea the same.

The elevator had slid down, now was between floors.

They saw Dr. Spots, sweating hard, panting.

Then the lift dropped another foot and forced them to lose their grip.

Dr. Spots banged on the walls with his sidearm and screamed, "Do something."

The lift dropped another foot. There was a sound from above, a whining, a harsh wail, as debris fell, the din of metal fighting metal, then separating from metal when cables snapped. The hydraulic elevator, which lifted and lowered elevator cars using a piston jack, failed.

The safeties that kept the lift from dropping no longer worked.

As if he knew what was next, Dr. Spots lowered his gun and whispered, "Fuck."

Then the lift plummeted, became a victim of gravity and height.

They were twenty floors up, twenty-one when the lobby was included. Force would equal mass times acceleration. The car was falling so fast the men were now on its ceiling. On impact, the car would stop and they would keep going, slamming into the floor.

Air from the falling lift pushed back up into their faces.

Señorita Raven gritted her teeth and prayed, "It'll stop, it'll stop, it'll stop."

The elevator was overspeeding. Metal shrieked. A safety device was supposed to grip the rails and bring the car to a safe stop. It should have happened within seconds. But the car stayed in free fall. Medianoche cursed aloud, sensed that all mechanisms that prevented the lift from staying in free fall had been tampered with, were completely disabled. That was virtually impossible to do, would take a genius and an act of God, but it had been done. Medianoche heard it falling. He looked up at the digital numbers. They had become a countdown to death. The Horsemen froze, hearts beating rapidly, praying to their gods for this to work out in their favor, because they were the goddamn righteous ones. The speed was too great. If it stopped suddenly, that would cause at minimum a fatal head injury. They yelled when they heard the heartbreaking crash, the explosion when it landed in the lobby. They yelled like they had been in that box with Dr. Spots and Black Mamba. Then the multiton elevator cable and assembly dropped for twenty-plus floors, pulled by gravity, and crashed down onto the elevator. It crushed the carriage and the men inside. Vibrations rose, juddered the edifice.

It shook dangerous men and women who were already shaken.

The gaucho had outsmarted a braking system that hadn't failed for 150 years, turned the elevator into a weapon. Dust rose from down below. The Horsemen sent curses, fired upward into the hollow of the elevator shaft, did their best to make a body drop. Medianoche wanted Gideon to have the same fall. He wanted to see him dropped; then he would shoot him until he hit bottom.

Medianoche shouted, "Get to the roof. He's not in the shaft. He's on the roof."

Tiburón, the soldier with six fingers and six toes, stopped and shook his head.

He was in the hallway and yelled, "Commander. Something dropped from the roof."

It was quick but felt like it was in slow motion. Tiburón pointed out the window in the apartment they had ransacked. Medianoche and Señorita Raven turned just in time to see a body fall from above. It dropped fast. Like a trapped man had jumped to commit suicide in order to face his fate, in order to prevent having what happened to Scamz happen to him. They ran to the window. They saw Gideon. Like the elevator had been, he was in free fall, dropping like a rock. Only this was different. A red-and-black parachute popped open and the winter winds carried him away, toward the mostly middle-class area called Almagro, in the direction of Avenida Rivadavia and Avenida Yrigoyen. While they were distracted, the son of a whore had gone to the roof and BASE jumped from the twenty-fifth floor. He floated through dreary skies, rain, and snow, maneuvered around concrete edifices that made Buenos Aires seem like the New York of South America.

Señorita Raven shouted, "He's bugging out."

The target was too far away to get a good shot. But Medianoche tried. Señorita Raven tried. And his six-fingered soldier, Tiburón, tried. Gideon landed in traffic, bending legs and rolling after the impact, like a professional. He missed being run over by a truck. Then his parachute was abandoned in the streets and he was gone, took off moving in the direction of the intersection of Estado de Israel and Estado de Palestina. It had been fifteen seconds from the roof to the streets, and like in New York, now he had a million places to chill out and plan his escape, or his next move.

In ten minutes, he could be anywhere. In twenty he could be on a boat crossing the river again. In an hour he could be on a plane flying to parts unknown.

Señorita Raven shouted into her headpiece, told the other Horsemen the location. "Get there fast. Get moving. Cobra, you're team leader. Break that bastard's back if you have to."

Tiburón said, "Only a madman would do a BASE jump from this height, in this weather. Only an insane person would attack us. But one did. He just called us out. Who the hell is he?"

Medianoche commanded, "Check the roof. See who is on his team. Shoot to kill."

They checked from pole to pole, found no one. There were boot prints from one man. This time there was no Russian. No one to replace the Landscaper. Looked like he was on his own.

Medianoche felt like the Beast was attacking him from his grave, Gideon his proxy.

When they hurried twenty floors down to the ground floor, freezing air, cold rain, and hints of snow blew in on the disaster. They stood, sweating. Rubble was everywhere, the front windows to the building blown out. The lobby looked like a building from the Middle East, one Uncle Sam had visited with a drone. The security guard had been injured. But two more Horsemen had to be taken to the morgue. He'd lost four good men in a matter of minutes. Jaw tight, Medianoche scowled at his failure. His men were badly mangled; both would be impossible to identify. Black Mamba had been lifeless when they went into free fall. Medianoche saw part of Dr. Spots's body in the wreckage, from his chest to his neck. His head was gone. It was like he had panicked and tried to jump out of the elevator between floors and decapitated himself. His head was up there somewhere, stuck in the shaft, or maybe down here bouncing around in the rubble.

Rattled and vexed, Tiburón shouted, "Who the fuck was that guy? A SEAL? A Russian? What nation is he from? A sniper who has the skills to make an elevator drop, but before all that, takes the time to leave a book, a prepaid phone, and a Father's Day card, then BASE jumps from a height that only an expert can handle? Who is he, Medianoche? Who are we fighting and how many?"

Eyes wide, blood boiling, Señorita Raven said, "Stand down, Tiburón. Not now."

The six-six, 235-pound albino snapped, "I wasn't talking to you."

"I'm talking to you, *Twelve Fingers.*"

"Go fist yourself!"

"Stand down, Tiburón. *And I will not ask again.*"

"I have twelve years of military service under my belt, and I want some goddamn answers, *Shrap Face.* Four of my brothers-in-arms have been put down by some tango, and I want some goddamn answers."

Señorita Raven ran, growled, leapt, and struck Tiburón in the mouth with a right cross. The sucker punch caught him when he was off-balance. The big man went down, tasted his own blood, then screamed like an animal. He swept her foot from under her and went after her, was going to show why they called him the Shark. His rage and indignation were greeted by a desperate and frantic elbow to the side of his head. He raised his fist and brought it down on Señorita Raven's rib cage, winded her. He slapped her and it sounded like thunder.

Medianoche exploded. "Stand down. Both of you, stand down now."

He yanked Tiburón to his feet, shoved him against the wall, his forearm across his throat.

"Señorita Raven is your XO, and when she orders you to stand down—"

"I have to stand down for your *bitch*? We all know you're banging Shrap Face. We can tell by the way she frowns at you when you put your eyes on Quiana Savage's sweet black ass. Savage is sleeping in your apartment, and we know she's in your quarters blowing you through the night. We know you're up there fucking that sweet black puss. You ever going to share the pretty one? You can keep the Shrap Face to yourself. That hajji's not worth a round of doggie."

"Stand the fuck down, Tiburón. You're losing it. Calm down and think straight."

"Get out of my face, old man. Kiss my six. I'm not high on some damn-ass hash. I believe in the plumbing theory in management; all the crap runs downhill. And we're knee-deep in bullshit. Old man, look at this disaster. Father's Day card aside, you and that goddamn raghead cockroach bitch who is sucking your cock better give me some fuckin' answers."

Señorita Raven managed to spit in Tiburón's face. Tiburón growled and pushed Medianoche away. When Medianoche wouldn't move so Tiburón could get to his XO, Tiburón took a swing, hit Medianoche on his iron jaw. Medianoche retaliated without hesitation, threw three rapid blows, the last landing on Tiburón's chin. Medianoche fought him like he was back in the pits. The giant staggered. Medianoche put his foot in the big man's gut, then gave him another blow to the side of the head, then one to the throat. Tiburón dropped, dazed. Medianoche moved behind him, put him in a headlock. Tiburón struggled. Señorita Raven pulled out her blade, snarled, and stabbed Tiburón a dozen times. Tiburón reached for his XO, was stabbed in his hands each time. Medianoche twisted Tiburón's neck until it snapped. Panting, Medianoche dropped his soldier. Breathing heavily, Señorita Raven was unhinged. She straddled Tiburón's body, stabbed him over and over, stabbed him and announced with each puncture that it was for every time she had been insulted since 9/11, stabbed him and told Tiburón her blade was because of what comrades like him had done to her, for what they had done to other women who served at their side and who were willing to die for them. Señorita Raven snapped, lost control, was no longer controllable. When she was tired, she stood, took out her sidearm, and put a dozen bullets in him, shot him in his manhood each time; then she reloaded.

The explosion had decimated the lobby. Spectators were looking, standing outside in the rain, too far away to see the fight. Vehicles stopped in the street. Sirens announced emergency services were on the way. Señorita Raven continued filling Tiburón's corpse with holes.

Medianoche exploded, *"Enough.* Señorita Raven . . . stand . . ."

An excruciating pain rose behind Medianoche's missing eye. His rage was a mountain, and that same rage fueled his blackout. Medianoche felt his brain catch fire. Heard it click and fight to whirr. Daguerreotype memories played at twenty frames per second, tried to shut him down.

Chapter 23

Like Father

Barrio Almagro. Avenida Medrano y Castro Barros.

Wearing a black backpack, I emerged from the Line A *subte*.

Face damp, sweat on my neck and palms, I came aboveground into cold air. Rain mixed with snow, but that didn't stop people from crowding the sidewalks. Heart beating fast, I took to the streets, hurried by fruit stands, *maxikioscos*, and *diarios*. *Colectivo* after *colectivo* passed by. The city buses seemed to run every three or four minutes. The thousands of cars went by at NASCAR pace. Hands in the pockets of my damp hoodie, gun in my right hand, something more powerful in my left, I moved by an uncountable number of businesses, maneuvered around a crowd trying to get inside McDonald's. At the intersection, I saw the name on the legendary eatery. Las Violetas. I pushed open tall glass doors that had golden handles, and walked past curved glass into a space that had ceilings high enough to be the roof of a second floor.

Las Violetas was huge. Old-world charm and sophistication.

Marbled columns, stained-glass windows and light fixtures, soaring ceilings, and tiled floors. I'd hoped it would be one of the smaller cafés. This place had too many entry points, and I had no idea what was upstairs.

Plants were on each side of every massive, polished column. Two small Argentine flags were on each column too, and a larger version was in the window. I noted each pillar because they were tall and wide, good spots for bad news to hide. Every unknown face was suspicious, even the people who browsed hundreds of cakes and pastries like they were shopping at a mall. Mostly Porteñas and others from South America were here. Tea and cakes were Argentine fare, nearly every cake filled with *dulce de leche*. Nothing gluten-free. Nothing light.

The café was at least half-full. I took a step back, paused to see if anyone had tailed me. Then I stepped forward and noted stairs, hidden corners, the exit to the kitchen. I plotted escape routes, none pretty. I would have to get to the roof and parkour my way to a better position. The glass on the doors and windows was thick enough to take a few bullets without shattering. But if a bomb or rocket was sent this way on my behalf, all bets were off.

I'd just shown the Horsemen that a sniper didn't give a shit about thick glass.

I stayed near the door for a moment. Waiting. Hunting for the hunters.

In a rush, heart thumping, aching from the landing I had made in the middle of the avenue and getting sideswiped by a car, still feeling pain from the fight I had had with Medianoche in the *villas*, I took my hood off and moved by the massive confectionary, went toward the swank bar, saw a stairway going up, counted thirteen steps in the blink of an eye, then passed the solid, marble-topped tables. Café Las Violetas was historic and elegant, but I wasn't here for the aesthetics. All its beauty was a blur. I might as well have been inside of a McDonald's on US 62 in Seminole, Texas.

White-jacketed waiters moved from table to table and served food on silver platters, but they were all in my way, all suspects. If one looked at me too long, my trigger finger might get itchy and my gun might get a case of the hiccups. I took a breath, moved around the red chairs and polished columns. Looked back behind me for the third time in ten seconds, didn't see men and women in black suits or militia thugs in bulletproof clothing. No one came at me with a sledgehammer. I was in the celebrated location where the *abuelas* of Plaza de Mayo had clandestine meetings camouflaged as birthday celebrations so they could plot a way to save and reclaim as many of their thirty thousand kidnapped and missing grandchildren as possible. *The disappeared.* That was decades ago. Back then the coldhearted government would have disappeared radical grandmothers as well. And since I had made that elevator drop and disappear, I was sure what was left of the Horsemen was bent on finding me.

The phone I had in my pocket rang. I recognized the number from the local SIM card.

I said, "Which Horseman is this finally calling from the phone I left behind?"

A woman said, "For what you have done, you will die. And it will be an ugly death."

"American accent. A woman. Let me guess. Señorita Raven?"

"You're fucking dead, Gideon. You are a dead man. Just like your mother will be dead soon. Just like your two brothers will be dead soon. Just like Scamz, all of you will be dead."

"Keep away from your windows. And tell your crew to be careful riding elevators too."

"Motherfu—"

I ended the call. The phone I'd left was an Android smartphone. Not many phones in Buenos Aires used GPS, but the one I had left was capable. He was in the area.

The Horsemen were coming. I wasn't sure how they were organized, if they were moving as a group or hunting in pairs. At least six of them were here. I had no idea how many had been added to the roster. And I didn't know how many were hunting prey in the USA.

I didn't know how many had gone up there and found Shotgun. I didn't know how they had located him.

I called Catherine's phone.

Again no one answered.

The criminal I was to meet was already waiting at the table most remote from the entrance. He wore a Colombian suit, one made for South American winters, and his shoes were Italian. The best of the best. He sat alone at a table of food. Tenderloin steak with mushrooms, grilled chicken, hake, salmon with Roquefort cheese, and a three-colored vegetable purée.

He said, "I assume you are Gideon. You worked with my associate Scamz."

"Do it right. Or this might be your last supper."

He nodded. "Sam I am. Green eggs and ham."

"Thank you."

"I provided Scamz with assistance a few days ago."

"I was here. The weapons came from you."

He nodded, then said, "I put him in contact with a man leasing a yacht."

"Hope he had insurance."

He was nervous. "You should try the Martin Carrera salmon. It is served with shrimp, mushrooms, and bacon. You will fall in love with Buenos Aires, if you have not already done so."

"No, thanks."

"I ordered it all for you. Take a moment. Eat. If you prefer bacon and eggs or some other sort of American meal, I can arrange that as well. But you must try the Maria Cala Victoriano."

He motioned at a cake, sandwich, and pastry platter. It was a mountain. There was a pitcher of freshly squeezed orange juice and a variety of teas, plus coffee and hot chocolate.

"Not today. Just give me what I need so I can go."

He shifted, nervous. "So, you're the one they call Gideon."

"And you're the man they call Assad."

"Never heard of you before a few days ago."

"Likewise."

"Like the white-haired Aussie Assange, neither of us can stay in one country too long. I change phones twice a day and rarely use the same computer for over a week. Someone would love to find and assassinate or send a drone after both of us."

"For different reasons."

"Word on the street is you're supposed to be the best at what you do. Even if half of what I have heard about you is true, you should be a Horseman."

"If my old man had raised me, who knows what I might have been."

"Who is your father?"

"No one I'd want to go to the Palermo parks and play ultimate Frisbee with."

He nodded. "Please, sit for a moment. All of this food, surely you want a bite. All of this running and killing, you must be starved."

"Stop stalling. Stop chatting me up. Give me what was arranged to be picked up."

"This will be the last thing. People are assuming that I have assisted you since you arrived. That would hurt my standing. I don't want to risk my relationship in this community."

He reached under his table and eased out a box large enough for a suit and a coat.

He said, "From Miguel Caballero of Bogotá, Colombia. The Armani of bulletproof clothing. The clothing of presidents, dignitaries, Horsemen, and very important gangsters. Specially made for Gideon."

There was a large briefcase as well. I went to the bathroom and came back three minutes later dressed in a dark gray suit and overcoat. My hoodie and old clothes had been trashed. I no longer looked like a hooligan. The suit was flexible, made for running, made for fighting. But most of all, it made me look top-shelf. Now I could walk into any bank and get a loan. My trigger finger's allergies worsened.

The arms dealer my London contact had reluctantly used was a broker named Benjamin Assad. The old man stood and shook my hand. His palm was damp. He was stress sweating, more than I was. Then I realized. Before there was chatter. Now I heard nothing.

I pulled my gun and turned.

Everything was wrong.

There wasn't a waiter on the floor.

The customers who had been here were gone, had left in a hurry, their hot meals abandoned.

The place was empty, silent, except for me and the international arms dealer. Sweat dripped from his brow. His hand was unsteady.

I looked down at the table at his cellular. It was facedown. I flipped it over. It was on. Probably had been on the entire time.

Someone was listening to us, to me, and I knew then.

I picked the phone up and said, "Medianoche."

The listener hung up.

I slammed the phone in Assad's face.

He'd stayed behind to stall me. I'd arrived sooner than expected.

I said, "You're a dead man, Assad. You're two-faced like Pakistan. You can't take my money, aid me, then give intel to the other side. It doesn't fucking work that way."

He quavered, "If I didn't let the Four Horsemen know, then I would be a dead man. I am only doing as I was instructed by their leader. For me this situation is a Kobayashi Maru. It is a no-win for me. They are an assassination squad. I have men, well-trained men, but they all refused to guard me today. Russians. French. South Africans. Middle Easterners. Men from Uruguay. *Dozens of assassins refused.* You have time to get away. You can escape. I will have to do the same. Like others, I'll seek asylum in the Ecuadorian embassy. I will have no other choice."

"I don't give a damn about your problems. Tell me. Did my London contact cross me?"

"No, no, she didn't. She has no idea. London is out of her league. She's a nobody."

"The rifle was as ordered. The rest of the merchandise you sold me is bogus?"

He shivered again. "No, it's good. If you live, remember I gave you what you ordered."

"So did Pontius Pilate. He gave the people what they wanted."

"Please have some consideration. I am simply a man who gives people what they need. I am a salesman. I am only a salesman."

"The safe house in Villa Pueyrredón?"

"They are there waiting in case you make it that far."

I put my backpack on my left shoulder, took the briefcase in my left hand, kept my gun in my right hand. Assad moved, pulled his jacket back, and went for a gun he had in his holster. I shot him in the right shoulder and he let his weapon fall, then raised his left hand in defeat.

I said, "That was stupid."

"Yes, yes, it was. My desperation got the best of me."

"How much did they offer you?"

"To be able to run my arms from here, undisturbed, for the next six months."

"You won't collect a bounty, not one on my head."

"I am an important man. I can get you what you need. I can arrange another safe house. There is one they don't know about in the residential area of Caballito, near Parque Rivadavia. It's in a classy, understated barrio with tree-lined avenues, cobblestone streets, and beautiful parks."

"Do I look like I'm here to be a tourist?"

"It's safe." He spat out the address, then stressed, "I guarantee you won't be found there."

"The problem is you know about it."

"Trust me. You can trust me."

"Ain't no trust between us, Assad. And that's bad. You had a nice first impression going there, especially when you offered me food, because I am hungry, but you blew it."

I ejected the clip in my gun, dropped it in my pocket, then loaded it with another one from my backpack. Sweat dripped down the back of my neck, but Assad sweated more. I swapped nine-millimeter bullets for RIP ammo, the same ammunition I had used when I took out one of the Horsemen in the elevator. The infamous bullet banned by the Hague Convention was the devil.

Assad held his wounded shoulder, stumbled by a red chair, huffed and puffed and tried to hurry away. The international arms dealer tried to scurry toward the rear of the restaurant. I didn't know what was back there. He could have been running to open a door for other Horsemen. I hit him in the neck with an RIP. He didn't even scream. The bullet exploded inside his body, sent metal in nine directions at once, to every point on a compass. He stopped moving. His body stood where it was, swayed a bit. Blood dripped from the gash in his head. He didn't know he was dead. But his ruptured brain figured it out because he dropped to the beautiful marble floor.

He'd taken my money and double-crossed me with a handshake.

As soon as I turned, two people hurried through the crowd moving up and down the avenue and rushed toward the entrance. They rushed toward the same heavy glass doors I had used, the *entrada* on the side where more than a hundred sweets were located. I was across the room, twenty yards away, on the restaurant side. The marble columns were why they didn't see me from the outside. Horsemen were galloping my way dressed in their trademark suits and overcoats. This time it was a man and a woman. The man looked like Hercules. He was on a raw-meat-and-steroids diet. The tall, dark-skinned woman had an Afro and looked like Pam Grier.

I recognized both from their photographs. All the intel I had received from my London contact had been good. I had tried to do the rest without Konstantin, and it was going sideways.

In my heart I wanted to go toe to toe with Hercules. I wanted to fight him hand to hand, elbow to elbow, and knee to knee and beat him down into the center of Hades. I knew I could do it, but I didn't have time. This was about bullets, not fists. I would be a fool to bring fists to a gunfight. I didn't have time to use fishing line to set a trap. I would have to go old-school. I pulled out earplugs, rushed to get them in. The next stage of the war was about to erupt.

As soon as Hercules put his hand on the golden handle of the heavy glass door, I pulled the pin on an M67 fragmentation grenade and rolled it in his direction. I stood behind a marble column, used that for cover. He'd seen me move. He rushed inside, threw smoke and flash in my direction. He pulled an AR-15 from underneath his coat, started popping. He had come to party and he wanted to party hard. Then Hercules looked down, saw the grenade I'd tossed, knew he had less than four seconds, screamed to his Horseman, tried to retreat, but it was too late. She had been on his heels. She was in his way. He stumbled into her. The muscle-bound man hit her like a wall, knocked her back. The explosion rocked the front of the café. The energy rolled over me, felt like a tsunami of air. Pastries were destroyed, glass broke, wooden tables became splinters that could do just as much damage as glass. The sound left me temporarily deafened.

Smoke from his grenade filled the air and tainted my lungs.

Aching, I removed my earplugs, rushed, gathered my things, stumbled toward curved glass doors, their French stained-glass windows shattered. The Italian marble floors were damaged. A historical landmark had been desecrated. I stepped over the broken glass, fragments crunching under my military-style shoes, and saw that a few people on the street had been injured. A near-death experience was a terrifying thing. Denizens were traumatized, some more by the sight of the historic building being damaged than by the Horsemen suffering on the sidewalk.

Even before I stepped into the frigid air, what I had done sickened me. I had visited many, but it had never been like this. I was slaying the devil's men as if they had the value of a dragonfly, because their mission statement was to do the same to me. The day was as violent as a production at the Parisian playhouse Le Théâtre du Grand-Guignol. This horror wasn't entertaining; it sickened me. But to defeat a Horseman, you had to be as cruel as a Horseman.

Hercules decorated the sidewalk. He'd lost both of his hands, and his left leg would never be any good. He had a sucking chest wound. He was unrecognizable. If not for the suit, it would have been hard to tell he was human. He had caught the brunt of the explosion, and Foxy Brown had been a victim of its energy, had been blown twenty feet into a car. A horrified Porteña in the crowd said the *morena* was upside down when she hit the car, had bounced off the car and landed headfirst. She'd hyperextended her neck, slammed the back of her head, then landed face-first on the concrete. In the middle of what looked like a jacquerie, I thought she was dead. Then she moved. Her eyes flickered. She twitched, moved like the pain was registering and coming in waves that rivaled a tsunami. She was down, disoriented, but she knew she was in trouble. She was blinded by agony and trying desperately to crawl to her gun. She was back on the battlefield. She moved two inches, crawled in the wrong direction. As more Porteñas came to see what had happened, I went to the gun and picked it up, dropped it in my backpack.

All eyes were on her, not the gun. Many had never seen a *morena*, or seen an Afro.

A little girl went to Foxy Brown and touched her hair, then ran back to her mother.

Foxy Brown and Hercules wore identical suits; both wore paisley ties, green the dominant color. They looked like Gladys Knight and a Pip who would never Pip again.

I put two fingers to the side of Foxy Brown's head and said, "Bang. Bang. Bang."

She was one of a kind down here. She was the third one I'd almost hit with the sniper rifle. Next to us, her friend Hercules did the death rattle. Sounded like his insides did the Harlem Shake. He did his final inhale, then exhaled.

Foxy Brown wheezed, coughed, choked, called out in agony. Tears rivered from her eyes. Shrapnel was stuck in her hands. Her palms and fingers bled. Her bulletproof topcoat had been almost blown off of her. Her suit coat had been blown open too. It revealed her plum-colored bra and her gun holster. I adjusted her blouse, closed her jacket, made her decent. Then I made sure she didn't have another gun before I took in the small crowd. If I'd been in the United States, everyone would have been recording, but people just looked and gasped. Some turned away from the horror. Someone thought there was a gas leak and told everyone to move back. Not everyone had seen the guns on the pavement.

I said, "This is what happens when you find Gideon."

Eyes closed tight, tears of pain falling, she spat out blood, cursed a dozen times, moved like she wanted to get up and become a Horseman again, made an ugly expression inspired by acute pain, then surrendered to her condition, panted like she was in the final seconds of labor, then replied, "Ears . . . hurting . . . ringing. Pulled a groin muscle. Oh God. My neck. Blew out my left shoulder."

Her nose was broken. Mouth bloodied. Front teeth broken. Afro damp with winter rain. She made a hundred sounds, like she was livid because pain was hitting her on many levels, agony a constantly changing pattern that put the hues of a kaleidoscope in her head.

Angry and frightened she whispered, "We fucked up."

"Big-time."

"We thought Assad had you. We fucked up and rushed in."

"You are consumed with assassinating me."

"We fucked up. But we are not done. We are not done."

I rubbed my face, sweat greasy and thick like blood, then squeezed her damaged fingers as tightly as I could, added to the kaleidoscope that had her begging. "How many Horsemen are coming for me?"

She kicked and yelled, slobbered and squirmed in the soft leather seat, then when I let her hand go, made a stream of whimpering sounds.

As my heart pounded, as stress poured from my pores, as my trigger finger kept hiccupping, I said, "How many are in your military convoy?"

In a rough voice she said, "Three."

"Including Medianoche?"

"Yes."

"How many vehicles?"

"I need medical attention."

"Get in line. How many are coming after me right now?"

She didn't answer. I held her fingers again, applied pressure.

Her pain ballooned. Again she screamed.

I asked, "How many?"

The pain made her leg tremble like she was delirious. "Two. One car. One motorcycle."

"Where is the Beast?"

"I feel blood coming out of my ear."

"Where is the Beast?"

"He's dead."

"Was he on the elevator? Was that who was with you?"

"No, no, no. He was KIA before I came. By the Scamz Organization."

"Scamz *Organization*? That British bastard wasn't *organized*."

"That's all I know."

"I'm glad the Beast is dead. One less for me to have to fight and put in the ground. And thanks for handling Scamz. Sooner or later I would have found him and done the same."

"Help me."

"Call the Red Cross. Or Africa Vive. I think that's Argentina's version of the NAACP."

"I'm hurting all over. I'm dying."

"Don't worry. The pain will stop when you're dead. I died once. I got over it."

I patted her down, removed a cellular and a black credit card. She had keys to a Mercedes. Cars had stopped; traffic was at a standstill. I looked at the window and door that had been destroyed, at the dozen people who were bloodied and wounded. It had been unavoidable.

I backed away, called the last number dialed on her phone.

Señorita Raven answered on the first ring. "You have him?"

"No, they don't. One is with Assad, the other is on her way to the same hell."

She said, "We know where she is. Thelma is Catherine. Her sons are Robert and Sven."

Then I hung up and took two more steps in retreat, then turned around. I stepped over Hercules and went back to Foxy Brown. In *castellano* I told the crowd she was my girlfriend, that she was from South Africa, a diplomat, and the embassy wanted me to take her to Hospital Alemán.

Hearing every tick of every clock created by man, I asked the Horseman, "Where is your goddamn car?"

She tried to motion toward the intersection of Avenida Medrano and Avenida Rivadavia. Sirens came this way. Sounded like alarms were coming from all directions. I carried Foxy Brown into a drizzle of rain and snow. Dim skies covered us. I transported her, my backpack, a briefcase, and more malice than any man should ever have tainting his soul. I became a man who was carrying his wounded lover to get medical attention. I dropped her in the passenger seat of the bulletproof sedan and sped away, took Avenida Rivadavia, my eyes on the rearview.

I had gone back to her for a reason.

I needed information. I needed the truth. Her life for the truth.

Heart beating like it wanted to escape my chest, I yelled, "Wake up."

"My head hurts." Her words slurred like she was drunk. "I can't stay awake."

"Wake up. Don't go to sleep."

She leaned forward, regurgitated on the floor mat.

Soon I raced down the widest avenue in the world, Avenida 9 de Julio. It was as if New York's Times Square and Paris's avenue des Champs-Élysées had an overweight baby and raised it on fast food and sugary drinks. The network of traffic was consistent and extensive but was made worse because plate-banging protesters had taken over other thoroughfares, had blocked traffic to protest Brazil, to protest a paper plant in Uruguay, were marching for the right to have abortions. There were many ways to go, plenty of places to hide and regroup, and I imagined them all. El Caminito. Plaza de Mayo. Plaza Dorrego. Teatro Colón. Museo Casa Carlos Gardel. Café San Juan. Museo Benito Quinquela Martín. Centro Cultural Kirchner. Jardín Zoológico. Risking being set up, I stuck to Avenida 9 de Julio. The streets were choked with garbage waiting on *cartoneros* while tourists took photos of a large painting of Eva Perón at a microphone. Argentina was filled with images: Carlos Gardel, Ernesto Che Guevara, María Eva Duarte de Perón, writer Jorge Luis Borges, and the cartoon character Malfalda. Crowds were by Teatro Colón, the Obelisk, and Plaza de la República. People walked fast, some had a gait faster than joggers. I was in the epicenter of Buenos Aires, with restaurants, hotels, and hole-in-the-wall shops all around. Armed police were near the Obelisk-watching tourists taking pictures. Criminals were out there too. The congested and polluted avenue was populated with pickpockets mixed in with homeless adults and children, all with hands out begging for pesos.

I was caught at a light, stuck in the vehicle-exhaust pollution. The moment I stopped, three guitar players came to the window and serenaded. There was a fire juggler and a guy inside a Hula-Hoop who rolled around in front of the stopped cars. When the light changed it was like the Grand Prix out of the gate. I zoomed with the madness of the city again.

I barked at Foxy Brown. "Wake up. Wake up. We have some talking to do."

She groaned. "I'm hurting. Feels like every part of my body is broken. I need help."

"You'll hurt worse if I open that car door and push you out in traffic."

She made a sound like death was dancing in her lungs.

"How many Horsemen are left in Atlanta?"

She treaded in pain, tried not to drown in her agony. "We lost three, but one is left. And the one left is the meanest soldier I've ever met."

I asked, "Do you know where Thelma is?"

"Outside of Atlanta. In Smyrna."

"Smyrna. She's in Smyrna?"

"We found her. Medianoche put an order out on her an hour ago."

"What's the order? *Wake up.* What's the order? Talk to me or get dropped."

"Black out. Whoever is in the house, whoever is with her . . . shit . . . I'm hurting."

My world turned bloodred. I said, "Thanks for telling me what I needed to know."

I pulled out my gun, aimed it at her head, itchy finger on the trigger, RIP bullet eager.

As she begged me to not pop her, as she begged me to not do to her what she and the Four Horsemen of the Apocalypse itched to do to me, a BMW motorcycle pulled up next to the car, same type of motorcycle that had tried to trap and kill the Scamz Organization days ago. The Horseman who rocked it looked at me, saw that Foxy Brown wasn't behind the wheel, saw her half-dead in the passenger seat, beaten down and bloodied like a POW. She groaned like she was being held hostage in the jungle west of Da Nang, South Vietnam's second-largest city.

That wasn't what he'd expected to see. As we moved like NASCAR in sixteen lanes of madness, the element of surprise was on my side. To defeat a Horseman, I had to be as cruel as one. Without hesitation I cut hard, rammed the BMW, hit him hard enough to make both of us lose control. I regained control, but the surprised *sicario* dropped and skidded on the damp avenue, then vanished underneath a speeding eighteen-wheel SUPERMERCADO JUMBO truck. The motorcycle was trampled by eighty thousand pounds; I saw that in my rearview. It happened quick. It was already over before the eighteen-wheeler slammed on its brakes. Wasn't easy to stop forty tons from moving. Some traffic stopped behind me. But many just swerved and moved around the accident, kept going like they had better things to do. While I sped with traffic, Foxy Brown groaned a dozen more times, struggled to breathe, suffered. Given the chance, she would have done the same to me, then gone to eat an empanada. Suddenly she went limp, like she had lost consciousness. Her chest expanded and contracted. She was breathing.

The windshield wiper glided back and forth as I snapped, "Wake up."

"Okay. Okay. Okay."

"Did Medianoche tell you who I am?"

"You're our enemy. You're a terrorist. You're our Taliban. You're the bad guy."

She gagged, threw up again. She made a mess, then sat back, eyes closed.

She was losing consciousness.

I yelled, "Wake up. We're not done talking. *Wake up, wake up, wake up.*"

I was so busy watching traffic and checking my rearview that I didn't see the knife.

Foxy Brown growled and attacked me. She attacked me with her eyes closed, had a blade in her bloodied hand. It must've been in a stash spot under the seat. Sneaky bitch had a combat knife, a five-inch. She stabbed me in my right shoulder. She had been trying to stick me in my neck. The strike was weak, but the blade was razor sharp. Then she tried to get the strength to stab me again. I squeezed her wounded leg, and her pain brought sense back to her head.

The blade dropped on her lap. I took it from her. Was tempted to push her out.

She mumbled, "You're my enemy."

I touched my shoulder where it ached. There was no blood. The Colombian suit I had gotten from Assad was legit. Too bad he wasn't. I looked over at Foxy Brown, ready to watch her bounce along the dirty streets. Her clothes had loosened. When she had attacked me, her left breast had tumbled free from her colorful bra. Dark nipple and dark areola. I reached over and hoicked up her jacket, closed it the best I could. She stopped groaning. I didn't have time to see if she was still breathing. Didn't care. If you pulled a thorn out of a lion's foot, it would still eat you alive.

Medianoche and Señorita Raven could track me. This car had GPS, and that was how the *sicario* on the motorcycle had found the car. He might've had time to tell them I had the car and had captured a Horseman. They knew where I was. That meant the family reunion would happen sooner than I had hoped. I drove for thirteen miles, went from downtown Buenos Aires to Greater Buenos Aires. Snow was on the ground. I was in a calmer, quiet suburban town named Ciudad Evita. I eased down Avenida José Mario Bevilacqua; soon I crept down España, did the same on El Yaguar. No Horsemen appeared. I eased by run-down apartment buildings in the working-class town. There were one-story brick homes. Parks. Woods. Sports center. Car wash. Bookstore. Passed garbage on the side of the roads in one section, then cleanliness and monuments of Evita and her husband, Perón, in another. The city was built for the workingman and when viewed from the sky was shaped like Evita's profile. Her name and image were everywhere, same as Elvis Presley's image and name dominated Elvis Presley Boulevard in Memphis, Tennessee. A welcome sign said Ciudad Evita was a National Historic Monument of Argentina. What stood out the most was a gigantic picture of Evita's face covered in a gas mask coupled with a sign that said TO BURY RUBBISH IS TO BURY OUR FUTURE. They wanted to use the sleepy town located away from the heart of Buenos Aires as a landfill. But no one was marching or protesting today. That meant today Ciudad Evita was a good place to bury a body. A damn good place.

I was four miles from Ezeiza International Airport. An escape plane waited for me. The cheeky arms dealer in London had arranged a Cessna 172 and enough fuel to get me almost 740 miles from here. Assad knew nothing about that, so that setup was still safe. If needed, a safe house had been arranged, and it was located on La Palometa.

I couldn't take this Mercedes there, or be seen carrying Foxy Brown to the door. She might be the only Afro-wearing *morena* between here and the underappreciated side of Brazil.

I stopped driving near the Buenos Aires Argentina Temple of the Church of Jesus Christ of Latter-Day Saints and eased out of the bulletproof car. Foxy Brown was either sleeping, in a coma, or dead. Gun aimed at her, I looked in the glove compartment. A red necktie was inside. I pocketed it. Cars passed by. People walked by. When the streets were clear enough, I checked under Foxy Brown's seat. A .380 loaded with hollow points was holstered there. Nice stash spot. I thought she had been trying to get to the gun but couldn't bend and grabbed the handle of the blade first. I went back to the driver's seat. Reached down. A Glock had been under my butt the entire time. I used the remote, opened the trunk, looked to see what other goodies were stored inside. It was a merc's treasure chest. A bloody war chest. Like before, they had come to battle. They had equipment that looked like it was made for fighting Blackwater.

I wanted to call Konstantin. I wanted to call Hawks. I wanted to call the Bajan. There would be nothing any of them could do. Not even the Queen Bee across the river could help.

My trigger finger had the hiccups. Wanted to finish this job. Head throbbed.

I couldn't blame Scamz. Was pointless blaming a dead man. I looked to the sky. I couldn't blame Arizona. She had always been my Achilles' heel. I had a million reasons to dislike her. She had come back into my life and reminded me of a debt, but I could have refused that job.

Hawks had been right. This was my shit. I owned it. This was started by my mother when I was a child. I had no idea what had happened before I walked in the room and saw Mr. Midnight strangling my mother. Again I was that child, gun in my hand, shooting evil in its head. I lived in his evil. This was the evil between her and Mr. Midnight brought back to life.

If I had stayed in Puerto Rico with Hawks, none of this would have manifested. I could have still been there with her, dancing, shopping, eating at Perla, the Atlantic Ocean roaring outside our window, sleeping naked. And each time I became distracted, Hawks would get on the bed, aroused, and make a come-here motion with one finger; then we'd act like rabbits in heat.

Or maybe I should have gone with her to do a job on the shores of Lake Chargoggagoggmanchauggagoggchaubunagungamaugg. It was impossible to change the unchangeable. Before we had left Puerto Rico it was too late. The last time we had sex, after I told her about Arizona and Scamz, was good-bye sex for her. She was an angry pit bull, lion, tiger, bear, and badger rolled into one big flaming ball of disappointment.

Maybe I never should have left Angelina at the End of the World.

I never would have let her down, and I never would have done the same with Hawks.

And I never would have resurrected Midnight.

I had woken the devil. I had kicked the dirt off his grave. I took full responsibility. Konstantin was in bad shape, worse than he'd admit, and I'd dragged him into this. And Shotgun was dead. This was my fault.

I called Catherine. Straight to voice mail. Voice mail was full.

I thought about Andrew-Sven and Robert.

I thought about my brothers with fear clawing at my chest.

Robert was as dark as the night, had strong legs, with roots in Africa, but had grown up in Europe. Before living in the red-light district on Berwick Street in London, he had witnessed the horrors in the darkest parts of his Fatherland. He had been in an area occupied by non-Arab Darfurians, had witnessed the armed Janjaweed, had seen them rape and murder. He'd seen his mother raped. He never talked about that, not to me, but I could only imagine what that does to the soul of a child.

Andrew-Sven was my brother by blood, his father unknown. He had blond hair and a strong build, his accent German. Steven was what we called him, so he could fit into the USA. But his accent told everyone he was from another land. He had had a hard life. Like me he had been dragged from brothel to brothel when my mother was on the run.

He had killed a man. Like me, he had killed to protect his mother.

My brother had tried to kill me once upon a time, before he knew I had been born from the same womb as him, again to protect his mother.

And my mother, the woman I'd grown up with and knew as Thelma, the woman who had become Catherine, the woman who only days ago had told me that once upon a time in Yerres, France, her name was Nathalie Marie Masreliez—I have no idea what happened there to put her on the run for most of her life. Her scars didn't show, and her smile hid her darkness, but she was damaged.

I remembered Hawks had told me there were two with the name Nathalie Marie Masreliez.

Maybe that was who she had been when she gave birth to me in a small, filthy hostel.

I was scratching scabs, opening old wounds.

I thought I had fixed it all. I thought I had given everyone a better life.

I was just trying to have some form of a fucking family.

I no longer had Shotgun to call to go handle my messy life.

With the dark history of America echoing in his every word, Shotgun had told me and my brothers, "A man has to learn to stand his ground, or get buried in the ground he's standing on. Government keep talking about terrorists overseas; I'm more worried about the rednecks in my backyard than bin Laden. Terrorism ain't nothing new to the black man. Not at all."

I knew he had stood his ground. Three Horsemen regretted crossing paths with him.

Seemed like it was just yesterday that Shotgun and I had taken the boys out to Woodstock. We had erected targets, fired off many rounds, our version of male bonding.

Like Evita Perón's profile, I looked toward the airport. If the Four Horsemen were following this car, they knew I was miles away and could escape in ten minutes. They also knew I couldn't make it to Atlanta in time to save Catherine and my brothers. I was more than five thousand miles from them.

I knew twenty-two ways to end a life. I just didn't know how to save three.

That was when I saw that I'd been found. A Mercedes that was the fraternal twin of the one I was in arrived in the area, came from Autopista Ricchieri y Puente, then entered the street I was on, heading toward El Cisne. It came speeding, was being driven hard. It saw me and braked. I was waiting for them. I had pulled a rocket launcher from the trunk. It was a portable, shoulder-fired missile, the kind that didn't have a recoil problem because the exhaust kicked out the opposite end of the launch tube. They had one that spat out grenades too. This had more bang. The Four Horsemen had come after us with these, and much more.

I was parked on the edges of Barrio Democracia, had turned off Colectora Autopista Teniente General Ricchieri on the side of the poor-man's housing facing a *fútbol* field.

I didn't know who was in that car. Didn't know how many. Didn't have a fuck to give.

I looked toward the barrios, only a quick glance. With that glance I saw faces in windows. Too many innocent people were nearby. I was a block away.

I threw the launcher in the backseat. I wouldn't murder innocents to get revenge.

I got back in the car and put the modified Mercedes in reverse. I wasn't trying to escape. I hadn't come this far to run. There was no mission, no funds would be transferred. This was revenge. Shotgun had died for me. And today I wasn't afraid to die for him.

I backed the Mercedes up thirty yards, looked at Foxy Brown, then put the luxury car in neutral. I revved the engine, made it curse and threaten my adversary. The other car did the same. The Horsemen made their weapon scream.

I pushed the button for the CD player.

A Frank Sinatra song came up.

I turned it up loud.

Ol' Blue Eyes sang that he did it his way, and I floored it, pressed the accelerator through the floor, charged toward the Horsemen, made the AMG move from zero to sixty in four seconds. They did the same and headed toward me. We played chicken in bulletproof cars. No one swerved. I moved in a straight line down the middle of the slick road. They did too.

Within seconds I was doing over eighty and moving toward the century mark. They didn't back down. The Horsemen never backed down. They galloped harder. They were American-made mercs gone bad. Americans never gave up. Never surrendered. In the middle of the block, as snow touched the ground, in the shadows of a church, two luxury chariots crashed.

Chapter 24

Finding Catherine

It had sounded like the Four Horsemen were under attack when she was on the phone with Medianoche. Whatever had happened, all Medianoche had said was to finish the Atlanta job.

"And don't fuck it up, Preacher. Do not fuck up the job. No blowback."

"Who else should I be concerned with?"

"Gideon is here. The Landscaper is dead. The Russian is unaccounted for."

"I'm not afraid of a Russian. I'd spit in Putin's face."

"Watch your six."

"'The Lord is my strength and my shield. My heart trusts in Him, and I am helped.'"

Parked, Preacher saw Catherine when she closed the plantation shutters. The trilevel condo units were in quads, and the one she was hiding in was the second from the left. It had windows in only the front and back. The back was the smaller bedroom. The larger bedroom faced the streets. Catherine had closed those plantation shutters five minutes prior.

Preacher had taken many photos of Catherine. Very lovely woman. There was something very elegant about her. Something magical. Reminded Preacher of the lover she had when she was stationed in Iraq. They had been at Alwat al Fasil Saiba, a few clicks from Basra International Airport. Too much drinking, off duty but still in uniform, and somehow she had ended up in an army tent with her lover, engaged in some game of truth or dare, a game that had them first kissing, then touching, then feeling each other's breasts while their male counterparts drank beer and cheered. In her mind it hadn't been any worse than what had gone on in college in the fraternity houses on Friday nights. Only a thirty-second video had been secretly made, and that had heralded the end of her military career.

"Your bad judgment is on the *Internet.* You are a disgrace to your country."

"The soldier who put Ecstasy in our beers and recorded the incident, the man who uploaded my personal moment for the world to see, will he be demoted and jailed? The circle jerk that was going on, will they all be reprimanded? Or will the men who stood and beat their meat and cheered go unpunished? They had their dicks out, and all you saw was my breasts. I didn't show my private parts. The men masturbated."

"That is not your concern."

"No disrespect, but this is my career, so it is my concern, sir. I've done three tours of duty. I have earned three promotions in six years."

"Now you are busted down in rank. Don't blame others. This is your doing. You've lost your rank and your money. Same for your pussy-eating partner. Don't open your mouth and make it worse."

But she did. She said she had done her job while others had died screaming for their mothers. Then she rattled off the names of two dozen enlisted men who were on the down-low. She ratted out a commander who had raped a nineteen-year-old soldier on the battlefield.

Her superior replied, "I didn't ask, so I'll pretend you didn't tell. And so will you. Things happen in war. Things happen to all of us."

"A soldier was raped in an active war zone by a man he was expected to go into battle with, and you want me to shut my mouth."

"And you will. Unless you are in love with solitary confinement."

"If I can't be myself, sir, then I am already in solitary confinement."

Being deployed was called TDY, and for some that also meant "temporarily divorced for a year." Many had a bed buddy, practiced endogamy until deployment ended. Even her superior slept with a military prostitute once a week. One hundred dollars for fifteen minutes. Everyone knew the game. Many married soldiers had safe partners. Men shared women. Some struggling soldiers were prostituting to buy food and diapers. A soldier from Brooklyn pleased four fellow military higher-ups while her husband watched and photographed. Superiors were cool with gangbanging or letting men fuck their wives while they watched and sipped beer.

But Preacher's romp with her lover was a crime to hang for.

She told her superior she was being judged by a country that had secret laws, secret courts, secret surveillance, secret prisons, secret killings. There had been airstrikes on journalists who had been mistaken for terrorists, long-lensed cameras mistaken for weapons, civilians and children killed, and no one reprimanded, only laughter. She stood up, said she was as proud to be a motherfucking *motherfucking* lesbian as she was to be an American, and *motherfucking* was used in the literal sense. Her lover had a child. She said she was lesbian and American and she would fight for both rights. She didn't regret what she had done, only regretted being betrayed and videotaped by a fellow soldier as if she were the enemy of the year. She was thrown in the brig, kept in solitary confinement for nine months, stuck in an eight-by-eight-foot cage in the Middle East. She was treated like she was in Nigeria, one of the most homophobic countries in the world, and given the Guantánamo treatment. Sleep deprivation, no blanket, bright lights at night. The only clothes she had to sleep in were a bra and thin boxers. Insult to injury, she had her rank reduced and was given a DD. There were no benefits waiting for her when it was all over. Not even enough coverage to go check on the irritable bowels she'd developed from the stress. She had served her country, was kicked out, treated like a traitor, and left on her own. And the lover had wanted nothing to do with her. Her old lover had a husband now, was married with two kids, another on the way.

Her lover betrayed her too. Blamed her. That heartbreak would never end.

She wanted to contact Rakisha Jones in Galveston, Texas. She wanted to tell Rakisha Jones that Joanne Baudry des Lozières still loved her. Wanted her back. Always would.

Preacher clacked her teeth together, wiped her eyes, then focused on Catherine's townhome. Whatever had been good in her, it had been sullied, destroyed, then taken away. So many revenge fantasies played in her mind. She had found an occupation in which she could act them all out.

She'd adapt to Argentina, meet a sexy Porteña, and learn to tango. Buenos Aires was one of Latin America's gay capitals. She'd done her research. She knew where the lesbian bars were located. Fiesta Plop, Pride Café, Casa Brandon, Verne Club, Flux, Peuteo, Rheo, Florería Atlántico, Doppelgänger. She knew about Bosques de Palermo. During the day it was a family-friendly park. Small lakes and paddleboats, pretty gazebos, stands renting bikes, and in-line skates. At night Sodom and Gomorra came to life and it became *zona roja travestis.*

Her Colombian jacket rested on the passenger seat. Feeling warm, she rolled her white sleeves up to her elbows. She adjusted her detachable clerical collar, shook off the six-year-old recurring nightmare of being booted from the military. She was twenty-nine now. Almost thirty. She was older. Wiser. But just as angry now as she had been then. When military life was over, she had become a gun for hire. She had done small jobs. And now she was a Horseman. She had taken care of the Landscaper, and now she had to handle a woman named Catherine. She looked at the images she had taken. Catherine was intriguing, a very pretty woman. Older, but looked much younger, and gorgeous. Preacher's weakness. Too bad Catherine had to be put down.

Preacher took out the dashboard camera that had been in the SUV when they followed the Landscaper. She played the recording from the moment they chased the Landscaper until they had caught him on that wide road near Mableton. She reviewed the shootout to see what had gone wrong. They had underestimated the Landscaper. He had been as quick as lightning.

An older, potbellied, bear-size wannabe hipster appeared on the walkway between the target's unit and the townhomes to the left. That caused alarm. He wore mauve shorts, a sepia tank top, and teal low-rise boots. Not exactly a trendsetter. The forty-something hipster was walking his little yapping dog. The hipster saw her car parked illegally, then looked irritated. He tugged at his long, stylish beard, went into Neighborhood Watch mode, and dragged his dog toward her. Preacher pulled her gun to her lap, the trigger aimed toward the stranger. Hit men came in all shapes, sizes, and wardrobes. He stared at her like he was ready to dial 911, until he saw she was of European heritage, saw her clerical collar, saw the Bible on the dashboard. White, blond, and Christian. Trifecta. The man's shoulders relaxed and he smiled, waved, and kept going. Now he looked shy. Like he wished he had the nerve to talk to a pretty woman. Probably was a porn-watching masturbator out peeping in neighbors' windows.

She watched him. Gun still aimed in his direction. He waited for his tyke to take a dump, then picked up the dog shit with plastic bags. She had always found that disgusting.

Maybe that was why that would never happen in Buenos Aires.

It was almost nightfall. Shadows elongated, but the heat remained powerful, over ninety degrees. The pavement was an oven, emanated additional heat. The humidity was suffocating.

Catherine wasn't coming out. Preacher would have to go inside.

There was a back door to each unit. Units on either side of Catherine's hideout had small decks, and those tenants sat out on their decks in the evenings. The decks were shaded by the sunrooms that jutted out above them. The rear door led to a bedroom that had been converted to an office space. From there thirteen carpeted stairs led to the main level, which had the entry, a small kitchen, a formal dining area, a living area with a fireplace, and a sunroom. Thirteen more carpeted stairs would take her to the third level. Two bedrooms were up there, on opposite ends.

Preacher would give it two more hours. Until it was dark enough. She would give the beer-drinking family on the deck time to be irritated by mosquitoes so they would go inside. If they didn't, while air conditioners hummed, Preacher's Plan B was to eliminate the family in the back, give them all brain-stem shots. Thirty seconds after that she would enter the back door where Catherine was hiding from the world, from the Horsemen, and she would take care of all who were in the townhome, giving them all brain-stem shots as well. Then Preacher would leave out the front door, walk out carrying a Bible, and get in her car and drive away.

Even if she walked out with a gun in her hand, no one would call the cops.

Blond, white, Christian.

A moment later the garage door to where Catherine was sequestered opened.

Preacher smiled like a prayer had been answered.

She whispered, "'If you have faith and do not doubt, you can say to this mountain, "Go, throw yourself into the sea," and it will be done.'"

Catherine's car was already started. She backed out. Her boyfriend wasn't with her. Only her sons. Catherine went around the roundabout in front of her unit, never looked toward Preacher's parked car as she headed up the mild incline. The car was loaded. It looked like she had packed up all her things and was once again on the run. She turned left, then hurried toward the exit for the condo units. Preacher followed, stayed back. No other cars were on the narrow road in the private community. The Park at Oakley Downs was a sixty-four-unit townhome neighborhood located off of Campbell Road between Atlanta Road and Spring Road in Smyrna.

When she made the left to follow Catherine down Campbell Road, she was stalled when people jogged in front of her car. Joggers went both in the direction of the Farmers Market at Spring Road and in the opposite direction through the tree-lined neighborhood that led to Atlanta Road. Preacher kept Catherine in sight. She made an easy left and followed, stayed close but not too close. She didn't want to spook her target. She didn't want to drive like she was anxious.

Two more cars passed going in that direction. That was good. She had a buffer.

Catherine wouldn't escape. Her fate was sealed. This was a wrap.

Preacher would make sure this was Catherine's last drive.

Medianoche wanted Catherine's eyes as proof of death. He wanted only her left eye but would take both of her eyes. God had made a way. No one to mess it up this time. Then Preacher would fly back to Argentina. She would make herself a top-notch Horseman.

Catherine was stopped at the red light, then made a right on Spring Road.

Preacher did the same, headed toward Cumberland Boulevard.

This time tomorrow, this job would be done, and she would be flying first class.

She would leave the country that had betrayed her, middle fingers high in the air.

She wasn't afraid. As long as God was on her side, she feared nothing.

Gun in lap, suppressor on, Preacher recited, "'Through You we will push back our adversaries. Through Your name we will trample down those who rise up against us.'"

She smiled, then chuckled.

That was the Bible verse she had recited two years ago, when she was in Maryland, the night she had broken into her ex-commander's home and gunned him down in his sleep.

Don't ask. Don't tell.

Rot in hell.

Rot in hell.

Chapter 25

Chattahoochee River

Preacher followed Catherine and her ebony and ivory sons through Smyrna, Georgia. They drove up Cobb Parkway, then turned around at the Big Chicken, headed back down US 41 until they were at Akers Mills, then turned left at the Barnes and Noble, took that street until it dead-ended, made a left followed by another right. Preacher thought they were going to one of the apartment complexes south of I-285. The complexes were as large as cities and sat on the Chattahoochee River. Catherine slowed, turned on her signal to turn right, paused. That pause forced Preacher to slow down. Then Catherine kept driving, her driving no longer smooth. She accelerated. Preacher realized she had been made. Catherine had sped up; then she turned left and went under the overpass, took the two-lane road north of Atlanta's I-285 perimeter highway.

Preacher knew Catherine was trying to lose her. That was impossible.

Then Catherine turned through a gate into an area where there was a park. A jogging trail that had closed. She was trapped, unable to turn around; then she accelerated, went deeper into the empty un- paved parking lot. As soon as the car stopped, Catherine's door opened; so did her boys' doors. They abandoned their car and ran toward grassland and marsh. They left the car open, engine running, and they ran. Preacher took her weapon, left her car in the same state, and chased. Preacher almost smiled. Underneath dark skies spotted with stars, in the heat of the summer night, surrounded by so many trees it was as if she was trapped in Sherwood Forest. She saw Cath- erine and her two boys up ahead, running together, fleeing.

Preacher took a shot, but they took to the woods, vanished. The forty-something Frenchwoman moved faster than a twenty-year- old; fear either froze people or made them move faster.

Preacher sprinted, sweated. Catherine and her sons dashed into the uneven terrain and topography of wetlands, riverbanks, grasslands, and forest. They ran for their lives, sprinted with so much fear in their hearts. They were being hunted. Preacher would make sure they never made it out of this section of the Chattahoochee River trails. They would never make it back to the car; they would never get to escape on I-285. Preacher was in top form, was a hunter and able to run incredibly fast. But running in a suit while carrying a weapon and being cautious slowed her down. She made it to an open area, saw Catherine and her boys just on the other side of the clear- ing, running into more bush, toward more trees, and Preacher raced as hard as she could.

Halfway through the clearing she fired more shots in the direc- tion they had gone.

There was a whistling in the air and then her legs tangled below the knees. She went down in the dirt hard, fell on her hand, twisted her right wrist. She dropped her gun. Dust rose. Bolas had been thrown, trapped her ankles, and took her down mid-run. Someone was rushing up from her six. She hadn't watched her six. Someone came from the forest. She looked up and saw a tall black man. Mus- cular. Handsome. Green eyes. Dressed in jeans and a T-shirt with the word ICHIROUGANAIM across his chest. His arms were the best guns she'd seen in a while. He held a bow and arrow, the arrow aimed at Preacher. Catherine and her boys took refuge behind the muscular man, the boys at each side of him, like they were his sidekicks, or his adopted sons. The boys were sweaty, and both held guns. Preacher saw that each had a nine millimeter and held it with the business end pointed at her. They knew how to hold a gun, so they knew how to use a gun, common for boys in NRA country. She wasn't worried about the firearms. Her suit would laugh at those. The impact would hurt like hell, but they wouldn't penetrate the Kevlar. But the arrow aimed at her gave her pause. The muscular black man stood at point-blank range and held it like a professional. He looked like an incensed, handsome, powerful Moor. A true warrior. He had a sidearm in the waistband of his Levi's. The arrow told her he knew the limitations of her custom-made uniform. Preacher looked back and saw who had thrown the bolas, then hit her with the Taser. Boots crunched dirt and gravel, eased up on her, and kicked her gun away. The darker boy hurried over and picked it up, then ran back to his position, as if this had been planned. He handed the .22 to Catherine, kept the nine millimeter.

Someone walked up behind her and carefully said, "I guess you're one of the Horsemen everybody keeps talking about."

Preacher looked up into the pretty eyes of a twenty-something woman with hair as long as the mane worn by the country-western singer Crystal Gayle in the seventies. The perspiring woman wore an Elvis Presley T-shirt, dungarees, and dusty cowboy boots. A crowbar was in her left hand. A nine millimeter in her right. Her expression said she was trying to determine which weapon to use next.

She said, "I don't know who you are, but my name is Hawks. We're in the same business. We work different ways, and you work on a higher level, probably make more money, but it's still the same business. The handsome fellow is called the Bajan. He said his children call him Old Man Reaper, but most just call him the Bajan. I call him my friend. We're good friends. Those other people, the ones you were chasing, I guess you know that's Catherine, Robert, and Steven. That woman and those two little boys are kin to someone near and dear to my heart."

Preacher nodded. "Well played."

"Well is the only way I play. You parked in the complex and watched them, and the whole time I was watching you. They led you and I was behind you. I had to make sure you didn't have backup. I know at least four of you were here. Didn't know if there were more."

"This matter doesn't concern you. Walk away and live."

"I know you don't think I'm going to let you put a finger on that Frenchwoman and her children."

Preacher said, "'None but the righteous. But the fearful, and unbelieving, and the abominable, and murderers, and whoremongers, and sorcerers, and idolaters, and all liars, shall have their part in the lake which burneth with fire and brimstone, which is the second death.'"

"Is that right? And which one of them that *burneth* do you suppose you are?"

In a mixture of ferocity and pain Preacher said, "Bitch, I could kill you with my bare hands."

Hawks frowned. "I don't like being called out of my name."

"The valiant only die once. Or is a bitch like you only good at attacking from the rear? Bitch, I eat pretty girls like you for breakfast."

"Bring it."

"Your black friend?"

"Ain't in it. This is between me and you."

"Bitch, you don't have the nerve."

"I really hate being called out of my name. My pet peeve."

Hawks tossed the crowbar to the side, tossed her gun to the Bajan, then backed away, let Preacher remove the bolas from her legs and stand. Preacher charged, threw hard blows, tried to fight the long-haired woman. She took a swing, swung over and over, but Hawks toyed with her, hit Preacher again and again, hit her with elbows, struck her eyes, her nose. Preacher was good, skilled in hand-to-hand combat, had beaten many men, but Hawks fought like an MMA champion, like she had been trained in Krav Maga by the Israelis, that training mixed with Russian street fighting. She was as deadly as she was pretty. Preacher went down, smiled, gritted her teeth, tried to get to her feet, but a blow to the side of her head sent her down into the dirt. Blood drained, turned her yellow hair red. Then she was kicked by Hawks. Kicked over and over. The pain. The agony. Preacher tried to crawl away from Hawks, but Hawks walked around, cut her off, and stood in front of her.

Hawks wiped sweat from her brow, adjusted her hair, then looked at Catherine and her boys. "Sorry for acting a fool in front of y'all. But this is the one who killed Shotgun. Shotgun got three of them, but this is the heifer who gunned him down and threw him in the Chattahoochee."

Preacher turned over, sat in the dirt, looked at her audience.

Hawks said, "The Bajan wanted to shoot you in the neck with an arrow, because he's really good with that thing, a real Robin Hood, but I told him not to. I tripped you up. American Indian runs in my blood. I got skills. But your funky little attitude is giving me second thoughts."

Preacher made it to her knees, then to her feet. The Bajan shot an arrow through Preacher's calf. She howled as she fell, then lay in the dirt unable to crawl an inch, in too much pain to scream. Preacher looked down at her leg. So much blood. She needed a tourniquet.

Hawks said, "Minister, this is done."

She motioned and the Bajan lowered his bow and arrow.

Catherine stepped forward. "Where is my son?"

Rocking with her pain, teeth clenched, Preacher refused to answer.

Hawks walked to Preacher. She stepped on the arrow in the open wound. Preacher howled louder than she had before. Hawks pressed harder, put most of her weight on the injury.

Preacher howled even louder.

Hawks backed away. Preacher panted with the agony.

Hawks said, "The lady asked you a question."

Catherine snapped, "Do you know where my son is?"

Then Catherine's expression darkened. She moved in closer. She held the .22 in her hand like she was about to shoot. But she did like Hawks, raised her foot to stomp on the arrow lodged in Preacher's calf.

Preacher trembled, and as sweat and blood mixed and ran across her face, she raised a hand. "Gideon is in Buenos Aires. Fighting my army."

Hawks snapped, "Are you serious? After all we did to get his half-dead butt out of that wretched place, he went back? We could've just left his butt down there the first time and called it a day."

The Bajan cursed. "I should have stayed with him in Brazil."

Hawks ranted, "Catherine, that boy of yours, I really don't know what to say. We have a team of people making plans to fix this, but . . . he's twelve doughnuts shy of a baker's dozen."

Stress sweating, breathing unevenly, Catherine shuddered and asked Preacher, "Is it true that you work for a man named Mr. Midnight?"

Hawks said, "They call him Medianoche down there, Catherine."

"Is it true?"

Preacher nodded. "I would advise you to back away, to let me go, and I will ask the Horsemen to show you the same mercy you show me."

Catherine shook her head. "There is no mercy with Mr. Midnight."

"And there will be no mercy for Gideon."

Catherine dropped the .22, then pulled her boys to her. Tears fell. Hawks took hard breaths but didn't cry. Preacher saw the .22, tried to drag herself in that direction. The Bajan shook his head, raised his bow, and made an arrow land next to Preacher's head.

Preacher said, "My team has gone after him. They knew where he was. Gideon is dead by now. Just hope the Lord lived in his heart."

Catherine cried.

The Bajan tossed Hawks a roll of duct tape.

Hawks put duct tape around Preacher's mouth, same for her

wrists and ankles. They all stood around her. They looked down at her.

In a mild German accent, the blond son asked, "Can I shoot her?"

Catherine wiped her eyes. "As much as I want to tell you to, as much as she deserves to be shot, no, Steven. Andrew-Sven, no, you may not."

"You said my whole name. You're mad."

"I'm not mad. I am afraid. She killed Alvin White."

The dark-skinned son with the British accent asked, "Then, Mum, may I? For what she did to Mr. Alvin, may I shoot her?"

"No, Robert. Son, please point your gun at the ground. Do as I say."

Catherine and the boys looked at Gideon's friends. Hawks listened to Catherine as she spoke to her boys. French. German. British. Everyone in the family had a different accent. And as they sorted this out, as they made sure no one had seen any of them in the woods, the Bajan's Barbadian accent and Hawks's southern accent added two more countries to what Gideon had once called his United Nations.

Hawks said, "Catherine, thanks for trusting me and the Bajan. I know you don't know us, but I know a lot about you. This heifer, I guess she tracked you down the same way I did, through Jeremy Bentham. Not sure how, but I guess that's what she and her hoodlum friends did."

"Was Jeremy part of this?"

"We will find out. Sooner or later."

"Will there be more people like this one? Four of them came. Four. They found Alvin. I saw it on the news. They know my home address."

"We don't know. I'll be honest; we don't know how this will play out. We just know that for now you're safe. You can pack up and move again. I can make a call and you can leave the country if you want."

The Bajan said, "I can get you from here to Barbados. There is a house in the Six Roads area. Or I can get you sent to Cuba. There is a place in Havana. It's mine. It's small, but no one is there. Same for Providence Island in Nassau. I have a place to hide you on Cable Beach."

Catherine shook her head. "I can't live this way. I have run from country to country. My boys have moved all their lives, almost each year. Living in fear is too much. I have to think of my boys. They need stability. They need to be safe in this world. I want to talk to Medianoche."

Hawks said, "To Gideon's father."

That shook Catherine. "I need to talk to Mr. Midnight."

"He is Gideon's father, right?"

"He told you."

"You're his mother and Mr. Midnight is his daddy, right?"

Without confirming or denying, Catherine said, "I need to talk to him. To Mr. Midnight."

"Why would you want to talk to a man who wants you murdered?"

"Because he has found my family. I am terrified, but if I have to go to him, if I have to surrender . . . I need to talk to him and the Beast."

"The Beast? Who is the Beast?"

"The Beast and Medianoche, they are like brothers."

The Bajan nodded, then lowered his bow and arrow. He pulled a nine millimeter from the small of his back. "Catherine. Sven. Robert. I will walk you back to your car. Follow me. I'll take the other woman's car and park it somewhere else; then I'll ride back with you, Catherine."

Catherine said, "Make sure to wipe away all of your fingerprints. Leave no DNA behind. The police are smart, but you have to be smarter."

The Bajan nodded. "Shrewd woman. You hide it well."

"I've done things I'm not proud of. And this night has reminded me of them all. The things we do, they catch up with us. They always do."

Hawks said, "Catherine, you and your boys don't need to see the next part. The Bajan will make sure you make it back home."

"I can't go back to Smyrna. They know about Jeremy's home. And I can't go back to my house. As far as I know, Mr. Midnight is out there."

"You have a safe room built in your basement."

"Yes. Alvin White built a safe room. But Mr. Midnight would burn down the house to get to me. That safe room would be our tomb."

"Jesus. What have you done to folks?"

Catherine wiped her eyes. "I need to get my boys someplace safe. They both need to eat, and they need showers and clean clothes."

The Bajan said, "There is a Knights Inn on South Cobb Drive. It's not much, but it's next to a Chinese restaurant. I can get you and the boys there, get what you need from Walmart on Cobb Parkway, and I'll be there and watch over you and the boys until this is straightened out."

Catherine nodded, her expression saying she had no choice.

Hawks said, "Wish I could've done the same for Shotgun and helped him stay safe. He was a nice guy. A man who kept his word."

The Bajan said, "He was supposed to stay in Alabama with his family. That is what Konstantin told me when I was in Brazil with Gideon. Shotgun wasn't supposed to go near Catherine's home."

Hawks said, "But it looks like he came back to check on you and the boys, Catherine. I'm not sure if Gideon told him to do that, because that goes against the Russian's order. But he came to check on you. He sang your praises in Uruguay. You and your boys meant a lot to him."

"We were family."

"He felt the same way."

That made Catherine cry. That rattled her boys.

Andrew-Sven said, "Mum, can we go to Mr. Alvin's funeral?"

Catherine wiped her eyes. "We'll see."

Robert said, "If not his funeral, then to his grave to leave flowers."

After a short pause, the Bajan said, "I think we're done here."

Hawks nodded. "I don't want to be rude and keep ignoring our guest. She's making all this noise and we're talking like she ain't down on the ground at our feet begging to get our attention."

Catherine's voice choked. "So my son might be dead."

No one said anything.

Catherine moved and stood over Preacher. She spat on her.

The Bajan went to her, put his hand on her trembling shoulder.

Catherine followed the Bajan, then frowned down at Preacher as she held her boys' hands. Both of the boys carried their guns and scowled.

Once Catherine and the boys left with the Bajan, Hawks waited a few moments, until it was quiet. Hawks dug in her jeans pocket, took out a pack of Juicy Fruit, popped her last stick of gum.

"You sure have pretty hair. Your attitude is ugly, though."

Hawks inhaled, looked out at the wide, flowing river, punctuated by angular rock shoals. As Hawks chewed her gum, she dragged Preacher by her feet. The arrow in her calf pulled along the earth and exacerbated the wound. Hawks hauled Preacher to the Chatta-hoochee River, down through the mud, and rolled her into the water. Preacher kicked, fought.

Three tours of duty. She hadn't come home to die like this.

Then Preacher refused to surrender. She was a Horseman. She fought and did her best to ignore the searing pain in her calf; she fought and it felt like half of her leg had been ripped away, fought until desperation and wariness set in and the pain in her leg was too much to bear. She fought until she didn't have the strength to fight anymore. Rakisha Jones returned to her mind. Preacher heard bugs flying near her ears. Mosquitoes landed on her sweaty face. Preacher was a Horseman. She wasn't afraid. She wouldn't show fear. She closed her eyes.

Mouth covered with tape, it sounded like mumbles, like nothing, but she was in prayer. Over and over she repeated, "'My desire is to depart and be with Christ, for that is far better.'"

Hawks said, "Sure is nasty tonight. I'm wet like a clam."

Hawks looked down at the woman in the minister's collar, watched the woman's nostrils flare as she inhaled the unique scents of the South. Hawks knew the woman was in pain. Her clothes were sullied from falling in the reddish orange ultisol—Georgia's famous red clay dirt.

The aroma of the damp red clay dirt danced with the scent the humidity brought from the forest as the Chattahoochee added its own fragrance. There was some butterfly bush and four-o'clocks in there too, same for common gardenia, moonflower, and confederate jasmine. Nothing smelled like the South but the South. Year-round, for each season, it made its own perfume.

Hawks wiped away sweat, inhaled air so thick it felt like she was breathing through a wet mattress. She was used to the heat. She was a southern girl. Elvis, country music, and buttery grits. She liked working with her hands. Liked working in gardens, liked working on cars. She liked fixing things to make the time go by. She could re-build an engine, then go into the kitchen and make the best sweet potato pie a man ever tasted. Then she could put on a negligee, some soft music, and be his sweet potato pie. She was never needy, was too independent for most men, but was girly when she needed to be girly. She was sweet, but could put someone in the ground and never blink twice.

Hawks said, "Time to get baptized and send you to the lake which *burneth* with fire and brimstone. Who uses the word *burneth* when they're talking? Crazy people, that's who. I usually do this in a bath-tub. Not as messy. And seems a bit more dignified than dying in the mud. The Chattahoochee ain't as nice as a bathtub, but under the circumstances, it's gonna have to do."

"'My desire is to depart and be with Christ, for that is far better.'"

Hawks said, "I don't know what you're saying, but it can't be a recipe to banana pudding. I've been craving banana pudding the last couple of weeks. Want some bad. Might make some later tonight."

"'My desire is to depart and be with Christ, for that is far better.'"

Hawks held Preacher under, her body jerking, bubbles rising.

Hawks said, "Since you like Bible verses, I have one for you. 'A good name is better than fine perfume, and the day of death better than the day of birth.' Something like that."

Preacher stopped kicking.

Bubbles stopped rising.

Another fifteen minutes went by, in case Preacher was an expert at holding her breath. Hawks could hold hers for more than ten.

Cicadas sang. The horny little crickets were louder. Insects buzzed. Common true katydids crooned back and forth to one another. Summer nights in the tropical climate of the South were noisy from sunset to sunrise. Bugs had a jacquerie every night. The Bajan had told Hawks that Barbados nights were just as loud. They had a lot of creepy-crawly things and frogs and bugs that danced all night long and didn't stop until the roosters and dogs complained at sunrise.

While bugs danced around her, as mosquitoes buzzed by her face, as the concert of creepy-crawly things ensued, Hawks checked the minister for a pulse. She was thorough.

Hawks said, "Hope you made peace with the Lord. Hope he's more forgiving than I am. But then, from what I've read in the Old Testament, probably not. He throws a mean tantrum. Almost as mean as mine."

Hawks reached to Preacher's neck.

With a jerk, she removed the cleric's collar.

She whispered, "You don't deserve this. My granddaddy was a clergyman and he was a good man. Never hurt nobody. I can see if you had issues with Catherine, or Thelma, or Nathalie, whoever the heifer is, but you wanted to hurt her boys? That's plain wrong. This ain't the Middle East. We don't do that here. Not on my watch."

Hawks chucked the cleric's collar into the marsh. Then she gave Preacher to the Chattahoochee. The river started in the Appalachian Mountains and ran more than four hundred miles. Hawks let the river carry the mercenary who had been sent to kill Gideon's family in the direction of Lake Seminole and the Georgia-Florida border. That was 245 miles away. Hawks doubted the body would make it that far. But no one would know where the Horseman had entered the winding river.

She was wet from her chest to her boots. Her boots were filled with water, covered in mud. She pulled those off. Pulled off her socks. Walked over dirt and rocks in her bare feet.

Chewing gum, Hawks exited the hiking trail, left the shadows, cowboy boots in her left hand as she headed toward Eugene Gunby Road. She took out her phone, put one earplug in, and listened to her new favorite country number by Chyyanna Lee. "Older Men and Whiskey" was on repeat as Hawks exited the Cochran Shoals part of the river. Sweating and not bothered by the perspiration, she hoofed it south, headed back up Interstate North toward Powers Ferry Road, headlights in her eyes. Her pickup truck was in the corner strip mall that housed Hillside Liquor and Harry's Pizza and Subs.

Cars raced by. Police cars passed too, sirens on, lights flashing.

She kept her walk summertime slow, but soon pulled her earplug away, stood shaking her head as she wiped away tears with the bottom edge of her Elvis Presley T-shirt, feeling that Gideon was dead.

She knew he was dead. She felt it in her heart.

She said, "Your dumb ass finally got yourself killed."

Muddied boots in hand, she went into Hillside Liquor and bought a fresh pack of Juicy Fruit. Underneath an announcement for a Stop the Violence party honoring the deaths of rappers Sledgehammer and his rival the Big Bad Wolf, the front page of *The Atlanta Journal-Constitution* had a small story about two local boys being found in the Chattahoochee. Hawks picked up the paper, read a few lines. Both boys were near the age of Catherine's sons. Her boys were as tough as steel. No one would snatch them out of their bedrooms at night and beat them to death with a blunt object.

She put the paper back.

Next to the newspapers was a display for BC Powder.

She picked up one, sighed, and bit her bottom lip.

When she was in Puerto Rico, her heart had the best of her.

She had started thinking about marriage. And babies. She was going to ask Gideon to come live with her, to shack up with her, to have a real relationship. She wanted to wake up with Gideon every morning. She'd thought about that while Gideon's mind was elsewhere. Even though it hadn't been true, Hawks would never forget Gideon's expression when he told her that Arizona was pregnant, when he thought it was real.

His face had said it all. What he felt was transparent.

He had an expression of jealousy.

He wanted Arizona's child to be his.

Hawks loved Gideon, but he would never feel for her what he felt for Arizona. Arizona was his whiskey. But Gideon had been her cocaine. That was the moment the fantasy ended. When she knew it had nowhere to go. She'd been chasing a man who was chasing someone else.

Hawks sighed the sigh of the foolish. Shook her head.

She spat her gum into a napkin, then threw the napkin into a trash can. She opened a fresh piece of Juicy Fruit, eased the sugary gum into her mouth. She hadn't chewed gum in years, not since high school.

She purchased a pint of Jack Daniel's and a bottle of Coke. After she was done with Catherine, it was going to be that kind of night.

When Hawks made it back to her dirty F-250, she threw her muddied boots in the cab, then tossed the box of BC Powder she had just bought onto the dashboard. She wiped away sadness, then let Jack and Coke get comfortable inside the armrest.

On the front passenger seat rested other business, a legal envelope.

Inside were papers, documents, copies of passports. She had a four-gig pen drive. And copies of birth certificates. She knew Gideon's birth name. Where he was born. Written on the legal envelope was Nathalie Marie Masreliez from Yerres, France. She was tempted to write Lying Bitch on the golden envelope, but that wasn't professional. Hawks wiped her eyes again before she took a satellite phone out of her glove compartment. Throat burning, heart heavy, she called Konstantin.

She had to tell him that the fool had gone back to Argentina.

If he died down there, they would never hear from him again.

He would just be gone, as if he had never existed.

Maybe it was for the best.

If he was dead, he would be spared the next level of his mother's lies. Nathalie-Thelma-Catherine had kept secrets inside of secrets.

While the phone rang, Hawks wished she had gone to Buenos Aires, to stop, save, or help that suicidal fool Gideon from going after those crazy revanchists. If she hadn't spoken her mind in Uruguay, she might've been able to talk some sense into his head.

Telling him they were no good then, it wasn't the best timing.

But it was the truth. And Hawks was a big fan of the truth.

She wished Gideon was here.

She'd take him away from all this, until it was sorted out, until there was a plan. She'd take him up to Memphis, to Tom Lee Park on the Mississippi River, make him sit on a bench next to her. They'd sit and stare out at the cars going across the Memphis-Arkansas Bridge while she told him the history of Mr. Tom Lee. Then she'd take him down to Beale Street. Make him listen to the blues. Then spend the night at the Peabody. Wake up and watch the ducks march off the elevator into the fountain. It was a southern thing. She had always wanted to do that with him. Would never happen now.

She loved Gideon. From first look, she loved him. She didn't like him, but she loved him so much she broke down in tears, and it took her two minutes to be able to say a single word Konstantin could understand.

Chapter 26

El Agua Fria

My heart hammered in my chest as I accelerated and screamed. As Frank Sinatra sang, I screamed like a madman charging into battle. We moved toward each other at breakneck speed. Two hard-charging bulls. But the Horseman chickened out and swerved, turned away from the head-on crash. The Horseman cut left, but I still caught part of the back end of their chariot. It was enough contact to send me out of control. By then both cars had too much speed on the damp street to not do any damage. The riled bulls built by Mercedes charged too fast, hard, and furious to make contact and not spin and hit something else. There had been two separate crashes. The air bag exploded in my face and the sound of metal, glass, and fiberglass coming apart filled my ears. Frank Sinatra had stopped singing. I was unconscious for a moment.

A true moment equaled ninety seconds. It would take a Glock 17 fewer than four seconds to spit out all seventeen bullets. I had been incapacitated long enough to be attacked and shot more than five hundred times.

I came back to life gradually, but within seconds the numbness faded. Pain became my alarm clock, and that shocked me back into this world. Right away panic took charge. My sense of time and place was distorted. I was light-headed and it felt like I was in a dream wrapped in a dream. Blood drizzled across my lips, its taste saturating my tongue.

My nose felt like it was broken. But it wasn't. It was bloodied. So was my mouth. It hurt to blink. My eyes would turn black. Didn't have time to assess the damage to my body, but I felt it all. Old wounds from fights in Antigua, London, Miami, and Buenos Aires danced. Fucking air bag had me trapped. Felt like I was in a chair being suffocated with a plastic bag. I didn't know what or who was outside the wrecked car, and I freaked out, growled, stabbed the air bag a dozen times to get free, then fought and kicked to get my jammed door to open, and when it gave, I fell out of the car to the damp road, landed on bulletproof glass that hadn't withstood the crash as well as the frames of the automobiles.

A light drizzle added to the snow that was having trouble sticking to the ground. I reached for my firearm. Didn't want to get gunned down. No one was on the road but me and the other car. It was forty yards away and looked as fucked-up as I felt. I scanned for the passengers of that car, looked for Horsemen on the ground, then I looked up at the windows, hunted for a sniper.

I saw terrified people.

Some came outside, but sensed danger, and didn't come near.

People in South America understood the ways of South America.

Feeling like the wind was knocked out of me, I struggled to inhale, then struggled to exhale, fought pain, and looked for Horsemen.

I expected another car to appear. Or someone else on a motorcycle.

I made it to one knee, groaned and cursed like I had been in a fight with all the Horsemen at once. The crash had destroyed both cars. Gun trained, I limped to the other AMG. It was upside down. The crash had blown the doors open. Medianoche wasn't in the other car.

There had been only one Horseman attacking me.

I stabbed the air bag and behind the wheel was Señorita Raven.

The crash had left her upside down, belted in, and unconscious.

I pulled her out. Dragged her away from the vehicle. Her face was bloodied, same as mine. Like bullets and bombs, the air bags weren't gender biased. The aches and pains in my body made her feel heavy. She was a solid woman, weighed more than I had thought. After I made sure she was still alive but hors de combat, gun in hand, I limped back to my wrecked AMG, opened the passenger door, and did the same for Foxy Brown. She was limp, disabled.

Still carrying my gun, I did a painful jog toward the apartments. Right away I stole a small blue van from inside the barrio, then sped back to the accident site. Both Horsemen were out cold, same way I had left them. I got them to the blue van. I grabbed hardware from the AMG I had been driving. I pulled out grenades and a rocket launcher, then hurried to get away. Both cars had caught fire.

The fire from the accidents reached the armaments in Señorita Raven's car first, but not before I had tossed both wounded Horsemen and the weapons into the van. Fire met explosives. As her car erupted, I returned to the *autopista* and sped north. Behind me the explosions from the luxury car I had been driving shocked Ciudad Evita.

I had gifted unwarranted terror to the world behind me.

But no one innocent had been hurt or died.

They might be traumatized, but they were physically unharmed.

It didn't matter to monsters, but that mattered to me.

A second later I heard the rise of sirens.

Firetrucks raced toward the car crash and explosions.

A squad of police were seconds behind them.

Señorita Raven was still among the living.

She struggled to breathe, but she was alive.

I checked Foxy Brown for a pulse.

The wreck had ended her suffering.

Not long after, I cruised down Santa María del Buen Aire and pulled up in front of a ramshackle warehouse near Avenida Osvaldo Cruz in La Boca. I was less than four kilometers from the Plaza de Mayo and two kilometers from the nightlife in San Telmo. I was in Capital Federal, not far from the colored artist house at Caminito de La Boca, sneaking into the area known as the birthplace of the tango. The sector had dwellings as colorful as homes in the West Indies. Used to be a major shipyard. The stench told me of the years of neglect and pollution in the water. Near La República de La Boca was where the Horsemen had executed men and women who had worked for the con man Scamz. That had happened hours before I had arrived here with Shotgun and Konstantin. Señorita Raven and Señor Rodriguez had laughed and tortured more than nine people who were part of Scamz's computer operations, then killed all but two. One had played dead, survived, managed to drag himself away from the murder scene, losing more than two pints of blood along the way. From a hospital bed, he had called and told Scamz his tale of horror. When we were en route, Scamz had briefed us on the things the Horsemen had done. The things the Horsemen were willing to do to other human beings made me feel like I could still become a saint.

I whispered, "Whoever fights monsters risks becoming a monster."

The concrete and wooden floors were marred, chipped, broken, and had been used to piss on and worse. Hooligans were hardcore *fútbol* fans. They were worse than thugs. They drank and stood in public and pissed on the stairs in the hallways at La Bombonera, the Boca Juniors *fútbol* stadium, so using the world as a toilet was par for the course. This wasn't the land of the rich, like Recoleta or Palmero. The pong of defecation was heavy-duty, but my aches were stronger. Single-pane windows in the warehouse were filthy or broken. My face hurt and my lip was swollen. I carried Señorita Raven up a narrow staircase, each stair uneven and disgusting. Her long hair fell back from her face. Dots peppered her skin. Shrapnel. She was tall for a woman. And she was both solid and soft.

There were nine rooms, debris scattered all over. Beer bottles. Cigarette stubs. Faint scent of weed. The scent of *paco*, Argentina's version of crack, was powerful. Mold spread like kudzu. Graffiti on every wall. An old wooden chair was in a corner. It was pretty clean. That chair was a tell. Before this roach nest was demolished, it was probably a place young hooligans brought naïve girls, that chair being where the hooligan sat with his pants at his ankles. Or where the girl pulled up her dress and got on her knees so she could doggie for five minutes.

Paco or *peso*, I'd bet that any girl who came here was paid in some way.

Winter air blew through shattered windows and underneath shabby wooden doors.

With my breath fogging with every exhale, I grunted as I put Señorita Raven down, then backed away, tried to shake off my discomfort. I spied out the front window. La Boca was full of tenements, large families living in matchboxes, so everyone was always on the streets long past midnight. They hung out in the streets, ate in the streets, owned the streets, until the sun came up and they were forced to go to work and tolerate tourists. It wasn't a sector where judicious sightseers would wander after sundown. Even if tourists were in a taxi, they would get stopped and robbed for all they had. Ten-year-olds killed adults in the *villas*, and I wouldn't be surprised if they did the same by the filthy river. Some Porteñas never went to La Boca and Hooligan-ville at any time. This was their Chicago, Compton, Detroit, Memphis, Oakland, and Saint Louis.

I took a deep breath and dragged Señorita Raven across the stained concrete floor, pulled her through trash, then tied her down, secured her on a dilapidated wooden table. It had been raised to have her at about a twenty-degree angle. It was the same table the Horsemen had used to torture. The bloodstains on the floor were probably from the Horsemen having fun.

On the table was a hammer, a nail gun able to drive nails all the way through concrete, and nails strong enough to put Jesus on the cross. A blowtorch was there too. So were a blade and a surgical scalpel. There was an IV line and a bucket large enough to hold the blood from a cow. The London arms dealer had come through once again. I took out my phone. I turned on music. I put on James Brown. He sang "Bad Mother."

After I tended to my nose, I turned to YouTube and played *The Best of Curtis Mayfield.* "Move On Up," "Pusherman," "Superfly," and "Freddie's Dead" played before I turned to her. I took out a secondary weapon, a simple .22. I shot her in her leg. Popped her in the thigh of her bulletproof Colombian suit. She jerked back into this world, yelled, eyes wide, in a panic. She returned to consciousness only to find herself in an unescapable nightmare. Her chest rose and fell as her eyes adjusted to her new reality. The Horseman scowled like she had the migraine of all migraines. The hate glowing in her brown eyes told me I didn't need to introduce myself.

As Curtis Mayfield sang "The Makings of You," I said, "You're Señorita Raven."

"Be advised." Her lips parted, the dark lipstick causing them to stick for a second, and I saw the small gap between her teeth. "I am the executive officer of the Four Horsemen of the Apocalypse."

"Oh, are we exchanging business cards? Sorry, I don't have one."

"I. Am. A. Horseman. I am a leader. I am prepared to give my life in their defense. I will *never* surrender of my own free will. None of us will. I will make every effort to escape. I will accept no special favors."

The soldier with the high cheekbones pulled her lips in tight, and her nostrils flared as she tested her restraints. I looked down at a dirty newspaper on the floor. Headline talked about the worldwide panic and Argentina's president, Fernández de Kirchner, having a measly twenty-nine percent approval rating. She blamed blue-eyed white people for the problems of the world. Señorita Raven kept fighting the restraints. She stopped. She realized she wasn't going anywhere, not unless I wanted her to leave. I went to her, loosened her black necktie. I owned her the same way they had owned the men and women they had tortured and killed when they were trying to defeat Scamz.

She cursed me like only a military person could, then said, "I'll kill you."

She caught her breath, gathered her strength, and struggled again. She did that twice more before she surrendered. Perspiring, she looked me in the eyes. Enraged. Belligerent.

I asked, "Why did you swerve? If you wanted to kill me, and you're prepared to give your life, why did you swerve? Why didn't you crash into me head on doing one hundred?"

"Because you had a Horseman in the car. I wouldn't kill her to capture you. Horsemen are not disposable. They are not bullet catchers."

"You swerved, barely missed me, lost control, flipped over at least six times. I lost control too. Spun out, but didn't flip, and hit a pole. Air bag got the best of me. Hit me like Tyson."

I picked up the water hose. Freezing water flowed. I put a towel over her face, and that caused her to pull at her restraints. She pulled like she expected to turn into the Hulk. She screamed. I let the glacial water flood over the cloth. That ended the screaming. She kicked, fought to breathe, but was immobilized. Instead of screaming, she should have held her breath. Then I stopped, let her breathe through the damp cloth, each inhale filling her lungs with water.

I said, "I know you've had SERE training. Survival, Evasion, Resistance, and Escape. So have I. But now you're in my world. There is no Geneva Convention. I can treat you the way you treated my friends. We were guests in this country, and from the moment we landed, you were not nice. Not at all. I can now treat you with the same barbarism inflicted upon me and my homies by lawless thugs wearing bulletproof suits while they peppered us with bullets and grenades."

"You think you're Medianoche's goddamn son."

"I was nice. I gave him a Father's Day card and a classic novel as a present. That was my first time ever buying a Father's Day card."

"He's rejected you. He hates you like he hates no other."

"You think I give a shit? Fuck Medianoche. Damn the man who had his hand in creating me."

"I doubt if it was his hand in your French whore for a mother."

"Let's see how long that sense of humor holds up."

"That's who you think you are, his son."

I told her, "This is my first time doing this."

"You want to be his son so fuckin' bad, it's killing you."

I paused. "You deserve this."

"You deserve worse."

"You're scum."

"You had no right coming here, interfering in our affairs."

"You should have joined NATO. You could have invoked Article Five. I think that's when member states have to come to the aid of any member state subject to an armed attack."

"*Fuck you.*"

"No, you're fucked."

She struggled to breathe through the saturated cloth. She was underwater on dry land. Adrenaline in overload, she pulled at the restraints hard enough to break her bones. Soon she breathed like her lungs were damaged. She shivered. She knew the dangers of waterboarding, knew brain damage wasn't far away, the same for death.

I said, "I'm not going to drown you. This is only the appetizer."

She coughed, gagged. Strong woman. A warrior. She'd never surrender.

I said, "I'm going to drain your blood. You're going to bleed to death in slow motion. After you lose three liters of blood, there will be no turning back. Up to that, you can probably survive."

She turned her head, regurgitated, coughed, wheezed, then fought to get a teaspoon of air.

I said, "I know twenty-two ways to kill a man. I've only done this form of bloodletting once. I tracked a member of the Mexican cartel to Juneau, Alaska. I'd rather pop and be done with it."

I moved the damp cloth from her face. She wheezed, chest rose and fell like she was in distress, in insurmountable pain. I didn't care. They had killed my friend. I wanted to do this to all of them. To defeat them, I had to become one of them. Kindness never defeated evil.

Kind men facing evil were sent to graves while they were still young.

She fought to get air, coughed, and her words were strained. "Wait, wait, wait."

"What am I waiting on? Godot? Is this supposed to have a logical conclusion?"

"Don't do this. Please, don't do this."

"I'm listening."

She swallowed, made a face like breathing was nothing but excruciating pain.

She managed to say, "There is a lot . . . you don't know."

"Tell me."

"A lot. You. Don't know. There is a lot Medianoche doesn't know."

"Talk and let's be done with this bullshit."

"I know about Margaret. I know about Thelma. I know about Medianoche and the Beast. I know things that you don't know. I know shit that nobody knows but me. If you kill me, that truth you want, it dies with me. I can tell you about the Beast and your mother."

I shook that off, said, "Maybe I'll be better without the truth. The truth is just a burden."

She found wind, coughed, then panted, "He raped me."

I paused. "Who raped you?"

"The man you think is your father. Medianoche. He raped me. And I might be pregnant."

"Liar."

"Don't do this. He threw money in my face like I was a slut. And he raped me."

"Desperate liar."

"I will tell you something. Something no one knows. I've never spoken it out loud."

"Make it good."

"I was raped in the military. By one of the soldiers on my own team. It would have been pointless to report the assault. One in five are raped, and it's rarely prosecuted, and a conviction would be un-likely. I was raped and . . . I set a bomb. I set an IED to kill that hy-permasculine, trigger-happy, ignorant redneck from Nacogdoches, Texas, and I only wanted to kill him, but I accidentally killed others as well. I killed him, my comrades, and almost killed myself."

I gave her rag more freezing water.

She fought, delirious, struggled to breathe, couldn't scream and drink water at the same time. She wheezed that she wanted to live. Or she wanted death to come faster.

It had to be horrible to want to live and not be able to. To want to die and not have control. That was what torture was about. She had broken down. She was broken.

I said, "Your new team killed my friend. When we fought days ago, when you bombed and destroyed the *villas*, he let you live. We had the briefcase, we had both of them, and he could have killed you in the *villa*, could've blown your head off, but he let you live. He was a fair man."

She coughed. "Why didn't you kill Medianoche then? Every-thing after is your fault."

"*That wasn't my mission.* I was hired to get the second briefcase. Not kill Medianoche."

"Bullshit. You had him. You let him live. You're weak. You're soft. You punked out."

I rocked, was being strangled, *renditioned* by my truth. "Because he's . . ."

"He's what?"

"He . . . *He's my father*. I could fight him. I fought him. It was my best fight, and it wasn't easy, but I beat him. I suffered a beating, but I beat a legend. I beat the monster that lived inside of my head. He tried to kill me, and he failed. But I couldn't kill him, no matter what he had done."

"You're afraid of him. You saw him and became the little boy who is afraid of his father."

"He's *Mr. Midnight*. In my mind, Mr. Midnight has always been larger than life."

"You idolized him."

"The way people idolize the devil. He was my goddamn boogeyman."

"Scared little boy. You didn't kill him then. And you won't do a damn thing now."

"It's not easy for a man to kill his father. At least it's not for me. Every boy wants a father. I've put others in the grave. But that was business. Those were contracts. I'm not a murderer. Anyone I sent to the pearly gates was a contract, or trying to put me in an unmarked grave."

"Hypocrite. Coward."

"No, it makes me human. I haven't lost my humanity. Not all of it. Most, but not all. I was focused, only killed my targets, only attacked my enemies. Like drone attacks, you killed innocent people on the street. Fourteen people died on the streets because of your bombs. *Fourteen*."

"You killed a dozen people in the *villas*."

"Two-bit soldiers who were armed by you and contracted to kill all of us."

"You're no different than I am. You ain't no different."

"I'm not phony. I don't drape what I do in any country's flag and call it righteous."

I remembered when I had gone to handle Thelma, my mother before she had taken the name Catherine. She was still a workingwoman then. I hunted her down, wanted to put her down for what she had done to me, and I was unable to follow through. She was my mother. She had another son by then. That meant I had a brother who needed protecting. That kinship bonded us and protected her from the darkness inside of me. It protected her from the midnight in my soul.

I said, "I do what I'm paid to do. No more, no less. I've exterminated in self-defense, and for pay, but I've never, never hunted someone down for personal vengeance, not until now. I'm the monster you created."

"You are the one who murdered my best friend on the goddamn train."

"Señor Rodriguez. It wasn't murder. That was business. Rodriguez was business. He would have killed me, Arizona, Shotgun, Konstantin, and anyone else who stood in the way."

"Don't you dare say his name with a goddamn smile on your face. He was my friend."

"You killed soldiers, your own comrades, you set a bomb and blew them the fuck up, probably got a medal for it, and you're upset about me killing a thug who was trying to kill me?"

"I killed my goddamn rapist during the darkest night with the moon shining bright. I killed a man who had raped me and stopped him from doing the same to any other enlisted woman."

"You lost the plot."

"I watched the bastard step on the IED and get blown into a thousand pieces. He was a low-IQ, immature piece of shit. He would throw flash and bang in the john when people were on the crapper. Had no respect for me, yet wanted to fuck me. I showed him. I was too close to the IED. But with my injuries, no questions were asked. Not one."

"I bet the Taliban was blamed. You probably blamed bin Laden himself."

"Four died after that bomb exploded. Soldiers had a field day. Men had died and other men went ballistic, were terrified, in a rage, and killed men, women, children, cats, and dogs. They killed dogs to keep them from eating the dead. You have no idea the things I've seen."

"You're crazy."

"Not crazy. Swimming in many levels of PTSD. But I never fall apart."

"The things we do for revenge. The things we do so we can sleep better at night."

"Sooner or later I'd do the same to the man you think is your father. I've dreamed that dream every night. Every day I am loyal to him, as I am to all soldiers, but at night, I dream about killing Medianoche."

"The man *I think* is my father."

"Sooner or later, he'll sit at his desk and find a Russian pressure plate under his chair."

"Sooner or later."

"He has it coming. He has no remorse. None whatsoever. He has no compassion. He married three women, and I feel sorry for each one of them. It had to be horrible being his wife."

"Why stay with the group?"

"Because this is all I have. I want to take over and control the Horsemen. I want to wear the red tie and sit at the CO's desk. But I have to learn from the best. Medianoche is the best. He is to killing what Marlon Brando was to acting. When he has a gun in his hand, it is like watching an artist. Medianoche the warrior is the ultimate alpha male. He inspires others. He influences men, makes them want to be like him. He understands war, understands what it takes to win, more than anyone I have ever met. I have fought by his side. I have studied him."

"You mimic him."

"I have mimicked him in all ways possible."

"You love him."

"Don't insult my soul."

"You sleep with him."

"He assaulted me. I won't go into detail. He's created a hostile work environment. He's choked me. Attacked me. Struck me."

"You've stayed. But you are dying for revenge."

"Best served cold. Best served cold."

"I like mine hot."

All she said had been emotional. Her anger was powerful. Her disdain was real. I popped my lips, the same way the arms dealer in London had done when she was thinking. I didn't believe two words from my captive's mouth. I couldn't afford to have empathy for my enemy. But like a man had done in London, she had wormed inside my head.

I whispered, "I watched Mr. Midnight try to kill my mother. That changed me."

"And you popped him in the left eye with a .22. That changed him."

I cleared my throat. "You're complex."

"I am very complex."

"You've been through a lot."

"Since I was born in Saint Louis."

"Maybe more than me. Our roads have led us here."

"You don't know my pain. You don't know my triggers."

"Your what?"

"Triggers."

"Oh. Triggers. Okay." I popped my lips. "I feel bad for you."

"I don't want your sympathy. What has happened to me doesn't define me."

"The others in your battalion, your friends, were collateral damage."

"Sometimes you have to destroy a village to meet your objective."

"Drone mentality."

"Drones are effective. They make others keep away from your enemy. Anyone who stands with your enemy is also your enemy. Like the men across the river are our enemies."

"The Men from Uruguay."

"They befriended you. Allowed you to pass through their country. Their day will come. I'd carpet bomb them to kill that *puta* Abeja Reina."

I popped my lips again. "Tell me what you know about Margaret."

"You first. What do you know?"

"She was my mother's best friend. That's all I know. Because of a lie, I used to think that Margaret was my mother. Never saw a picture of her. Just know she's dead. They found her body in a Dumpster."

"Is that right?"

"She was killed in North Carolina. By Medianoche. By Midnight. I have no idea why."

"Hadn't heard that one about Margaret the Jamaican. Not what I read in the files."

"Jamaican?"

"From Montego Bay. Margaret was her whore name. Thelma was the designation your mother used. Margaret took her name from Margaret Thatcher. You didn't know?"

"Tell me what I don't know. Tell me about Thelma. The Beast. And Medianoche."

"Fuck you."

"Where's the Horseman called the Beast? Is he really dead?"

"You're the beast. Motherfucker, look in the mirror. You're the goddamn beast. You walk like a beast. You talk like a beast."

I stood and picked up the damp cloth. She had talked, rambled, argued so she could breathe.

I said, "I've always been a beast. Now I've upped my game and I'm something less than human, but a man capable of being as vicious as an animal. The Horsemen did this. I know a Horseman has found my mother and my brothers."

"They're dead. Three more coffins. One large, two small."

I turned the water hose on again, faced her, and as she struggled in vain to break her restraints, I whispered, "Every war is the same. It starts off being about something, but soon it devolves into the need to win. Every war loses focus, takes on a life of its own. So here we are. Only one of us can win. Otherwise, the war continues. Sorry for what I'm about to do. But this is what you deserve. For Shotgun. For my mother. For my brothers. For the innocent comrades you killed with an IED."

She struggled; then I let the calm arrest her.

I spoke assuredly. "As your blood sewers out of you, Señorita

Raven, your body will try to counterbalance for the gradual loss. Your heart will beat faster and try and get oxygen to your tissues. You'll get weak, feel light-headed, drunk, then turn pale. Your skin will stop feeling warm. You will be on the way to becoming as cold as your heart. Don't worry. That's only the first level. Three levels to go. When you've lost about thirty percent of your blood, around three pints, there will be no other way out, and you will need a blood transfusion. I think that I am remembering this right. I might be off by a pint. And the blood that came out of you, that will be no good. It's a one-way trip. The bleeding will be deplorable and unpardonable. Your heart will start working overtime, straining to get enough oxygen to tissues. You will feel weaker. Your blood pressure will drop. There aren't any machines here to tell you where you are, but you will know. Everything inside of you will be fighting to keep you alive. The body is designed that way. Smaller blood vessels will constrict and try to force the blood to circulate. They will do that to keep the circulation going. But you will still be bleeding. After you've lost forty percent of the red fluid that keeps you alive, it will be pretty fucked-up. You might need help restarting your heart, the kind of help you can only get at a hospital. The distress on your body's circulatory system . . . you won't survive. Not long from now your heart will no longer be able to maintain blood pressure and circulation. You know what happens next? Everything starts to shut down. It's your end. You'll see Death standing in the corner. Organs will fail one by one. You'll fall into a coma. Then you will die. The same way my friend . . . my best friend . . . died, but your death will not be as quick. You will feel it to the end. You will know what it's like to die, one drop of blood at a time."

I went to the other equipment, pulled it and the bucket closer.

She said, "Don't do this, don't do this, don't do this."

I took a breath. "Be honest."

"What do you want to know?"

"If I let you go, would you one day come after me?"

"That would be my mission. You killed my best friend."

I barked, "You killed mine."

"And he killed three of my soldiers."

I asked, "Would you go after my family?"

"There is no way to turn this around."

"We are too far gone."

"Your family. The Russian. The Scamz Organization. And especially you."

"And Medianoche will only get more Horsemen."

"There will always be Horsemen. *Always*."

"Then you leave me no other choice. To defeat evil, you have to become evil. To defeat a Horseman, you must behave like a Horseman."

The process began. The fluid of life drained from her. She watched for a moment, then turned her head, stared at the ceiling, nostrils flared, teeth tight. Her lip trembled. A tear fell from her left eye. Then her right.

I whispered, "You're two pints short."

Soon she shook like she saw the Grim Reaper standing in the corner, pointing his scythe at her. She trembled the way I did when I was a child and had nightmares about Mr. Midnight. It also reminded me of when I was killed in London. Gun in hand, I went to one of the filthy windows, spied down on the dirty streets, looked to see if Horsemen had tracked her. The silence and knowing she couldn't escape finally broke her.

She lost it, screamed, "*No no no no no no.*"

"I am the wrong one to fuck with. You will soon meet a room of people who learned the same lesson. Politicians. Rappers. An assassin with a broken nose. And other Horsemen. Tell them Gideon said hello."

Chapter 27

Last Exit Before Death

Alvin White had told me and my brothers, "A man has to learn to stand his ground, or get buried in the ground he's standing on."

That stayed with me as I drove past San Telmo; only one thing was on my mind. I sped down José Antonio Cabrera in Palmero Viejo. Zoomed by stands selling *La Nación*. I drove as far as San Isidro Cathedral, then came back toward the Hilton in Puerto Madero. I crisscrossed La Reina del Plata. No one followed me. No one attacked me in *la ciudad de la furia*. Had to be sure I was safe. It was just me, my paranoia, and my guns against a league of madmen and their guns. Not long after, I was on Francisco Acuña de Figueroa, coming up on the Sanatorio Güemes building. The building where the Horsemen kept their quarters was close.

I navigated what felt like rush hour at one in the morning, avenues filled with cars, buses, and Radio Taxis, then pulled the van into a parking garage on the nearest corner. I smelled empanadas, but the scent wasn't as profound as the stench from the Four Horsemen of the Apocalypse. I smelled Los Cuatro Jinetes del Apocalipsis, the aroma stronger than fear.

I gathered weapons I had tossed into the stolen van. I had saved an M84 stun grenade. I had also saved a flash grenade. It wasn't much. But it was all I had. I adjusted my suit, put on the red tie I had found in the Mercedes, pulled on the overcoat, eased on a fedora. The hat had been in the Mercedes too, recovered after the crash, then tossed into this van.

I patted my pockets to make sure I had what was most important. The black card that I had taken from Foxy Brown was in my inside suit pocket. At first I had thought it was a credit card, but it was a card like a hotel key. It opened gates and doors, no fingerprint required.

Only a fool would attack a country on its own soil.

Only a fool.

I became part of the night, on the hunt for soldiers and psychopaths.

I became a fool.

The card opened the security gate without a hitch. Two guards in the booth looked up, saw a man dressed like a Horseman. By the time they realized I wasn't one of the maniacs in black, they had been hit with flash and bang. As they stood blinded, I eased out a gun, attached the suppressor, and sent both to a permanent sleep. The gate closed behind me. I headed down the walkway to the building, shooting out security cameras as I moved toward my final destination. I had to get to the seventeenth floor. I had thought about flying the Cessna, then bailing out, but that would have been a suicidal move. As I floated toward the building on a parachute, they could've had target practice, and that would have been all she wrote.

I swiped the door to the edifice. The light turned green. I went inside, headed toward the elevators. The ones the Horsemen used were around the corner. Before I could make it that far, another security guard came from that direction. He was as big as the Hercules I had seen earlier at Las Violetas. I had my gun trained on the center of his head. He dared me to put the gun down and fight him hand to hand. He called me a chicken; he called me a coward.

My body ached from the car crash. From having so many fights to the death.

Fighting was the last thing I needed to do. I could kill him and be done. But I would always wonder if I could have kicked his ass. No one was here to talk my ego down.

I took my fedora off. Eased out of my overcoat. I put my weapons to the side.

Wearing brass knuckles, I told the big, muscular motherfucker to bring it.

He came at me, came at me hard, threw a vicious left jab paired with a right cross, but my right hand went out fast, caught him on the chin. He staggered, didn't like that. He threw a haymaker, a punch meant to knock my head into the middle of the next millennium. It was a death blow. He missed but kept swinging. I bobbed and weaved, each of his blows missing me by a hair, each getting closer. Each miss frustrated him and made him swing harder, faster. The powerhouse threw twenty-one punches in less than ten seconds, and like Muhammad Ali had done with Michael Dokes, I had dodged them all. He was winded and tried to restart his rampage, but in that one-second break, my right went out fast, caught his chin; then my left hook went to say hello to that same chin. I wore knuckle busters made of iron. I had hurt both hands fighting Medianoche. My hands couldn't take a bare-knuckle brawl. I hit him hard, and it was a one-two combination, then caught him with a roundhouse kick that made his face turn on his neck like he was part owl. He looked groggy, didn't know what had hit him.

He refused to go down and stay down. He staggered at me like he wanted to catch me in a bear hug to keep me from beating him, and I gave him the uppercut from hell. I went at him with a controlled flurry, became Sugar Ray taking down Tommy Hearns. I treated him to two lightning-fast left hooks. I hit him so hard I thought his neck had snapped. He was dead on his feet and I laid in, gave him hard, accurate punches, switched up and gave him elbows and knees. Made his face a bloody mask. I beat him like I had Shotgun's spirit giving me guidance. Blood gushed from the guard's nostrils, but he refused to fall. I hit him hard and his features morphed as his neck hyperextended. His face was broken. It was lights-out for him, but I was on fire, kept swinging as he fell, connected more times before the pavement abruptly stopped his fall. I stomped his groin, tried to shatter his nuts. There were no rules; there was no referee. This was a fight until the end. I pounded him, attacked his face, stomach, arms, tried to make each punch deliver two thousand pounds of pressure. I pounded his head, punched his brain until he looked like no man I'd ever met.

I pounded him, remembering a monster beating my mother. A monster they called Mr. Midnight. He was trying to choke the life out of her. That was something a child never forgot. He screamed at her and was killing her. He had her by her neck, her body raised sky-high. My mother was naked and kicking. Kicking and suffocating as he rag-dolled her around the room, kicking over lamps as she clawed at his hands. Kicking. Kicking like I was punching. Punching. Punching. Like I was an army man, a man who jumped out of planes, a man who had sniper training, a man who wanted to kill the man on the ground in front of me as badly as Mr. Midnight wanted to kill my mother. I tried to beat my history out of my body and into that man's face.

The first time I had shot a man, when I thought I had killed Mr. Midnight, I asked my mother if I'd done wrong. A man had tried to kill my mother, and I had killed him in return and was afraid I would get a spanking. I was a child, confused, afraid, and I remembered that moment. I was scared because I had gotten out of bed when I knew I wasn't supposed to.

"Did I do a bad thing?"

"Some people deserve to die," Catherine had said when she was still Thelma, then shook her head. *"Your daddy told me that bad people need to die. It makes the world a better place."*

I had saved my mother. I had felt like a superhero. I was proud of myself.

Now I realized that she was the bad person my father was trying to kill.

Mr. Midnight was the man she told me was my father.

My father had become a madman and wanted her dead.

He had told her that while he tried to choke the life out of her. He had screamed that some people deserved to die, and killing people like her, bad people like her, made the world a better place. I beat my opponent until that memory left me alone, until it let me be.

My bloodied opponent was done. But I wasn't finished.

Once upon a time I walked away from my first enemy, only to have him resurrected. I wasn't going to be careless and walk away without being sure evil was deep in its grave.

I was a gladiator in a Colombian suit. A bloody mess after the gruesome fight. When an opponent stepped into the ring and challenged my life, I was a merciless warrior.

Panting, I grabbed him by his hair, took out my blade, and without pause, I pulled my blade across his throat, gave him a Colombian necktie.

Then I stood over him wheezing, my body still in a state of disrepair from fighting Medianoche days ago, here in the heart of the slums of another corrupt South American dystopia.

My breathing evened out, and I stood still, my trigger finger moving back and forth.

They could've killed Scamz bit by bit every day for the rest of their lives, but they never should have gone after Shotgun. Or my family. By now a Horseman had found my mother and brothers. They would learn that I was the last man on earth they wanted dying for revenge.

I picked up my coat, my jacket, my weapons. I eased my suit coat on, adjusted my necktie, then eased my fedora back on. Became Mr. Bespoke. I went to the Horsemen's private elevator. I swiped the black card. A green light came on and the elevator door opened.

A soft, feminine, programmed voice announced, *"Piso cero."*

I stepped inside and felt like I was trapped in a coffin. I didn't know who or what would greet me when the doors opened again. I shot my hand out before the door closed, and it opened again without a problem. I stepped off. To the right was an unmarked door. I went there. Used the black card, swiped, and the door unlocked. I opened the door on a stairwell.

The elevator could rise, then drop back to the earth. Or when the door opened, I could be greeted the same explosive way I had greeted Hercules and Foxy Brown at Las Violetas.

I took the stairs, went floor by floor, shot out security cameras along the way.

I would pull the sword from the stone, or I would die trying.

Chapter 28

Piso Diecisiete

Seventeen levels. Maybe thirty steps between floors. Legs burned like fire. No booby traps had been in the stairwell, but that didn't mean there wasn't a silent alarm. The black card opened the door on the floor eighteen stories above the ground, and I eased out, the barrel of a gun loaded with RIP bullets leading the way. No one greeted me. All I heard was music. "Last Night When We Were Young." A Frank Sinatra song. The kind aging men listened to, to reminisce.

There were four apartments on the floor.

I expected those doors to open at the same moment, guns blasting.

I followed the music, crept to that door. It was ajar. I looked for a tripwire. I found nothing that was connected to a grenade. I eased the door open, and it was the same flat I had all but destroyed with sniper fire. It was Medianoche's apartment. What was left of it.

He was there. Dressed in Four Horsemen apparel, seated at a desk.

He sat at a desk, in a shattered room, while Frank Sinatra sang of days gone by.

Medianoche raised his head, squinted at me when I opened the door. He saw his oldest living enemy and tried to stand up but couldn't find his balance, then sat back in the chair. A gun was on his desk. He reached for it, but I put my hand on top of the weapon. He didn't have the strength to wrestle it from me. I took it from him, then backed away, took three steps back.

Cold night air blew in from the shattered patio windows. I saw the holes I had shot in the walls. My shoes crunched broken glass while I made sure no one was in the kitchen or the bedroom.

Weapon trained, expecting the unexpected, I said, "Medianoche."

It took him a second, but he struggled and finally said, "Gideon."

"Must be the cleaning lady's day off."

"I clean my own quarters. Always have."

"So here we are."

"Again, gaucho. Again."

"Round two?"

"If I could, I would stomp you into the floor."

"If you could."

"The situation has changed. Temporarily."

His eye patch was off. I saw the damage I had done to him years ago. I saw where I had shot him. It was ugly. It was enough to make a man hate another man. A fake eye was on the desk, an ocular prosthesis, in a small box. He struggled to put it into the vacant socket in his scarred face. His hand wouldn't work. The eye dropped and rolled over to where I was standing. I picked it up, went over to him, rinsed the eye in a solution to prevent contamination, then helped him put it in the cavern in his head. A vial of cocaine was on his desk too. He'd spilled it, made a mess. Something was wrong with him. The right side of his face was slack. He'd blown a fuse. No one could fake a slack face. That didn't make the psychopath any less dangerous.

I asked, "Get the card I left for you, Mr. Midnight?"

"I'm not your father."

"I was going to leave one for every year since I've been born."

"I am not your fucking sperm donor."

"My mother said you were."

"Thelma lied. The Beast might have been your father. Not me. You have a little bastard brother born in Germany. Beast was that bastard's dad. But face it, your mother is a whore, boy. Your brother is a trick baby, just like you're a trick baby. And any other baby she might've had is a trick baby. Thelma is a whore. And a good one. The line to get to that pussy was like the line to get into Disney World. She was a house favorite. Thelma, the French whore in Montego Bay."

"Thelma was. Catherine isn't."

"Once a whore, always a whore. Changing your name doesn't change your character. Like I told you before, any man you pass on the street could be your goddamn sperm donor."

I looked around the room. DVDs with Cagney, Bogart, Garfield, Hayden. Mitchum, Wells, Macready. All gangster films. A saxophone was on a sofa. I picked up the horn. I gripped it tight with my hands. Wanted to hit him. Wanted to beat him until his head was mush.

I put the horn back down.

I asked, "What happened to you?"

"A transient ischemic attack."

"You had a ministroke."

"Few hours ago. After the sniper attack, the luck of the draw worked in your favor."

"I'm fucking disappointed. I showed up ready to rumble."

"Same here. I wanted the same. I wanted to crush your skull."

"Lack of blood flow to the brain."

"Already had issues. The fight we had in the *villas* didn't help my case."

"You're done."

"I'm not done. It took me out of the fight. But this will resolve itself within twenty-four hours."

"So, it's not permanent."

"It didn't kill brain tissue. Won't have permanent disabilities. I will be good as new."

"You're sitting here, dressed, waiting on it to pass."

"So I can join my team and lead them to victory."

"So, should I come back tomorrow? Should I have made an appointment?"

He coughed. "You made it past the guards."

"I went Horseman on two. Went Gideon on the third."

Medianoche said, "You are proficient with weapons. You are good at hand-to-hand combat. You're cunning. Ruthless. You have balls. You should have been a Horseman."

"Sorry. I have ethics."

"It's not too late. I could make you a Horseman. You could complete the Nunca Más contracts for me as a start. You could help me close the Caprica Ortiz account."

"I don't murder wholesale. Not even now."

"I can't say that I'm not impressed."

"Well, you're pretty impressive yourself."

"Military?"

"No. Not like you. Just a simple assassin."

"Who trained you?"

"Hard times, bad luck, and a few dangerous people who will remain nameless."

"The Russian?"

"He was one."

"Was he an asset?"

"Classified."

"Who trained the Landscaper?"

"The streets."

I picked up a chair that had been overturned. I sat facing Medianoche. We both wore dark suits and red neckties.

He motioned toward his missing eye. "You did this."

I asked, "Why did you try and kill my mother with your bare hands?"

"It was my mission."

"Your mission?"

"The Beast sent me into the whorehouse to kill her."

"The Beast."

"He was my leader. He was the CO. That was the mission assigned."

"Why didn't he do it himself? All of you seem like DIY kinda guys and dolls."

"He couldn't kill the slut."

"Why?"

"You don't want to know all the things your mother did, the things we paid her to do. Let just say, no matter how many were in the room, she pleased them all, man or woman, and she was the best. He rode her raw and knocked her up. He loved her, I suppose. As much as a man can love a whore, he loved her. She loved his money. Fair exchange. Maybe he had a kid by her and couldn't look in the face of his unwanted child's mother and choke her to death."

"The Beast told you that he impregnated her?'

"He might've done it twice, if the first time was with you."

"She never mentioned the Beast. Only you."

"Women lie. Don't you watch *Jerry Springer* up there in the States?"

"Never been interested in trash television."

"She thought I was dead, so lies could be put on my name. The whore told you I was your old man because she thought I was dead, and she could close the door on that issue."

I shifted, confused. "What about Margaret?"

"Margaret."

"You killed her."

"I don't remember. That part hasn't come back to me. Not yet."

"My mother said you killed her and left her rotting in a Dumpster."

"Do I seem like the type to leave a woman in a Dumpster?"

"Yeah. Yeah, you do."

"What did Thelma tell you?"

"She told me that my mother was a prostitute named Margaret, and Margaret had been found dead in a Dumpster. She told me . . . when I was young she said I'd killed my father."

"And you take her word when she tells you the man she thinks is dead is your father?"

"Either way, you killed her best friend. You killed Margaret."

"I loved Margaret. When I was capable of loving, I loved her. I fell in love with a whore. But I had forgotten about her. I forgot about her when you popped me in my head. When I lost my memory, the Beast rewrote her in my mind. He told me she was from Eastern Europe, a Slav. For years I thought she was Russian, Belarusian, or Ukrainian. Another lie. Another damn lie. She wasn't a Slav. She was a black girl, from the islands. I remember that much now."

"You're a liar."

"The Beast and Thelma were liars."

"If the Beast is dead, you can tell any lie you want."

"Go look in the Beast's quarters, gaucho. Go fucking look. Tell me I'm a liar."

I motioned. "Lead the way."

He struggled to get up, failed again. I helped him up. He moved like half his body was numb. Years of wars, of being a warrior, and this was what it had all added up to. This.

While he struggled, I asked, "Where were you from?"

He said, "I grew up in El Pueblo de la Reina de Los Angeles. My father was a detached drunk and my mother was a beautiful Romanian actress who died in the Baldwin Hills flood. He took my mother's death hard, but he didn't cry. What was done was done. He was a rough guy, physically rough and mentally rough. My father married the Beast's mother. The Beast's father had died. My dad needed a woman to take care of the house and cook and clean. She needed the security. And a woman needs a man to protect her from other men. Well, women used to. It was that way when I was growing up. Things have changed. Women are in the Middle East, fighting and protecting men now."

Then we were at the door to the Beast's quarters. Again I was cautious, felt like this was a setup. I pushed the door open, saw no one inside. The apartment was as quiet as a tomb in the middle of the night, the temperature cool but not cold. I sat Medianoche in a chair.

He said, "Now look around and tell me what you see, gaucho."

Tiled floors sparkled. It was a white-walled museum. Flags. Trophies. Valuable coins. DVDs. Many military books, novels on all the wars. Other novels as well. *Las venas abiertas de América Latina* and *La noche de los lápices*. Cuban cigars. Stainless steel flask and lighter.

He was a well-read warrior and had a weapons qualification badge.

I was surrounded by the Beast's belongings. There were photographs of him in the apartment. He looked like a powerful military man. A man who jumped out of planes and fought bulls with his bare hands. La Bestia de Guerra. It was like staring into my brother Andrew-Sven's face. My brother had the same face. Had the same strong build.

I asked, "What's the other room?"

"It's where his servant slept. A gunsel named Draco."

"A gunsel."

"Your hoodlums killed him at the roundabout the night I kicked your ass."

I touched the books. "Who was this guy? Who was the Beast?"

"He was my best friend. He was my brother. He was my commanding officer."

"Why haven't I ever heard of him?"

"The Beast was a *pathicus*. A *cinaedus*. He was a powerful soldier, an excellent warrior, but he was a weak man. That's the nut sack you might've come from. Not mine, gaucho. He had a wife. Had children. But he just did that because that is what men are supposed to do. He was with your mother because that is what men are supposed to do. That's what women are for. It never stopped him from being who he was."

"You claim he sent you to kill my mother."

"He betrayed me then."

"We left you for dead."

"On the floor of a whorehouse."

"You die where you die. You die however you die. Be it kicking and suffocating with a plastic bag over your head, or with a bullet to the brain. Or in a falling elevator."

"Well, someone found me, an ambulance came. My memory was gone. For years, decades, sections of my memory were gone. Now, bit by bit, it's starting to come back."

"You didn't die. I shot you in the face, point-blank, and you didn't die. That .22 should have rattled around inside of your brain. You shouldn't be here. I saw you fuckin' die."

"You saw what you wanted to see. You saw what you needed to see. Maybe your whore-mother lied. I didn't fucking die. Just part of my brain. Just part of my memory. But it's fighting to be reborn. This cavern where my eye used to be, you did this to me, gaucho. You did this."

I barked, "For trying to kill my mother."

He tried to snap, "I was under orders. That was my assignment."

"An assignment you failed."

"I failed."

"And here we are. I shot you with your own gun. That has to hurt."

"That gunshot, you gaucho fuck, has caused me problems. Now this ministroke."

"You tried to kill my mother."

"She is nobody. If she had died, the world wouldn't have missed her. I would have killed her, then put a bullet in you to shut you up. Maybe you would've been the one with one eye and a bad memory."

Trigger finger moving back and forth, I stood staring at images of the Beast.

I compared my features to his. Same as I had already done with Medianoche.

"You said he had a wife and other children?"

"He did. But he didn't give a rat's ass about either. All he cared about was the Four Horsemen. This was his brainchild. He was an excellent warrior. He was brilliant. Together we were hungry lions chasing gazelles through fields and across rooftops around the world."

I paused.

I said, "And Arizona killed him. She killed the Beast with her blade."

"No. I killed him. I killed the Beast."

"Arizona hit him with her blade."

"She wounded him. Then I put a bullet in his head, like you put one in mine."

I stopped starring at the photos of the military man gone rogue.

I faced Medianoche. "You sent a team after my mother."

"I did. And fate led them to the Landscaper."

"They attacked Alvin White."

"And Preacher filled him with lead and dumped him in the Chattahoochee River."

"You sent the Preacher to kill my family."

"Smyrna, Georgia, on Oakwood Trace. Townhome owned by Nia Simone Bijou, but being rented through an agency by Jeremy Bentham. He'll catch a bullet if he gets in the way."

"You found my mother and my brothers."

"Hours ago. Thelma and those two trick-baby bastards should be done by now, gaucho."

"Those are my brothers."

"They are the spawn of my goddamn enemy."

"She is my mother."

"Do you think I give a shit? You see this hole where my eye used to be?"

"I guess we're done talking."

"I guess we are."

"The only reason I didn't kill you before was because I thought you were my father. My mother told me that after I had shot you the first time. I had to live with that anger and guilt. Thanks for taking that off the table, Media-fucking-noche. It will make doing this much easier."

"You're nothing, gaucho. Just like your whore-mother, you're nothing."

He battled through his stroke, his weakness, stood up like a bear, roared, became ten feet tall. His rage echoed, and he became the devil in my nightmares, the man I feared.

Mesnatë. Mitjanit. Middernacht.

Hanner Nos. Gece Yarısı.

Medianoche.

He cursed me, came at me, lunged, and promised me death.

He conquered his stroke and became Mr. Midnight.

Chapter 29

El Fin de la Guerra

And our war would end.

But when one bloody war ended, a bloodier conflict was born to take its place. Peace was the enemy of those who loved war and the spoils of war.

After it was done loading the information I needed, then downloading a worm that would corrupt their systems when activated, I pulled the pen drive that had software intelligent enough to be able to crack open any computer's system from the Horsemen's main computer. I dropped the pen drive into my jacket pocket. I finished drinking a Quilmes Cristal, then went to the bathroom. I took a leak, then picked up a comb that was in the Beast's immaculate bathroom. It had hair follicles. It had his DNA. Had to be his. After I dropped the comb into a plastic bag, I looked around at the things the Beast had owned. I took pictures of his images and awards, of his books, and then I pulled three photos from inside silver frames. I folded those and eased them into my inside suit pocket. Then I sent a text message to a number with 809 as its area code. Done but not safe, I left the apartment of the Beast of War, gun in hand. No Horseman or guard was in the hallway. I kept my eye and gun on the door to Medianoche's war-torn apartment while I pushed the button to call the elevator.

My fingers had left blood on the lift's call button.

I looked at my bloodied hands, wiped that print away, same as I had done everything I had touched. Blood covered my expensive suit, none of it mine this time.

A soft, feminine, programmed voice announced, "*Piso diecisiete.*"

With the lobby being the zeroth floor, I was eighteen floors aboveground.

An object falling on earth would drop at 9.8 meters per second faster every second. Would take but a moment to reach maximum speed. I felt that when I had BASE jumped to escape the wrath of the Horsemen. A parachute changed the physics of falling, kept me from plummeting like a cannon ball. It wasn't the fall that killed a man. It was the sudden deceleration. It was the abrupt stop. One hundred percent of people died after falling eighty-five feet.

The pedophile at the Gherkin never had a chance.

The men I have thrown from planes never had a chance. One target had been dropped from only two stories. He was the exception. The order was to make sure he didn't die. It was a South American job I had done years ago after I had vanished without a trace and left Angelina sobbing and worried at the End of the World. Off the shore of Brazil, over the Atlantic Ocean, less than one hundred miles from the epicenter of São Paulo, sits Ilha da Queimada Grande. Snake Island. No sane man went there; it was overrun by snakes and remained undeveloped. The island had between one and five poisonous snakes per square meter. They said at least four thousand poisonous golden lance heads slithered in a population of more than a quarter of a million snakes. Some said it was closer to half a million snakes. I just knew it was too many snakes to fit on a plane.

If I could've, that was where I would have taken Medianoche.

I would have dropped him from a Cessna on that island. But with my luck, he would have survived. Snakes would have bitten the devil and died. He would have swum to Brazil.

I thought about a dozen ways to kill Medianoche as the elevator descended.

The programmed voice announced, *"Piso cero."*

The door opened and I was armed, had a loaded gun and an itchy trigger finger.

I anticipated another guard, another Horseman, or Medianoche himself.

I had descended eighteen levels much slower than it had taken me to BASE jump, much slower than a two-hundred-plus-pound man would fall.

Eight floors would have been enough. I had been twice that height, plus two floors.

The guard I had fought was where I had left him. He hadn't moved an inch. I knew he was dead. But I had known a man was dead before. I put two RIP bullets in his head to be sure. If he rose from those two shots, Jesus would finally be impressed by the devil's work. When I opened the glass doors and exited into the cold, in front of me, as a light rain drizzled across this section of Buenos Aires, I saw Medianoche. I stopped moving when I saw Mr. Midnight.

I saw the man who, since I was a boy, I believed was dead. I found he was alive, had survived a point-blank shot to the head, and believed he had the powers of Jason Voorhees, Freddy Krueger, Chucky, Pinhead, Tall Man, and Michael Myers.

He could be part Dalek.

Or a ninth-series Cylon.

Or just be the devil.

Gun trained, I took tentative steps until I saw the bulletproof raiment of a man who wore only the best a Bogotá clothier had to offer. Today, I wore a suit by the same clothier.

We had fought upstairs. It wasn't close to the battle we had had in the *villas*. But it was a fight. He was temporarily weakened by a stroke, but he was still strong. I went back to his quarters, dragged him with me, and I beat him with his saxophone. I beat him for every time he had called my mother a whore, for every time he had called me a trick baby, for every time he had called my brothers the same. He had dehumanized us all. Once dehumanized, the object wasn't worth living and was easy to kill and feel nothing about it. It was the way nations had been taken out.

He told me I wasn't his son. He told me he had killed my brother's father. He told me that my mother was dead. And so were Robert and Steven. I dragged him out on his patio. I threw him over the rail. I grunted and threw him, and the old soldier had fallen without a sound.

Now I stood in front of his body. Twisted, he looked so small.

He didn't look like him anymore.

His body was broken, but I couldn't tell how badly.

Most of the damage would be internal.

His head was misshapen, his face now unrecognizable.

Blood came out of his ears and mouth.

But other than that, he looked okay. He looked like he could get up. Wipe away blood. Pop a BC Powder. And start a war. He reminded me of the body of Evelyn McHale resting atop a crumpled limousine after she jumped to her death from the Empire State Building in the forties.

Only he had hit the ground. It was dark, the thick of night. If anyone had seen him, they hadn't screamed.

I looked up, did the math in my head. Calculated his speed at impact. He had tumbled, gone end over end, then smacked into the concrete walkway at more than a hundred miles an hour.

At some point, the height didn't matter. A man dropped from a height would achieve terminal velocity and wouldn't be able to fall any harder than he was already falling.

If Señorita Raven hadn't swerved her car when we were on the damp streets of Ciudad Evita, our head-on car crash would have been harder. No one would have walked away.

I went to Medianoche, took out a white handkerchief. I took some of Beelzebub's DNA. I still wanted to know what I was to Mr. Midnight, if anything. The comb I'd found in the Beast's bathroom, his DNA, and mine would also be sent to my contact at DNA Solutions.

I kicked Medianoche; then I jumped back like a frightened child.

Expected him to groan and get up, rise like a riled bear once again.

He didn't move. He was in permanent hibernation.

I took a few pictures with my phone.

The photos were more tragic than gruesome.

Then I unloaded my gun into his body, let my trigger finger hiccup, then reloaded, and unloaded again. RIP bullets exhausted, I wiped the gun down and threw it on his corpse.

I said, "Come back from that, motherfucker. Come back from that."

Covered in sweat and blood, I spat on the devil and limped away.

Chapter 30

La Reina

I went back to the building, used Foxy Brown's black card to open another unmarked door. This one led to the Horsemen's private garage. It was like stepping into a well-appointed Batcave. There were three more Mercedes-Benz. Four more BMW motorcycles. And armament that had probably been furnished by the traitor Benjamin Assad. I commandeered a Benz. I turned the car on and it purred. A CD started to play. I pointed the AMG toward Greater Buenos Aires, toward EZE, their Ministro Pistarini International Airport. Or Ezeiza International Airport. Whatever they called it meant nothing to me. I had bigger issues. Bigger than the Porteñas who marched the streets for the right to abortions, bigger than the protests against Brazil, bigger than the protest against paper plants in Uruguay, bigger than the protest against part of Avenida Pueyrredón becoming a two-way street. Bigger than the world falling apart and the banks collapsing in Reykjavík. They were bigger because they were my problems, and now I felt like Atlas with the world on my shoulders. My head throbbed as I sped by graffiti, public housing, *cantinas, farmacias, locutorios, remises,* and Shell gas stations. Tears formed in my eyes. I imagined one large coffin and two smaller ones. I no longer had Shotgun to keep an eye out for me. I had failed him. I had failed my brothers. And my mother.

I should have gone to Atlanta first, saved my family, not come here.

I remembered what Señorita Raven had told me.

Three coffins. One large. Two small.

My throat tightened, then it burned.

My eyes watered and I could barely breathe.

I wept.

Back in jeans, a sweater, trainers, and a leather jacket, carrying a backpack, I boarded a Gulfstream G650, a plane that could fly close to Mach .90. Cream leather seats. Sofas. Meeting area. Bed. Might have had a shower so when you landed you left the plane fresh. It was a flying mansion. When I had come down here with Shotgun and Konstantin, we had been on this plane flying above fifty thousand feet at seven hundred miles per hour, moving a mile every five seconds. A pace that would leave Usain Bolt in awe. The same slender Ethiopian, modelesque Russian, Arabian princess, and gorgeous Brazilian flight attendants greeted me at the door of a plane large enough to transport a party of eighteen. They smelled nice, refreshing after inhaling the stench on the streets of Buenos Aires. The Ethiopian's scent was smoldering aldehydic amber with floral notes, the kind that melted into your skin. The modelesque Russian smelled like luscious nag champa and mind-altering musks. The Arabian princess—one inhale made a man smile and think of buttery tuberose, tropical frangipani, and indolic white florals. The Brazilian had a butt that would win awards in her country and the aroma of animalistic chypres. I had met them before. This was the jet Scamz had sent to bring Shotgun, Konstantin, and me from Atlanta down into the den of trouble. The flight attendants had no idea how much my world had changed since then. Their combined scents were subtle, perfect. If a city smelled that good, I'd never leave, would stay in bed, masturbating. They asked me about Konstantin. I told them he wasn't coming on this trip. They asked me about Shotgun. I told them that he wasn't coming either. Left it at that.

Classical music played. Flat-screen televisions were on CNN, the international version, the sound on mute. The scent of cloves assaulted my senses the moment I stepped on the plane. That aroma came from Djarum, an Indonesian kretek. It was a clove cigarette made in Kudus, Central Java. It was as classy as wearing a two-thousand-dollar Italian suit while playing Beethoven on a baby grand piano. Djarum was Scamz's brand, his trademark smoke, as it had been his father's brand and trademark. I smelled cloves and knew the legacy of Scamz hadn't died with him at sea. A woman spoke in Tagalog. She was angry, yelling at someone. I knew her voice. I knew her Filipina voice well, better than I knew my own voice. Used to hear her voice in my dreams. It was Arizona, the woman many knew as Queen Scamz. To me she would always be Arizona. She was at the back of the plane. When I stepped on the Ferrari of airplanes, I felt an ache in my heart.

Shotgun should have been here taking this trip. He'd have a funeral and I wouldn't be able to attend. If I did I would still feel so much anger.

As soon as I moved beyond the smiling flight attendants, I saw a different Filipina woman. She wore a short white blouse. Tight black skirt. High heels with red soles. Sierra was slightly darker than Arizona, in energy and complexion, owned a fuller body, more ass and tits to serve as a distraction, her meanness and coldness boundless, her damage deeper than the average sociopath. She was a woman who disturbed men, destroyed men, left them coming back for more. That Pussycat Doll had dyed her hair from black to strawberry blond since I saw her last. Usually she wore it pulled back in a ponytail, so her face looked ten years younger than she was, but now it was half-up, half-down, in a gorgeous style. Even with the schoolgirl face, she had a body that said she was a woman. A diabolical, cunning woman who had barely survived Buenos Aires. She was Arizona's sister. She was Queen Scamz's younger sister, so I guess that made her the Princess Scamz.

Her perfume was musky and sweet, an olfactory negligee.

Last time I saw Sierra, it was after she, Scamz, her sister, Arizona, Konstantin, and her brother had been in a shootout with the Four Horsemen. She had been shot and beaten, was almost dead. She was fucked-up. Her hair was matted from almost being blown up in the streets of Buenos Aires, lips chapped, face battered and bruised, lips and cheeks swollen, on a stretcher, a victim of a gunshot wound, shivering from pain and cold, and being loaded onto a yacht in Puerto Madero. I wasn't sure she had survived. I thought she was on the yacht with Scamz when the Four Horsemen had hunted them down, then sank them like the *Titanic*.

It was nice to know that while I was fighting for my life, while my family was being attacked, while Shotgun was being hunted and murdered, she was out getting her nails done and her ass waxed.

I nodded once. My expression remained no-nonsense.

She nodded once and maintained her stoic countenance.

I said, "I need a laptop and the Internet, please. As soon as you can."

She moved out of my way.

When I looked back at her from the next compartment, Sierra was still watching me.

We looked at each other and held eye contact for half a minute. She had a way of looking at a man in an expressionless way that made him feel like he was less than the scum on the bottom of her shoes. Then she turned, and the woman I had been ordered to kill once upon a time walked away, moving her ass like it was talking in code, her tight skirt making her butt cheeks wink left and right with her bipedal stride. I saw what father and son had seen in her. Arizona had been the brains, the one giving orders. Her sister was a quiet seductress. Neither was weak. I had seen both of them put men in the ground. When we had been in a shootout in Miami off I-95, I had seen Sierra kill a man in the most horrible of ways. Then she went and had ice cream.

Arizona's hair was the same as it had been before, long, dyed light brown with highlights. Her perfume was the kind that gave men erections before they ever laid an eye on her. Her perfume wore stilettos, had Kathleen Turner's voice in *Body Heat*, and could get a man to kill for her. Last time I saw the woman who used area code 809, the area code used by con men and con women around the world, she had been fucked-up too. Had damn near been FUBAR. It was after she had given birth to her and Scamz's so-called baby in a safe house across from the Thelonious Club in Buenos Aires' Centro Armenio. Her face had been crushed into the street when the Beast had used his foot and tried to grind her face into the concrete. Her face had been marred, lips swollen and busted, had cuts all over. It was hard to tell now, not without looking close, beyond the makeup. Her sister looked like lust, but Arizona looked like love unrequited.

One woman a man wanted to fuck; the other he wanted to marry.

She said, "Sit."

I didn't move.

She softened her tone. "Please, have a seat."

"That's better."

I sat while the luxury plane hit the runway and glided upward toward the skies.

Arizona said, "Pardon me for being curt and on edge. Don't want to be still too long. Especially in Argentina."

When we were at forty thousand feet I glanced at my Rolex, saw the time, then looked out the window and said, "You're safe. Unless someone attacks you in a military jet, you're safe."

"Safety is an illusion, a luxury not many can afford."

She had a device the size of a PalmPilot. The light flashed green. No high-tech surveillance was pointed her way. It told her that I wasn't wired, or trying to wirelessly steal any information from her. A second device, the same size as the first, was on the table too. It lifted information on all cell phones, laptops, and PalmPilots. She could be robbing me.

Knowing she had Wi-Fi, I motioned to it. "Turn that off."

She said, "Sorry. Was lifting credit card information from people at the airport."

She also had a Thuraya satellite phone made in the United Arab Emirates and functional in more than 120 countries, from the high seas to the North Pole.

I said, "You've been working since you fled Buenos Aires."

"Money never sleeps."

"You lost seventeen million a while ago. When all of this began."

"I've gotten a third, close to a half, of that back working other opportunities."

"You mean cons."

"As they say, a sucker is born every minute."

"Don't end up on the Ten Most Wanted Fugitives list with Semion Mogilevich."

"I'm smarter. Much smarter. I could hit his pocketbook and he'd never realize it was me. But there is an honor among thieves. More or less. Stealing from the government is easier."

She handed me the Thuraya, from the Arabic name for the constellation of the Pleiades. It was also known as Seven Sisters and located in the constellation of Taurus. I had no idea what that had to do with a phone. Didn't care. Was too hard to think about nonsense.

I asked what I already knew. "From Queen Bee and her rogue's gallery in Uruguay?"

"She will contact you when she needs your services."

"How do you know her?"

"I know her. That's all that's important."

"You told her we were in Uruguay."

"I wanted to make sure you made it out okay."

"You didn't trust Scamz."

"No, I didn't. So I made sure you were covered the best I could."

"What do you know about the Men from Uruguay?"

"They want to be the Four Horsemen of the Apocalypse."

"I left a few job openings available."

I put the phone on the table in front of me.

A tall, rounded vase with a base and a stem was on the chair next to Arizona. It was the type used for storing the ashes of a cremated person. It was seated and buckled in with care.

I asked, "Your brother's remains are in that urn?"

She nodded. Emotions rose, but she suppressed them. The ashes of her brother. The Four Horsemen had killed him during a battle on the streets, the same one that had left Sierra tapping on death's door. Arizona had been tapping on that same door. I hadn't been with them at that moment. The Beast had killed her brother. And she had thrown a knife into the Beast's back. She thought she had killed the Beast. I knew the truth, but I would let her go on believing that lie.

I said, "We watched you have a baby. An ugly baby."

"Not my finest moment."

I said, *"Faber est suae quisque fortunae."*

She nodded when I recited the first part of the password from the Buenos Aires job, the one that, in combination with the briefcases, allowed access to the king's ransom.

I said the second of three passwords. *"Audaces fortuna iuvat."*

She nodded; then she said, "And the third password was your name. It was Gideon."

"That surprised me."

"It surprised everyone."

"Especially Scamz."

"He hated you. He was jealous of you."

"He had everything. Why would he be jealous of me?"

"Me."

"He had you."

"Did he?"

For two blinks Arizona softened, looked like the ingénue I had met in North Hollywood. I saw the girl I had fallen in love with. Then she was back to being Queen Scamz, all business, seated on her throne.

She said, "I could've died with my brother on the streets, at the base of *General Justo José de Urquiza*. I could have died in the rain with my brother. I could be in an urn."

"We all almost died."

"Medianoche and the Beast. Never saw any motherfuckers like them in my life."

"Were you afraid?"

"Yes. From the start. When I tried to save my sister, I knew I was dead."

"The baby bump."

"Saved me."

"If only they knew."

"Wish I could have seen the looks on their faces when they realized they'd been conned."

"By the queen."

Arizona inhaled and exhaled her brown cigarette, tinted the confined space with the scent of cloves, puffed only twice; then she put her cigarette out. She sat quiet for a moment, breathing the scent preferred by two of her lovers, legs crossed, a queen on her throne.

She said, "Gideon, I've been thinking about when I met you in North Hollywood."

"Back when you were wearing off-the-rack clothes and driving a broken-down Hyundai."

"You were pretty broke yourself."

"I was new to the business. I saw you and I would've done anything to have you."

"Been watching *Battlestar Galactica*. Been listening to Miles and Coltrane. Been thinking about us at the Parker Meridien. Same for the day we had in North Carolina, the day we went to the theater and saw that horrible Sharon Stone movie, then went to the Carolina Inn."

"You remember what you told me you had forgotten. You said they never happened."

"They happened. I remember. Never forget either time."

"That's a new song you're singing. Last time you denied New York and North Carolina."

She said, "They are always on my mind, especially when I bathe and listen to Coltrane."

"The jobs I did for you must have been on your mind. The men you needed handled."

"No, us together. Making love. I remember the first time we made love."

I corrected her, "Fucking. The first time we fucked."

"I should have given you the chance."

"To do what?"

"You wanted to be my boyfriend, for lack of a better term."

"You didn't want that."

"I should have been your girlfriend. After the first Scamz died, I should have come to you. You had a ranch with horses in California. You had other properties. I should have been with you. We could've done something. I've been wondering what that would have been like."

"Hindsight."

"There was a job, the Lakenheath job, but I had also come to London to be with you."

"Back when you wanted me to go to Amsterdam and kill your sister, Sierra."

"I had felt like everyone I knew had betrayed me. Everyone except you. I think I needed you. I was outside your hotel room door. I went to the MyHotel located near the British Museum, was going to shower, get in bed with you, feel safe while I put my heart on the line, but I heard her. I heard you. She was loud. You were with another woman. A woman you'd met on the plane. You hadn't known her eight hours, and as soon as she left the plane, you fucked her."

"You snooze, you lose."

"I was angry. I had no right to be angry, but I was. I should have just told you how I felt."

"Might have changed a few things."

"Is it too late to put all of that behind us?"

"You tell me. Is it too late to put two men named Scamz in the rearview? Never know when another Scamzito might pop up. I'm sure the original Scamz had more than one son. Next one might be from Iceland. Or Thailand. Men like him spread legs, breed women, and move on to the next. They leave namesakes scattered all around the globe."

"The first Scamz was my boyfriend."

"He was sleeping with you and your sister."

"It was complicated."

"He used to knock you around."

"I was a foolish girl. Like most girls who came from nothing and grew up in the streets, I mistook abuse for love."

"His son?"

"The second Scamz, he was all business. He had connections. He was more ambitious than his father. He took me to another level. I learned a lot dealing with him."

"You loved him too."

"There was no love."

"Then you used him."

"He was a means to an end."

"A means to an end, not an end in itself."

"He's dead. I didn't shed a tear. Actually, I know it sounds cold, but I felt relieved. One less motherfucker to deal with. One less backstabber."

"His properties and money?"

"Will become mine. I might keep a house here and there, but the bulk will be converted to cash and moved to my offshore accounts."

I shook my head. "He thought he could escape the Horsemen by staying at sea."

"I stayed in the air. Since I left him, I have been on this plane. If I needed to land to refuel, I never left the plane or went into the airport. I let airport security be my first line of defense."

"You slept with him to use him. He slept with you to use you. He fucked you, softened you up, and convinced you to call me, and you convinced me I owed him a debt. I sense no robbery, not between you and him. You pulled me into a world of trouble, Queen Scamz."

"Call me Arizona, same as you always have. Just call me Arizona."

"Is that your real name?"

"No. I haven't used my real name since I was a teenager. I've been Arizona so long, this is the only name I answer to. This is who I've become."

"Why the name Arizona?"

"Because a man saw me in the Nordstrom's in Montclair, California. I had already done a Doris Payne number and distracted the salesman long enough to steal two rings from a jewelry store, and then we were trying to shoplift a dress. We had purses that were lined with aluminum foil, so the alarms wouldn't sound at the door when we boosted tagged clothing. He came up to me and asked me my name. I didn't tell him. Wouldn't tell him. Then he told me I was hotter than Arizona in July. He told me that security was watching me, said they had been on my tail since I'd left the jewelry store. He offered to buy the things I had in my bag so I didn't end up in jail. He told me that if I wanted to steal, if I wanted to become a grifter, he could teach me to be smarter at the game."

"And I bet that man was Scamz. The original Scamz."

"Yeah, it was. For a moment I felt like I had been saved by Prince Charming."

"I won't ask how Sierra got her name."

"She was with me when I met Scamz. He drove us home. We lived off the Sierra Avenue exit in Fontana for a while. He called her the 'PYT from Sierra Avenue' because of that. Then he just started calling her Sierra. She liked it. And she's been Sierra ever since."

"Never knew that."

"No one does. We had a mother on drugs. A father MIA. We raised ourselves. My brother. My sister. Me. We were girls and a boy from the gutter. I use to drive through middle-class areas like it was Disneyland, told myself I'd be on their level one day. Now I realize they had nothing. Back then I hustled, stole, did things to make sure my little sister and brother had food to eat. Stealing was a survival skill. We didn't have it like the middle-class people. Anything I stole, I sold for food. Nothing was for me. Paid more than minimum wage. Stealing is how white people became rich. The rich have left many dead bodies behind."

I nodded. "I've worked for the rich. I know their secrets."

"Then Scamz took me to the pool hall in the valley."

"I remember that place. Eight Ball Corner Pocket, run by Big Slim."

She smiled. "Scamz taught me the basics of the game."

"Big Slim's pool hall was a witches' brew of gangsters and con men."

She said, "Thieves, pickpockets, and swindlers."

"And killers."

"And killers."

"Will never forget the electricity I felt when I saw you that first time."

"What was I wearing?"

I nodded. "You came in wearing your flight attendant uniform. You were a flight attendant by then. You changed. Came back in booty shorts. Sandals. A tank top with a white girl giving the world the middle finger."

"You remember."

"I remember. I could tell you were a hedgehog and a man had to get past the quills to get to the soft parts. I wanted you. I didn't care if you were using your job to be a mule for Scamz. Thought we'd have some sort of Bonnie and Clyde, Romeo and Juliet thing going on. You told me to be with you, I needed to have a million dollars in the bank."

Arizona asked, "Is it too late for us to see what this energy is that exists between us?"

"Yeah. It's too late."

"Why?"

"I could give you a million reasons."

"I hurt your feelings. Rejection makes men become petty."

"I'm not being petty. Just being real. Things are clear now. Back then, if you had made me that offer, I would've gone on *Oprah* and jumped up and down on her couch. You've changed. I've changed. So it's like the night in New York and the day at the Carolina Inn didn't happen."

"They happened."

"But they have no currency. They mean nothing."

She gave me a wounded smile. "You'll want me again."

"We're done, Arizona. We were done before Scamz the younger. We never really were because you never got over Scamz the elder."

"When you want me, remember this moment."

"Is this a watershed moment?"

"I lowered my wall for you, Gideon."

"From the moment I first saw you, I used to dream about you. All I wanted was you. I tore down my wall for you. Now it's been rebuilt."

"Parker Meridien. Carolina Inn. Coltrane. Miles Davis."

"Just moments in our past."

"You'll want to make love to me again."

"You don't make love; you only know how to fuck. And the better a woman fucked a man, the more a man was convinced she was making love to him. I learned that from you."

"Don't throw my words back at me."

"Don't think I'm a fucking fool."

"No one called you a fool."

"Don't fuck with me. I have a lot of blood on my hands because of you."

She sipped her watermelon martini. "Scamz's son meant nothing to me. I only slept with him after I came to the hotel room in London and found you with a woman. I stood at your door, heard you fucking her. A stranger you met on the plane. Not until then, not until I found you sleeping with a stranger did I even consider him being my lover. It would have been you. You saved me from men my sister had sent to kill me, and you saved me from Lakenheath. Well, no need for us to review all of that. We know how it went. I was thrown in the Thames. You were killed. I killed a few people. If not for Scamz, you would have stayed dead. He saved the man I cared about at the time and I guess he became my hero."

The Russian came by with drinks. I took a beer.

When she walked away, Arizona said, "Shall we talk business?"

"The pen drive will have all the files, accounts, and passwords for the Horsemen."

"Did you extract the information? Will I be able to get the money they stole from Scamz?"

"Money never leaves your mind, not even when blood is all over the dance floor."

"I don't like losing. Not to a woman you met on a plane, not to the Horsemen."

"Medianoche did a swan dive and I didn't have time to get the information."

"They killed my brother."

"They killed my friend. And they have killed my family. My mother and my brothers."

She took a breath, modified her tone. "Do you want to negotiate?"

"I don't negotiate."

"You have it. You have what I need to take back the money they stole from Scamz."

"Yeah, I do."

"But you're not going to give it to me."

"You don't deserve it. You're no better than the Scamz resting at the bottom of the sea."

She gave me half a smile, then stood, threw her martini glass against a partition, and walked away, each step hard, her ass sending me a negative message, that she was the queen, that there would be consequences. The music changed. And old-school jam played. Kelis was screaming, "I hate you so much right now." Arizona sat in a recliner in a different section, legs crossed, one bouncing, high heel halfway on.

The Brazilian flight attendant came to me with a laptop. She cleaned up the mess Arizona had made. Everyone stayed away from the queen. I logged on to GoToMyPC and connected to Powder Springs. What I saw made me bend over, and the tears came strong.

Catherine was in the house. The boys were back at Powder Springs.

They were alive.

Then I was surprised.

Hawks was there, and so was the Bajan. Hawks was sitting up under the Bajan and he had his arm around her. I used the satellite phone and called the house number.

On the computer I saw everyone jump when the phone rang.

Catherine ran to the phone, looked at the caller ID.

She answered, afraid, hopeful, unsure, "Hello?"

I cleared my throat, wiped my eyes. "Hey. It's me."

"Jean-Claude?"

"Yeah. You're okay. You're okay, right?"

Catherine jumped up and down, shouted, "It's Jean-Claude."

Hawks and the boys made it to Catherine's side first. The Bajan went to them and stood to the side. A gun rested in the waistband of his jeans. I didn't let her know I could see them all. Hawks knew there were cameras in the home but didn't know I was watching them all right now.

Steven yelled, "When are we roller-skating on MLK again?"

Robert ran and picked up the other line. "Yeah, we want to go roller-skating."

My mother with her French accent. My brothers, one who sounded German, the other who sounded British. The United Nations was safe again. After my brothers told me hello, Catherine made them get away from her and get off the other line. They always did what she said.

I asked, "Catherine, are you okay? Did anything happen down . . . up there?"

"Are you okay, son?" She was crying. "Are you okay? I need to know you're okay."

"I'm okay. I'm okay. I had some bad intel on you guys. You're safe."

"Am I? Are we?"

"Medianoche is dead. Mr. Midnight is dead."

Her voice shook. "All of the people he worked with?"

"All gone. The one who was the leader, the Beast, is dead too."

She paused and looked at Steven.

I waited for her to talk about the Beast.

She said, "Alvin White was murdered. It was on the news. The newscaster you like, Jewell Stewark, she reported it three nights in a row. It was on Facebook. It was in *The Atlanta Journal-Constitution*."

"He was my friend. He was my first best friend. Never had friends growing up."

"He was a great man. I admired him for trying so hard at everything."

"I know what they did. One by one or two by two, they all paid. Not that it will do any good for him or his family, but they paid." Then I added, "Yeah. Medianoche is dead."

"Where are you?"

"On a flight. Leaving the epicenter of hell. Heading back to North America."

"Will you come here? I need to see you, face-to-face."

"Since you're okay, New York for a day or two, then there. I hear Steven and Robert in the background. Tell the boys I will come there and take them roller-skating; then we can go to Funtime on Buford Highway and bowl a few games. Friday I can take them to a baseball game."

"Here in Atlanta?"

"In Chicago. Friday we can fly to Chicago, spend the night, spend Saturday at Wrigley, then fly back Saturday night. They can bring their homework with them. If you approve."

"As long as they are back in time for second service at church."

"You go to church?"

"We go to a Catholic church. They need church."

"I'll have them back from Chicago in time."

"I would like to go. I would like to get away from here."

"You can go too."

She paused. "They thought you were dead too."

"I'm fine."

She dabbed her eyes. "Will you take your brothers to Woodstock to practice shooting at cans and bottles?"

"No, I won't do that anymore."

"No, take them. And I want to go too. I need to remember how to use a gun."

"What happened down there that has turned you pro NRA?"

"I want them to know how to use a gun."

"In case people like me come in that direction."

Silence sat between us.

I said, "You need to *remember* how to use a gun. When have you used one?"

She paused. "Never. I have never touched one. Not since I was very young."

I let that contradiction go, but that excited utterance went into my memory bank. There was a lot I wanted to talk to her about, but now wasn't the time. I needed to know if she had known that Medianoche was alive, and I needed to know about her and the Beast. She had never mentioned the Beast. I needed to know who my mother really was, and why all the lies and secrecy. Catherine took the phone and went to the kitchen. She told me about how she had run to the townhome where Jeremy Bentham was staying, had taken the boys there to hide.

He wasn't there with her. I didn't know how much he knew about our lives.

Catherine, the woman formerly known as Thelma, handed the phone to Hawks. I never would have imagined them ever being in the same room, let alone inside of Catherine's home.

She told me she had drowned a preacher in the Chattahoochee River.

I said, "Thanks, Hawks."

"Have you called our *jefe*?"

"No. Are you crying? Is he okay?"

"You went off grid like an idiot. He's not happy about that."

"You're crying."

"Just my allergies. Just my allergies. They act up when I get too worried about a fool."

We talked for a moment. The Bajan had gone back to the living room.

Hawks said, "Jeremy Bentham."

"What happened?"

"When your momma got to his townhome, she asked him a few

questions. Asked him why there was no record of him existing until recently, as if he had just been invented."

"How did she know there weren't any records of him? What was his answer?"

"Well, you had told your momma to look around his stuff, and she did what you asked. Not long after, he got in his car, drove away, and vanished from the face of the earth."

"You made him vanish?"

"The Bajan did. We had Horsemen coming out the ying-yang; Shotgun had been killed up on South Cobb Drive, and I wasn't taking any chances. Shotgun managed to take out three people in the same kind of suits, left them all so they'd have to have closed-casket funerals, and I knew they had to be associated with the Horsemen. I just didn't know if more were already here."

I said, "Jeremy Bentham. So I won't get a chance to meet him."

"Not without a séance or a Ouija board."

"I told Catherine to be careful."

"Too late for that. She found out the hard way. Stubborn woman. Not good at listening. Real nice, but has her ways. At least I see where you got your hard head from. I will say one thing; she loves her children and she is real protective of her boys. And they are real protective of her."

"Who was Jeremy Bentham after? Her or me? Both of us?"

"No idea. But all of his identification was fake. Real good forgeries."

"How much ID did he have?"

"Your momma found six passports in his house. And about one hundred grand in cash."

I asked, "What currency?"

"Most was American money. Some British pounds and euros."

"No reals from Brazil or Argentine dollars?"

"We didn't see any. What does that mean to you?"

"He wasn't out of South America. Someone from across the pond put him there."

"He could've been like your momma. He could've been a man with a past, some kind of a nasty past and had come to Atlanta to start over. A lot of folks go to big cities to get lost. In the South, the ATL is the best place for that. He might've liked the name Jeremy Bentham because of the English philosopher, or he might've just been a fan of the television show *Lost*. Hell, I asked him if he chose the initials because of James Brown. But he refused to say, got real angry and combative when he was confronted. He doubled up his fists. So the Bajan kicked him in the head three times. That changed his attitude. When we hogtied him to chat, he told us to eff the eff off. We didn't have time for no foolish games."

"You did the right thing. I wouldn't have been that nice."

"Was he part of that blackmail thing against you?"

"The guy who blackmailed me, he's at the bottom of the ocean."

"Well, who was this one? Where did that roach come from?"

"I never met him. He never tried to contact me. Only Catherine."

"And now you never will meet him."

"Was one of the passports from France?"

"Sure was. France. Germany. Russia. And one for here in the USA."

"The other two passports?"

"Belgium and the Netherlands."

"And she didn't know him from France or Europe?"

"She said she didn't. Said it was her first time meeting him when he flirted with her."

"She was his target."

"I guess. But your momma is real pretty. Coulda just been that he was a con and liked pretty women. Her accent gets men's attention too, especially down here in Bubba-ville. And she has a nice figure too."

"Any weapons in his house?"

"None that we could find. Everything else was normal."

"Computer?"

"He didn't have one. He didn't even have Wi-Fi at his townhome."

"He could get Wi-Fi at any Starbucks. He might have been someone's eyes and ears."

"He was seeing your momma. He was sleeping with her. She's broke up about it, but I told her, then showed her all the evidence. We went over it all together so she could be clear. She felt like a fool behind it, I will tell you that much. And she got real angry. Real angry."

"I'll talk to you when I land in the USA."

"Well, since you're okay, and everything is handled, we're going to leave soon."

"We?"

She whispered, "Gideon, I know you're probably looking at the cameras."

"Not yet."

"Well, the Bajan helped. Konstantin didn't want to take no chances and sent him down here . . . *up* here after they got Shotgun."

"Where you off to?"

"Have to break out my passport again and go to Wales."

"Need backup?"

She hesitated. "MX-999 is going with me."

"Who is MX-999?"

"The Bajan. That's the name he uses when he works with some collection agency called RCSI. He's got some issues with them."

"He mentioned that to me. How bad?"

"Big-time issues, so I might end up trying to help out."

"MX-999. What does that mean?"

"Long story on that one. That RCSI group, they are some horrible people. Anyway, the Bajan is going with me. But thanks for the offer."

"He's still there?"

"He's been here, locked and loaded, watching over Catherine and the boys. We didn't know how many Horsemen were up this way. She was staying in a motel with the boys, but decided to come home, as long as the Bajan and I stayed around and helped her look for trouble. We just got here a few hours ago. The Bajan came first, made sure it was safe."

"He's a nice guy. Konstantin said that 007 was a nice guy."

"It's MX-999. Smartass. He's different. And before we go, there is this other thing."

"What other thing?"

"The information I have on Nathalie Marie from Yerres. Y'all been through a lot, and I think y'all need to make sure y'all are in the right mind before you look at what I have for you."

"What did you find out about her connection to Yerres?"

"Some lies are prettier than the truth. That's why some people have to lie."

"She's earned your empathy."

"No, you have my friendship. You trust me and my judgment?"

"Yeah. I do."

"Put some time between this and that. Let them be happy you're okay. And you can spend some time being glad they're out of danger."

"So you know something about me that I don't know."

"We're done with this. For now."

I paused, soaked in reality. "Thanks for the help, Hawks. Thanks for everything."

"You get beat up? You fall off another building?"

"You know how I roll."

"I have an extra box of BC Powder. Will leave it here for you."

"I still owe you for the last box."

"Think of it as an early Christmas present."

"Okay."

"Can I say something?"

"Sure."

"Thanks for Puerto Rico. I mean that. I really did have a good time."

"You're a woman who means what she says, and says what she means."

"Learn to be that kinda man, Gideon. Not for me, but for yourself."

I said good-bye, ended the call, and went to Arizona. I reached in my pocket and took out the pen drive. She sipped her martini, then looked at me like she could no longer trust me.

I told her, "You get into the Horsemen's systems. The money they forced Scamz to transfer into their account, it's yours. The rest is mine. Every dime. Don't leave enough in that account to rub two quarters together. No money, then there can't be any more Horsemen."

She nodded. "That works for me, Gideon."

"I'm doing what I promised I would do, that's all."

"Thanks for being fair. Lakenheath tried to rip me off back in the day on the Katrina scam. And Scamz, didn't trust him as far as a monkey can throw shit. That's why I kept the passwords to myself. He would have stolen it all and left me out to dry. I needed you down there."

I told her, "I want all of the Horsemen's files. Only for me, my eyes only, not for you."

"Agreed. No problem. You can watch me if you want."

I handed her the pen drive. She pulled out a laptop and went to work. Amazing how any laptop with Wi-Fi could be used to break into any system that had the same.

I asked, "Mind changing the music? That song gives me a headache."

Soon Miles played. When his song ended, Coltrane began.

Arizona said, "You killed your father. Same as Scamz, the first one, did."

"If I did, it wasn't the same."

"If?"

"Or maybe it was. Maybe it was the same."

I left her to working, to cracking into systems and stealing money.

Soon she had her millions, the money that had once belonged to Scamz.

The Horsemen's war chest was sent to my offshore account.

I had millions.

I'd find a way to get more money to Alvin White's widow and kids. Maybe have an accountant send a stipend each month. Set up college funds. And some would go to Steven. And Robert. And Catherine.

I had the comb with the Beast's DNA. I would get Andrew-Sven's DNA and send it all in.

As I had been before this fiasco in Buenos Aires, I was back to X.Y.Z.

I'd call Medianoche's DNA and mine A.B. Asshole and Bastard. Those would be sent to DNA Solutions in a separate package. Right now my blood brother's truth was the most important. The truth about my father had bothered me most of my life. Even though Andrew-Sven never said anything, I know it bothered him. One day Steven would want to use his real name, would want to only be Andrew-Sven, would want to know about his identity, and would start asking Catherine questions about his father, who he was, how they met, and what happened. He knows what she did when she worked on Berwick Street, but he would want something definitive. He should know who his father was, or who he wasn't. I could give him that truth.

If there was any truth in what Medianoche had said, I could look my brother in his eyes and tell him that his father was a strong man, a military man, a leader who jumped out of airplanes and went on secret missions. I would say he had died in battle. He had paid the ultimate price protecting his army in a war down in South America. That would be my spin. I wouldn't ever tell him I was part of that war. I would never tell him I was his father's enemy. And I hoped my brother would never find out.

When Arizona was done, she pressed a key and the Horsemen's files were purged from their system. Then the hard drives were written over with hexadecimal code that was nothing but gibberish. When the Policía Federal Argentina finally broke the codes and went to the seventeenth floor, the computers would be paperweights. From the seventeenth floor to Las Violetas to Ciudad Evita, Policía Federal Argentina and *los bomberos* had work to do.

My job was done.

For a second I had a flash of Señorita Raven and Foxy Brown.

I told myself that I had done the right thing.

I went to the back of the plane to go to the bathroom. I washed my face like I was trying to scrub away my personal horrors, my PTSD. When I came out, Sierra was waiting at the door. I went to move by her, but she blocked my path. She gave me eye contact. The stoic, silent siren gazed at me the same way she had a few days ago, like rabid lust chained to a stake, growling, struggling to get free, but under her control.

She kissed me, put her tongue inside my mouth, pushed her breasts against my chest. Then she sighed and walked away, her bowed legs doing a slow sashay by her big sister. That soft exhale was the only sound I'd ever heard her make.

Arizona's back had been to us when that sexual harassment had gone down.

Days ago, I had gone to rescue Sierra when she was wounded in Argentina. I had transported her to Scamz's yacht. Maybe that was her version of a thank-you kiss. Or maybe because I had refused to put her down years ago when Arizona had sent me to Holland.

The stoic brown-skinned Filipina had surprised me.

I had stood up to Scamz, and Scamz had pulled a gun on me, and without a gun in hand, I had made that bitch back down. He was dead. Maybe in her eyes he had died a king, but I had been a warrior. And even a king never rose from his throne to battle a warrior.

She knew I had pulled the sword from the stone.

Maybe she wanted to be my reward. Many queens became enamored of warriors and wanted to be pleased by what they saw as a real man.

Princesses did the same, and some were more cutthroat than queens.

They knew kings had power but were weak men.

Without warriors there would be no kings.

Without warriors, there would be no presidents, no emperors.

I sat near Arizona, let the chair recline back, and closed my eyes. Sierra came back in our section, sat across from us sipping a chocolate martini. Her energy ran through me, made me open and close my hands. I smelled her fragrance and the subtle scent of the chocolate in her drink. Felt her lust without opening my eyes. She smelled so good my toes curled. She smelled like bad news dancing with trouble.

She changed the channel on the flat-screen, began watching *Breaking Bad*.

Arizona snapped, "Who the fuck told you to change the channel?"

Sierra threw the remote at Arizona.

From oil and vinegar to oil and water.

Arizona shot her sister a look. "Pick it up."

Sierra picked up the remote, put the television back on CNN and the news about the world financial crisis. She then took her drink and walked away, her ass moving like it was screaming and cursing, but she was back in less than a minute, fresh drink in her hand. She put the urn in the seat next to her and sat next to her brother, legs crossed, calm, stoic.

She blamed Arizona for their brother's death. Soon they would be in another civil war that rivaled the war between the noble families in Westeros.

As Coltrane played, I sat between sisters with the scents of angels and demons, con women who had tried to kill each other once upon a time. And who might do the same again.

Friends close.

Enemies closer.

And family closer than close.

What the assassin called Hawks had said stayed on my mind.

She had proof that there were more falsehoods from Catherine.

Thelma still existed. She was hidden in plain sight.

Then, as Sierra had done, only for a different reason, I sighed softly.

I said, "Do you know what a moment is?"

Arizona looked at me like I was a fool. "A moment is a moment."

"A moment is a medieval unit of time and equals ninety seconds. Back in the Middle Ages when they used sundials, they measured time in moments. So an hour had forty moments instead of sixty minutes."

"Why are you telling me that bullshit?"

"So I can get my mind off death and killing. For a moment."

"Is that supposed to be a joke?"

"Not really. Just needed to put something else in my head."

My trigger finger moved back and forth, hiccupping.

Sierra stared at me. She sipped her drink and stared.

Man or money, she wasn't afraid to steal from a con woman.

Again I saw what Scamz the elder and his son had seen in Sierra. I understood why they took thirty pieces of silver.

Arizona saw her sister looking at me; she jumped up and slapped her, cursed her out in Tagalog, then in English told her younger sister if she ever crossed her again she'd end up back in Amsterdam doing live sex shows.

Sierra picked up the urn that housed the ashes of her dead brother. Ass wagging, enraged, she marched to a section in the rear of the G650.

I was right.

One war had ended; another had started.

But that war wasn't my war. I still had my own.

Chapter 31

Gotham

Wearing jeans and a T-shirt, I moved through summer heat and battled traffic on I-95, crossed the Hudson River, and made my way to the Upper East Side of Manhattan. It was almost ninety degrees and muggy, each inhale disgusting, like sucking on the exhaust of a car, but being in motion felt good. I rocked a Ducati Streetfighter; being on two wheels kept me from feeling trapped. I threaded the needle, dodged cars, pedestrians, buses, and a sea of yellow cabs. An hour ago, with a handshake good-bye, Arizona had left me on the tarmac in New Jersey at Teterboro, just across the George Washington Bridge, a short distance from the Lincoln Tunnel, in a city that had as much traffic on its streets as it did on the sidewalks, a Gotham that was always in a hurry.

I sped and threaded the needle through traffic until I was near Central Park, not far from the Met Breuer museum. I found a space to park in front of my destination, then reached into my backpack and pulled out a New York Yankees baseball cap, eased on dark

Wayfarers. While he was distracted, I slipped past the Upper East Side doorman, didn't look back toward Park Avenue and Seventy-Fifth Street. I hesitated before I stepped on the elevator, then backed away and found the stairs. Cameras were in the stairwell, so I kept my head down, climbed to the twentieth floor. I eased down the hallway and tapped on the door for unit B.

A woman opened the door. She was in her twenties, slender, dressed in black. Her hair cascaded over her shoulders. Like I had done on the plane, I noticed her perfume. Gucci. She told me her name was Yana.

In Russian I said, "My name is Gideon."

"Do you have a weapon, Gideon?"

"Several. In my backpack."

"I will need your backpack."

I handed it to her. She handed me a claim tag.

She asked, "Do you mind?"

"Go ahead."

She searched me. Found nothing.

She said, "Remove your baseball cap and sunglasses, please."

She stepped aside and I entered the gracious entry gallery. It felt like the home of a diplomat. Yana led me into an elegant living room. Russian Mafia music played and could be heard in the seven rooms, was piped into the five bathrooms of this fourteen-million-dollar property. Many Russians were in the apartment, all dressed in suits and ties. Food and drinks were being served by Russian waiters and waitresses. There was an open bar. People chatted and some danced their Russian dances.

The Man in the White Shoes entered the room to loud applause. He was holding hands with his smiling wife. He looked like Cary Grant and she looked like the Italian actress Gina Lollobrigida.

Konstantin had finished his chemotherapy. This was his celebration.

He came to me, shook my hand, then pulled me to him, and we hugged like family. He sighed, looked relieved.

In Russian he said, "Son, you vanished and had me worried. I thought they had you."

"I know, Konstantin. I know."

"You didn't follow my orders."

"I had to go. They would have found us all, one by one."

"Not for the cancer, I would have been at your side."

"I couldn't let you go back."

"Now sit. Drink. Tell us how you killed those motherfuckers."

I was in a room filled with people in the same business. Husbands and wives. Most were over sixty. Their days doing wetworks were behind them. I was the youngest face in the place. First we damned cancer and toasted to Konstantin's kicking its ass. Then gangsters and their lovers heard my tale of David fighting many Goliaths. They toasted me with drinks raised high. They chanted my name. They said my name like I was the Gideon from the Bible, the military man, a leader who, despite having the numerical disadvantage, had defeated the Midianite army. I drank with them like they were family, and celebrated Konstantin being better.

He treated me like I was his son.

I respected him like he was my father.

Then I needed to see my brothers. And confront my mother.

Days later I went back to Atlanta. I went to visit Alvin White's gravesite. I went to Atlanta Memorial Depot and paid for a marble headstone. Then on an overcast day, I sat there with my friend's spirit for a while. I assured him that his children would be taken care of, but money was no substitute for a father like him. Money would never fix his wife's devastated heart or lessen her unmeasurable grief. Then I had gone to see Catherine and the boys. I upgraded the panic room with reinforced walls. I installed a vault door that led to that space. The door was hidden behind a mirror. I put televisions and a MacBook Pro in the panic room. It was stocked with food, guns, ammo. The boys helped me. I took the boys to skate, took them bowling, took them rock climbing, and then I drove them and Catherine out to Woodstock. I took them to the field we used to go to with Shotgun for target practice. We set up bottles and cans to gun down. There wasn't a house for at least a mile in any direction. Out where conservatives and the NRA roamed, I showed my mother how to load and use a gun. First I let her try popping off with a .22, then switched to a .380. She killed a few bottles, but missed four out of five shots. My brothers were hitting seven out of ten. They were becoming little marksmen. Catherine didn't like guns.

She said, "So much violence and machismo."

While the boys were target practicing she walked a few feet away.

I followed her, then stood next to her and watched the boys.

She said, "Hawks and the Bajan saved us."

"They did. They watched over you."

"He had sent people to slaughter us. To kill me and my sons."

"That was the plan."

"Is he really dead? I know I have asked you that so many times. But are you sure? I am still afraid. Very afraid. Is Mr. Midnight really dead?"

I took out my phone. I showed her the images of Medianoche after his fall from grace. I studied her fear. Her face lost its color.

"You should have dismembered and burned his body. You should have dragged his carcass through the streets for what he has done."

Her anger, the fear and coldness surprised me.

I popped my lips. "Mr. Midnight was my father."

She pulled her lips in, but said nothing as her mood changed.

I said, "Let's walk over there and talk."

"About?"

"Lies that have been told."

Forty yards from the boys, when I stopped walking, she stood next to me, gun in hand, lips twisted, much on her mind as she kicked dirt.

Her voice was uneven. "What lies, Jean-Claude?"

My mother wore slim jeans. Pink chucks. White T-shirt. Atlanta Braves baseball cap. She looked young, small and delicate. I had on worn Levi's and an aged Batman T-shirt. Brown steel-toe boots that had seen better days. Everything I had on I had picked up at Goodwill.

I said, "I need us to be honest with each other."

"What have I done wrong this time?"

I told her there were hidden cameras in the house. I told her that was how I was able to look inside of her home. I used my phone, connected to the system, and let her view what I could see when I had monitored the house in Powder Springs. I revealed where each camera was located.

She was outraged. "Why would you put cameras in my home?"

I put the phone away. "To protect you and my brothers."

"You are far away, and somehow a camera is supposed to protect us? You lie. Why would you violate my privacy in such a way? You bring me back to America, give me a house, then put cameras in almost every room so you can spy on me? Is that house my prison or my home?"

"I will give you the codes. The password. And you can change it to whatever you want it to be. You can look in the house before you come home. At night you can monitor outside and be sure you're safe."

"Secret cameras. That was how you knew about Jeremy."

"Yeah, that's how."

"You will not be able to spy inside my home after this day?"

"Not unless you want me to keep surveillance."

"Why would you do that to someone?"

"You know why. Because of what you did to me when I was a boy."

She shuddered. "I am not that person. I was young. Stupid. Afraid."

"Tell me about Nathalie Marie Masreliez. Tell me about Yerres."

She kicked dirt and shook her head. "Leave my past in the past."

"Is there any secret you have I need to know?"

"Alvin White is dead. Let that be enough. Let that be your guilt. Let that be the pillow made of rock you try to sleep on each night."

My jaw tightened and my trigger finger began to hiccup.

She said, "Robert's mother and Alvin are dead because of you. Live with that. Lose sleep over that. I have every night. I suffer every night."

"*I suffer both day and night.* I will take the hit on Robert's mother. I was careless. That was my fault. Alvin White is dead because he came back here to try and protect you from all of this bullshit you've created."

"Shot many times. Pulled from the river like he was a dead animal. I was his teacher. You involved him in that ugly part of your life, not me."

"I don't want to fight with you."

She snapped, "Then stop whatever you're doing."

"I just asked a couple of simple questions."

"Stop interfering with my life. Stop spying on me."

"Sure, Nathalie. Sure."

She looked me in my eyes. *"Va te faire foutre*, Gideon."

She cursed me and called me *Gideon* as an insult.

In French I asked, *"Who was Jeremy Bentham?"*

"I don't know any more than what I have already told you."

"He wasn't a Horseman. They don't take you on dates and buy you popcorn before seducing you. They blow your brains out and move on."

"Then who was he? Why me? What did he want from me?"

"Don't know. Not yet. The truth always shows up. Remember that. Sooner or later. Every lie has an expiration date. Every lie, large or small." I took a breath. "Did loverboy Jeremy ever use your computer?"

"When we were at Barnes and Noble, yes, for a few minutes."

"Did you watch him?"

"No. I was reading a novel and drinking café. I trusted him."

"Either he planted a virus or stole your personal information. Your computer is no good. Give it to me. I'll get you another one today. Change your e-mail address. The banking I set up for you and the boys, any account you have, change all of your passwords, including Wi-Fi."

"Jesus. This is too much. All of this, this is too much."

"Has anyone contacted you looking for him?"

"No one. I did like you told me to do. Once or twice a day, I have called his number pretending I was looking for him. Today I will call and say I am hurt that he has not returned my calls, sound sad, be angry, tell him I can take a hint, cry, and say that I will never bother him again."

"Good. Good."

"Where is his— Where is his body?"

"It will never be found, not without an archeological dig."

She took a few hard breaths. "He used me. Like every man I have ever met, he used me. When a man does that, when he lies to have sex with a woman, when it is done, the woman feels as if she has been raped."

"He was after more than sex. This was deeper. Sex was his fore-play. He wasn't around long enough for you to feel like you'd been fucked."

Her voice cracked. "He found me, tricked me, used me."

"Get over it. You've used many people. In your own way."

"I don't use people."

"You sent me to kill. *You did that*. My mother put a weapon in my hand and sent me to kill. Then she lied and kept most of the money."

She clacked her teeth twice. "Let's not do this, Jean-Claude."

"You put a weapon in my hand and sent me to kill."

"Fucking get over it."

"There she is. Thelma. Hiding behind Catherine's smile."

She regarded her gun, then deepened her scowl.

I said, "You know how to use it. It's loaded."

"You are cold and abusive, no different than Mr. Midnight."

"You don't like my tone? Then kill me. End this shit. This is who I am. I've gone too far down this road to turn around. I can't put my gun away and become an electrical engineer. That was my dream when I was a kid. You put a knife in my hand. *You sent me to kill.* And the things I have done to save you . . . You don't want to know the things I have done."

"When you are angry, you sound like him. That terrifies me."

"Like who? Medianoche? Or the Beast?"

She dropped her gun like it burned her hand, let it land in the dirt. Dark secrets made her lip tremble.

I asked, "Who is Andrew-Sven's father? You've never said."

Catherine hurried away from me, ran hard, then slowed when she was near the boys. I watched her and wondered what information Hawks had found. I wondered what she knew about my mother's life in Yerres. I wondered what Hawks was refusing to tell me. I wanted to know what the fuck my mother was hiding. I felt Mr. Midnight and the Beast were part of a bigger secret. I picked up her gun, took a few steps, then jogged and stopped near her. She told Andrew-Sven and Robert it was time to end target practice. The boys ran over to her, saw she was crying.

Robert asked, "What's wrong, Mum?"

"We were talking about Alvin White, and I became sad. I told Jean-Claude how beautiful the funeral was. I told him about Alvin's brothers. They are big men, boxers like Alvin, and they cried like they were little boys. His wife cried. And his children cried out for their daddy and that made everyone in the church break down. A hundred people came to see him off. He did nice things for so many. I told your brother how everyone spoke and said Alvin White was a good man. I told him how the tears started again when they put dirt on his coffin. Now I am crying again."

Andrew-Sven hugged his mother as she wiped away her tears.

My mother was as good at lying as I was at killing. Her lie was powerful enough to make me need to step away and wipe my own eyes.

Chapter 32

Strangers

As I'd done night and day since the battle in Argentina, I snapped awake and grabbed the gun stationed on the nightstand. Within a blink, I was on my feet and the nine millimeter was trained in the direction of the abrupt sound. The problem didn't reveal itself, hugged the darkness.

I was seven years old again, and Mr. Midnight was in the shadows.

The noise came back, and I saw my enemy.

The sound that had pulled me from my nightmare had come from my phone. A new text message alert had made it vibrate on the desk.

I exhaled, eased the tightness in my chest, the same for the pressure in my head, then I moved by Tumi luggage, stepped over a T-shirt that said ABOLISSONS LA PAUVRETÉ and other clothing scattered on the carpet, over three pairs of shoes, and picked up my work phone. It was next to the satellite phone, the Thuraya I had been given on behalf of Señorita Reina Abeja.

```
WOTCHER UP TA? I'M NOT ONE TO COCK ABOUT SO I JUST
WANT YOU TO KNOW THAT I MISS YOU ALREADY. HOPE IT'S
OKAY TO SAY THAT SORTA THING. GLAD I GOT TO SEE YOU
AGAIN.
```

It was a text from the arms dealer in London. Zankhana. Zed. Bolshie. She was reaching out to me over a secure network isolated from the mainstream, a network that required special software to enable communication. Another coded message came while I held my phone.

```
ENJOYED SPENDING TIME SNOGGING WITH YOU AT ROSE PUB
AND KITCHEN, NEW CROSS. HAD A BLAST AT STAR WARS THE
MUSICAL. I'M ABOUT TO SEND YOU SOMETHING, HOPE YOU
DON'T FIND IT OFFENSIVE. I'M HAVING KITTENS ABOUT IT,
BECAUSE IT'S NOT THE KIND OF THING I NORMALLY WOULD
DO. BUT I WANT YOU TO STAY AS RANDY FOR ME AS I HAVE
BECOME FOR YOU.
```

I texted her back a smiley face. She sent me another message, a nude photo. Her tattoos, the scorpion that ran down her body, her hair, her skin. Zankhana was a fit work of art. One of the best bods I'd ever seen.

```
FOR YOUR EYES ONLY. ☺ DON'T WANT YOU TO FORGET ME. ☺
I GUESS I'M TRYING TO SAY I FANCY YOU. HOPE THAT
KEEPS THINGS FROM BEING WOOLY. WILL TAKE MORE AND
SEND MORE PICS IF YOU WANT. WELL, I DID TAKE MORE,
JUST SEND A SMILEY FACE IF YOU WANT TO SEE THEM. ☺
YOU ARE DEVASTATINGLY HANDSOME WITH YOUR FACE HEALED.
```

Weapon at my side, I sent the arms dealer a dozen smiley faces followed by *X*'s and *O*'s. For a moment I wished I had stayed in London.

She was in this business. She understood me better than most. I had done what I had to do. I had told her about the nightmares. I saw enemies both new and old when I closed my eyes. The nights I was with her, I had jerked awake at least a dozen times. Once I woke up screaming.

I took slow breaths. Chest was wrapped in steel bands. I broke free, then shook off a chill and looked at the shoes and clothing on the floor. I went to my backpack, took out a BC Powder, downed it with water.

For six days this suite in Paris had been my five-star safe house.

I put the phone down, crept back to the window, cracked the thick curtains. Europeans who were out wore heavy coats, parkas, gloves, scarves, boots. Snow fell and the grandness of Paris twinkled at me, the well-lit Eiffel Tower minutes away. I was hiding at the Shangri-La Hotel.

I wished Shotgun had lived to see this city. He would have loved to be able to see the black Americans and Africans speaking French in Paris.

I caught my reflection in the glass, then saw someone behind me.

The sudden movement jarred me; my trigger finger tensed up.

"Boo, you a'ight over there?"

A light on one of the nightstands clicked on. Living in a mental hell, I saw heaven. Sweet brown skin, virgin white covers pulled up to her small waist. Two shades of makeup had stained the saintly sheets.

She turned on her side, faced me with her eyes barely open.

I lowered my weapon. "Didn't mean to wake you up, Lola Mack."

"Were you about to sneak out without saying good-bye again?"

"No, wasn't leaving, not about to bounce, not yet."

"You're going to that other part of Paris to handle your business?"

"Yerres. Yeah. Soon. Later today. Before nightfall."

"Want some company? You said it's a short train ride from here."

"You can't go with me. Might not be safe."

"You okay?"

"Give me a moment." Shotgun was on my mind. "Just a moment."

"You've done that every night. Stood in the window. You're look-ing at your reflection over and over like you've never seen yourself before."

Over the last few weeks I had reached out to women I had left with-out saying good-bye. I still hadn't called Angelina. The look she'd had in her eyes when she ran into me in Brazil haunted me. The instant tears troubled me. Weeks ago when I was in Atlanta I had called Jewell Stewark and left a message. She was ATL's top newscaster. We had met in a jazz club a while ago. Sambuca Jazz Café. Two hours after that we had a room at the W Hotel by Perimeter Mall. We had had dinner in the room, talked, laughed, had sex, then rested on the bed and watched the news. Boys who had been outraged and needed revenge after 9/11, boys who were eager to kill the Taliban had ended up in Iraq.

Everyone was fighting a bad war. Everyone was in the wrong war.

When I was passing through Miami, I had reached out to Miki Morioka, a waitress I had met at Tootsie's Cabaret. She had married two weeks before, was just getting back from her honeymoon in Las Vegas. I congratulated her, and she waved it off. Wasn't excited about being hitched. She told me it was a marriage of convenience, so her child could have some sort of a father at home. And she needed the financial security. Kids were expensive and private schools weren't cheap. She told me that as we sat naked on a towel placed on the sands of Haulover Beach in Miami Beach, Florida. It was my first time at a nude beach.

Miki said, "Let's go to your room and, you know, get busy. Don't mean to rush you. Have to get my kid from the sitter, then make dinner."

When we were done having sex, before she kissed me good-bye, she had said, "*Saikou ni yokatta.* It is always so good to see you, Jean-Claude. Always. Next time I'll cook something from my recipe book."

Then I had felt like I was in the world alone and called Lola Mack.

She heard my voice and made me feel like it was Christmas. I told her I was in Miami wrapping up a few things, but had to go to Paris. She was in between acting jobs, had been busy planning her own wedding, but dropped everything because she wanted to meet me here. She hadn't seen me in years, not since I had left the Cayman Islands suddenly. She wanted to be with me again.

My world was safer now. Not safe, but safer.

Not every question had been answered.

So I had booked the actress Lola Mack a first-class ticket.

At Charles de Gaulle Airport, she had run and jumped into my arms. Dinner at Le Grand Véfour, a show at Moulin Rouge, and a shopping spree on Champs-Élysées, rue de Passy, and rue du Faubourg Saint-Honoré had made up for any perceived wrong I had done. Bags from Gucci, Yves Saint Laurent, and Christian Dior were all over the suite.

Lola Mack whispered, "Put your gun down, Boo. Come here. It's cold out there. Colder than a witch's tit in a brass bra. Your balls are gonna shrink."

"You're tired. You've only been asleep two hours. Rest."

"I'll give you a head-to-toe, deep-tissue massage."

"You know how that will end up, right?"

"I'll end up on my back with my feet on your chest."

"I was thinking with you facedown, ass up."

"I love it when your balls slap against me over and over."

"You're incorrigible."

"I like big balls and I cannot lie."

"Simply incorrigible."

She smiled, her mouth wide and generous. "Don't argue. Let me put you to sleep."

I picked up a cup of café I had left on the dresser, took two swallows to get the taste of BC Powder out of my mouth, then eased back into the large bed. I kissed Lola Mack. Her tongue was sweet, like expensive wine. My skin was cold against hers, as cold as my dreams, as cold as the men I had fought since I was a little boy. Her warmth felt like heaven.

"Boo, I didn't come all the way to Paris to sleep without you."

"You came to sleep with me."

"When I leave here I want to be bowlegged."

I sucked her ear, sucked her neck, kissed her shoulders. She put me inside her. Slow and easy, I filled her up. Lola Mack covered her own mouth, muffled her moans, but with each stroke she set free soft cries.

"*Lola Mack*, what are you doing?"

That drowsy voice came from the other side of the king-size bed, beyond Lola Mack. Mrs. Jones pulled the sheets away from over her head and yawned. Lola Mack was a few years younger than I was, and Mrs. Jones was a few years older. She was young, but a more mature woman.

Lola Mack sang, "Wake up, wake, wake up, wake up, and help me."

Mrs. Jones fluffed her hair, sat up, picked up the glass of 1999 Domaine Leroy Musigny on her side of the bed. She was an attorney, divorced, born in Jamaica, but raised in middle-class Los Angeles.

"Good Lord." Mrs. Jones sipped liquid power and finesse that cost four grand a bottle, then chuckled. "He's going to blow your back out."

Mrs. Jones leaned in, slapped Lola Mack's beautiful brown booty over and over, playfully gave her corporal punishment for waking her.

Mrs. Jones whispered, "So erotic. Sensual. It's beautiful."

I said, "You're next."

"Don't you dare threaten me with a good time."

Lola Mack made me turn over. She took me in her mouth. The warmth pulled my mind away from thoughts of killing and death. This was better than morphine. My breathing no longer felt trapped in my chest. I took long, intense breaths, ignored the flashes behind my eyes, hummed, held her long brown hair, felt her breathing deeply, slowly.

Mrs. Jones said, "Damn, Lola. Damn. Look at you."

I reciprocated, went down on Lola Mack, gave her tongue and

fingers until she told me she wanted more. I eased between her sweet, brown thighs, grinded against her, sucked her neck, kissed her shoulders.

She eased me back inside. It aroused her and calmed me.

Mrs. Jones whispered, "I love watching you two make love."

Soon it was Mrs. Jones on her belly, facedown, moans rising.

Lola Mack sipped wine and watched, then joined in.

All of us together in the same bed, this felt like yesterday as well. Once upon a time, years ago, for a season, I'd retired and lived the perfect hedonistic, decadent lifestyle with Lola Mack and Mrs. Jones.

We made love like we were trying to escape pain and find something better than the world had offered. I fucked to calm the noise in my head, to make the flashing go away. We moved around the bed, evolved from position to position, from triangle to triangle, until Mrs. Jones mounted me reverse cowgirl.

As Mrs. Jones rose and fell, Lola Mack kissed me again. It was one hell of a honeymoon kiss. She inhaled my moans, then she backed away, crawled, and faced Mrs. Jones, singing. Lola Mack was playful. She touched the attorney's face and lips.

Then Lola Mack went to her bags, pulled out two vibrators.

After playtime with the toys, after being upside down in my arms, both of them were on the bed, exhausted.

I was an assassin, but I had also grown up in many brothels.

I had my father's blood. And I had my mother's blood.

I knew just as many ways to please as I did to kill.

But that hadn't been enough for Arizona, not at the start.

And it hadn't been enough for Hawks, not in the end.

Lola Mack asked, "Did you come?"

I shook my head. "Just wanted to please both of you."

"You're pretty hard."

"Yeah. Still."

"It's not good for a man to be that excited and not finish."

"Not good for his health?"

"Not good for my ego."

Mrs. Jones whispered, "Touch yourself."

Enthralled, still wiggling her ass from side to side, Lola Mack looked at me and said, "I love it when you jack off and come."

Mrs. Jones whispered, "Masturbate for us."

"Yeah. Make yourself come."

"Do like we used to do on Seven Mile Beach."

"Hell yeah."

I sat on the edge of the bed and the goddesses were on their knees, their hands on my thighs, watching me, giggling, waiting.

They ran their hands over my skin and kissed my flesh.

"Slow it down."

"Yeah, like that."

I did what they asked.

Like a good whore.

Mrs. Jones whispered, "I love it when you stroke yourself."

"The way it sounds."

"This shit is so fuckin' hot."

"I'm calling dibs."

"Oh, we're about to fight."

My orgasm made me moan in pain and pleasure. It didn't want to end. They moved my hand away and took control, stroked me and imbibed until I was dry. While I lay on my back, panting, struggling to come down, they laughed and said I fed them well.

Not long after we had showered again and sipped water, Lola Mack was on the bed, nude, finally sleeping. I stood in the window, still naked. Mrs. Jones was in my arms, her back to my chest. She held my gun, like she was my protector. Or to keep me from leaving la Ville-Lumière anytime soon.

She rocked in my arms. "Will it be dangerous in Yerres?"

"Everywhere I go, danger waits. Blade sharpened. Gun loaded."

The gun was in Mrs. Jones's left hand. She put her right hand behind her, between my legs, then held on to my cock like it was a leash.

Argentina. Medianoche. The Beast. Catherine. Yerres.

Mrs. Jones interrupted my thoughts. "What are you thinking?"

I rocked her, made my smile turn upside down. "Nothing."

"Your breathing changed. You stopped blinking. I watched your reflection in the mirror. You were gone. You were no longer in this room."

"I'm here, Mrs. Jones. I'm right here."

I told myself that one day I'd leave this occupation again. For good. Before the hangman found me and put his noose around my neck, I'd get a woman. Make her my wife. Have a child. Buy a house. Be a square.

And never have to run again. Not even from the IRS.

Across the room, Lola Mack stirred, then turned over.

Mrs. Jones leaned back into me, again serious, and took nervous breaths. I held her a little tighter, absorbed her anxiety, added it to mine.

Mrs. Jones hummed, then twisted her lips. "Lola Mack loves you."

"I know."

"She will cancel all her auditions and her wedding if you ask her to. She will leave the life she knows and run away with you if you ask."

"I know."

She whispered, "I adore you too. I've missed you so much."

A woman told me I only knew how to fuck. And the better a man fucked, the more a woman was convinced he was making love to her.

Mrs. Jones put the gun down, hand-combed her bushy hair, then turned to me, put her arms around my neck, kissed my lips a dozen times before she put her head against my chest. I looked at the window again, stared at my reflection as I enjoyed the kindness of her skin against mine.

Behind us, a phone vibrated. At first I thought it was the satellite phone that Abeja Reina had given me. It was the other phone.

She said, "Just when I had you to myself."

She gradually let me go, let me go to the electronic leash.

The message was coded. It had bounced through a dozen servers in twice as many countries. I turned on an app and decoded the gibberish.

```
You don't know me but I am identified as MX-401. It
is possible that I may need your assistance in
liberating MX-999, the man you know as the Bajan. I
will know within the next five to seven days. This is
to put you on notice that your skills and help may be
needed. Please advise.
```

The West Indian man who had saved my mother and brothers was in trouble. Like I had been in trouble, the Bajan had problems.

Shotgun had never turned his back on me.

I would be the same way with the Bajan.

I replied. SEND CONSULTATION FEE. A REPRESENTATIVE WILL CONTACT YOU FORTHWITH.

Ten seconds later the phone buzzed again.

I didn't have to pick it up.

I knew the message. FUNDS TRANSFERRED.

My anxiety level jumped from level 4 to level 7.

Whoever the fuck MX-401 was, he was unknown to me.

He was on the Bajan's team. That was all I needed to know. I would go now if I could, if I was needed. They would contact me soon.

That meant I needed to rush and take care of business in Yerres.

Maybe I never should have invited Lola Mack and Mrs. Jones to Paris and gone to Yerres six days ago. I could go bundle up, walk out into what was once called Paname by the locals, and Lutecia by the Romans.

Yerres and the secrets it held were why I had come back to France.

Hawks had turned over the right stones. It felt like she had turned over a boulder. That boulder was on my shoulders the way Atlas held the world. The information she had, she had given it all to me months later.

She had found what could be my birth certificate.

I was born in France. I was born in Yerres.

Birth certificates don't have photos. Birth certificates have the name of the subject at birth, the date of birth, place of birth, parents' names, file date, and tell if it was a live birth, tell if it was a multiple birth.

What Hawks gave me said I was born a twin.

It said that both twins were born alive.

The truth of truths could be in Yerres.

When I looked in that direction, the hairs on the back of my neck stood up. My guts were telling me that there was trouble. I detected danger. Had no idea what kind.

It scared me. Someone had run my mother out of Yerres.

And I might have a sibling.

One war ended, and another always rose to take its place.

I held a mature woman in my arms, but looked at my reflection.

Behind us, Lola Mack asked, "Are you leaving?"

She was on her side. Watching us. Her lips pulled in.

Lola Mack frowned. "I heard that special phone vibrate."

Mrs. Jones whispered, "He's leaving us again."

I said, "Yerres. Need to get there as soon as I can."

"Then you'll come back? We want to keep you safe."

"Then I have to go off to parts unknown to work."

"From danger to danger."

"Yeah. Danger to danger."

"Without us."

"Without you."

Lola Mack took a deep breath, looked unhappy as she rose from the bed. She moved around bags and luggage, stepped over the results of our shopping spree, came to Mrs. Jones and me, put her arms around us.

Lola Mack said, "Mrs. Jones, you hold on to one of his legs and I'll hold the other. We should hobble him like they did Kunta Kinte."

I kissed Mrs. Jones; then I kissed the tears on Lola Mack's face.

As Paris began to rumble, as the rising sun broke through winter smog and reflected against the whiteness of snow, silence covered us.

I wouldn't leave them abruptly, not the way I had before. Not the way I had left Angelina Maldonado at the End of the World. Angelina hated me. I could tell she would always hate me.

Hawks was gone. Arizona was in my rearview.

Lola Mack and Mrs. Jones kept me anchored.

I would stay with them as long as I could.

Yerres would have to wait a little longer. The truth wouldn't change. Truth was concrete, fixed. Only lies changed with every conversation. Thelma's truth would be there whenever I arrived.

Many had tried to kill me. And I had killed more warriors than a soldier did in a war. Because of Mr. Midnight. Because of Medianoche's rage. *Medianoche*. His name would be forever etched into my brain.

I had already killed a monster. *Monsters*. I wasn't ready to shake awake another one. Because even the first monster wasn't fully dead.

The packages from DNA Solutions were back. Had been back a while. Both were in FedEx boxes at the home in Powder Springs.

They were locked in the panic room in the basement.

X.Y.Z.

The answer to my brother, the Beast, and me was there.

And there was A.B.

The answer to Medianoche and me was there.

The Beast. Or Medianoche. Maybe neither was my father.

I was a grown man, told myself that my answers didn't matter.

I told myself that every day.

I was doing this for my brother.

For Andrew-Sven.

Yerres would be for me.

Paris was colder than the souls of men.

Colder than a whore's heart.

But this room felt like heaven. A man like me, with the things I had done since I was seven, this was as close to heaven as I'd ever get.

I got back in the bed with Lola Mack and Mrs. Jones, and more soft kisses were shared, and for a moment we were a lazy three-headed beast.

I said, "One more day. Then I'll pack my gun and go to Yerres."

Lola Mack pouted. "Three more days?"

"Okay. Three."

"Five?"

"Four."

"For real?"

"Four."

"Four more days. We can kick it at Au Petit Fer á Cheval, Le Sancerre, Chez Prune, and Pause Café. We can go dancing again too."

Mrs. Jones smiled. "After you go to Yerres, then to parts unknown, you'll come back to us soon. I hope."

I didn't make a promise. They were too hard to keep.

Then we were quiet, cuddled against each other, sleeping as the City of Lights screamed to life. Two million people were in the city. I focused on the two in this room. The gregarious attorney and the loquacious actress held on to me. Gun on the nightstand, within reach, gradually, reluctantly, I closed my eyes. I surrendered to the weight of exhaustion, to the need for rest.

As I took shallow inhales and exhales, my trigger finger twitched. With each twitch, there were a dozen flashes in my mind.

Then my mind lit up like Dubai at midnight on New Year's Day.

And with each flash, I saw Mr. Midnight.

Whenever a room was too dark, I saw Medianoche in the shadows.

Dreams always became nightmares and I saw our last fight.

I relived that battle over and over.

He was a warrior.

A man who parachuted out of planes.

A soldier who had gone on countless missions for his country.

He was a man who had beaten bulls with his bare hands.

He was the strongest man I'd ever fought.

Injured, he was still as powerful as a raging bull.

I had killed many, and that battle troubled me.

I remembered how Medianoche had tumbled eighteen levels.

He fell and all I could hear was my own angered breathing.

I had listened for some sort of outcry.

There was none, not a sound from him.

Only the sound of rain and the din of Buenos Aires.

We had battled, and he had barked, cursed.

He had fought like a warrior who would never surrender to death.

But Medianoche had fallen soundlessly.

Without a scream.

Without fighting the fall.

That disturbed me.

It fucking disturbed me.

It always would.

Like Mr. Midnight himself, it always would.

Chapter 33

Los Últimos Recuerdos

Mind sharp, body weakened by the stroke, Medianoche had fought Gideon. Medianoche hadn't given a shit about his faulty brain; he would be a warrior to the end. He had been a soldier most of his life. One arm was numb, wasn't strong enough to wipe his ass clean with a roll of Elite Premium Triple Hoja toilet paper. The other arm wasn't deadened, but it wasn't much better. But he fought his oldest living enemy. Medianoche had screamed as he struggled, had tried to swing his good arm, shouted the way a soldier did when he was on the battlefield attacking his enemy head-on. This would be their final battle. He would kill Gideon.

But Gideon was powerful, much stronger than he looked. Gideon was as focused as he was talented. He was angry, but the surge of energy from his wrath remained under his control.

This was the man who should have been a Horseman.

With Gideon as his XO, they would have won every battle.

Gideon threw blows, connected with his chin, and Medianoche went down on one knee.

It felt like he had been kicked by a horse.

Gideon let him go, then returned, beat him with the saxophone. Medianoche couldn't stop him, because once again his mind lit up.

The inside of his head clicked and whirred.

Memories rose. Daguerreotype memories came in black and white.

He saw himself now as he was then. Barely out of high school, already enlisted, gun in his hand, fighting for his country. Had never killed a man before, but learned how to do it and walk away. After two bombs had been dropped over Japan, but before there were drones, he had fought teenagers with guns. Those teenagers had been slaughtered by teenagers with bigger guns. That summed up every war. That summed up the rich man's and politician's entertainment. War was all he had known. He had left California and the war in his own home, had left the beatings put on him by his old man, and went to Uncle Sam. War was what he lived for. He lived to beat others as his father had beaten him. He loved the feeling. Not the war, but the feeling that came with victory. He had fought African children wielding guns manufactured in the US, guns now being used to slaughter American soldiers. He had almost been killed by Middle Eastern women and children turned into walking time bombs. He had smelled the scent of many deaths.

But none had smelled like the arrival of his own.

Blood dripped down his face, across his goatee, turned the gray hair red.

Medianoche's words were garbled. "Caprica Ortiz . . . three more jobs . . . Nunca Más."

His words went unheard.

Gideon was in a rage. The whore's son had become a monster.

A powerful monster. The child of a beast and a whore.

Medianoche felt Gideon pull him to his feet, heard the gaucho yell and curse. He told Medianoche he had no right to call his mother out of her goddamn name.

Bloodied, incensed, words slurring, Medianoche said, "Your mother . . . brothers . . . dead."

"Then you better fucking apologize when you see my mother in hell."

The enraged gaucho grunted and dead-lifted him, picked him up like he had the strength of Atlas. The gaucho held Medianoche over his head as if he weighed no more than a folding chair.

That was the first time Medianoche had ever felt amazement dance with fear.

Now he knew what other men had felt like when he had done this to them.

He tried to fight, tried to at least make the gaucho drop him on the floor.

The headaches that had marched into his life and become more frequent, more severe, the pain that heralded the blackouts, all of his troubles were caused by a tumor in his brain.

A goddamn brain tumor. Frontal lobe. Made a man swear a lot, become aggressive, and lose inhibitions. But he had always cursed like a sailor, had always been aggressive, and didn't have any inhibitions left to lose. He rejected that prognosis. Walked out of the hospital.

Men like him lived forever, or died in battle and became mythical. Men like him didn't die in a hospital, withering away and shitting in a bedpan and being spoon-fed oatmeal.

Medianoche had planned to take a fertility test, to see if his vasectomy had come undone. But after the news about his brain starting to rot, he didn't care.

He didn't care if he had fucked it undone and had kids all over the globe.

The gaucho stepped over broken glass, grunted again with each step.

Medianoche was thrown from the terrace out into the darkness of the night.

As Medianoche fell from eighteen stories aboveground, his brain set fire.

And he remembered everything in color. Beautiful color. He

remembered it all. Back then he was married to his first wife. The Beast was married as well. His wife was pregnant.

He remembered that Thelma had two children, twins, and she had given one to someone else to care for, had left a child overseas because she couldn't afford to feed two. The French whore told the Beast and Medianoche that one of them was the father, and the French whore had called the Beast's wife, had called Medianoche's wife, had told both women everything. She demanded money to care for her love child. Her love children. One million for each child. Or she would go to the courts and file papers. It was all fun and orgasm until a whore was pregnant.

Margaret had put Thelma up to calling the wives. The Beast was pissed off, livid, and in anger he had grabbed Margaret, caught her in the kitchen, trying to use the phone. She threatened to call the police on the both of them, threatened to tell the police they were assassins, threatened to give names of people the Beast had revealed during pillow talk, threatened to tell all the secrets she knew to the police and the news. The Beast struck Margaret with his fist, struck her hard, like she was a man, and then he had wrapped the telephone cord around her neck, begun strangling her. Thelma had screamed, tried to save her friend, had gone after the Beast with a butcher knife, but Medianoche had jumped in the way, had knocked her silly, and when she had made it back to her feet, Thelma had spat in Medianoche's face, had bared her teeth and yelled that she was not afraid of him, yelled that she was not afraid of anyone, not anymore, and yelled that she had killed men before, said that she had killed men in Paris, had killed them and run away. She started stabbing at Medianoche, stabbed at him over and over like that demonic doll in *Trilogy of Terror*, stabbed until Medianoche caught her wrist and wrestled the blade from her hand. He took it and twisted her arm, made her yell in pain. The Beast had ordered him to kill one whore and he would kill the other, because he was not going to jail, and his brother Medianoche would not go to jail, not for this, and he would not pay for a whore child, would not give a dime, not to a prostitute. As two women screamed for their lives, the Beast dragged Margaret out in the backyard, dragged the West Indian woman down three concrete stairs, then across high grass, dirt, and more concrete.

As he fell soundlessly, Medianoche remembered.

Remembered.

Remembered.

He had taken his gun out, then paused to watch the Beast in his ruthlessness.

The Beast had beaten Margaret until she was unable to scream, had beaten her as dogs barked, then thrown her in the trash, in a Dumpster, threw her on a bed of nasty food, maggots, and flies, then fired off five rounds into the container. He pulled his weapon from underneath his coat and put five slugs into the West Indian woman. He shot a woman he used to be fond of for years. This would be the cause of Medianoche's first divorce, the cause of the Beast's separation.

They had never seen the second child. They didn't know for sure if there was a second child, if it was really in Europe, or if the French whore was just trying to get more money. A whore getting pregnant was an occupational hazard, not the fault of the john. The whores had crossed the line, called wives, disrupted families, demanded money, made threats, and signed their own death certificates.

Breathless, mouth bloodied, Thelma tried to get up, tried to race for the front door, but Medianoche caught her. He put his gun to her head, then put the barrel down her throat, made her gag. The French whore pissed herself. Piss rained all over Medianoche's polished shoes.

He put the gun down on the table, made the French whore lick his shoes spit-shine clean.

She pleaded for her life, asked, "Why why why? Why are you doing this?"

Medianoche replied, "Because some people deserve to die."

"Please . . . I beg you . . . Please . . . I am a mother . . . I have children. I have a son sleeping in the next room. He could be your child. *Your* son."

"And that's the problem. That's the goddamn problem."

"Please . . . no."

"You'll be where you belong in a moment."

"Please."

"Out back."

"Please."

"In the Dumpster with Margaret."

Then Medianoche strangled Thelma. Strangling was an intimate act, forced the one being asphyxiated to look into the killer's eyes. The murderer could watch the soul leave the victim's body. It was an intimate act of hate. Medianoche had stared into Thelma's eyes, let her see his anger as he saw her fear. He had her suspended in the air. He was her hangman, his hands her rope. The room in her house of ill repute was her gallows. Eyes filled with tears, the French whore gagged, coughed, spat, and stared at Medianoche's face. She tried to claw him, tried to fight with all her heart to live. Suffocating, dying a slow, certain death. He smiled, let her breathe. The Beast came back inside the slut's house and Thelma's reddened eyes went to him, begged to be saved, but the Beast turned his back on her, turned his back on the whore he had cared for the most, the beautiful French girl he had made love to more times than he had his own wife, the whore who claimed to have birthed his children. The Beast told Medianoche to kill her, to do it slowly, to make her suffer for the phone calls, for the blackmail. The Beast told Medianoche to make her regret what she'd done, and then walked out the front door. The Beast stood guard on the front porch, didn't want to see Thelma's well-earned death. He closed the front door. Medianoche held Thelma by her fragile neck and manhandled her petite frame around the room. She kicked over lamps, eyes wide because now she knew she was seconds from death. This would be her end, his face the last face she ever saw. But as he choked her, Medianoche looked to his left and saw her snotty-nosed son, the bastard she had fed NyQuil like it was fresh orange juice. Medianoche saw that the trick baby had picked up and was holding his gun, saw his own .22 aimed at his face, at his head, and before Medianoche could drop Thelma and attack and break the neck of the fatheaded cereal-eating NyQuil-drinking son of a whore—*BANG*—*Gideon* was born.

Acknowledgments

¡Hola, amigos! ¡Hace mucho tiempo desde he escrito un libro que se trata Gideon!

In other words, it's been a long time for the Gideon fans. Sorry it took so long, but not a day has gone by when Gideon didn't pop into my mind. And I do hope it was worth the wait.

I had done a few false starts; once it started in the Bahamas, another time in Barbados, and neither approach worked out. For each I had done a time jump, allowed a few years to go by, but what seemed to work for me was simply continuing the story where I had left off. The need for revenge seemed so immediate and so much like *fiyah*. It wasn't done. It had only started. So basically, *Resurrecting Midnight* and *Finding Gideon* will read like a serial novel.

As an homage to the series, I tried to include bits and characters from every part of the series so far. Even the arms dealer in London was first seen in *Sleeping with Strangers*. Her part was much smaller then, but equally important. There are a lot of Easter eggs. I had to reread the series to make sure I could keep things as consistent as possible. That was a challenge. If I slipped up, forgive me. A lot of characters have been in and out of the series. It was great to revisit them all.

Drumroll, please. Thanks. Let the shout-outs begin!

I want to thank my agent, Sara Camilli, once again, for going on this ride with me. It was a roller coaster and I hope the journey was worth the cost of the ticket. I have written Gideon being on the run many times, but this was the first time I wrote him as the one in search of revenge.

Thanks for the final title!

And thanks to Jacquie Lee in South Carolina. She was the woman who made things happen at Books-A-Million for many years. She messaged me months ago, when the book didn't have a title, and said, "Gideon's name has to be in the title. It has to be."

I had never considered that for the next novel. I was looking for something with the word *Midnight* in the title. And Jacquie said, "It's Gideon's series, not Midnight's."

I told my brilliant agent, Sara. And then we were *Finding Gideon*.

Thanks to my amazing editor, Stephanie J. Kelly. You made Gideon shine. Thanks for the hard work. I am really excited about Gideon being back on the shelves in the brick-and-mortar stores, as well as being available online for the fans. When the last offering came out, it was before the '08 elections were over. I didn't know if Obama or Clinton would be in the White House, so there were no mentions of the president. LOL. I think in Gideon's absence a lot of readers have finally caught up and new readers have come on board. Okay, I'm rambling. I just wanted to give you your well-earned props, and many thanks. You have made this novel rock!

To everyone in publicity, thanks for all the hard work. Thanks for all the help on social media and spreading the word. I've been working with y'all since the days of licking stamps to put on letters. LOL. Shhh! Don't tell the millennials we've been kicking it since the nineties.

Nah, tell the millennials. They rock. They are *woke*, run social media, and rule the world.

Last time I dropped a Gideon novel, I had a (yikes!) Myspace account in the acks. Damn! And pretty much everyone at the publishing company I thanked then has moved on to other things. But they remain as important to me. They always will. Thanks to all, past and present.

Kayode Disu, my Nigerian brother, thanks for reading and rereading and rereading umpteen chapters as I worked on this novel. I think it all came together in the end. I need to get back across the pond!

As usual, I get in a rush and accidentally forget someone. It's never intentional. So let me give you some space. First, accept my apology. Now grab your favorite pen and scribble your John Hancock.

Hear ye, hear ye! I want to give super-duper thanks to _____ _____ for helping a late-night-writing bro out, big-time. You had to help me remember the details of Gideon, because it had been a minute. I had to be a man of my pen and keep my word and bring Gideon and Medianoche back. Without your help, chicken soup, and laughter, as well as your comments on social media, I would not have made it out of this one with my sanity. We had to make some hard choices in the third act! ☺

November 24, 2016. Green cargo shorts, blue Dr. Seuss
T-shirt, Puma socks.

Latitude: 13.116910, Longitude: −59.474249

84°F, partly cloudy, 72% humidity, 4:46 P.M.

Carolyn's son.

Miss Virginia's grandson.

Mrs. Gause's godchild.

Miss all of y'all.

Every day I miss y'all.

Eric Jerome Dickey

ERIC JEROME DICKEY is the *New York Times* bestselling author of twenty-four novels and is also the author of a six-issue miniseries of graphic novels for Marvel Enterprises, featuring Storm (*X-Men*) and the Black Panther. He also penned the original story for the film *Cappuccino*, directed by Craig Ross Jr. Originally from Memphis, Tennessee, Dickey is a graduate of the University of Memphis, where he pledged Alpha Phi Alpha, and also attended UCLA. Dickey now lives on the road and rests in whatever hotel will have him.